An Invitation to
THE CAPTAIN'S TABLE

a novel by

ELLEN FRAZER-JAMESON

FOURTH DIMENSION
of South Beach

Published by
Fourth Dimension of South Beach
MIAMI, FLORIDA
www.ellenfrazerjameson.com

© 2020 Ellen Frazer-Jameson

The right of Ellen Frazer-Jameson to be identified as author of this Work has been asserted by her in accordance with sections 77 and 78 of the Copyright, Designs and Patents Act 1988

ISBN: 978-0-578-73338-8

Cover design and typesetting: Gary A. Rosenberg
www.thebookcouple.com

"Not all who wander are lost."

—J.R.R. TOLKIEN

$\rightthreetimes$

*To the wanderers, the armchair travelers,
and the free spirits—you enrich my life.
Thank you, family, friends, and colleagues
for your love, support, and wisdom.*

Other Books by Ellen Frazer-Jameson

THE LOVE TRILOGY

Love Mother Love Daughter

Love Refuses to Die

Love Kills with a Kiss

Once Upon a Lie

Flame Island
(originally released as *Dark Hole in My Soul)*

NONFICTION

Seven Steps to Fabulous

Seven Steps to Cruising Fabulous

Travels with Otto

Slim with the Stars

Contents

CHAPTER ONE

M/V *Vision Star* sails from Southampton, UK—
Grand Round the World Voyage   *Day 1* 1

Amsterdam   *Day 2* 1

At Sea   *Day 5* 4

Ponta Delgada   *Day 7* 12

Gala Night   *Day 10* 19

Bridgetown, Barbados   *Day 14* 28

At Sea   *Day 16* 38

Gala Night at the Captain's Table   *Day 16* 41

Oranjestad, Aruba   *Day 18* 51

Panama Canal   *Day 22* 58

Puerto Quetzal, Guatemala   *Day 23* 64

Acapulco   *Day 25* 68

SOS—Rescue at Sea   *Day 30* 71

Bora, Bora, French Polynesia   *Day 32* 78

In the Zone   *Day 34* 94

Bay of Islands, New Zealand   *Day 39* 101

Christchurch, New Zealand   *Day 40* 114

At Sea   *Day 44* 120

Sydney, Australia *Day 48* 127

Sydney—Day 2 *Day 49* 133

Pain and Healing *Day 50* 141

Kuranda, Northern Territory, Australia
    Day 55 147

Soul Searching at Sea *Day 58* 152

Rabaul, Papua New Guinea *Day 60* 159

At Sea *Day 64* 166

Captain's Table *Day 66* 173

Free Spirit *Day 66* 180

Searching Questions *Day 67* 186

Tokyo, Yokohama and Kagoshima, Japan
    Day 68 193

Confidants *Day 72* 200

Tianjin, China *Day 73* 207

Shanghai, China *Day 76* 215

Singing from the Same Hymn Sheet *Day 77* 222

Hong Kong, China *Day 79* 227

Ha Long Bay, Hanoi, Vietnam *Day 82* 237

Bangkok and Ko Samui, Thailand *Day 86* 245

Singapore, Malaysia *Day 90* 253

Captain's Farewell *Day 96* 262

Mumbai, India *Day 100* 268

CHAPTER TWO

Adrift on the Shore 273

"Go Around Again" 275

At Sea   *Day 3* 278

At Sea   *Day 4* 281

Captain's Table   *Day 10*. 290

At Sea   *Day 12* 299

At Sea   *Day 13* 301

At Sea   *Day 15* 304

At Sea   *Day 18* 305

Cartagena, Colombia   *Day 20* 308

At Sea   *Day 22* 313

At Sea, Sunday   *Day 25* 315

Captain's Table   *Day 30*. 318

At Sea   *Day 35* 323

Nuku Hiva   *Day 38*. 325

At Sea   *Day 39* 327

Bora Bora, French Polynesia   *Day 40* 331

Gala Night   *Day 41* 337

Suva, Fiji   *Day 42* 343

At Sea   *Day 45* 348

Tauranga, New Zealand   *Day 46*. 351

At Sea   *Day 47*. 354

Captain's Table *Day 49*...........................357

At Sea near Sydney, Australia *Day 52*..............360

Sydney, Australia *Day 54*........................364

At Sea *Day 55*......................................372

At Sea *Day 56*......................................375

At Sea *Day 57*......................................379

At Sea *Day 58*......................................381

At Sea *Day 59*......................................383

Night-time *Day 60*..............................386

CHAPTER THREE
"What Goes Around, Comes Around" 395

With Gratitude.......................................414

About the Author 415

Chapter One

**M/V *Vision Star* sails from Southampton, UK
Grand Round the World Voyage, Day 1**

Amsterdam

Day 2

"Would you cut off your ear for love?"

Helena de Croy Ringold continued to stare at the life-size Van Gogh self-portrait in the museum of his art in Amsterdam. Although they had not been introduced, she was confident she knew the identity of the male voice, the soft-spoken man who stood behind her, out of her line of sight and whose question pulled her from her self-reflection.

Master of the selfie, back in the nineteenth century, Van Gogh painted his own image over forty times. "It is hard to know yourself," he explained in a letter to his sister, "I am looking for a deeper likeness than that obtained by a photographer."

Helena related to his need to identify himself. Vincent, the tragic artist, fascinated her.

As she stood before his legendary painting, *Starry Night*, for the first time in the Museum of Modern Art in New York, decades before, Helena had broken down in tears. Deep, choking sobs escaped from her body, and the ability to control her deepest emotions was lost. Crying for the man, for herself and

1

for all the troubled souls in the world who would never find the means to express themselves. Echoing Vincent's despair, many were driven to commit the final act of human destruction: the sacrifice of their lives.

"You have given the question some thought?" the accented voice challenged her.

Without turning around, she shrugged and hoped that the smile on her face was not visible to her questioner. Careful to judge the delicate balance between genuine indifference and a misleading message of disinterest, she leaned her head on one side to show acquiescence and to subtly indicate that she was considering the proposition.

Helena brought to mind the garishly colored tarot card of *The Fool* blindly about to step off a cliff into the unknown. That same feeling of exhilaration and anticipation had welled up in her the previous day when she boarded a luxury liner in Southampton and set sail for the trip of a lifetime. A Voyage Around the World. Amsterdam the first port of call.

She contemplated the scenario whereby the individual whose presence, of which she was acutely aware, had chanced upon her by accident. After all, it was hardly unusual for visitors to Amsterdam to make a pilgrimage to the Rijksmuseum and the Van Gogh Museums, both located in Museumplein, a public square.

An opportunity to experience the world's largest collections of the greatest artist in human history and gaze upon hundreds of premier examples of his full works of 850 oil paintings, 1300 watercolors plus 750 written documents was never going to be passed up by those who are moved by the imagination, memory and observation of Vincent's phenomenal artistry and creativity.

Certainty fixed itself in her mind and heart; this was not a random encounter, soon to be discarded and forgotten. Here was the embodiment of a dream she had created. The physical manifestation of her desire and quest.

She knew perfectly well the identity of her questioner. She observed him checking her out the first time they shared space in the luxurious interior of the ship the day before. They had not been introduced. From his observation post, high on the top gallery of a gleaming polished silver staircase, she could have been just one in a thousand who congregated in the reception area after joining the ship that would be home for the next four months. But she knew that was not the case. The look that passed between them, though it spanned three floors, told her all she needed to know. He was the one. The one who would share her journey.

Helena pivoted on her heel and, caught off balance, spun herself right into his arms. Their eyes locked.

"Yes? No?" he asked.

Taller than her by almost twelve inches, she raised her head and now let her smile show.

Casually dressed in dark-colored denims, a well-aged leather jacket over a white shirt and wearing shiny black boots, he exuded confidence. Standing erect and relaxed, close up he was even more handsome than she had been able to observe from a distance. A strong, mature, patrician face proudly chiseled out a classic silver fox appearance, hair the color of midnight sprinkled with flashes of steel, not too long, not too short, black eyebrows and penetrating ebony eyes.

He did not let her off the hook and, instead with a laugh, insisted, "Now, an answer. You must know. Would you cut off your ear for love?"

She resisted the temptation to appear too clever by half and point out that it was debatable whether Van Gogh cut off his ear for love or was simply driven by madness—and absinthe—to mutilate himself and present the bloody specimen to an acquaintance at the local brothel, a lady of the night. It is claimed he told her, "Keep this object carefully."

Helena decided that the story was so well-known that he probably already knew it, and she instead responded to his question.

"No, Captain, I would not cut off my ear for love. However, I would not stop you from cutting off yours to prove your love for me."

At Sea
Day 5

"Captain's coming. Captain's coming."

Across the ship, this refrain echoed through the decks, corridors, lounges and restaurants. People slowed their pace, looked around discreetly and maneuvered their position to put themselves in a direct line of engagement.

Whispered words were exchanged and eyes signaled the message, "Captain's coming."

Everyone on a vessel of over a thousand people reacted to the advance warning.

Officers and crew members straightened and prepared for instructions, waitstaff adopted an enhanced manner of attentiveness, ready to serve if called upon to do so. Passengers reacted according to their agenda for the day. To greet the Captain cheerfully with a compliment for a successful berthing or an exit from a new port, or to take the opportunity to voice a complaint that the gentle motion of the ship put them to sleep or kept them awake. Complaints about the weather were also addressed to the Captain.

Women passengers preened in the hope that he would acknowledge them. They were desperate to present themselves in their best light. One appreciative smile from the Captain could induce a feel-good factor that lasted for days. Single, married or otherwise engaged these women harbored a secret desire that his attention would shine on them. Unspoken fantasies and desires reverberated around the proud vessel and lived to ignite one more daydream.

"Captain's coming," all eyes turned toward the pathway of his entrance several minutes before he appeared; the expectation produced a stirring, like Chinese Whispers, another chance to impress the Captain of the ship.

Officers and selected personnel, especially those in uniform, regularly become the subject of enhanced popularity and attract a fan following onboard ship. Specific individuals generate more attention than others. The Captain is the ultimate authority, the man closest to God when it comes to saving souls at sea. A pair of safe hands to guide several thousand passengers and hundreds of crew members through the storms of life on any given voyage. Certain Captains are veritable rock stars, projecting the best of what it takes to induce fantasies, wild imaginings, and hero worship. On the Marine Vessel *Vision Star*, Captain Grigory Petrovich was such a man.

He approached, walking with purpose, striding out, his long legs covering deck after deck, climbing stairs, traversing open spaces, completely focused. His head turned from side to side, his eyes observed everything, taking in at a glance the minutest detail.

He talked into his radio, issuing orders, "Painters to Deck Seven. Officer to Navigator Deck. Restaurant manager to Atrium."

His rubber-soled, highly polished, white leather shoes made

no noise on the scrubbed decks or carpeted common areas. His tread was steady, even; he strode out, a pathfinder.

His eagle-eyed visual inspections were unscheduled and random. Moving so fast he often caught up with or overtook the jungle telegraph. Nodding, smiling, extending handshakes he was in control of every movement on his beloved ship. Taller than any of the men, he stood heads and shoulders above everyone—even the notoriously tall Dutch ladies—but looked down on no one.

An easy laugh, which engaged his whole face, was bestowed on those who amused him. Small tidbits of information or an accurate observation could reward the teller with the full force of his good nature and his appreciation of a joke.

Passengers stepped out, halting his progress. Hardly breaking his stride, he engaged, responded, offered a handshake or a shoulder clasp and moved on.

Dressed head to toe in white, his starched uniform fit perfectly, not a wrinkle on his lithe frame, with a freshly laundered shirt, pressed trousers and a slim, white leather belt that separated trousers and shirt. Four gold braids adorned the epaulets on his shoulders. He carried the uniform with pride, and, though tall, he moved with ease and grace and gave off an air of total confidence and assurance. In profile his face showed signs of aging that made him appear handsome and distinguished. Age and experience showed on his face and added to his appeal.

Few men on land or at sea commanded the degree of authority he achieved with his presence. The whole ship reverberated to the words, "Captain's coming."

Along with the other cruise line passengers and company, Helena held her breath in anticipation. Stretched out on a sun lounger, book on lap, she effected an air of nonchalance as she angled her body in the direction of his approach.

A quick once-over of her black-and-gold designer swim-suit, her body and legs artfully arranged, she ran a hand through her hair and a tongue over her dry lips.

He stopped directly in front of her, casting a shadow.

"Hello, Captain," she smiled.

A huge grin lit up his face. "At last I've found you. I've been looking all over the ship for you. Where do you hide yourself?"

Delighted to discover he had been looking for her, she smiled mysteriously.

"I plan to add you to the guest list for the next Captain's table. Would you like to come?"

Knowing that an invitation to the Captain's table was a coveted prize on any cruise ship, Helena assured him, "Wouldn't miss it for the world. Thank you."

"See you then," he acknowledged and before she could regain her breath, he moved off and disappeared down a set of sweeping silver-gilded stairs.

Wearing a Cheshire cat grin and wagging two puppy dogs' tails, she gathered her belongings and almost broke into a little dance as she made her way back to her cabin.

First things first. What to wear for this glamorous event? Fortunately, her full to bursting wardrobe contained a dazzling collection of evening wear designed for such occasions. Four cases were hand delivered by courier to the ship when it was still in the embarkation port.

By the time she arrived at her suite on the top deck toward the rear of the ship, an official invitation had been delivered from Guest Services.

"The Captain cordially invites Madame Helena de Croy Ringold to dine at his table. Drinks in the Cocktail Lounge. Dress Formal."

The pinnacle of social cache in the cruise world. She had arrived. For all the fancy events, black tie dinners and red carpet events in her many social roles, this was one Helena had never experienced but it had long been on her wish list. Now it was coming true. And with the invitation, the added excitement of a devilishly handsome Captain.

Memories of a sighting of the new moon on the balcony of her home in Spain flashed across Helena's mind as she remembered lighting a candle, saying a prayer and asking the universe to send a romance to add to the abundance of her Grand Around the World Cruise.

"It has been seven long years since my husband died," she reminded whichever guiding being might be listening. "There has been no one. No one I have been remotely interested in romantically. Please send a worthy contender."

Now she lifted the embossed invitation to the Captain's table to her lips and kissed it.

"I believe magic is about to happen," she said out loud. "I am ready to be amazed."

A glittering prize. Thank you, God. Thank you, Universe. Thank you, Captain.

* * *

It was noontime and over the shipside PA system came the announcement:

This is your Captain speaking from the bridge. Here is the current information of your ship's direction and speed. Today we are cruising toward the Azores at a speed of seventeen nautical miles. Skies are cloudy and heavy rain is expected this evening with temperatures at fifteen degrees Celsius. The wind is south-south easterly fifteen to twenty knots, increasing to twenty-five and, locally, thirty. We hope you enjoy your day at sea and please take care as you move about the ship. See you around.

The broadcast ended and the information was assimilated for those who made it their business to follow these matters, usually male and often with recreational sailing experience. The passengers are assured that the ship is heading in the right direction. Now, the chosen direction for many passengers was directly to the dining rooms, buffet or on-deck barbecue.

Queues form outside restaurant doors even though the lavishly appointed dining rooms and services of the ever-efficient staff can more than accommodate all comers.

Cruise ship days revolve around eating and the three main meals, breakfast, lunch and dinner, are supplemented with afternoon tea and late-night pizza parties, plus room service and coffee shops for pastries and snacks. Elaborate chocolate fountains are set up to operate at midnight to draw crowds, and the late-night snack service circulating in the lounges and bars do a good business among those who still have an appetite for a little bit more. It is said that, onboard, those who really try can easily gain five pounds a week.

Helena was fast establishing her own lunchtime routine, coincidentally running into the Captain in the buffet line in the Terrazza at lunchtime. Aligning the optimum time with her own morning agenda, she made her way to the upstairs bistro, and sat within a designated area at the same table at the same time each day. The dining room was almost empty, but the serving staff stayed at their stations knowing that before they closed the line, the Captain was likely to appear. On the days when they hung green curtains over the counter she knew that the Captain was not coming. She heard the message that was passed between staff after a phone call and listened for the instruction, "Close the line." That meant for that day she would not bump into him.

A man of habit, he arrived for lunch most days not more than twenty minutes before the lunchtime session was over. Serving himself from the extensive buffet, he collected salad, soup, fresh fruit and bread as he walked up and down the counter, examining the food and questioning the servers about the dishes. He called for the chef to question and compliment him.

Special tables that had been set up with international dishes or speciality foods drew his attention and he graciously accepted invitations to try the various dishes, knowing that whoever served him would generously overload his plate and watch attentively to see how the meal was received.

The headwaiter, knowing his preference, collected from the bar a glass of ginger ale.

The Captain positioned himself at a high table in a prominent position in the restaurant.

He ate alone but was open to being approached by passengers or staff and often called over members of the waitstaff for a spontaneous briefing.

"Is all good with you?" he would ask and listen intently to their response, and close the conversation with a polite, "Thank you for letting me know."

Helena judged her entrances. Since reciving her prized invitation to the Captain's table, she endeavored to make herself available for a developing relationship. She wanted to ensure he was in no doubt about who she was when she turned up for the gala dinner.

If by chance she and the Captain moved through the buffet line at the same time, they would have a brief conversation and she would retreat to a distant part of the restaurant to eat her meal. Often venturing outside to a deck-side table or behind the glass wall that shielded diners from the sea breeze.

Although her back was to him, her low-key position-ing held a secret. The glass acted as a mirror and she could observe him from a distance. She built up a picture of his character with every new piece of information. She noted that he made the sign of the cross before eating his food and never ate dessert. She usually left the restaurant before him to ensure that, should he want to talk, he would need to be the one to initiate a conversation. And he did. Day after day he stopped by her table, positioning himself behind a chair as he stood with his hand resting on the back of the chair. His body was relaxed, and he gave her his full attention as he talked, joked and flirted.

Helena thanked him for the upcoming invite. "I am hon-ored to be invited to the Captain's table," she told him.

"The honor is mine," he said and sounded sincere, but she didn't really believe him.

"Only special people are invited to the formal dinner, and you are not simply on the list," he told her, "you are a guest of the Captain."

Helena hugged her secret to herself and did not divulge to any of her regular dinner companions that she been chosen to attend the table.

"I wonder how they choose people to go to the Captain's table?" asked a lady guest at dinner one evening.

"Only VIPs are invited," her companion told her. "You have to hold Diamond or Platinum or Princess status. Or have a title. Like Lord or Lady or Professor or Doctor."

Helena smiled and said nothing. She was used to fending off questions about why she traveled alone. "No husband, no boyfriend, no prospects," they teased her, "we will have to see if we can find someone for you. Surely going all around the world, there must be a man for you somewhere."

From across the table, one dinner guest nodded at her and made the others laugh with a joke. "If looks count, then I bet you'll be on the list," he told her.

Ponta Delgada
Day 7

San Miguel Island, the largest city in the Azores, Ponta Delgada, is known for its pineapples. A Portuguese colonial town located on a remote archipelago, the area was often referred to as the Hawaii of the mid-Atlantic. Visitors are drawn by the world-class whale watching, sailing, diving, hiking and canyoning and excellent opportunities for surfing and other water sports. The Azores contain two of Portugal's fifteen Unesco World Heritage sites—the vineyards of Pico and the old town of Angra do Heroísmo on Terceira and three biospheres: the islands of Graciosa, Flores and Corvo. The islands boast an abundance of natural parks and marine reserves to safeguard the unspoilt environment and pride themselves on being world-leading examples of sustainable tourism.

Sustainable tourism was a cause Helena supported, in principle. In practice, she headed for the local retail area after having walked ashore from the ship's landing quay.

On entering and exiting harbors, a small crowd gathered to watch the Captain in action on the bridge as he guided the huge vessel safely into its berth. Most dockings took place early in the morning and Helena left her bed at sunrise and watched all the activity as officers and crew and shore workers maneuvered the ship into its dock.

Passengers who sail, gathered together to discuss the tactics and debate whether the Captain had chosen the best approach to achieve his goal. They shared amongst themselves a running commentary: "He could have held it there," "I would have turned the ship sooner," "Too close to the dock for my comfort."

On a retractable bridge one deck below the enthusiasts, the Captain and his senior officers carried on with their tasks as they worked at the control panel, study charts and the computer-generated technical information they needed for a successful docking. The Captain was in control, relaxed, assured and totally engaged as he steered the ship into dock. For every arrival and departure, he was in his place on the bridge.

"To steer the boat is my favorite part of the job," he replied when asked about his duties and obligations. "It is the craft of the master."

Mission accomplished, the Captain looked up to his audience and acknowledged their interest. Helena stepped back out of the way and attempted to shield herself behind an oversize, bearded, rail-gazing amateur sailor who had been particularly vocal, determined to impress with his knowledge. She didn't move fast enough and what she had hoped would not happen happened. The Captain saw her and, with an almost imperceptible nod of his head, acknowledged her.

Helena separated herself from the other watchers and made her way to her cabin to collect the outerwear needed for a visit ashore. She took the stairs two by two, having promised herself at the start of the voyage not to use the elevators.

There were two reasons to avoid the elevators: for physical fitness and to avoid the overcrowding that occurs when hundreds of passengers are on the move. On a cruise ship, most people are heading to the same place at the same time.

The ship docked and everyone headed to the gangways to disembark. When the ship was ready to set sail, everyone headed back onboard for tea and refreshments. With plenty of theater, lectures and movie options, the majority of travelers would be in the communal areas.

Savvy cruisers soon established their own patterns to move on the side-lines and secure their places. It was an art, a game and a source of pride for many strategically minded passengers. Helena hurriedly collected her jacket, bag and hat and headed for the gangway. Today there were two designated points of exit; she took the least busy one, which was away from the main reception. Much as the leisurely pace of life onboard ship suited her, she enjoyed the freedom of being off the ship and taking a stroll into town. At this port of call, no tenders from the ship were required and no taxis were onshore.

Shops and restaurants in Ponta Delgada displayed signs welcoming the cruise ship passengers and offering discounts. Helena was willing as a visiting tourist to spend some money and contribute a token amount to the island's economy as she bought gifts to take home. The overriding motif of the gifts, as expected, was pineapples.

Not too much in the way of retail temptation, the shops were small and mostly featured handcrafted goods and simple local clothes.

In a small town on cruise days, fellow passengers intersected in the shops and restaurants. Information was swapped and shared: "Free Wi-Fi in the café top of the road," "Good home-made food in the restaurant opposite the church," "Currency exchange open, banks closed."

At a quiet outdoor restaurant in the square with a fine view of the church and the faded colonial architecture of government buildings, Helena ordered a pastry and coffee. She had not

tirelessly to achieve recognition in his chosen profession. Her lifetime partner had been powerful, intelligent, compassionate, accomplished and totally confident in his ability. The Captain reminded her so much of him and for the first time she truly felt she had met her match. Who could blame her for hoping that there was a bond, a connection, that could be developed?

My heart opens to him, she wrote in her journal on the night of their encounter in the museum in Amsterdam. *Every time I see him, my deepest intuition tells me that he feels an attachment to me. I have always believed in love. I believe in love at first sight; that's what I experienced with my husband. We both knew straight away that we were meant to be together. Whatever sacrifices had to be made to make that happen. Now I have identified that sensation again. I have to give my heart free rein to follow where this experience leads.*

She resisted the temptation to walk to the dock and see at what time the marine tour was due to return.

What good would it do to find out who has accompanied him? Once you have the information, what would you do with it? she questioned herself. *The journey has barely begun. This relationship, if it is to develop, needs to have the participation of two people. Let him be his own person with a driving force, thoughts and actions. Two grown-up, mature adults with all rights and opportunities to behave as their best self. Refuse to doubt yourself over a situation about which you do not have the facts.*

Walking back alone to the ship, Helena continued her inner dialogue. She knew that nothing could deflect her now. But she was also aware that caution was needed.

Like a bad fairy at the feast, she felt the words of the warning, and the shadow overpowered her. "Remember what happened last time. Protect yourself."

Back onboard, Helena made the decision to go to the sail-away party. She would not go to the railings where she could see the Captain and watch him at work on the bridge. "Give him space. He singled you out for an invitation to the Captain's table; count that as a victory."

A favorite saying came into her head, "If you love something let it go, and see if it returns." With the two of them together on a ship going around the world, the possibilities were endless; this adventure was to be savored. Helena remembered her heartfelt plea to the new moon, "Please send me a romance."

She danced to calypso music at the sail-away party up on deck. As the sun sank and the ship left Ponta Delgada, Helena made herself a promise: "To be myself, to present myself to him as a fully formed, worthwhile human being who knows her own value and behaves with dignity and integrity. This adventure is truly to be enjoyed, not endured. Dismiss negative emotions of jealousy, doubt and fear and embrace your highest self with love and honor."

Lost in her affirmations and the rhythm of party music that celebrated leaving port, Helena found herself dancing next to the couple from the restaurant.

"We went to see the marine tour boat come in," they told her. "The Captain wasn't onboard. He left early. They put him down in one of the inlets and he took a car back to the ship. The professor was pleased to see him go. She said he made her repeat word for word the lecture she's to give at the next presentation about the ecology of the sea. She says he has an insatiable appetite for facts and figures and knows almost as much as she does. But the best thing about the trip, she said, was after our Captain left.

"The skipper of the marine tour shouted out, 'Whale ahead,' and there it was surfacing and descending in the ocean. A beautiful blue whale putting on a show and blowing out spouts of water. Of course, it made us wish we'd gone on the trip."

Norman looked sad.

His wife Norma interrupted, "It's my new mantra, always say 'yes' to the experience. It may not come around again. And you'll miss the whale."

Norman and Norma finished each other's sentences and appeared to be joined at the hip. It was as rare as seeing a blue whale to ever see one without the other.

Helena laughed; she liked this couple. They were both retired schoolteachers who now had the freedom to travel the world, and they claimed they intended to spend their children's inheritance. "And the payoff is that the children get rid of us for half the year."

"Good for you," Helena said when they imparted this piece of information. Everyone on a cruise ship has a story, a reason for being there, and theirs seemed as good as any.

"Eyes right," said Norman suddenly, "Captain's coming."

Gala Night
Day 10

Helena had her own reasons for embarking on the world cruise. She compared it to getting back on the horse again after an accident: a purposeful intention to replace bad memories with good ones.

For at least a decade, she and her husband, Antonio, had spent Christmas and New Year onboard cruise ships. Their favorite was the famous Queens fleet of the prestigious Cunard Line, elegant, sophisticated and international. It was the perfect time of year to escape the cold British weather and be part of a celebration at the holiday season. The Mediterranean island of Madeira had built a global reputation for presenting a magnificent fireworks display over Funchal harbor on New Year's Eve as a thank-you to all the cruise lines and ships' passengers who visited their cities over the course of the year.

New Year's Eve onboard was an extra special occasion. Showcased with a Gala and Masquerade Ball, Helena loved the chance to splurge on a grand New Year's Eve ball gown. She loved the spectacle and the aura of glamour; it was truly as she imagined living in a perfect, fantasy world. An added bonus she admitted was that in a tuxedo, all men looked like movie stars.

Fortunately, her late husband, Antonio de Croy had a head start in that department, his dark Italianate good looks meant he was already handsome—though the pronounced scar down the right-hand side of his face could be construed as menacing or mesmerizing.

He conjured up stories to explain the scar and frequently the explanation verged on the totally unbelievable. To amaze or impress he really simply needed to tell the truth, which was as outrageous as any story he could make up.

"My friend pushed me off a cliff," was the true story.

The tragic accident in his teenage years left him with multiple broken bones and a scar inflicted by the jagged cliff edge as he dived from a craggy rock face on a remote part of the Italian coastline. He had made the jump many times before; it was a favorite summer pastime for him and his friends. The difference was that this time he was pushed before he could jump and was caught off balance so that he misjudged the trajectory of the dive.

Months of care in the hospital repaired the bones, and reconstruction work on his face put his smile back together.

Friendship with the individual who had caused his accident was not healed. "He must pay for what he did to you," demanded his distraught mother.

"They are friends; it was an accident," said his father.

Antonio had no say in the matter because he was in a coma; no one knew if he would recover, but the debate raged about whether criminal charges should be brought. As he regained consciousness and started the long road to recovery, his family finally agreed that no good purpose would be served by bringing charges.

"Of course it was stupid and reckless but not malicious," they concluded. Antonio forgave his friend and on occasions over the years they had met and even jointly presented papers at professional seminars and conferences.

Both were internationally recognized as world authorities on developments in the field of cancer research. Antonio often declared, "The accident made me a better doctor, scientist and person. I have compassion and empathy and I know what it means to be in pain and despair of ever regaining health and strength." Not a religious man, he was deeply spiritual and guided in his life by a profound faith and desire to be of service to humanity.

On their cruises, Helena treasured the precious time they spent together.

"At least in the middle of the ocean, I generally have you to myself," she had joked.

Though she asked, she knew he would not consider cutting back on his totally committed life of lecturing, hospital consultancy, clinical research and the presenting of his findings in academic books and professional publications.

"I have only one life," he explained, "I must spend whatever years I have giving back for the good of medicine. My work changes lives; I am duty bound to fulfil my mission."

Secluded in their luxury suite on a cruise liner, Helena learned to give her husband space when required and company when needed. The couple had no children, through choice.

Helena had a standard answer. "I was never blessed. Thank God."

They both knew that many marriages and relationships crumbled under the pressure of frantic work schedules and the compromises required for raising children. Helena was reconciled to never being a mother, and she gave thanks that she and Antonio had such an idyllic lifestyle.

There was one major challenge, as is usual in everyone's life, but she and Antonio had long since given up discussing the issue that devastated them both and threatened to destroy their marriage.

Antonio betrayed Helena. She thought her heart would break the day he told her about his affair. She remembered every moment of that pain-filled day when he came back from a lecture tour. Helena had joined him for a few days, earlier in the schedule, but returned to oversee construction work on their London home, a beautiful town house in St. John's Wood where they were adding a conservatory and an extension to the kitchen.

Antonio phoned from the airport to say he was on his way home. Helena heard his key in the door and expected him to join her upstairs.

"Hello, darling," she called, "I'm in the bedroom."

The staff who worked in the house had gone home for the day. She was surprised when he did not make his way upstairs to shower and change his clothes and instead headed to the open kitchen to inspect the progress of work on the conservatory.

Totally out of character, he left his briefcase in the hall, threw his jacket over an armchair in the reception area reserved for patients and met her at the bottom of the stairs. Together they walked to the conservatory overlooking the garden to check out the building work.

After a few perfunctory questions, Antonio lost interest and pulled up a plastic stool left behind by the builder. He looked dejected and out of place as he sat in the rubble and residual dust of the half-finished conservatory. He tugged angrily at his cuff links as he struggled to roll up the sleeves of his shirt.

With a deep sigh, he exhaled and, as the breath left his body, he faced her.

"Before I tell you the beginning, I will tell the ending," he said softly. "It's over. Truth to tell it was over before it started." Helena struggled to follow his reasoning. "You met her at the dinner you attended during the conference. She presented a paper that afternoon and came to ask my advice on a position she was offered by a well-respected university in Brazil. The position would mean giving up her research fellowship. We talked and I found her engaging but not much more so than many of the other young colleagues who seek my counsel."

Helena steeled herself, she already intuited what was coming next. She leaned against the half-finished kitchen counter and when Antonio held out a hand to encourage her to come close, she resisted. Antonio bit the inside of his cheek and took a long time before he resumed speaking. She tried to plead with her eyes. Helena felt as if all the oxygen had been sucked out of the room. If she allowed him to go on, she was bound to hear what she didn't want to hear.

Perhaps they could stop now. She wanted to scream out but, instead, calmly said, "Don't say another word. Let's end the conversation now. I don't want to hear what you're going to say."

Antonio, usually so in control, looked stricken. "If only that were an option," he almost whispered. "But it's too late for that. She and I have history. At a previous conference, she approached me and, over drinks and dinner, we . . . " he hesitated, "we got to know each other. Helena, I won't insult your intelligence," he told her. "One thing led to another. We've exchanged a few texts, had a coffee together when I ran into her at the hospital, but we never again . . . never again . . . " he let the words trail off.

"You know I've been faithful to you, all these years. I promise," he pleaded, "this has never happened before. And if there is any way back for us, it will never happen again."

The temptation to throw an object across the room or run from her place of safety was so strong, Helena felt herself clinging to the counter.

"If I start screaming, I may never stop," she warned him. "Don't push me. There is no after, for now, there is only this moment." Despite her best efforts, she raised her voice, "And what, what now? Why are you telling me all this?"

Her beloved Tony looked down at the floor, twisted his hands together and dropped the bombshell. "She's pregnant."

At that revelation, Helena lost it. She rushed across the kitchen, her body like a whirlwind, kicking up dust and flailing her arms wildly. She ran at him and beat him across the head. "How dare you? How dare you do this to us?" she screamed.

Antonio took the blows and then reached out, grabbed her around the waist and clung to her, tears running down his face.

"I'll make it up to you," he tried to negotiate. "Tell me what you want me to do."

For a long time they held each other, then he took her hand and walked her to the couch in the lounge. The early evening had turned to night and still they sat side by side in the darkness. Helena cried and buried her head in his shoulder. Tony held her close and stroked her hair as she let out the pain in huge wracking sobs. Her pain was mirrored in his eyes, but he did not cry.

He retained his composure and told her again and again, "I'll make it up to you. I never meant to hurt you. I'll make it right again, I promise, if you give me the chance. I don't want to be without you. Please don't leave me."

"What about *her*?" Helena spat out.

"She doesn't figure in our future," he assured his wife. "I have no relationship with her. I will fulfil my financial obligations to the child and have a legal agreement drawn up that will bring the matter to a close."

They talked till dawn and, when they were all talked out, shared a small snack and a glass of wine. "Let's go to bed, I need to be near you," said the husband she had loved and trusted since the day they met. Later, sharing their marital bed, they clung to the familiarity of years of intimacy. Rational and controlled, Antonio asked Helena to forgive him and allow them to move on from this major interruption to their previously perfect relationship.

"I've been a bloody fool," he admitted. "I bitterly regret that I've hurt you. Please allow us to rebuild what we hold so precious. Remember our vows and work with them. For better, for worse, till death do us part. I ask your forgiveness like I forgave my childhood friend. My life was shattered, but I healed and my spirit was stronger for the challenges."

Helena could cry no more, though, she knew the deep well of sadness would continue to threaten to overflow and disturb her sense of security and well-being.

"I need time," she said. "You're the doctor. Tell me, how long does it take to heal a broken heart?"

However, she had no intention of leaving Antonio, and he had no intention of leaving her. They would present a united front and work together to rebuild the trust in their relationship. This was not a matter to be discussed with anyone else except those that needed to know, mainly their family lawyer.

Helena sealed her lips against asking for details of the woman who had almost shattered everything she loved. Whatever decision that person came to about their own future, they would be well provided for but they would have to take responsibility for their choices. She felt anger that there was premeditated manipulation in the situation. How could a grown, mature woman allow herself to be caught in this situation if she hadn't wanted it to happen? But that was not a question to which Helena chose to devote too much energy.

Antonio was her husband and, as he had stated, they vowed to be together, "Till Death Do Us Part." "As far as I can accomplish it, I propose to behave like an emotionally mature adult," Helena told Antonio. "I will not put you under pressure or punish you for what can't be changed. Our life together continues. We are man and wife."

With love and understanding, they had weathered the storm together and were relieved when the date of their long anticipated New Year cruise arrived. The evening Gala and dinner were glittering, the fireworks spectacular. Helena's gown outshone all the other ladies, and she and Antonio danced in each other's arms at midnight and kissed. As always, they toasted to their future: Helena and Antonio together forever.

They returned to their luxury suite. Helena was in the bathroom when she heard the cry.

"What's happened? Tell me. What's wrong?" she called as

she made her way into their living room area. Antonio lay on the floor still wearing the gold-and-black mask he had worn at the Masquerade Ball.

Helena panicked when she saw him stretched out on the floor. Hitching up the layers of petticoats and the black fishtail of her ball gown, she kneeled down beside him, removed the mask and loosened his scarlet evening necktie.

He had removed the jacket of his evening suit. Antonio's face was a ghastly grey. Helena cradled his face in her hands and instinctively began to blow into his mouth and give him the kiss of life. She pounded his chest as she recalled the training she had received on how to administer CPR. The instructor had told her, "Apply pressure to the chest, repeat the rhythm of the Bee Gees song 'Staying Alive.'" She had hoped she would never need to perform the life-saving procedure on anyone, especially not her strong, hearty husband.

Antonio was silent. He did not respond to the physical pounding on his chest or her frantic entreaties. "Antonio, can you hear me? Please answer me."

Helena stretched across his body and with an effort reached the phone that had fallen from his hand. It was already mid-call, "Who is this?" Helena demanded when she heard an unfamiliar female voice on the other end repeatedly asking, "Hello. Hello. Tony, are you there? Hello."

"Who is this?" Helena's voice was cold as ice; her insides twisted with fear. "Get off the line. Hang up NOW. It's an emergency."

She dropped the phone, gathered up her heavy skirts, crossed the room and picked up the landline. She hit the "0" button for reception and told them, "Emergency. Get a doctor here now."

Antonio had not moved a muscle or said a word. She lifted

his wrist and felt for a pulse. There was none. She kissed him on the lips.

"You're going to be okay," she repeated over and over again.

The New Year was less than an hour old when Professor Antonio de Croy Ringold was declared dead by the ship's doctor. His body was removed by tender from the ship and flown home from Madeira for burial.

Helena sat alone in the first-class window seat of the British Airways flight as it took off from Funchal airport headed for Heathrow. Antonio's body was in the hold. She had tried to argue that she needed to be beside him. It was not possible. Death had parted them.

Bridgetown, Barbados
Day 14

Bridgetown was a bustling colonial town and the first-class shopping areas along Broad Street and Swan Street buzzed with the rhythms of local culture. The entire downtown area and the Garrison comprised a World Heritage site and were preserved for their historical significance. The capital of Barbados, Bridgetown, offered duty free shopping at the cruise terminals and upscale boutiques. Tourists and locals alike passed their time yachting, fishing, watching cricket matches and joining the party atmosphere of the nightlife in the town square. The Barbados Museum offered a history of the island, and visitors to the island loved to see the house where George Washington had stayed and the church he attended. The island was also home to the oldest Jewish synagogue in the western hemisphere. Tradition, local culture and world-class shopping were all major attractions, but most tourists chose to bask in the warm sunshine and head for the beaches. Sounded like a plan. Helena decided there was a spot in the sand with her name on it.

She walked off the ship in Barbados. She hadn't yet had to undertake a tender ride.

Seven years before she may have thought that she had taken her last cruise. Instead the idea began to grow that she needed to get back on the ship. The mythical seven-year cycle had proved to be true for her.

For the first year after Antonio's death, Helena would catch herself gazing into the mirror to ask, "Did he die or did I? The existence of my life makes me feel like a ghost."

She told friends, "I understand why half of all widows and widowers die within six months of their partners." She certainly questioned whether there was anything she chose to live for. As the years moved on, however, she rebuilt her life.

In year two, she felt the weight of the blackness lift and began to believe life might be worth living. There were cultures in the world where, apart from the one year of morning in black clothes, the second year of widowhood was marked with restraint. Full black dress was not required, and navy and grey were considered appropriate colors to wear. Still it was frowned upon for widows to attend social gatherings. Without the need to be indoctrinated, Helena felt her body and mind and spirit resonate to these time frames. Subconsciously she chose subdued clothes and social gatherings, even those that were not torturous held little attraction. She liked the close company of family, except when she didn't. Arriving with her overnight bag, she would accept an invitation to stay away from home for a while, then in the middle of the night, change her mind and leave. She found it almost impossible to settle anywhere. When she thought she had cried the everlasting well of tears dry, again, out of the blue she would break down sobbing, in the cinema, a restaurant, out shopping.

By years three and four, normal life began to be resumed. Helena found she was ready to get back into the stream of life. "Okay, I will accept the date you suggested," she told her friend. "He's very respectable," her friend said, "I know him through church friends." Helena agreed to go to a performance of one of her favorite musicals, Andrew Lloyd Webber's *Evita*.

At the interval as they sipped tea in the bar, she complained to her companion of a headache. "I'll call an Uber," she said. "I'll be fine. You stay and enjoy the second half."

Sweet man that he was, he invited her out again, but she refused. It was two more years before she agreed to another date. On that occasion, a lawyer, the friend of mutual friends suggested a visit to the Royal Academy Summer Exhibition. "Good choice," Helena agreed. The show, with its breath-taking collection of diverse styles of art, was fascinating and culturally stimulating, as always. Her companion was knowledgeable and charming. After, they had one more cup of tea in a delightful French restaurant in London's West End; she knew she could have tried harder but instead refused a follow-up invitation.

The seventh anniversary of Antonio's death approached and Helena made a bold decision: to go on a cruise, and not just any cruise, she set her sights on an around the world voyage. Months at sea allowed her to acknowledge that now, seven years after Antonio's death, she had been renewed.

For years it had been a source of intrigue to her that every seven years the whole body renews itself. Every single atom, proton, neutron, cell and fiber in the body had been replaced. Helena felt a new energy burst forth.

"After seven years, I am ready to re-join the human race," she said celebrating the achievement.

To ensure her commitment to the process, she performed a new moon ritual. She had performed this ritual before and been lucky enough then to receive the desires she had indicated to the universe.

"The only thing that my life lacks is romance," she decided.

As always, Helena honored the process whenever she made the sacred decision to ask for help from the universe. She wore a rose-colored goddess gown to match the rose-pink candle and choose the all-pervading smell of rosewood incense. She held a scroll in her hand on which she had written her affirmation and performed the ritual on her balcony overlooking the sea on the Costa Blanca in Spain.

"Hear my plea," she said out loud as she lit the candle and incense sticks and prayed like her life depended on it. "I desire romance with a beautiful handsome man. Someone worthy of me. Someone who will value me, will know that I am special and allow me to share their life and make them feel special in a loving relationship."

Faith is required for such a venture and Helena never doubted her request would be met.

*　*　*

Two weeks into the world cruise, she walked off the ship and headed for a beach that was recommended by someone who had insider knowledge. It was close to the town and within walking distance of the harbor. Waves crashed on white sand, and the surf rolled gently across the beach.

Helena chose her swimsuit with care, not too reveal-ing but not too sedate, one that showed off her tanned, slim figure and enhanced her well-developed breasts. A suit that was perfectly appropriate should a suitable swimming partner happen by.

She set herself up at a quiet spot close to the water's edge with a good all-around vision of the beach and sea. He had told her he liked swimming. This particular beach was his suggestion. She scanned the oceanfront.

No sign of him, though, she did spot a couple of cruise ship passengers some distance away. Time for a quick selfie on the beach in Barbados to send to the family back home, then she paddled in the pounding surf and plunged into the inviting bath temperature aquamarine water.

Helena swam farther and farther from the shore until around a curve in the beach she could see the cruise ship docked on the quay. She flipped on her back and allowed herself to drift. She was sure he would show. If not, why did he tell her that he loved to swim and direct her to the exact spot?

Helena righted herself and began to swim for the shore. Suddenly she realized, she was not alone in the water. A familiar figure was headed toward her. The tousled black hair was unmistakable. She stopped swimming, planted her feet down on the silky sand and waited. The ocean gently tugged and pulled at her and she had difficulty keeping her balance.

"Hello, Captain." She smiled as he came alongside her. "Lovely day for a swim."

They swam together, treaded water and talked. Only once did they touch. When Helena appeared to lose her balance, he put his hand out to steady her.

It was hard to hide her disappointment when it became obvious that he had no intention of staying. They spent only a short time together before all too soon he was gone again.

"Time for me to get back to the ship," he said. "You don't

have to rush. You have lots of time. Onboard time is 5 p.m. Enjoy your day. See you around."

The Captain made his way quickly to the shore and toweled himself off. Her eyes assessed his tanned, lithe body. She watched him dress. Jeans, a T-shirt and a baseball cap. Not inclined to follow too closely, she made her way slowly to the shore. He waited for her to catch up and reminded her, "Captain's table tomorrow."

Helena flopped down on her towel and tried to keep the scowl from her face. "Yes, of course, see you there."

She realized that all else was expectation. He had not invited her on a date, only given her local guidance on the best beach and place to swim. Certainly, he is his own man; Helena was forced to accept that. Eyes closed, she drifted into a meditation so she could ponder upon the intentions of the man who now consumed so much of her thoughts and try to discern if there was a way of moving closer to the hopes she had for a relationship. A shrill voice broke into her reverie.

"Was that the Captain?" the female voice asked, and then repeated, "the Captain, was that who you were talking to in the water? It was, wasn't it?"

Into view came Meredith, a particularly annoying fellow passenger. Helena did not want to have this conversation, not here, not now.

"Hello, Meredith," she said as she sat up and adjusted her body to lean back on one arm. "Yes, it was him," Helena admitted.

"I kept trying to catch up with him," Meredith said, "but he was swimming too fast for me. How come you got to talk to him?"

Meredith and Helena were not friends. They were dinner companions. Reluctant ones certainly as far as Helena was concerned. Meredith had become the thorn in her side. An annoyance from which she could not escape without being totally rude and asking to move tables. Not a course she wanted to follow, particularly as she enjoyed the company of her other dinner companions.

The cruise ship offered the usual choice of dining tables: six, eight or ten. Helena judged that, being a lady traveling alone, ten was a sensible choice as she met new people, socialized at the end of the day and had an opportunity to share experiences and trade stories. Meredith was also traveling solo and assumed that she and Helena would become bosom friends, joined at the hip.

"We can do things together, go on shore excursions, hang out and party."

Helena was all for being sociable and sharing activities with friends when appropriate, but she did not choose to become exclusive with anyone.

Well, maybe one person, she thought as she smiled inwardly.

Meredith was determined that they should team up and most days mentioned an activity—art classes, amateur dramatics, deck walking or, heaven help her, knit and natter—where they could get together. As politely as possible, Helena refused most approaches but, on occasion, in the spirit of harmony, she would agree to meet up.

Although she had the potential to be an interesting companion and was certainly very accomplished at many of the skills that eluded Helena, like quiz shows and crafting, there were some very distinct differences in the women's characters.

A horse rider and country dweller, Meredith was the outdoor type. She was a fitness enthusiast and deck walker in all weather. Helena, a town dweller, wasn't sure how to program her Fitbit and her insistence on wearing high heels meant that most of her deck walking was down carpeted corridors from cabin to restaurant.

Probably the same age as Helena, but Meredith didn't wear it quite so well. She was supposed to have traveled with her sister, but there was a change of plans.

Meredith had taken to making comparisons between Helena and her sister. "Yes, my sister is a wimp, like you," she remarked when Helena refused to join a deck quoits team.

"For goodness sake," she exclaimed on another occasion, "setting a cell phone to different time zones is not rocket science."

At the dinner table, Meredith baited Helena. "How many red outfits do you have? On informal nights, you don't have to dress up so much. Where did you say you buy your clothes? High-heeled shoes are going out of fashion. I read that, on the catwalk, flats are the new heels."

Helena brushed the remarks off as a joke, not wanting the other dinner table guests to feel uncomfortable. Cruise ships attract all kinds of allegiances and antipathies. With a thousand people in close proximity day after day, not everyone is going to get on, but, like in the playground, it is a responsibility for everyone to play nice. Helena always played by this particular rule: Stay close to those you like and stay away from those who rub you up the wrong way.

Funny thing, in all the years she had cruised with Antonio, personality clashes with other guests never happened. Perhaps because they were all mature people, couples mostly with whom they had become friends. Now, as a single woman, she attracted different kinds of social interactions, not always pleasant ones.

The last thing Helena wanted to do as she lazed under a sunny sky in an island paradise was to share the afternoon with

Meredith. And she definitely had no intention of discussing the Captain with her.

"Can I join you?" asked Meredith as she unloaded the large beach bag and towel she was carrying.

"'Fraid not," said Helena, "I'm leaving. Promised myself to check out the boutique shopping before I head back to the ship."

Dressed in a shocking-pink swimsuit with matching skirt, her bag in hand, Meredith seemed to debate whether to stay or to suggest that she, too, wanted to go on the shopping expedition. As Helena stood up, Meredith sat down.

"You're not planning to buy more clothes, are you?" she goaded Helena.

Helena slipped a short, white silk dress over her red-and-white-striped swimsuit, which had dried quickly in the afternoon sun, and put on a pair of large, round white sunglasses.

"Maybe," she called over her shoulder as she walked away up the beach.

"Make sure it's not red," retorted Meredith, "blondes look better on the blue spectrum."

"Thank you, I'll remember that," said Helena, but she was too far away for Meredith to hear.

Helena's journal entry: *Sailing out of Bridgetown. A message of Hope. Sailed away from Barbados and have a sea day on way to Aruba. Tomorrow is the day of the long-awaited Captain's table. Obsession with the Captain continues. After our swim this afternoon, I am more smitten than ever. I look for him constantly. And when he's nowhere to be seen, I look for signs. Like the black-and-white bird flying past my balcony, swirling and swooping and floating on the breeze. A sign that I am to enjoy my freedom. Have faith the universe knows my wants and needs. Believe I'm not destined to be alone. Believe I have found the one.*

* * *

As the ship sailed out of Barbados, Helena dressed for dinner and made her way to the restaurant. She was hungry, having had no lunch. She was more than a little pleased with herself as she prepared to make an announcement to her dining companions. She chose her moment. Main meal over, a waiter used a miniature silver brush and dustpan to sweep the snow-white linen tablecloth clean of crumbs. A quiet oasis in the ritual of the daily five-course dinner menu. Between the main course and dessert, another waiter refilled wine glasses and set out fresh silver cutlery.

Helena paused for dramatic effect and failed to keep the excitement from her voice as she said, "I've been invited to the Captain's table. I will be dining with him tomorrow."

Meredith, always slightly behind the others in finishing her courses, a delaying tactic that seemed designed to draw attention to herself and to hold up the other guests, almost choked on the bread stick she was nibbling. She slammed down her napkin and ran from the room. The male guest who had predicted that Helena would indeed be on the VIP guest list winked at her from across the table.

His wife nudged him, "Find out how we can get an invitation."

An elderly lady, who generally listened more than she talked, which she explained by the fact that, in the busy cross talk of conversation at a full dining table, she could not hear very well, beamed with delight. "I've always wanted to be invited," she said.

"You're so lucky. You must tell us every detail," said one of the other guests.

"You can bet on it," Helena promised.

At Sea
Day 16

Helena awoke and, without opening her eyes, smiled at the sun that streamed in her stateroom window. Wherever she was in the world, she never closed her curtains. She counted herself fortunate that her natural inclination was to throw back the covers, jump from her bed, already alive, awake and ready to face the day.

It hadn't always been that way. In the times of her darkest depression, she had pulled the duvet over her head and denied the arrival of the day.

Gratitude that she was able to celebrate the dawning of a new day never left her. When the demons were upon her, she had no resources to change the way she felt. There had been times when she thought her life would be like that always. But she had come to believe in the adage, "This, too, shall pass." Good and bad, all pass. We just need to hang in there.

"Today's the day," she said out loud. Her husband, Antonio, would have told her she had watched *Titanic* too many times, or *Death on the Nile* where the beautiful people gathered at the Captain's table to be wined and dined and have a life-changing experience. Antonio preferred a quiet dinner for two. He had more than enough excitement in his life and career. Helena lived her life by Tennessee Williams's motto, "I don't want realism. I want magic! Yes, yes, magic! I try to give that to people. I misrepresent things to them. I don't tell the truth, I tell what ought to be the truth. And if that's sinful, then let me be damned for it!"

Antonio adored his beautiful, elegant wife and loved that she was a romantic. High on love, she shared it with her chosen person. For all the years of their marriage, her avowed mission was to make him feel loved, spoiled and special. She showered him with cards and letters and gifts. In return he sent bouquets, never missed a birthday or anniversary and lived by the motto, "Happy wife, happy life."

After her husband died, Helena was left with a gaping hole, not only of his physical absence but of a person-size place to direct her love. Family friends, home, pets, church, work all offered and received her affection, attention and, yes, love, but she was forever conscious that nothing can replace the light that reflects in a loved one's eyes for that light validates, inspires and ignites life itself.

Helena reflected on her situation as she showered and allowed the water to wash away the sleepiness of the night and energize her body. She wrapped herself in a silky mint-green robe and tied her hair in a messy bun on top of her head.

Room service delivered breakfast while she was in the bathroom, and the room steward laid a table in the picture window alongside the balcony.

The ritual of breakfast appealed to her and she could not start the day without that first cup of tea. Otherwise, she avoided the temptation to start eating too early in the day. In cruise ship world, the food was endless. A glass of freshly squeezed orange juice and a small bowl of oats with berries scattered on top were all she generally ordered for breakfast. She read the ship's daily program and listened for announcements of special events.

Somehow, she had almost expected the entertainment manager to announce in his early morning broadcast, "Madame Helena de Croy Ringold is dining with the Captain today."

Helena checked the appointment times for her day spa body treatments, manicure and pedicure, hairdressing and professional evening makeup, all designed to ensure that she would look her best. The news that there was a full lunar eclipse that night excited Helena further.

She did not doubt that this was to be an auspicious day. The phenomena of a blood moon was anticipated. The stars aligned. Her heart was not mistaken. She resisted the temptation to play on YouTube the legendary Celine Dion *Titanic* love song: "My Heart Will Go On and On."

A warning voice made itself heard in Helena's deepest reasoning: *Let go of the obsession. Enjoy what is to come, but be prepared for the fact that you may have magnified this beyond the realm of possibility. Take heed of the words, and keep it real.*

The Ocean Spa presented a sanctuary of calm, peace and luxury. The air was perfumed, and the sweet smell of incense and the sound of meditative music combined to create a relaxing atmosphere. "This is heavenly; you have the touch of an angel when you give a massage," Helena told the lovely young Eastern European massage therapist.

Helena sank gratefully into the deep, warm towels and allowed her body to be pummeled with a deep tissue massage and polished with seaweed, before being smoothed with the finest lotions. A rejuvenating facial with an exclusive three-step caviar cream elixir readied her for the professional glamorous makeup process. During her treatments, a conditioning mask enriched her hair and added volume in preparation for the experienced Gala night hairdresser to create an intricate up do with curls, swirls and intricate accessories.

"You look fabulous," said the therapist. "I am going to take a photograph and put it up at the reception to show our other clients."

Helena had to agree because the spa team did a wonderful job.

"Thank you so much," she said, "now I am red carpet ready."

The effect was show stopping: her body had sprinkles of glitter on the shoulders and back; her hair was a crowning glory; and the evening makeup highlighted her smoky eyes and red lips. The hairdresser and makeup artist took their photographs, and the other therapists came to admire the work of their colleagues.

Helena was about to leave the spa and return to her room, ready to step into her oh so carefully chosen dress when the elevator door opened and out stepped Meredith. She held in her hand Helena's treasured Captain's table invitation.

"How do you come to have that?" Helena asked, furious and mystified.

Meredith's face gave away nothing. "It must have dropped out of your robe pocket in the sauna," she explained. "I went in there after you. Sorry, it's a bit soggy."

Helena took the damp invitation. "Thank you, though, I'm sure I won't need it. The Captain knows who he has invited to dine with him."

Allowing her to make a dignified exit, the glass door slid open right then, and she turned her back and walked into the elevator. As the door closed, Helena watched in the mirror as Meredith fired her parting shot, "Your hair looks ridiculous."

Gala Night at the Captain's Table
Day 16

Helena's face burned with rage and embarrassment. The carpeted walk from the elevator to her suite had never seemed longer. Helena prayed that she would not bump into anyone she knew, not before she'd had a chance to review her fancy hairdo.

"What was wrong with it? Did it look ridiculous? Was it over the top?"

Helena slumped onto the double bed and pulled a large tasseled cushion into position, avoiding her hair. Taken completely by surprise, the unprovoked attack from Meredith had knocked the wind out of her sails. She didn't know whether to laugh or cry. Reluctant to look in the mirror in case her attacker was right, she reflected on the Cinderella moment. Ugly sister Meredith knew exactly where to aim to deflate a woman's confidence. It was a mean, wicked thing to do, but Helena refused to stay wounded for long.

As she jumped up for a 360-degree look in the mirror, she declared. "You shall go to the ball, and no-one has the power to stop you."

Years ago she had been advised that, if she received an insult or a compliment, she should check from whence it came. She had the power to accept or reject it. Did she value the opinion of the person? The answer to that was obvious. *Thanks, but no thanks, Meredith, you can have your meanness right back at you.*

Determined not to waste any more time on the unpleasant incident, Helena checked her hairstyle. She opened the bathroom cabinet to ensure a wide-angle view of the back. Okay, she decided, it was elaborate and designed for effect. She patted the crown down, just a little, and pinned the sides up. *Thanks, Meredith.* She smiled; the hairdo benefited from these small adjustments. Ones that Helena would no doubt have noticed herself, as, like most women, her hairstyle always needed a little personalizing after the hairdresser did her job.

Breathe deep, she told herself. Nothing was allowed to spoil this evening. She stepped out of her robe and walked naked to the wardrobe recess alongside the marbled bathroom. The underwear she had especially selected was laid on top. A black lace corset and red-ribboned panties.

Perfectly offsetting her blond hair, which was piled high on her head with tiny spiral curls framing her face, her chosen dress for the evening's event was a fitted strapless column of silver-and-black sequins with a fishtail net skirt flaring out from the knees. Around her neck she had an antique diamond pendant and chandelier diamond earrings. To draw further attention to the light-gold frosting on her bare shoulders, a marabou stole was clasped on one side. She carried a silver-jeweled clutch bag.

A vast collection of evening shoes was available to her, but she already knew what she would select: the highest heels she possessed—scarlet five-inch Louboutin heels with a metallic silver filigree decoration. The Captain's height meant he was a man not to be intimidated by a woman standing as tall as him.

Her reflection in the full-length mirror gave her reassurance that tonight she was definitely dressed to impress. And some. Antonio used to call her the "Belle of the Ball" when, like now, she pulled out all the stops.

"Let's go, Cinderella," she winked at her reflection.

The invitation directed her to be at the exclusive Commodore's Club for cocktails at 8 p.m. Before she had reached the entrance, she was met by a senior officer who escorted her to join a small party of guests already seated in a semicircle in the center of the room.

He offered her a glass of champagne, but she declined. "Sparkling water with ice and lemon for me," she told him, and he called over a waiter and gave her order.

"The Captain is on his way," the officer announced to the guests as he did the job of introducing them to one another. Three couples, three nationalities.

Helena knew some of the couples by sight from activities around the ship. One lady was from South America. She and Helena had taken dance and fitness classes together; her husband had also attended salsa class at least once and tried to follow the steps, but he didn't come again. An American couple, Merv and Candy, from Austin, Texas, greeted her like a long-lost friend and she knew the German wife of the last couple from choir club.

All conversation ceased as the Captain appeared in the room, dressed in his formal black evening tunic respendent with gold braid, and flanked by two senior officers. He walked to the empty forest-green chesterfield leather armchair next to Helena, seated himself and nodded welcome to all. For Helena, he reserved the widest smile and a quiet, "Thank you for coming."

Like her, he declined the champagne and asked for sparkling water, ice and lemon. In a toast to his guests, he clinked glasses and laughed when he noticed she, too, drank water.

When it was time to move from the Club to the main restaurant, the two senior officers led the way and two others brought up the rear. Alongside the Captain, as his party was escorted through bars and lounges onto the silver staircase where they stopped for an official photograph, Helena experienced the sensation that her feet did not touch the ground; she truly believed she floated on air.

Passengers turned to watch the party progress, and Helena basked in the glow of the openly admiring looks directed toward the Captain, his party and herself. The most handsome and respected man on the ship was her date and she could not have loved the attention more.

Into the dining room and beyond the occupied dinner tables, the officers stopped at an entryway of which most passengers, even though they passed it every night, were unaware. Floor-length glass doors partly concealed behind discreet white voile curtains were offset from the main area and led to the private dining room. Glass, chrome and a glittering chandelier reflected in a wall of mirrors showcased the exclusive collection of the finest bottled red, white and rose wine. A long oblong table covered in pristine white linen was artfully laid with gleaming silver cutlery and shining crystal glassware. Tiny artificial tea lights flickered and twinkled as bright as stars. Open flames were not allowed onboard ship.

Helena's gold embossed place card was opposite the Captain's in the center of the table. A waiter held her chair, took her stole and arranged it on the back of her high-backed, upholstered chair and, when she was seated, spread the white linen napkin onto her lap. With a flourish, the headwaiter offered the menu card and drew attention to suggested wines to accompany each dish.

Helena studied the menu and as she did so was aware that the Captain's eyes never left her face. "I am very familiar with the menu," he said as he watched her make her choices.

On the ten-course menu, she identified several dishes she was familiar with and others she looked forward to tasting. The menu was a delight to read:

Amuse-bouche: Pineapple Ravioli with smoked salmon
("mouth amusement," a small appetizer popular on French menus)
Appetizer: Cherry Valley Smoked Duck Breast Carpaccio
Soup: Asparagus Cream with Carrot Flan
Salad: Eggplant and Kolovi Olive Tartare
Sorbet: Lemon Basil Sorbet
Fish: Seared Truffle Infused Sea Bass Fillet
Surf and Turf: Beef Tenderloin, Half Lobster Tail
Dessert: Macadamia Nut Chocolate Mud Pie
Cheese Board: Crackers, Dried Fruit and Strawberries
Coffee and Tea: Homemade Petit Fours

* * *

The Captain looked amused at her obvious delight as she perused the menu.

"You approve?" he asked.

"I certainly do," she assured him.

"That is good because I approve of you," he told her. "You look beautiful; your hair up suits you."

Helena smiled at his gracious comment. "Thank you, kind sir," she joked.

Seated opposite each other across the table, they held an animated and private conversation even while surrounded by ship's officers, guests and waitstaff. They were constantly smiling with pleasure to be in each other's company. The evening was everything she had hoped and dreamed. She was on Cloud 9.

She gloried in the fact that he was truly the most handsome, striking, cultured, intelligent, good humored, accomplished man she had ever met. The only rival was her late husband. Antonio had been a proud Italian; the Captain, an exuberant Russian. They were both men who had their sense of identity firmly rooted in heritage, culture and homeland. In their larger than life personalities, they shared many character traits. Fearless, full of life and with a flair for the dramatic, both were dynamic, powerful, assured men. Constantly fascinated by the world and its people and able to command respect yet remain humble. When talking with someone, they possessed the ability to be present and to give the gift of listening.

What more could she say about the man who sat opposite her except that she was hypnotized by his charm and dared to hope that he was enamored of her. She had waited a long time to fall in love again and she could think of no more worthy contender.

One of the best nights of my life, so far, she thought, then added, *and not over yet*.

Throughout dinner and the parade of gastronomic delights, they smiled with delight at each other. To amuse his guests, the Captain insisted she recount a story she had told him. It was one her husband had liked to tell.

"The chief executive of a global corporation had lost the favor of the board and while they headhunted a successor for him, he was sent on a Grand Around the World Cruise. In his absence, they failed to find a suitable candidate and the search continued. On arriving back after months away, the chief executive was flattered to identify the chairman of the board waiting for him on the quayside. He waved enthusiastically from the railings but only when the ship was close enough to the dock could he hear what the chairman was shouting up to him. 'Go around again.'"

The story had become a favorite since Helena had first shared it with the Captain; now she was flattered to be asked to share it with his guests.

It did not escape her attention that he used her to deflect a potentially embarrassing situation. The South American guest, who may have had a little too much to drink or thought he was being amusing, started a particular line of conversation. Seemingly unaware that he had committed a faux pas, he embarrassed his wife by telling the assembled guests, "This Captain is the most popular I have ever known. All the women passengers have crushes on him. Including my wife. All the women want to kiss the Captain."

The Captain shrugged and raised his eyebrows, the wife glared at her husband and Helena realized her good fortune that, if that was true, she was the one who was partnered with him, at least for tonight.

Wine flowed and the Captain and Helena were the only two who drank water. Like co-conspirators, he smiled every time they raised their glasses. A final toast was proposed to a fine evening and for good conditions for the rest of the cruise. "Thank you all for coming," said the Captain. "May you enjoy the rest of your cruise."

The guests finished their coffees and said their thanks as the Captain excused himself.

"A table is reserved in the Club and the Captain will join you for a nightcap," the officer explained as he pulled back her chair. In the Club, Helena sipped a cup of tea and awaited the Captain's return.

"I have to get back to my office," he told her. "Other duties call." He did not overstay his return and refused a drink but he urged his guests to linger over their nightcaps, assured that all had enjoyed their special evening. Addressing Helena, he stood by her chair as was his habit at their lunches. He gazed at her and spoke quietly, making it obvious that this was a conversation addressed to one special person, "Thank you for your company. I am always pleased to spend time with you. We will do it again. Tonight, I intend to open a new page in my logbook for you."

Though she had no idea what he meant, Helena decided indications were that she should take it as a compliment. She smiled. "Good night Captain, and thank you for a wonderful evening."

She wanted to add, "And I hope it's not over yet," but knew that would have been totally inappropriate. While the other VIP guests continued to drink and talk, Helena excused herself.

She made her way onto the deck and stared out over the railings up into the night sky looking at the moon that would later be eclipsed by the shadow of the earth. "Something's wrong with the picture," she reflected sadly. "In all the advertisements for romantic cruises, a couple share the night under the stars."

Waves pounded the side of the *Vision Star*, whipping up the foam as she ploughed ever onward. One of the greatest pleasures of a cruise is that there is no standing still. Every day a new worldview, another port, hello, goodbye. Sail away. Go to bed in one country, wake in another. Forward momentum driving every experience. No regrets.

Helena strolled upstairs and down decks, restless, unwilling to go home and take off her beautiful party dress. "It's not even midnight," she lamented as she checked the clock on her cell phone. She even checked her messages in case he had tried to make contact.

Strangely unfinished, she refused to feel any disappointment. She recalled that on the night she and her husband had met, they had left the party hand in hand, spent the night together and never parted again.

This is a different story; a different time and place and different rules—she had no choice but to accept. Putting personal feelings aside, she was all too aware of the integrity of the man she had chosen. *The Captain is not like other men*, she told herself, *he has responsibilities and obligations and needs to act appropriately at all times.* The life and safety of thousands of people were in his hands. His was a noble calling and he was not about to jeopardize that for an act of disrespect. He was a man of honor.

Helena acknowledged the thought to herself as she passed one of the late-night bars and heard the ballroom music playing. On a secluded deck in the moonlight, she hugged her fur stole close to her body and danced—alone. She was startled when a white-suited officer passed by on the deck above and descended the stairway. For a moment she dared to hope, but it was not the man she longed to see. It was an officer she knew by sight.

"Is everything okay, Madam," he asked. "is there anything I can help you with?"

"That's very kind, but I'm perfectly fine," she assured him. "I'll be on my way to bed after I've seen the eclipse. Good night."

Later, with the moon shining through the window of her room, Helena refused to allow any unrealized expectations to spoil what actually had taken place. The voyage around the world had only started. She was hardly two weeks from home.

There were still months of cruising ahead with adventures, exotic locations and opportunities, plenty of time to get to know each other. Helena's heart filled with happiness as she remembered how it felt when his eyes gazed into hers, the sensation of pure joy when she could smell and watch and breathe in his essence as she succumbed to the powerful attraction of his strong physical presence.

She wrapped the crisp, perfumed sheets of her cozy white bed around her and lay her head on the soft pillows. She replayed the night in her imagination. Dreams do come true, she was sure. She made magic happen as she conjured up this amazing experience. Her desperate desire for a romance had drawn her to him and him to her. Surely it was not only in her imagination. Of course not, she had been a guest tonight at the Captain's table.

Sleep beckoned and she drifted off with dreams of his arms wrapped around her, his hands caressing her body and his mouth covering hers in a never-ending kiss.

Oranjestad, Aruba
Day 18

Aruba's capital city, Oranjestad, is a bustling island town, showcasing the traditional in colorful colonial buildings and the modern in shiny new shopping malls. The cruise terminal in the downtown area allowed easy access to boutiques, upscale chain stores and street vendors and a wide range of casinos, restaurants, dance clubs and bars. In addition to shopping, dining and entertainment, the island's capital city offered museums, a butterfly farm, art galleries and a marina. A colonial history modeled in the formal Dutch architecture was enlivened with the brightly colored styles of the Caribbean. The guidebook description of the ship's next port of call reminded her that she had visited this particular island many times before. A shore excursion to Aruba's town and beaches presented opportunities for sightseeing and a friendly beach with music and food that encouraged a party feeling.

Helena joined the other cruise passengers as they danced with locals on the sandy beach. The laidback music made her feel game for anything and kept her spirits high. She was acutely aware that all the fun, sun and sand she had signed up for by joining a world cruise was threatened with being overwhelmed by her mind's constant desire to think about *him*.

She knew only too well the nature of obsession and addiction to people, places and things and was determined to safeguard her mental health by projecting outward onto happy thoughts and not inward to a longing and desire that may well not be satisfied.

The last time she lost control over an obsession, she almost lost her mind. A mania had set in and the only thing she could focus on was her obsession. It had started when she came across a photograph on Facebook. No matter how often she told herself to delete her account and to refuse to engage in the gossiping and intrusive elements of the social media giant, she still found herself sucked in.

When Antonio died, she was consumed by desperation to check out his contacts and see who featured on his friend list. She knew what she was looking for, though, she had told herself that was not the reason for her interest.

"It's not your business," the few people who knew of his indiscretion warned her. "Do not pursue the people, places and things of his private life. No good can come of it."

Daylight always brought clarity but, in the wee small hours when she couldn't sleep, while she actively mourned Antonio and felt desperately alone, she followed the path through passwords and email addresses to check out who he called his friends. Playing a dangerous game, she pretended she was not looking for one particular person. Many of the names of friends from all over the world were familiar to her. Work colleagues, family friends, and members of clubs, associations and professional bodies to which he belonged. Antonio always claimed it was necessary to keep up with the network of social media; it had kept him connected and offered useful information. Occasionally he would tell her that someone had reached out via a friend request.

"Why would you want to keep in touch with them?" she'd ask. "We hardly know them and I've certainly no interest in getting friendly over the internet." She feared the intrusion of people into their lives and dreaded that even old friends would reunite.

Her own childhood friends, past work colleagues and distant family members held no interest for Helena. When it was time to move on in life, she walked away without a backward glance. The excitement of the new was her driving force, not the hold of the past.

"Move on, let go" was her motto, and she had always been eager to find out what was beyond the next bend in the road. Apart from the closest members of her immediate family, whom she held dear, extending a welcome to friends of friends was not the way she operated.

Antonio held fast to the connections of his past; it was the way he had been brought up. Community was the guiding principle of the close-knit Italian town where he had been born and bred. Though most of his immediate family had passed, he took very seriously his commitment to ensuring that the legacy and reputation of his aristocratic family lived on. Unfortunately, the richness of his heritage had long since lost its grandeur, and there were no palaces or lands or titles to covet. However, the upcoming generations shared his passion of ensuring that the proud tradition was never forgotten and would live on in the ancestors. Her husband's family had a long and noble history; they had won and lost lands, titles and reputations.

Antonio shared the enthusiasm of the younger generations and provided guidance and encouragement. For these distant family members, he cultivated a rich network on the Web even if his life and work meant that he rarely had the opportunity to return to his roots.

In his lifetime, Helena accepted that her husband was a man who needed to cast his net wide in his search for knowledge and his desire to embrace humanity.

"I became a doctor because I love people and want to serve them," he explained. "Even though most of my work is now in a laboratory, my life's work is directed at individuals and my need to help alleviate their suffering."

In a gesture of maturity, to prevent herself from prying into his personal business, Helena had initially closed down Antonio's Facebook account. Then the thoughts began to gnaw at her. She tortured herself with details of an imaginary relationship. She needed to know the truth. She needed to know if he was in touch with that woman. Wanted to see a picture of her. Was desperate to find out if there was a child. Was Antonio a father? Did he communicate with the mother?

Helena knew she was crossing a boundary that threatened to lead to hurt as she trawled through his contacts to find the woman. She had always refused to hear any details. She did not want to know the name or whether she was still in Antonio's orbit. As they had agreed in the beginning, only the lawyer would have the information. There was to be no personal contact.

Night after night, Helena checked out the streams on Antonio's social media accounts. She considered and dismissed dozens upon dozens of young women who may have had a personal connection to her late husband. She scrutinized photographs, read the messages they sent, followed the comments and looked into his history.

Obsession consumed her. Night after night she stared at the screen. She tormented herself with the questions. At a time when she was expected to be recovering from the trauma of Antonio's sudden death, she sank deeper and deeper into a pit of despair. She called into question every aspect of their lives together. The pregnancy was a trap, she convinced herself, certainly not a scenario in which Antonio colluded. Now she was not so sure. Had there been others? Had she deluded herself, lived in denial, refused to see signs, been like Pollyanna and refused to acknowledge what she didn't want to see?

In the dark, like a criminal, a dark Web hacker, she clicked and scrolled and stared.

"I'll find you," she muttered to the screen, to the unseen presence. The ghost in the box. "I know you are in there."

Helena took up smoking again and used tranquilizers to hold her anxiety at bay. In earlier years, she had suffered bouts of depression and debilitating feelings of impending doom that rendered her unable to perform normally. The symptoms had manifested in an eating disorder and she had accepted professional help to get her life back on track.

Now she felt the control and discipline she had learned to exercise slipping away.

Tears of frustration had flowed down her cheeks as she focused her attention on the screen.

Even though she was actively searching, it came as a shock to finally come face-to-face with her quarry. A mirror image of herself: blond and blue-eyed with a heart-shaped face, full rosy lips and a delicate nose. Her smile was beautiful and showed off her dimples. The photograph could have been of a younger sister of Helena's and beside her sat a young, smiling, handsome dark-haired child. To deny the similarities between the boy and Antonio was impossible.

"How could you, Antonio?" she gasped. "It was never all over."

The photograph burned its way into her heart and mind.

Tears and fears tormented her. Long, lonely hours of crying and questioning. Helena saw no way out. "This time my heart really will break."

The photograph haunted her. She blew it up, printed it out and stared at it for hours.

She heard Antonio's voice in her head, "Now you have the information, what do you plan to do with it?"

Helena was filled with anger and confusion, she wanted to rage and scream. "How dare you?" she asked over and over again.

Threads of online conversation and photographs between the woman, Avaleen, her son Tony and Antonio were easy to follow. Helena wrote and deleted message after message. She called the lawyer who dealt with the initial arrangement and subsequently took care of all of Antonio's legal affairs. His counsel was straightforward. "This is not your business. I can give you no information. You can let it ruin your life, or you can forgive Antonio and move on."

A consultation with the therapist she had visited when she suffered the worst effects of her eating disorders, years before she met Antonio, left her with the same message.

Have the therapist and the lawyer discussed me? she wondered. *They both have the same advice. Did they talk and decide what to say?*

After a prolonged period of self-torment and hopelessness, Helena responded to the guidance of her counselor, and self-preservation eventually overcame the debilitating effects of sadness and grief. It was not easy, but she made the decision to follow all the necessary steps to take care of her emotional and mental health.

"I am worthwhile," she told herself. "I deserve to be well. Trying to create problems or hurt for people whom Antonio loved will only bring me more pain. I don't want to give power over my life to anyone. I've worked too hard on my own recovery."

"I need to take affirmative action," Helena reported to her therapist. "I've permanently closed down the Facebook account."

"Sounds like a positive development," the therapist confirmed. "You already look lighter, more free."

Helena enjoyed the positive reinforcement but did have one small confession to make,

"I did send a message before I disconnected," Helena admitted. "After much consideration, I simply wrote, "There's enough love to go around.""

Journal entry: *Aruba. I've been here before. Not only to this place but to this mind-set. The Captain consumes my every thought. I want to spend every minute of the day with him. I am obsessed. Wherever I am, I am conscious that he may appear. I treasure the memory of last night and the photograph of him and I, together, in the official pose on the way into dinner. The original photograph showed the full line-up of guests and officers. I cut it down so that now it features him and me. It takes pride of place on my dressing table. The room steward smiled when he arrived to do evening turndown service on my bed. "He is a very popular Captain." He nodded his approval.*

After a long day ashore, Helena decided not to dress up for dinner. Instead she followed the informal dress code and went upstairs to eat dinner in the Terrazza. And there he was. No fancy dinner tonight. He ate alone in the restaurant at his high table. He called her over. "How are you? Did you go ashore today? I didn't. Too much work to do. In my office studying charts and replying to emails."

Helena gave him a quick rundown of her uneventful visit to Aruba. "I wanted to get an early night," she told him. "After last night when I spent half the night on deck waiting for the eclipse."

"I could have told you there was too much cloud to see the eclipse," he smiled. "I, too, wanted to see it. I am a big fan of celestial phenomena. I watched from the bridge and even waited to see if the aura would go red. No luck."

"It's the last such red moon eclipse for about fifty years," said Helena.

"Well then, I guess we won't see it next time either." He laughed.

"I'll leave you to finish your meal," Helena told him, "I know you have a busy day tomorrow."

"One of the show parts of the cruise," he explained, "crossing the Panama Canal. I will be up at 4 a.m. You can stay in bed till 6 a.m."

Helena felt a shiver inside as he discussed their separate sleeping arrangements. She resisted any temptation to remark or even look as if she had noticed.

"Always good to talk to you, Captain," she nodded. "Enjoy the canal. I'll be up there on deck at dawn with the other thrill seekers."

Before retiring for the night, Helena made her way to the reception desk and left a "Private & Personal" letter to be delivered to the Captain.

On a gold-embossed Cartier card, she wrote, "Thank you so much for a wonderful evening as your dinner guest at the Captain's table. You are a most gracious host and your other guests were excellent company. It gives me great pleasure to know you have opened a new page in your logbook for me. It sounds like a most auspicious recognition and I intend to accept it as such unless, and until, anyone tells me differently. With kindest regards and admiration, Helena de Croy Ringold."

Panama Canal
Day 22

Passage through the Panama Canal lasted from dawn to late afternoon. The Captain was on the bridge the whole time even though all vessels transiting the canal are required to have a local pilot in charge of guiding the vessel through the locks.

The canal is one of the two most strategic artificial waterways in the world; the other is the Suez Canal. Ships sailing between the east and west coast of the United States, which otherwise would be obliged to sail around Cape Horn, shorten their journey by almost 8,000 nautical miles when transiting the canal. Savings of up to 3,500 nautical miles are made on voyages between one coast of North America and ports on the opposite coast in South America.

Passengers hugged the rails and watched every minute of the long and complicated journey through one of the largest man-made structures in the world. With endless fascination they watched the pilot, the crew and the Captain as they maneuvered the cruise ship through the lines and narrow gates of the Gatun Locks (passing in the east lane), Pedro Miguel Locks (through the west lane) and Miraflores Locks (west lane). Ships passing in opposite directions were visible, like on a motorway.

"Tell him to mind the paintwork," called one passenger to the Captain. "He came a bit close on that last lock gate."

Never taking his eyes off operations for a minute, the Captain smiled good-naturedly.

He stood at ease, his body balanced, feet crossed and leaning on the steering wheel, a man comfortable with himself and his responsibilities.

This was not his first rodeo; he had made this journey dozens of times but still never tired of the magnificence of the spectacle and admiration for the incredible feat of engineering.

Helena made sure she was not visible to him even as she spent hours on deck savoring her maiden voyage through the Panama Canal. She passed the time between locks by writing a report using research she gathered from Google. She decided to post it on the ship's Facebook page where passengers were invited to share photographs and comments.

A MAN A PLAN A CANAL—PANAMA (read it backward or forward)

The Panama Canal has earned its place on the ultimate list of the great journeys of the world, featuring as it does on the wish list of many new and seasoned travelers. For that reason, the vast majority of passengers through the Canal and into the Gatun Lake were determined not to miss the experience, even though it took place at ridiculous o'clock.

The Captain announced the arrival of not one but two pilot boats to navigate his 93,500 ton, 965-foot ship through the hundred-year-old Panama Canal. The historic canal fascinated man with the idea, but not the execution, of building a route that would join the Atlantic and Pacific, as far back as the Spanish arrival on the land mass back in the early sixteenth century. Now it is hailed as an international trade route and maritime shortcut that saves time and costs by transporting a world of goods via the 50-mile waterway—a man-made passage through the two oceans at one of the narrowest points of the Isthmus of Panama and the American continent. Since its official opening in 1914, more than one million ships from all over the world have transited the canal. And more make the journey every day.

An eagerly awaited expansion opened offering two gigantic new lock complexes, one on the Pacific and one on the Atlantic, thereby facilitating an improved route alongside the previous ones. The phenomenal engineering feat upgraded shipping patterns in the region with the Canal as an ever-greater driving force for global trade.

The United States managed the canal from its official opening in 1914 up to the start of the millennium in 1999 when Panama took over full operation, administration and maintenance of the canal. The latest expansion consolidated Panama's position as the most important transportation center in the Americas.

As *Vision Star* prepared to take its place and join the never-ending twenty-four-hour stream of vessels traversing the canal, the passengers' enthusiasm and sense of awe made the journey into an adventure. They were informed by officials that all toll and license payments—totaling a quarter of a million dollars for their 2,000 passengers—had to be completed and paid into a Panamanian bank twenty-four hours before the vessel was allowed to start its passage—cash or bank orders—no checks.

Sleepy passengers, many still in pyjamas and clutching steaming cups of coffee, crammed the rails on the observation deck to claim the best view of entering the first set of lock gates.

Awaiting our turn in the narrow entryway to the first of three concrete locks that would take our cruise ship from the Atlantic to the Pacific, the view of the surrounding area was lush, tranquil and isolated. Rising majestically on the first bed of rapidly swirling water, we were elevated eighty-five feet to the top of the water mountain.

The interoceanic waterway uses a system of locks with two lanes that operate as water elevators. In these lanes, the ships are transported from sea level to the level of Gatun Lake, twenty-six meters above sea level. This process allows smooth crossing through the Continental divide and then lowers the ship to sea level on the other side of the Isthmus.

Water used to raise and lower the vessels in each set of locks is obtained from Gatun Lake by gravity and poured into the locks through a main culvert system that extends under the lock chambers from the side and the center walls. The lock is 467 yards long and 60 yards wide, the size of more than four football fields. Once inside the concrete channel, our main understanding of the hydropower propelling the boat forward was by observing the ships laden with towering steel cathedrals of cargo and goods in containers who entered the lanes before us.

Emerging from the locks, Gatun Lake resembled a maritime car park with shipping vessels moored as far as the eye could see. This sight reinforced the wonder of hydropower and produced in observers an exhilarating sense of accomplishment. Man conquers the mighty oceans.

Passengers gave rapt attention to the close-up views of the hydro operations construction station—a series of tracks and trains and giant engineering machines. The bi-oceanic journey through the Panama Canal proudly conferred a sense of accomplishment on travelers, as well as produced another check mark on the bucket list.

Panama Canal. Been there, done that; bought the T-shirt, the Panama hat and the fridge magnet. And to cap it all—a chance to quote one of the most famous palindromes ever: **A MAN A PLAN, A CANAL—PANAMA**—forward and back—it's the same!

"Impressive," said the Captain, as he met Helena in the buffet line the day after the Panama Canal passage. "I read it online. You made a very good job of explaining the incredible experience of traveling through the canal, an amazing achievement for man. Also, I never heard before about 'A Man A Plan A Canal—Panama.' Thank you for that."

Helena basked in his praise and smiled as she finished helping herself from the vast selection of salad dishes. The two of them stood side by side and waited patiently as the serving team set out a fresh tureen of piping hot soup.

Served first, Helena headed for one of her usual tables by the rear window, far from his now rarely used lunchtime high table. The restaurant was almost empty of passengers.

She watched as he was handed his tray and the bowl of steaming vegetable soup was added to the tray containing his salad. Tray in hand, he walked across the restaurant headed for his table, then as if suddenly remembering something, he stopped and changed his direction. The headwaiter, about to deliver the Captain's lunchtime order of a glass of ginger ale with ice, stopped to watch and wait to see what would happen.

Helena thought she knew what was about to happen.

Straight ahead, the Captain crossed the vast dining room. Balancing his tray, he stopped by her four-seater table next to the floor to ceiling windows overlooking the ocean. "May I join you?" he asked.

"Of course, Captain," she said, hardly able to contain her excitement.

The thrill of an invite to the Captain's table was almost surpassed by him inviting himself to her table. She tried to concentrate on her breathing and not make a fool of herself.

"This must be what it means to be lost for words," she said under her breath as she challenged herself to pay total attention to the moment. She focused her attention on her food as if it was the most natural thing in the world for him to share her lunch table. He smiled his trademark grin and watched as she attempted to process this new development.

Never had she seen him join anyone at their table. How special she felt that he had singled her out. She felt sure her eyes registered her total surprise and her smile was wide as that of a Cheshire cat.

"One thing I have to ask you," he said with a serious look on his face. "When we have lunch together, please call me Grigory. Not Captain."

"Of course, Captain," the words were out of her mouth

before she could stop them. Together, they laughed and shared the joke.

Across the restaurant, the headwaiter looked on in amazement and the serving staff watched to gauge his reaction. He was trained to react discreetly whatever the circumstances, but if asked, he would have to admit that this was one situation he had never seen before.

The Captain's table was taking on a whole new meaning.

Puerto Quetzal, Guatemala
Day 23

Puerto Quetzal is a large industrial port, a gateway to some of the most fascinating and beautiful places in the country of Guatemala. Northward, the air is scented by sugarcane and coffee and the mountains overlook the beautiful Atitlan Lake. Macadamia nuts are one of the most important exports of the country.

Guatemala, and its indigenous Mayan population, was ruled by Spain from the mid-1500s until it gained independence in 1821 when it became part of the First Mexican Empire and subsequently part of the Federal Republic of Central America. In the late twentieth century, Guatemala experienced a series of authoritarian governments until 1944, which led to a popular uprising and a ten-year revolution. Military rule led to civil war between the government and the guerrillas that lasted almost forty years, until Guatemala established a representative democracy in 1997.

For centuries, the Mayans mined jade and the Jade Maya Factory and Museum has evolved as a world leader in reintroducing Maya Jade to the world through the discovery, mining and working of Guatemala's fine jadeite jade. Guatemala enjoys the distinction of being one of the major sources of this fine stone.

A woman with a passion, American archaeologist Mary Lou Rending and her husband, Jay, made the decision to re-establish a jade carving industry in Guatemala, using native workers who implemented the carving traditions of their ancestors. Mary Lou still runs the Jade Maya Factory and Museum, and visitors can hear the story direct from her.

She proudly displayed a signed photograph of President Clinton on his visit to the museum.

"I am passionate about jade," she explained. "It is my life's work and I am very proud of the tradition we have established here. The raw jade is mined and transformed into pre-Columbian style museum quality replicas and exquisite handmade jewelry."

Seduced by the beauty of the jade, Helena engaged Mary Lou in conversation and received an invitation. "We always have need of guides who can conduct tours of the museum," she explained. "If you are interested, one of my team will train you and you can join us here in our important work to spread the word of this ancient and traditional art."

"If I ever have the chance to come and live in Puerto Quetzal, I will take you up on your offer," Helena assured Mary Lou. "In the meantime, I will take home a reminder of your wonderful jewelry exhibition by purchasing a jade necklace—and having a photograph taken standing beside the life-size statue of a Mayan warrior." The centerpiece of the warrior's costume presented a vibrant display of the brightly colored feathers of the quetzal bird, the national symbol of Guatemala, whose feathers were in ancient times used as currency.

The Mayan culture has been preserved, and the country

and Port are alive with color from the brightly painted colonial buildings that line the cobblestone street to the traditional costumes of the local people. Thirty volcanoes, three of which are active, cover the country of Guatemala.

Lunch at the excellent restaurant, confined within the ruins of the sixteenth century Casa Santo Domingo, released in Helena an intention that at some time in her life she would spend time connecting with the deep spiritual and cultural heritage of Guatemala.

"It's all very well being a tourist," she reminded herself, "to visit for a day, then move on but some places deserve more time and attention to explore and become embedded. I would like to be a traveler still passing through but stopping long enough to absorb the atmosphere, the culture, the messages emitting from rocks and stones of the very land."

Lost in wonder, she imagined herself attending one of the classical musical events and traditional performances that take place around the medieval stone altar. Then Helena lit a candle and sent out the intention that she desired to return to this sacred and enchanting place.

With a sense of reverence and awe, she examined the collection of Mayan Colombian archaeological pieces and the artfully lit collection of superb glass treasures from masters such as Baccarat, Daum and Lalique. In the ruins of the former monastery, a private collector devoted his time and resources to ensuring the feeling of contemplation and spiritual connection that touched the soul in the hallowed display of exquisite works of art and in the rock faces and secluded crevices.

"Only art and culture truly move my soul," said Helena to the volunteer guide, who struggled to understand her spoken language but knew the language of the heart when presented with it.

"Maybe I will come back one day," she told the taxi driver who had taken her on a private tour of Puerto Quetzal, "but please be mindful of the time I am due back onboard. I don't want the ship to sail without me."

She was right to be concerned, the drive back to the ship was unpredictable and subject to diversions because of a recent volcanic eruption and disruption to the road systems.

"But the tour is not over yet," the taxi driver admonished her, "you need to feast on the best tastes of Guatemala."

He was not to be dissuaded and stopped his "seen better days' car" by a small roadside stall and urged Helena to buy the main exports of his country. Some of the world's finest coffee is produced in Guatemala, and, alongside the export of macadamia nuts for which the country is famous, these products drive the local economy.

Arriving back at the ship, Helena accepted a gift from her newfound friend. "Chocolate was invented by the Mayans," he informed her. "For you, a gift of a chocolate doll."

Tucked into a brightly colored, woven woolen purse, which may or may not have been specially made by his wife, as he said, was her gift, a smiling doll.

"She makes your wishes come true."

He waved goodbye as Helena walked toward the gangway to join the other passengers returning from their shore excursions, and, like the many friendly, hospitable people she had met that day, he urged her to come back to his country.

Helena smiled and promised it would be on her wish list—and she also had a special wish for the chocolate doll to grant: to one day share a special day of sightseeing, like the one she had enjoyed, in the company of the Captain. She planned to ask her magical chocolate doll to make it come true.

Acapulco
Day 25

"Going Loco down in Acapulco," a global hit by superstar Ricky Martin, blares out from every bar, and the crowded beaches and high-energy nightclub culture attracts tours from all over the world, with cruise liners stopping in the port every day of the week and bringing in thousands of visitors.

Helena hailed an SUV and shared the ride to the famous Flamingo Hotel with other cruise ship passengers. Acapulco, a major seaport on the Pacific coast in Mexico, had a reputation as a dangerous place. Murders occurred every day, usually committed by local gangs and drug traders.

"Don't go alone," the cruise line representatives warned. "You'll notice when you arrive that the streets are lined with armed policeman. There's a reason for that. Keep safe and travel with other cruisers."

One of Mexico's oldest and best-known beach resorts, located in a deep semi-circular bay, Acapulco first gained its reputation and became popular in the 1950s. It was a celebrated spot for partying celebrities and millionaires. The north side of Acapulco is traditional and authentic, with history and local Mexican street life; the southern part of the city is dominated by new luxury hotels built for tourists.

Hollywood stars of yesteryear, such as Cary Grant, Gregory Peck, Errol Flynn and John Wayne, spent their holidays in the stylish villas and apartment blocks high up on the hills overlooking the city. Those days are long gone, but the area known as Diamond Zone still features impressive hotels such as the Fairmont Acapulco Princess, which has a unique Aztec pyramid architecture, and the Mayan Palace, which was constructed using the shapes and symbols of Mayan culture.

One downtown hotel features, on its rooftop, a larger than life statue of a warrior princess armed with a bow and arrow, which is visible high above the main city street.

One of the most famous of the Hollywood stars who invaded Acapulco in the '50s and made it fashionable was actor Johnny Weissmuller, the original Tarzan. Johnny was the owner and promoter of a garish pink hotel, Hotel Los Flamingos, perched high on a cliff that provides spectacular views of the bay and Pacific Ocean. The hotel is an homage to the golden days of Hollywood with black-and-white photographs of the movie stars who visited the hotel and enjoyed cocktails in the rooftop bar. These days Johnny's private quarters are rented out to tourists and the winding tracks between secluded guest rooms attracts vacationers from all over the world.

In looking for danger, Helena had to concede that the most dangerous thing she encountered at the modern-day Flamingo Hotel was a lethal cocktail overflowing with fruit, umbrellas and plastic flamingo twizzle sticks.

From the profane to the sacred, Helena and her companions moved on to the Chapel of Peace, a modern custom-made church designed and constructed 1,250 feet above sea level in an idyllic setting that overlooks the harbor and La Roqueta Island.

Reminiscent of the visual impact made by the Statue of Christ the Redeemer when arriving in Brazil, whether by air or sea, the chapel features a towering 138-foot Trouyet Cross, which is visible across the entire city and bay. At night the cross is illuminated, an everlasting monument to the sons of a wealthy Acapulco couple, Mr. and Mrs. Trouyet. Their children died in an air accident while returning to the city fifty years ago. The chapel is reverentially preserved and maintained by a family trust. Helena prayed in the Chapel of Peace and dedicated her devotion to her departed husband, Antonio.

Then came the visit she had been both dreading and longing to experience: the black SUV containing her and her fellow passengers arrived at La Quebrada, a headland high above the sea. Timing was crucial as the ritual they were about to see was performed only at certain times of the day. Here the famed Acapulco Cliff Divers leap from rock formations, some as high as 130 feet, and plunge gracefully into the sea below.

Before they make their death defying dive from the cliffs, they kneel at a little shrine to pray. Hundreds of tourists hold their collective breath while they watch the young men line up to dive from the cliff tops. The dives are choreographed by age, and the entire crowd burst into rapturous applause as the youngest one kneeled to pray, then settled his feet and held his body perfectly balanced on the stony ledge.

Helena held her breath, crossed herself and prayed along with them, imagining what it must have been like for her husband, as a young man in Italy, to perform the daredevil feat of cliff diving.

The fact that he had forgiven the school friend who pushed him over the cliff always reminded her of the special person she had been lucky enough to marry.

Show over after performing their sky-high antics, the cliff divers make their way down to meet their admirers in the waiting crowd. Selling photographs of their spectacular dives and having photos taken with tourists funds the young men's activities and gives them a wage to continue the daredevil activities where they challenge and survive death on an hourly basis.

Helena pushed her way through the crowd. She wanted to offer a donation to the boys and purchase a photo from the small makeshift table top a supporter set up and covered with photos. Having bought a set of photos of the boys diving, she moved in to get an extra personal memento. The boys hovered around; this was the only chance they had to make their money for the day.

"Would you take a photo of me with this dashing hero?" Helena asked one of the cruise passengers from her tour. Embraced by a handsome, muscle-bound young man still dripping seawater from his dive, Helena smiled for the camera and explained, though, she wasn't sure she was believed, "My husband was a cliff diver."

SOS—Rescue at Sea
Day 30

Helena armed herself for war. Determined not to be intimidated, she wore a slinky, scarlet dress and black patent-killer heels as she prepared to face her regular dinner companions for the first time since the news of her special relationship with the Captain became public. News of her lunch date with the Captain had spread throughout the ship like wildfire. All eyes were on her, and she heard a whispered, "Captain's girlfriend," as she walked around the ship.

Not that she minded, far from it. She would have been proud of the fact were it true. Instead she had no idea of what relationship, if any, would develop. All she hoped was that being the subject of such gossip would not drive him away, a man of his integrity was likely to steer clear of controversy.

Head held high, she walked into the restaurant and acknowledged the greetings of the hospitality and waitstaff who lined up to welcome the passengers every evening. She saved an especially warm "Hello" for the officers whom she had gotten to know at the Captain's table.

"Thank you, you're very kind," she said as one of the

senior officers offered his arm and escorted her to her table. This courtesy was extended to many of the single women onboard when they arrived at dinner alone, but tonight Helena was especially glad of the company as she walked through the crowded restaurant.

"Good of you to join us," said Meredith, as Helena took her place at the circular table. "Presumably you did not receive any more important invitations for dinner tonight. Thank you for gracing us with your presence."

"Always glad to see you, Meredith," said Helena as she tried hard to keep the sarcasm out of her voice. She looked around at the other passengers with whom she had always had friendly relations. "I highly recommend you accept the invitation if you are invited to dine at the Captain's table. It's a wonderful experience and one not to be missed. However, I'm very glad to be back here among friends. Thank you for keeping my place for me. I promise not to bore you with details of the other place and I appreciate you not asking questions."

Meredith fumed, but the rest of the guests smiled as they got back to discussing important matters and much more interesting conversations about their own lives.

Helena remembered the advice from a wise teacher of hers: "You wouldn't worry so much about what people think of you if you knew how rarely people actually do think of you."

Guests shared their experiences of recent shore excursions and looked forward to up-and-coming port calls in French Polynesia in the South Pacific Ocean. Stories of ancient tikis, cannibalism and swarming sharks fired their imagination.

The last ocean to be discovered by the Europeans, the Pacific Ocean covers 63.8 million square miles of sea and extends from Asia and Australia to the Americas and from the Arctic Ocean in the North to Antarctica in the South. It is so vast that it covers more area than all the land masses in the world put together. The name Pacific originates from the Latin word *pace*, which means "peace," and was named Mar Pacifico, which means peaceful sea, by Portuguese explorer Ferdinand Magellan in 1521.

Dinner over, Helena made a tour of the ship. She followed a route that allowed her to check out the bars, lounges and communal areas to see whether by good fortune she would run into the Captain. She was familiar with many of his regular routines and, in her journey around the ship, up stairways, across decks, through communal areas, she was ever alert to the possibility of seeing him.

Their relationship appeared to have moved up a gear after enjoying lunch together, but where this would lead she could not envisage. He was nowhere to be seen. She refused invitations to join friends who engaged in after-dinner activities: dancing, drinking, testing their knowledge in quizzes. She would have denied it, if asked, but Helena's mind had room only for thoughts of him. Another fruitless tour around the ship assured her that they were not destined to meet.

Reluctantly Helena returned to her cabin. She checked her emails, texts and the landline. No communication. Events were not moving quickly enough to satisfy her.

On her knees, she searched under the bed for a small traveling bag. In that were the secret elements she used to add impetus to her desires. Her magic kit was an essential element in her spiritual practice—she never traveled without it. Helena dimmed the lights and put on soothing meditation music. She carefully laid out the symbols of the candle ritual: a bowl of crystals to focus the energy and a small electric candle because open flames were not allowed in cabins. The flickering light symbolized the experience of being in several existences at once. It was an ancient method of transcendence, a natural and ideal tool to make a connection with the universe. Focusing on the light quiets the mind and directs attention to manifesting desires.

She prayed out loud, "May this sacred intervention and holy meditation bring positive energy to attract the relationship my heart desires. I channel the color pink as a symbol of unconditional love and offer the petals of a rose to show my purest intentions. I give thanks for the wish that is to be granted."

Magic empowered Helena and focused her mind with clarity on her goals. As long as her heart was pure and her desires came from a place of love, she was at peace with her belief that she could manifest and articulate her desires to the universe. She called herself a cocreator.

A master manifestor. Alongside traditional prayer, she found her rituals to be a powerful contributor to attracting the life that she chose to live. She saw no conflict with her faith in traditional religion; candles, incense and prayer are universal methods of gaining the attention of the divine forces that are responsible for our life situations.

With care she packed away her paraphernalia. Her mind was in a happy, hopeful place. Sleep came easily, and she drifted into dreams full of promise and peace. Perhaps being in the Mar Pacifico, the peaceful sea, had induced the profound feeling of well-being with which she awoke. Happy to face another day and undertake an exploration of the exotic pacific island of Nuku Hiva.

But for one vessel, the peaceful sea had not proved so peaceful.

Overnight their cruise ship had altered course and sped to the rescue of a yacht that had gotten into difficulties. Joining the crowd who had gathered on the upper deck, Helena asked several passengers what had happened, "Why have we stopped sailing?"

With so many eager to recount the news, she soon heard the full story.

"We answered a May Day call," they told her. "We were the nearest ship and the Captain changed our course to go to the rescue."

"And where is the yacht now?" she asked. A laugh went up from the watching crowd.

"Down there," replied a fellow passenger she knew, an amateur sailor who was always first to assess the situation.

Helena leaned over the railing and was more than a little surprised to see a yacht drawn up alongside the cruise ship. She recognized the uniforms of several of the ship's officers onboard the yacht.

"What happened? Was anyone injured?" she wanted to know. "Are they coming onboard here?"

"The Captain's on the bridge; he's talking to them from there," her friend explained, "and he's not very pleased. Seems he was told the yacht was in distress and had an injured person onboard. Now he's learned that the injury is minor and they have run out of fuel. Not a legitimate reason to send a May Day and have another vessel go to their rescue."

The Captain was on the radio speaking to the skipper of the yacht. "What do you need?" he asked. "You have refused the assistance of our ship's doctor. My officers will provide your other requests."

The three people onboard the yacht, two men and a woman, looked relieved. The Captain looked resigned. Aware that many of his passengers were observing the exchange, he looked up to his audience. "They require fuel, water and food," he told them. Then with an ironic laugh, he played to the gallery, "They'll be asking for dancing girls next."

During dinner the Captain made an official announcement, "Due to our responding to aid a ship in distress at sea, our position is so far off the original course that we cannot make a port call to the island of Nuku Hiva. I have made the decision to sail straight on to our next scheduled stop, the island of Tahiti, which I am sure you will enjoy. Thank you to all the crew and officers who assisted in the operation today and thank you, the passengers, for your understanding."

The whole restaurant responded with a round of applause, and, even though a few disgruntled passengers claimed that a visit to Nuku Hiva was the main reason for their taking a world cruise, most reasonable people agreed that no other course of action was possible.

Later that evening, the Captain, accompanied by two of his officers who had been involved in the rescue mission, made the rounds of the communal areas and stopped to talk to passengers.

Helena was with friends enjoying a drink in the lounge when he passed by. He made his way over to talk to her companions, and she asked, "Okay if I write up a report?"

"Of course," he smiled, "I look forward to reading it."

Helena gathered information and shared her report on the ship's comments page. A fellow passenger provided a photograph of the disabled yacht moored alongside the liner.

Cruise passengers awoke to find themselves at the center of a drama on the high seas in the middle of the Pacific Ocean. They had been expecting to make a port call on the tiny French Polynesian island of Nuku Hiva in the Marquesas Islands. Instead, in the early hours, their ship answered a distress call from a US sailboat that had become disabled and had sent an SOS stating they had an onboard medical emergency and required fuel and water. From their position a few miles south of the equator, the cruise ship altered their course and sped over one hundred sea miles to answer what the Captain called a "Matter of Honor."

"One we take very seriously: to come to the aid of a vessel in distress, no matter the distance or conditions. The cruise ship Vision Star offered the two men and the woman onboard the services of the ship's doctor and provided fuel and water, enabling the disabled yacht to continue their trip, which began in Mexico." Captain Grigory thanked the passengers, officers and crew for their understanding and support. "Everyone did an excellent job," he announced. "Life at sea is unpredictable and can be challenging. Following our intervention, the vessel we assisted resumed their journey, and we are back on course to our next port of call, the Islands of Tahiti."

Helena's report was posted on the ship's website and on several travel blogs. She was overjoyed to receive a text message, "See you in Tahiti. I look forward to hearing the inside story of *Mutiny on the Bounty*."

Helena prepared her research before the port stop, knowing that, when they next had lunch, the Captain would ask her what she had uncovered. He listened to BBC news and had an appetite for documentaries, especially about history and the sea.

Mutiny on the Bounty: Royal Navy vessel *Bounty* left England in 1787 on a mission—collecting breadfruits—Mutiny happened in South Pacific April 28, 1789—Acting Lieutenant Fletcher Christian seized control of the vessel from Captain Bligh. They set Captain and eighteen loyalists adrift in an open launch and Captain Bligh completed the journey of 3,500 nautical miles across the Pacific Ocean. *Bounty* had been in Tahiti for five months and the mutineers formed relationships with the local women. Bligh reached England in April 1790 and the Admiralty despatched HMS Pandora to search for Christian and the mutineers. Fourteen were captured and court-martialed, four were acquitted, three were pardoned, and three were hanged. Christian's group hid on Pitcairn Island where Christian was later murdered by natives.

Previously Bligh had sailed with Captain Cook to the South Pacific. In 1806, Bligh was appointed Governor of New South Wales and in 1814 made Rear Admiral and Vice Admiral in which capacities he commanded several ships. Bligh was subsequently arrested and overthrown in the Rum Rebellion. He was not offered any further naval appointments and died in 1817 at age sixty-three.

Helena concluded there was plenty of food for thought to inspire an interesting lunchtime conversation. Even she did not expect to simply sit, gazing into his eyes every day.

Bora, Bora, French Polynesia
Day 32

Storms lashed the ship and all open decks and the swimming pool were closed for reasons of safety. Walking around the ship was treacherous, and the restaurants were less busy than usual as many passengers succumbed to seasickness.

Helena swallowed her sea sickness pills, put on the wrist bands she had been assured were effective and hoped to keep the feelings of queasiness at bay. "Hold on to the handrail and be very careful on the stairs," the cabin steward warned her as she left her cabin and headed up to the restaurant. "You must wear boat shoes, no heels."

The Captain was forced to abandon the shore stop in Tahiti. After six days at sea, some passengers began to suffer from cabin fever. Despite constant activities onboard ship, they longed to be ashore exploring new lands and meeting new people. Tahiti was an especially popular destination and the cruisers looked forward to a visit to the fabled south sea island.

Helena's expectations had been to meet up with the Captain on the island, and she was bitterly disappointed that stormy conditions had canceled her plans. In her mind's eye, she imagined a picture-perfect day on a paradise island and a chance to move their relationship to the next level.

It had been days since she had seen him. The adverse weather conditions meant that he hardly left the bridge. On the last day of the week, he arrived in the restaurant and appeared at her table, obviously under pressure.

Without preamble, he shared her table in the center of the busy restaurant. Passengers had little better to do than eat. Some even took ownership of tables and, with their friends, played cards or board games. Helena felt sure that he would not join her at the only table she had been able to secure, a low-level table alongside a busy passageway in an open area of the restaurant.

He looked tired. "I can't stay long," he told her. "I have been very busy. Hardly getting any sleep. There are other senior officers who can take charge, but I feel the need to be present. I can't sleep anyway when I am concerned about the weather. Constantly I am checking the weather forecasts and adjusting and studying the conditions."

Helena loved the easy way he confided in her and treated her as a friend and someone with whom to share the reality of his situation. Other passengers stopped by the table, and he reassured them. "It's all good. We are monitoring the conditions constantly. Yes, it is sad we could not go to Tahiti. Next time, maybe."

Interruptions to his meal appeared not to faze him, but most passengers respected his mealtime. His demeanor was charming, interested and attentive, no matter who was asking the questions.

"What have you been doing?" he asked Helena, putting down his knife and fork to listen to her answer. He never assumed that only his role as the Captain of the ship was important. He displayed a genuine interest in other people. Helena was grateful she commanded so much of his attention.

She stared into his eyes, captivated to be so close to him and every fiber of her being longed to reach out and touch him. His presence and proximity intoxicated her, risking that he would not respond, she took a chance and said, "What do I do? I think of you. Knowing that your responsibilities must be particularly challenging, I send out thoughts and prayers."

"Thank you. That is good," he told her and smiled. "Now, I must get back to work. Keep well and I will see you soon. You are on vacation. You have the opportunity to do whatever you want. Enjoy yourself. Remember, tomorrow is always better than today."

As he left the table, he stopped long enough to touch her arm. "Take care," he said.

Helena sat at the table and accepted the offer of a cup of tea from a passing waiter. As the restaurant cleared after lunch, she moved to a table overlooking the sea and gazed out at the waves as they splashed and washed up high on the windows.

What does it all mean? she wondered. *It feels like we've missed something. Our relationship has jumped to a level of familiarity and ease. We are friends, more than friends but not lovers. We share no intimacy and avoid talk of personal matters. He knows I am a widow, but I studiously avoid asking any questions about his relationships. Of course such a man must have a history, but I don't want to know. I don't want familial connections to come between us.*

Helena was aware that every aspect of their friendship

had been played out in public. No secret trysts, no personal messages, no late-night phone calls. Always his approach was respectful and he conducted his business in full view, but there was no denying the powerful force of attraction at play. Passengers, waitstaff and officers, or other company members, who visited the restaurant could see where he was and his dining companion. Helena treasured every moment she spent in his company. Her heart was filled with a deep longing for him. The more she saw him and learned about the kind of man he was, the more her admiration and attraction grew. She had never known a more cultured, interested, intelligent man.

She longed to ask, "What happens next?" but was determined to maintain her dignity and sense of self-respect. To be her own person, to show herself as a mature, independent woman, to not overreact or act like a love-struck teenager. Even though that was exactly how she felt. "Stay calm, centered, and do not make assumptions about what is to be."

After so long in a loving marriage and with only a couple of brief dating experiences in the seven years since her beloved Antonio passed, Helena felt ill equipped to know how to handle the situation. Her own feelings were crystal clear to her, but she knew the Captain was not a man to behave inappropriately. His whole demeanor was controlled, mature, self-contained.

The look in his eyes seemed to indicate his interest. At times he looked at her and smiled in a way that melted her heart, but, as for words of love, there were none. Helena fingered the pink-stoned necklace she had taken to wearing. A love amulet, a physic token designed to bring him close to her. Was the magic working? She hardly knew anymore. But she could not dispute that every time she saw him, her feelings grew.

"How do you know when you are in love with someone?" she questioned herself. "If it's when thoughts of them overwhelm and consume every other aspect of your life, I guess that must be some indication. Or is it an obsession? Compulsion?"

The restaurant was empty of passengers. A few of the catering staff worked to prepare afternoon tea. So deep in thought was she that the hypnotic waves induced a meditative effect and hours passed by. Suddenly, as if released from a spell, Helena came back to earth with the realization that the high seas had abated, and the sun was shining.

The following day, the ship made land and the atmosphere was carnival-like. Enthusiastic passengers embraced the new port of call as if it had been six months, not six days, since they had been ashore.

Tenders ferried the passengers ashore, and a glass-bottomed boat waited by the small village pier to take guests on a ride deep into the blue waters to see an underground world of exotic fishes.

Bora Bora, one of a small island chain in the middle of the Pacific Ocean in French Polynesia, discovered by the legendary explorer Captain Cook, is set in a sea of turquoise, sapphire and indigo and protected by soaring rain forests. The island lies just west of Tahiti and is close by the neighboring island of Papeete. The islanders welcome visitors with floral leis and friendly smiles.

Bora Bora is a favorite with honeymooners from all over the world, with direct flights from Los Angles, and idyllic palm-fringed holiday cottages on stilts in the middle of the ocean offer privacy and an enchanted fairy-tale start to married life. Mount Otemanu towers over the island with its crystal-clear shallow water and white, soft sand.

Reluctant at first, Helena was finally persuaded to jump off the side of the glass-bottomed boat into the translucent blue waters. Head down, mask on, she swam in the ocean, surrounded by fish of every imaginable type, size and color. The skipper of the small boat, a local boy with waist-length hair, stripped down to his shorts, dived into the water and encouraged her to drop from the side of the boat into the warm, blue waters. He swam close by her side and guided her adventure.

"Keep your head down, stay very still and let the fish come to you. If you splash, you'll drive them away."

They laughed together as he stirred up the fish so that the passengers still onboard could see the rich display though the bottom of the glass boat. Back onboard he handed her a towel and dried off his own jet-black locks.

"There will be time when we get back to the dock to have a drink together," he said.

"I'd like that," said Helena graciously, "but I plan to go and check out the island shops. I'm looking for South Sea pearls to buy myself a gift. I have always wanted a rare black pearl."

"Good, I can help," he told her with a wide grin that showed off his snow-white teeth. "My sister owns a jewelry store in the village. She will give you a good price. Come, I will take you. We need to sail; it is nearby. Wait till the other people leave and we will go."

Helena hesitated for a few moments and then seized the moment.

"Okay, I love an adventure," she said, "but you must make sure I arrive back in time to catch the ship. Or I will have to stay in this island paradise forever."

"Okay," the skipper smiled and seemed unfazed by the suggestion. She guessed that was how so many sailors were seduced and ended up staying and making new lives with the natives of the South Sea islands. He sailed to an inlet where pearls were harvested and marketed. Wanita, the skipper's sister, guided her around the farm and explained the process whereby cultured pearls were manufactured in an eco-friendly system designed to protect the environment. At the end of the tour, a gigantic treasure trove of brilliant South Sea island pearls dazzled Helena's eyes as she entered Wanita's palm-fringed shop.

Laid out under glass counters, she was invited to inspect an ocean's feast of tray upon tray of pearls of all shades and sizes that had been cultivated around the island of French Polynesia. Blue, green, purple, brown, grey, silver, peacock, Helena was not to be deflected; she knew what she was looking for. She had long coveted a black pearl and now she had the expert guidance and insider knowledge to make a considered decision.

Wanita delighted in telling the story of the pearls to the many visitors and holidaymakers who visited her shop on the secluded island. Generally, only cruise ship passengers had the resources to buy the precious pieces of jewelry, most of which was locally made.

Helena held in her hand one shining necklace as Wanita told her, "Black Tahitian pearls are rare and unmistakably beautiful. Once upon a time they were so rare that they were considered the *Pearl of Queens*. They are highly sought after because of their larger size, brilliant lustre and classically perfect, round shapes. They come from the warm water of our islands here in the South Seas and are grown in a black lipped oyster."

Helena listened as Wanita explained that the saltwater pearls grown in bays and inlets in Tahiti and the South seas were considered more valuable than freshwater pearls. Naturally grown pearls whereby the oyster produced the pearl were more highly regarded than cultured for which a shell bead nucleus was created and inserted into the oyster, thus irritating the oyster to produce a pearl.

"Pearls are considered classic and contemporary and designs

range from the traditional to the modern. Natural, freshwater, cultures and shell pears are all valued for their beauty and ability to add elegance to outfits.

"Look I will show you how to tell if a pearl is real," said Wanita, whose love of pearls came out in her storytelling. "To discover if a pearl is real or fake, place it on a piece of white paper and check with your eyes to see whether it is blemished; is it regular in size and shape, does it have wrinkles, ridges, chalky spots, pin prick inclusions?

"Cultured pearls are a product of nature, and the mollusk, the oyster, leaves its fingerprints on the gem during its creation so you'll always be able to find some kind of imperfection. Synthetic pearls feel smooth, like plastic, because man-made gems lack the crystalline produced naturally in the real pearl."

Armed with this specialist information and guided by an expert, Helena choose a piece of jewelry that she had fallen in love with as soon as she saw it displayed in the showroom window. A necklace made of a single row of black Tahitian pearls with a diamond clasp that felt uniquely suited to her and perfectly complimented her skin tone and graced her long, slender neck.

Delighted with her purchase, and glad of the skipper's family connection in helping her choose her necklace, the skipper returned Helena through the inlets and pink sand beaches to the pier launch point for the tender back to the ship. She carried the gift box with the beautiful black pearl necklace inside.

"I have the perfect dress to wear to show this off," she told the skipper.

"Sorry I am not on your ship to see such a sight." He smiled.

As she waited on the quay for the tender that would return her to the ship, the skipper appeared carrying a fruit and flower–filled cocktail. He handed her the glass and taking her other hand in his, he insisted on swaying close to her as he danced to the happy island sounds of a small local band.

Helping her step onto the makeshift stairway leading onto the tender, he told her, "Come back to Bora Bora. I will look out for you and your ship."

Helena promised to remember him and his glass-bottomed boat.

At the end of the half-hour trip back to where the ship was moored offshore, Helena glanced up at the bridge that was extended over the tender gangway. Officers watched as tenders arrived home in preparation for the ship sailing to its next port of call.

The Captain was on the bridge, attending to his duties as always.

Helena was forced to accept that she was not the main priority in this scenario. There would always be three in the relationship: him, her and the ship.

"Please be sure to follow all instructions and observe the rules of health and safety while on the tour," a young administrator from customer services told the small group of passengers who had gathered in the anteroom of the main restaurant.

"Welcome to the Behind the Scenes Tour of the ship, we will visit the engine room, the photographic department, the computer room, the kitchens, the stockroom, the laundry and, last of all, the bridge where the Captain will be pleased to answer your questions. You are not permitted to carry anything during this tour, for your safety. Many of the staircases are steep and you are required to hold onto the guardrails.

"There is to be no photography or video recording, but the Captain will pose for a group photograph just before we take you down to the restaurant for a lunch the chef has specially prepared for you."

The hotel director, a senior officer who had worked on cruise ships for decades and undertaken every post, starting with the most junior barman, ran the entire operation of the 1,200 passenger vessel and all the ancillary services of accommodation for more than a thousand passengers and more than 600 staff members. He stepped in to start off the tour.

"Welcome to the tour and before we start to fortify you for the onerous task of visiting all the departments, let's start with that most important of places. The Captain's table where my staff will serve you speciality morning coffee, croissants and pastries.

"I ask only one thing," he said displaying the jokey disposition for which he was known. "When you meet up with the Captain at the end of the tour, do not tell him you have eaten at his table. He takes very seriously the fact that, when guests are invited to his table, he should be there to ensure they have a memorable experience. But for you, today, we have made special arrangements and breakfast will be served in the private restaurant inside the main restaurant where we serve eight thousand meals every day."

Helena smiled inwardly, warmed by the fact that she had already had her memorable experience at the Captain's table. Now she was looking forward to the first coffee of the morning and an in-depth tour of the ship. In every department hard-working crew members proudly showed off their specialized areas and answered questions from the visitors. After breakfast, the tour members were escorted to the theater where most passengers spent every evening of their cruise watching high-class production shows. Guests were invited to examine all the audio/visual equipment that went into presenting the hi-tech performances. The theater on the *Vision Star* had a seating capacity of 600 and two shows a night ensured that all 1,200 passengers had the opportunity to see every performance.

In the dressing room, guests were able to see up close the dozens of costumes used by the singers, dancers and entertainers over the course of a world cruise.

"Are shows exclusive to this ship or bought in from other cruise lines?" one guest wanted to know.

"No," the cruise director proudly explained. "All our shows are original, conceived, arranged and choreographed right here on the ship. We have our own musical director who also leads the *Vision Star*'s orchestra and oversees the musical presentations all over the ship, including the classical performances in the atrium, the guitarists and the singing duos in the bars and lounges. Our entertainment teams are professionally trained in all aspects of dance, music and acting, and hundreds of hours of entertainment are provided for our guests, catering to all tastes."

In the galley, the head chef proudly introduced his staff and explained that each individual was responsible for their specialist dishes. Attended by assistants, they produced different types of hot food and cold food: soup, dessert, pastry, bread, sauces.

"Everyone in the kitchen works a split shift," the head chef explained. "Early morning till afternoon preparing and cooking meals for lunch and dinner, then they return after dinner and work the late-night shift.

"There are no full days off on a ship for the whole voyage, but team leaders allocate one regular shift off. Everyone on a ship is there by merit. They work their way up, and we offer extensive training and opportunities for promotion."

All that cooking and preparation ensured hundreds of dishes needed to be washed.

Helena accepted the invitation to stick her head in one of two empty dishwashers, a long tunnel of which she could hardly see the other end as the cylinder was twenty feet in length.

The laundry room, a steamy hive of activity, was filled with washing machines and industrial-size dryers churning out a constant stream of linens, tablecloths, napkins, bedding and towels, plus crew uniforms and passenger room service orders. Lines of cabin stewards queued up to collect their daily supplies.

One ecologically conscious passenger asked about the methods the ship used to reduce waste and pollution at sea. "Do you recycle?" she wanted to know. "Where do you dump the ship's rubbish? Is anything thrown over board at sea?"

The crew member in charge of the recycling rooms happily showed the process used for the tons of rubbish generated every day by a vessel the size of a small village.

"Here is the bottle crusher," he explained, "and the can flattener for items that will be offloaded in ports where we have an arrangement for them to be removed and disposed of. There are eight categories of waste and recycling. All food is pulped and dumped into the sea twelve miles out from land, and this acts as food for the sea life."

Storage, iceboxes, fridge-freezers and freezers deep in the lower decks of the ship contained supplies. "There are alarms inside the storage rooms," the crew member explained. "It has never happened to our knowledge, but only a couple of minutes inside the freezers would result in death."

Helena caught her breath and tried not to listen to the answer as an overzealous passenger wanted to know, "I guess that's also where you put the body if someone dies onboard?" Helena turned away, and it was not only the cold of the open freezer that made her shiver.

She listened as the conversation continued. The crew member talked about the fact that fresh food supplies were taken on in ports all over the world. Supplies of meat, fish, vegetable, fruit were stored onboard for up to fifteen days. In the galley, there were three sections: hot, cold and bread. One person prepared salads/appetizers/canapés. All food is discarded after four hours if not eaten.

"Next time you complain about having no fresh bananas at the buffet table," said the storeroom chief, "you may remember that we are dependent on what supplies the market has or our agent delivers. We can't pop down to the local store or make a grocery order out at sea."

The tour members laughed and promised to be more understanding in future if their favorite food was not immediately available.

Galley members are identified by scarves: a green scarf signified responsibilities for preparing foods; green/red meant sauces and dressings; and a white scarf meant fetch and chop. Fifty-two chefs on three split shifts worked in the kitchen, which operated twenty-four hours a day. All cooking is done on steam and electric, no naked flames. Onboard all water is desalinated seawater, tested for safety and health by the medical teams and also by outside testing, including health inspectors in port.

The executive chef oversees the cooking of 8,000 meals per day with thirty different dishes served in seven passenger restaurants under the authority of a restaurant manager and three restaurants for the company: crew mess, staff mess and officer's mess. There are 750 guests at each sitting—and in a typical day they use 3,000 eggs, 2,200 pounds of rice, 66 pounds of meat, 44 pounds of chicken, 165 pounds of vegetables and 143 pounds of fruit. "The chef chooses the daily dishes from a standard list of fifteen thousand menu items."

The tour continued to the engine room where they were greeted by the chief engineer. Far from being a noisy, greasy dark place containing heavy equipment, the engine room was, in fact, a bank of computers providing real-time images of four engines with eight pistons.

"Maintenance men do still sometimes have to climb into the engines and adjust a piece of equipment, but most of what we need to know can be seen on-screen," said the chief engineer.

Helena observed that his white uniform did not look as if it had ever been stained by grease or grime. The Russian chief engineer gave Helena a friendly smile; he had met her once when he was having a drink in one of the lounge bars with his friend the Captain. "These screens are replicated on the bridge," he confirmed. "The Captain needs to know everything happening on his ship."

In what would have once been called the darkroom but was now filled with light, the ship's chief photographer was also surrounded by computer and digital equipment. "So far, one third of the way through the world voyage, the official photographers have taken 36,000 photographs. We expect to hit over 100,000 before we arrive back in home port."

Most of the tour up to that point had been conducted on lower decks, but now the passengers were escorted upstairs to the top deck, the bridge.

The chief engineer offered an observation as he bid the tour farewell and they left his area of command: "The ship is a living, breathing creature. The engine room is its lungs, the kitchens are its heart, and the bridge is the brains."

Helena liked that; it was one of the things she admired about the Captain—his intelligence and all-encompassing knowledge about so many subjects.

The Captain was waiting. He warmly welcomed everyone to the bridge and thanked them for attending the tour so as to better understand the behind the scenes operation of the ship. Helena stayed at the back of the tour members as the rest jostled for a position close to the Captain. Being so tall, he could see over all the heads, and he smiled and nodded in recognition when he saw her. He leaned casually against the arm of his tall chair next to a bank of computers, a place from which he could see the whole vista outside the panoramic windows.

Four officers were also on duty and three of them scanned the horizon with binoculars.

"As you can see, we run a paperless ship," the Captain explained. "Everything about our navigation is controlled digitally, but I do have charts and navigational aids in my office in case of failure, though, we have very sophisticated backup."

He laughed when he was asked, "In an emergency would you able to steer the ship by the stars?"

"Since I was a boy, I have been sailing," he replied. "To navigate by the stars is a necessary skill for a seaman. Of course, we still have a sexton that we can steer by, but I hope it does not happen."

"What is the difference between a ship and a boat?" asked one passenger.

"After giving it some thought, well," he said, "one way you can tell is that a ship can carry a boat, a boat cannot carry a ship."

"We see you on the bridge every time we enter and leave a port," observed one of the men Helena recognized as a regular when the passengers gathered at the railings to watch activities on the bridge.

"I am the ultimate authority. It is my responsibility," said the Captain without hesitation, "to ensure that the vessel arrives and leaves port safely and efficiently."

"What is the favorite part of your job?" he was asked.

"I like to steer the ship," he said, and the sailors in the room nodded in agreement.

"Also," the Captain told them," I like to be up here on the bridge looking out at all the wonderful things of the sea. I must have seen hundreds of them, but I still enjoy the sight of a beautiful sunrise or sunset and the sea creatures who play around the ship: the whales, dolphins, the birds. The sea is my life. I never tire of it."

Helena's heart melted at what she took to be declarations of spirituality, his awe at the natural phenomena of the universe and the creatures that inhabit the natural world. She observed also the framed photograph of the Russian Orthodox God that was displayed prominently on the wall behind his station.

"How many times have you been around the world?" asked one female whom Helena had noticed was determined to attract the Captain's attention.

"More times than I can remember," he admitted, "and I plan to keep going for several more world voyages."

"Ladies and gentlemen, your lunch awaits," said the administrator from customer services, who had guided the party on its three-hour ship's tour. "Let's have a group photograph taken with the Captain as a memento of today's visit."

Helena fixed herself to the end of the line, and the woman who had asked about his world travels positioned herself right next to the Captain. He looked in Helena's direction and raised his eyebrows. "I think we need to move everyone in a little more," he said. "Please, come here and stand by my side."

Perfect, thought Helena, *that will look great when I cut everyone out except him and me.*

As the other passengers headed for their specially prepared fancy lunch in the main restaurant, Helena headed for the buffet. She was determined to miss no opportunity to share a table with her special lunch companion. He was already sitting at "their table" when she entered.

"Sorry I'm late." She smiled. "I had an important meeting on the bridge with the Captain."

* * *

Alone in her cabin that afternoon, Helena sipped a glass of sparkling water and studied the information she had received about that day's tour.

> *Fascinating facts and figures about the Grand Around the World Cruise.*
>
> *The ship is expected to cover over 35,000 nautical miles.*
>
> *Items of passenger linen to be laundered: 350,150, comprising 48,000 bed sheets and duvets, 55,000 pillow cases, 112,000 towels and 67,200 bathmats. Add to that 10,000 similar items for the crew, 17,200 tablecloths, 162,300 napkins and place mats, 21,000 crew uniforms plus 10,500 articles of guest clothing.*
>
> *Over the course of the cruise, guests consume 37,150 bottles of wine, 3,600 bottles of spirits, 3,500 bottles of champagne, 4,800 liters of juice, 21,000 bottles of water and 31,000 cans of soft drinks*

"I'll raise my glass to that," she said, waving her glass in front of her, "and thanks to all the hard working crew on this voyage. And of course, the officers."

In the Zone
Day 34

"This is your Captain speaking from the bridge. We are crossing the international date line. Tomorrow will be erased from the calendar. There is no February 13 on this ship."

The noon time announcement was Helena's signal to start to prepare herself for her lunchtime assignation. Nothing else was more important to her. The daytime activities she enjoyed onboard were all designed to fit around her desperate desire to spend time with the Captain.

"Got a date?" asked a choir member as Helena excused herself early from daily rehearsals.

In the cabin, she applied fresh makeup and dressed with care, choosing clothes that she judged would illicit one of his small approving smiles. She made her way to the restaurant. Her routine mirrored his. "I love the way you dress," he told her once. "I love the way you look. In fact, I love many things about you."

She settled herself at their favorite table and prepared to wait. A member of the serving staff brought her regular pot of tea, and she nibbled on biscuits and cheese. To eat and talk and concentrate on him was too much of a distraction.

"Captain's coming," declared the headwaiter and all crew members waited expectantly. Helena sat perfectly still trying not to overjudge her expectations. There was no rule that said he had to eat with her every day, but certainly it had become more than an occasional occurrence. Helena watched the various entry points from which he could appear and when he came into sight, her heart skipped a beat. It never failed. Her body tensed and she avoided making it obvious that she was looking in his direction.

Discreetly she watched; she could not bear to miss a moment in his presence. Confident, unhurried, observing all, he greeted the staff and selected his food. Eyes down, Helena waited.

Plates of food in hand, he approached her. "May I?"

For certain he knew he would be received with a smile and a welcoming greeting.

"Of course," she said and sighed. Her day was already complete. Time in his company had become the highlight of every day. She failed to hide her delight that she was to share precious time, conversation and his physical presence.

Day after day, he chose to join her and she endeavored to be grateful for each day without projecting or attempting to decipher whether they would ever be more than lunch companions.

"How are rehearsals going?" he asked. She knew he observed from the gallery as the choir ran through their repertoire. There was little that escaped his notice on the ship. "When is the performance?"

"Valentine's Day," she told him. "As you can imagine, we are singing love songs," she informed him.

"I will try to attend," he said.

Conversation was relaxed, easy, and he showed interest in all that she was doing and shared about his day. But there was an underlying tension. Helena struggled to understand what was happening, what was not being said. He looked at her intently and often seemed to be on the verge of saying something important, but he resisted. Instead long pauses ensued while they sat in companionable silence and gazed intently at each other.

"How are you?" he asked. In response to her cheery, "Fine, thank you," he persisted, "How are you really?"

Helena struggled to know what he was asking or what answer he was expecting.

She was confused. *Did he want her to admit her feelings? Open the door to take the relationship deeper? Where would it go if the polite restraints of Captain and passenger were removed?*

His eyes gazed at her with longing. Occasionally he reached out and, as if by accident, brushed her arm. The touch of his strong hand made the hairs on her arm stand on end but she did not return the touch. She gazed instead into his eyes and hoped her eyes translated her message as she wordlessly pleaded, "Tell me what you want."

"He is the Captain," she reminded herself over and over again. "He is steering the ship. He will decide where we go next. He knows what he wants; he knows what is permitted."

Day after day, the ritual continued. For an hour, rarely more, because he needed to return to his duties and occasionally less if he heard something on the radio to which he chose to react. The two sat locked in their private world.

With their heads close together, oblivious to other people in the restaurant, they talked, laughed, within touching distant but not breeching the unspoken protocols. The boundaries of their intimacy discouraged outside intrusions. Their daily conversations, as befitted two travelers on an around the world voyage, were global. History, culture, geography, politics and any and every aspect of the passenger experience on the cruise. Even the weather.

"Three passengers warned me that it was cold out today," she told him. "Captain's got his sweater on."

He laughed good-naturedly. "Maybe is cold for me but not for them," he said.

"Well, I went back to my cabin and put on a sweater when I heard the news," Helena told him and he laughed even more.

Helena had a question that she longed to ask. Maybe now was not the time.

He had told her that she would be on the guest list again for the next formal Captain's table. Meredith had been the bearer of gossip.

"So you're not invited to the Captain's table tonight?" she asked with glee when Helena arrived at their regular dinner table.

Helena smiled, and gave nothing away that would provide more ammunition for Meredith's malicious and sarcastic remarks.

As it happened, her news was out of date. Helena's question was answered when a fellow guest approached the lunch table.

"Sorry to bother you, Captain," he said. "I can come back later, but the headwaiter said you were looking for me."

"Yes, I want to apologize for having canceled your invitation to dinner. I was too busy to host the table; you will be on the guest list for the next one."

The guest smiled happily. "No problem, Captain," he said, "I look forward to it."

Helena affected an air of disinterest because she did not want to be seen to listen in on his conversations. He soon brought her up to speed.

"You are also to be on the list," he informed her, "next time, I promise. It is my pleasure to see you sitting across the table from me, at the formal dinner, at this table, anywhere. I want to watch you."

Helena was tempted to reach out and touch his arm but resisted. Instead they sat in silence, breathing in each other's closeness. How she wished he would make a move and initiate real physical closeness. Her longing for him had become an ache, an unsatisfied need. Now that she was left in no doubt about how he felt, Helena longed to know when this impasse would end.

His radio, active on the table between them, offered a stark reminder that he was not like other men. He was not free to follow his desires and pursue a passing attraction.

"Duty calls," he told her. "I need to go." He touched her arm lightly. "Enjoy your day." He left the restaurant and stopped a few feet away from the table. He came back and said quietly, "Look after yourself. I will see you tomorrow."

The bitter sweetness of the knowledge that he was feeling at least a semblance of what she felt carried Helena through the day.

She jumped when he reappeared one more time. She hoped it meant he could not bear to leave her. "I will come to your Valentine's Day choir concert," he said.

"Then I will sing you a love song." Helena attempted to keep her tone light but failed.

"Thank you," he said.

★   ★   ★

Journal entry: *I'm out of my depth. This has never happened to me before. I thought I was a mature woman, one who had experienced many levels of intimacy and relationship. But always attraction has been closely followed by physicality. I've had one-night stands where we have ended up in bed straight off the dance floor, and even long-term relationships where old faithfuls have returned at different times in my life, sometimes after a break of years, and we have resumed a physical relationship. I've had many years of a happy marriage and, I am ashamed to admit, one night of passion with a stranger whom I met on a plane. I thought these encounters and experiences made me sophisticated, a modern woman, one who was in tune with her sexuality. Still, I don't know what to make of the current situation. I feel passion, obsession; I burn with longing for him. In his presence I am excited, joyful, hopeful and uplifted. Without him, I am disappointed, restless, discontent. He makes me feel alive, appreciated, worthwhile.*

Am I so programmed to the baser instincts that I cannot imagine a relationship without sex? Is this courtly, spiritual, platonic love for real?

Seven long years since the death of my husband and I finally find a devastatingly attractive man; am I to be deprived of his touch, his kiss, the feeling of holding his body close to mine?

Is this friendship, is this relationship, is this romance?

I feel like a Victorian lady or a medieval maiden longing for her lover, her suitor and knowing that she will never feel his manhood grind into her, never cry out in ecstasy at his prowess, never feel his sex inside her, never drown in his kisses. Knowing they will be forever condemned to longing looks, loving gazes, unfulfilled desires.

How the hell do you express love when there is no sex?

* * *

Helena could find no peace as she tried to settle down to sleep in her big, empty double bed. Surely he could phone to whisper sweet words and say good night? A text with kisses, a smiley face or a simple red rose?

* * *

One hundred members of the choir club took their final bow on the theater's main stage and accepted the enthusiastic applause of the packed audience. The Valentine's Day performance had been long awaited and cruise ship favorites like "Moon River" and "Sailing" took their place in the repertoire alongside specially selected numbers such as "Can't Help Falling in Love with You" and "All You Need Is Love."

Helena, from her prime front-row position, anxiously scanned the audience, especially for men in white uniforms. After a group photograph and hugs all around with friends and choir members, Helena left the theater. She had enjoyed the show. At least there was one thing that took her mind off constant thoughts of a certain someone. She was unsure whether she had identified him up on the top balcony.

The Captain stood outside the theater doors congratulating the choir masters and musicians.

Helena fell into step beside him as he made his way down the spiral stairway.

"Did you enjoy it?" she asked.

He looked embarrassed. "Sorry I missed the performance," he said. "I meant to get here in time but I arrived to see only the last number, 'Hallelujah.' I am familiar with it."

Anxious not to show her disappointment, Helena joked, "Were you worried about me singing love songs to you?"

"No, I would like that," he said looking straight at her, "but not in front of all those people."

She wanted to vent her frustration and ask, "Where then?" but she'd promised herself to play it cool at all times, to maintain her dignity. A small group of fans had attached themselves to the Captain. Helena detached herself.

"Enjoy New Zealand," he called out as she said goodbye. "We have several stops in that country. Maybe I will see you there."

Helena walked away and was annoyed to find that she was on the brink of tears. Her feelings were running riot, and she was on a roller coaster of emotions. She hardly knew what to expect.

"I've sailed halfway around the world," she acknowledged, "and still I don't know if I am on my head or my heels."

Bay of Islands, New Zealand
Day 39

As picturesque a place as to be found anywhere on earth, an archipelago of almost 150 islands, Bay of Islands languishes in turquoise waters boasting a rich marine and terrestrial ecosystem. Most of the action takes place out on the water, whether yachting, big game fishing, kayaking, diving or cruising around in the company of whales and dolphins. It is also a place of enormous historical interest. The site of New Zealand's first permanent settlement, on the island of Russell, was the birthplace of European colonization in the country. In 1840 New Zealand's founding document was signed in the Bay of Islands. As the most northern region in New Zealand, the climate is subtropical, which allows for various flora and fauna that do not flourish anywhere else in New Zealand. The islands are a tourist hot spot due to the diverse number of small islands and untouched beaches.

Enthusiastic and passionate islander's welcome visitors and their love for their country and islands drives the many family-run businesses who offer exploration and unique adventures on land, in and on the sea and in the air.

Totally unhurried, the vendors on the white-washed pier present their opportunities to share what they call, "Unique experiences in amazing places." The atmosphere is tranquil and unpressured. As an example, free follow-up trips are offered to any visitors who do not see dolphins on their excursion.

"We don't often need to offer the free trip," claimed the sporty young lady taking bookings and selling tickets on a range of boat trips. "Our visitors see dolphins on over 90 percent of our trips."

Helena signed up for a trip to the Hole in the Rock, an iconic landmark on the island and in sight of the Cape Brett Peninsula and Cape Brett Lighthouse. She traveled in comfort on a black-and-yellow catamaran through the huge opening in the rock.

"There are some things you only need to do once in a lifetime," said a native New Zealander who took the seat next to Helena and introduced herself as being "from the city,

Christchurch, fifty miles away." She made it quite clear that she was a little less than impressed with the Hole in the Rock. "While my husband goes out big game fishing, I make yet another trip on this boat. We've been coming to these islands every year since we married ten years ago. Far as I'm concerned, I've been here, done that and bought the T-shirt. But I don't think he'll quit until he's visited every one of the 144 islands."

The vibrant-pink T-shirt that covered her ample bosom carried the message, "You're lucky I'm here, I could have gone fishing."

"Don't ask. Yes, it was a gift from him. Don't know why I allow it," she admitted.

Helena liked the woman; she wasn't sure she would be as tolerant of her partner's hobbies. They said goodbye as they left the boat, and the woman told her, "I gotta hurry. Need to be there to welcome the fisherman home from the sea and hear those big fish stories."

Having no partner to welcome home from the sea, Helena took a shuttle bus to the Waitangi Treaty Grounds high on the headland overlooking the Bay of Islands. The historic treaty house and museum proudly display the document that officially founded New Zealand and, in videos, exhibitions and art works, tells the history of the country and the birthplace of a nation.

On display on the grounds there stands a ceremonial canoe and here is a studio where native carvers practice the ancient art that is passed down from generation to generation.

"This is a sacred place, please remove shoes and leave all weapons outside," said the Maori tour guide who welcomed visitors to a traditional cultural performance. "Traveling back in time, the show features stories and traditions that shape our unique and special culture."

Michelle, the guide and a proud wife and mother, welcomed everyone to the *fahne*, the meeting house and eating house. "It is here we take care of people," she explained. "The carvings on the wooden walls are the knowledge that needs to be passed on to the next generation. Our ancestors are not dead; they wait on the other side ready to guide the new generations. In this space, we eat and sleep communally. There is room for all the family. No one is ever turned away."

"We celebrate the dead," explained Michelle. "This house is used for welcomes, weddings and funerals. The four faces of the carving posts showcase male attributes and female skills. It is read as a book, the Maori tribes write down information through artwork and painting. The lattice work is made out of flax; the square blocks define a stairway to heaven. The journey of each individual is transmitted through designs from the original meeting houses."

Michelle called into a sacred circle her husband and a teenage son to help her describe the work undertaken by master carvers from all over the country.

"Carvings with their tongues out are used to ward off evil spirits and the colored stones are Power Eyes—a source of light," her son explained.

"Meeting houses are our library; they hold archives and photographs and keep the legacy of our tribes alive. The knowledge of the tribe surrounds and sustains us. The traditional carvings represent nature and are all hardwood timbers, sourced from our land. The red colors are produced with mud and clay; the black is ashes and yellow plants. All work builds on a foundation of uniqueness and tools of integration."

Sitting on low wooden benches, the visitors listened to the origins of the culture of the Maori tribes and their Confederation established under the first Maori king and continued through the current community population of some 60,000 Maoris.

In a collective, the chiefs are considered advisors and they appoint nominated representatives. Michelle explained the Maori philosophy that lives and moves in two worlds.

"Missionaries taught us to read and write using the Bible," she explained. "Therefore our religion is often described as a cross between Catholic and Maori.

"The Maori religion can be summed up as 'Be nice—look after parents and enjoy life.'" While Michelle talked and educated the visitors, older members of the tribe entered the meeting house to offer their welcomes.

"We are a product of our grandparents," Michelle's son stated. "There is nothing more disappointing than to disrespect the elders. They are fonts of knowledge. We are honored by their presence."

"The spirit of love and tolerance within the meeting house invokes an atmosphere of peace. There is an energy that lives and breathes in the plants, the weather, the Devi God, Sun God and Summer Maiden. The good energy that visitors bring by taking time to visit our community is a blessing. We thank you for being here and allowing us to tell you about our people, our culture and our community."

The whole village lined up to say goodbye and shake hands—and rub noses. A farewell performance was held outside in the campground.

Under the statue of a Maori king, warriors, older chiefs and young men showed off their skills with sticks and spears while the women played drums and danced. After a high energy performance, the performers asked for audience participation. "Please stand up and join in our dance. It is traditional and we will teach you," said one of the young girl dancers. "It is very easy."

Following instructions, visitors were encouraged to clap and follow the steps. Helena thought the tune and even the words in the Maori language sounded familiar. The dance movement accompanied by drumming and clapping directed the dancers to "Put your right leg in, your right leg out, your right leg in and shake it all about." It took a little while for the visitors to see the joke: They were being instructed to "do the Hokey Cokey and turn yourself around." Much laughter ensued.

Making ferocious faces and waggling their tongues, the warriors attempted to scare off enemies. But the highlight of the display was the photo opportunity presented outside the meeting house when a traditionally dressed Maori warrior, in robes and grass skirt, offered to show Helena the traditional greeting and how to rub noses.

"Like this," he said. "Stand very close and stare into my eyes. Make connection, we have to be sure that we are friends not enemies. See me, don't just look. Be still. Now lean in and press your nose against mine."

The gesture felt strangely spiritual, and Helena was moved by the encounter. She actually did feel "seen," even in the midst of a crowd of people.

The high energy dancing, drumming and chanting offered first-class entertainment but also a connection on a deeper level. The guide pointed out the intricately carved walls and explained, "This book contains all our names. It lists our ancestors and family members and tells us who we are. No strife is brought to this sacred place, but guidance is sought from the elders of the tribe in all matters of life. We are bound by codes of conduct reaching back thousands of years. All family members are loved, supported and held in the circle of the tribe."

"Thank you, it is an honor to have met and been welcomed by your people." Helena made it her business to seek out the native guide as the visitors left the Treaty Grounds and the performers prepared for their next show. "Being offered a glimpse into the lives of a proud people like the Maoris, still living and practicing the culture of their ancestors, is a privilege."

Lost in thoughts of her experience, Helena stared out of the window of the coach at the wild, rugged land that had belonged to the Maori tribes long before the Europeans came to conquer and settle. Helena was conscious that all too brief visits to set-piece presentations often raised more questions than they answered, but still she was grateful for the opportunity to glimpse into other people's lives. And if it did not amount to a full-scale expedition, it did offer a chance to share communality with strangers on the other side of her world.

When the pace of global life became too hectic and world troubles took away peace of mind, Helena knew her thoughts would return to this peaceful, beautiful city.

But for now, she was about to raise the bar on adventure and excitement.

Having satisfied her need for culture, history and tradition, she was ready for the daredevil helicopter ride she had promised herself.

A *Lord of the Rings* flight was high on her agenda. A family-run helicopter company promised to fly passengers to the rugged locations of the blockbuster film.

"We are the crew who personally flew the actors and technicians during the filming of the blockbuster film," said the pilot. "This tour is scheduled to land on Mount Olympus, to view the strange pinnacle rock formations that were used to portray the storyline set in the fictional South of Rivendell.

"Mount Olympus sprouts rocky outcrops, which over time have been eroded by weather to form incredible columnar shapes. A farther stop in Mount Owen showcases some of the oldest rock in New Zealand, with priceless geological properties. A landscape of glaciated marble karst is exposed and defines the challenges the film crew working in the harsh alpine environment experienced. You are about to have an amazing cinematic experience."

As she climbed into the helicopter, Helena realized she was the only passenger—only the pilot and she were on this exciting trip. "Buckle up," said the pilot as he directed her to the seat in the back of the chopper. "It's noisy in here and can get bumpy, so hold on to your hat."

"I'm ready," said Helena. "Good to go."

"Yup, waiting for one other passenger," said the pilot. "My office got a call from your ship. He's on his way."

Helena had looked forward to a one-on-one exclusive tour but pushed her bag farther under the seat in front to make room for the other flyer. Even though he was not in uniform, there was no mistaking him. Striding out, tall, confident, assured, wearing dark glasses and a baseball cap. Her heart leaped and she said a small prayer of thanks. "In all the helicopters in all the world, he is about to climb into mine."

Her eyes followed his every step as he crossed the small landing strip, ducked his head under the already rotating blades and opened the door. In a glance he saw her and gave a huge grin. "You said you might take this ride," he said as he settled himself beside her in the back seat. "Looks like I got lucky and chose the right flight."

"All set?" the pilot asked as he looked back over his shoulder and pointed to his earphones. "You might want to put yours on," he said, "it gets noisy."

The Captain removed his baseball cap and sunglasses and put on the ear protectors. Helena followed his lead and then directed her attention to the spectacular view as they flew out over the island and headed high into the mountains.

Side by side with the Captain in the rear seat of the aircraft, flying high in the air, Helena truly felt like she had died and gone to heaven. Conversation was impossible and, with the distraction of words removed, the eyes were designated to do the talking.

Back-to-back they each stared out of their windows and settled into the comfortable familiarity of their closeness as the pilot explained the landscape. "We're on Mount Olympus. Look down there," he commanded, "that's where the nine rested and cooked a meal, and the crebain crows of Saruman, searching for news of the one ring, spied the travelers down below. Hurriedly extinguishing their fire, they hid behind the pinnacles in an attempt to escape discovery. You are familiar with the scene?" he asked.

The Captain nodded eagerly, as he did also when the pilot pointed out the film location on Mount Owen. "The Mines of the Moria," said the pilot, and then he described the scene in the film that had taken place down below. "It was here, distraught at the loss of Gandalf, that the remaining members of the Fellowship of the Ring escaped the mines and threw themselves to the ground in grief."

The pilot explained that for many months he and other members of the helicopter service had become integral members of the film crew.

"It was an exciting time," he recalled. "We all became really good friends. The film company put on a special screening of *Lord of the Rings* for all the local people here who had been involved with the film, and our company had our name on the film credits. We were all treated like movie stars for a while.

Now people still come from all over the world to see where the scenes were filmed."

Flying above the clouds in the wild blue yonder with the man of her dream by her side was excitement enough for Helena. The pilot's shouted explanations were hard to hear, but she didn't care.

"I'll watch the film again," she shouted above the noise in the cockpit, "now that I've seen the location where the scenes were filmed."

"Yes, it will be good to remind ourselves," said the Captain.

He glanced at Helena and his depthless black eyes stared straight into hers.

She was reminded of the encounter in the Maori village where she rubbed noses with the young warrior and he urged her, "Don't look, see me."

A chill ran through her and she shivered. "Are you cold?" asked the Captain and reached out to touch her hand.

Briefly their hands touched and, unlike in the restaurant where he would withdraw his hand quickly, he held his hand on top of hers and placed his other hand underneath. He squeezed her hand between his palms. They sat hand in hand, not moving, not talking. He seemed about to speak, and Helena strained to hear what might be said, but, with a sigh, he stared hard at her and shook his head.

The helicopter headed for home, and Helena regretted that the trip was destined to come to an end. Reluctant to break the spell, she knew that all the words she wanted to say were unnecessary. They were connected, they understood each other on a deep emotional level; together, they shared a special bond.

In the private space of the helicopter, high up in the sky, almost alone, Helena wished he would kiss her, hold her close to him, whisper words of love in her ear. But somehow she knew that what they had experienced that day transcended earthly considerations.

"Thank you," she said to him as they unbuckled their seat belts. "I had one of the best days of my life. You sure know how to show a girl a good time."

He laughed. "I always have a good time when I am with you," he admitted.

The blades of the helicopter whirled and slowed, and he held out his hand to help her alight.

"Helena, you are a special lady," he told her. "Excuse me, I must go. They are waiting for me. You have transport back to the ship?"

"Yes, I'm fine," she said. "It's not far to the tender pickup point. I have time to get a coffee on the dock. The Captain won't set sail without me."

* * *

Back on deck before dinner, a compulsory passenger lifeboat drill was scheduled. Helena knew the drill. To be sure of the time, she checked the daily bulletin: "When you hear the ship's alarm bells, return to your cabin to collect your life jacket and some comfortable clothing. Then proceed to your assembly station as noted on the back of your cabin door. Please listen carefully to the announcements. During this drill, all services onboard will be suspended. Thank you for your cooperation."

Life boat drills were held regularly and the Captain and his crew took especially seriously the SOLAS (Safety of Life at Sea) regulations. A roll call was taken and instructions were given in the fitting of life jackets. Crew members inspected the lines of passengers gathered at assembly points beside the numbered lifeboats they were designated to use in the event of an emergency. The Captain walked the decks, eagle-eyed, checking everything.

"Why doesn't that man have a life jacket?" asked the Captain. A crew member answered, "He said his wife told him not to bring his; she said he could share hers."

The assembled passengers laughed and even the Captain had trouble keeping a straight face.

"Sir, tell your wife," he said, "on this ship you follow my instructions, not hers."

★ ★ ★

Auckland is New Zealand's largest city and main transport hub, an urban environment with beaches within half an hour of the city. Helena signed up for an official shore excursion and joined cruise passengers on a coach trip to explore the many diverse landscapes of Auckland.

Traveling as one party in four or five coaches with maybe a hundred other cruise ship passengers was not really her favorite way of sightseeing but it had its advantages. All main sights and points of interest could be covered efficiently. Photo stops and lunch made the best of what was generally limited time.

Helena planned to explore all points of the islands. In the west, lush native rain forests plunged down the hills to meet the sea on dramatic black-sand beaches while the east's sheltered golden sands were fringed with red flowering pohutukawa trees. To the north, the rolling hills of wine country met stunning coastlines, and, in the south, there are picturesque country gardens, unspoiled forest and tranquil bays to explore. Auckland is dotted with forty-eight volcanic cones that provide spectacular panoramic views of the city and harbor.

At Rangitoto Island, a twenty-five-minute ferry ride from downtown Auckland, Helena walked through the lush parkland and posed for a selfie alongside the crater of a volcano.

"Best not stand too close," a fellow cruise ship traveler told her, pointing out the sign she had failed to see, DANGER, THIS IS AN ACTIVE VOLCANO.

Back in the city, Helena met a friend with whom she had previously agreed to go up the Sky Tower, a telecommunications and observation tower. Housing the Sky City Casino complex, the top floor is 782 feet high and provides panoramic views of the city and harbor.

Helena enjoyed a spectacular skywalk outdoors, fifty-three floors up the Sky Tower, but refused the offer to bungee jump. She was adamant, "I've had quite enough adventure for one day." She tried to make her friends understand, "A skywalk and active volcano are quite enough excitement for me."

From the sky deck of the tower, she stared out to sea and was able to identify the cruise ship, *Vision Star*, docked in the harbor. To cruise ship passengers on journeys short and long, including Helena's Grand Around the World Cruise, whatever explorations, excursions or attractions are available in strange and exotic new lands, the cruise ship on which they sail is the mother ship and quickly becomes home away from home.

"I'll come and watch your bungee jump," she told her friends. "But I'm saving myself for tonight's sail-away, the Abba Goodbye '70s party. I never lose the thrill of being up on deck waving goodbye. Arrival in the morning generates feelings of anticipation and the farewell at night celebrates a day well lived; it teaches me a lot about attachment and detachment," she tried to explain. "I love knowing that tomorrow we will have sailed across the ocean and be miles away. No regrets. Keep moving on."

"Your poetic reflections are all very well," her friends told her, as they neared the front of the queue. "We are people of action. Sure you won't join us? Take a leap into the unknown."

"I've already done that," Helena assured them. "My life is one great, long mystery."

Christchurch, New Zealand
Day 40

The sleepy French-inspired provincial town of Akaroa is invaded day after day by hordes of cruise ship passengers. The site of the first French settlement, the coastal town on a peninsula, Akaroa is known for its rolling hills and farmland. It is situated on the South Island of New Zealand, which is populated by one million people and 50 million sheep.

An hour outside Christchurch, the town strives to re-create and maintain its French heritage and culture and retains street names and houses that invoke all things Gallic. In the French tradition, Akaroa is passionate about its cuisine and has become a destination for food and wine festivals. Under azure-blue skies, sky-high fir trees hide the hairpin bends of the coastline around the harbor.

The tiny permanent population of just over 600 is over-whelmed, especially in the summer months, by domestic and international visitors. The local economy is dependent on the visitors, and most people in the town are welcoming and friendly. However, there were those who liked the town the way it was before a hurricane forced the cruise lines to find a new anchorage after damage to their regular port of Lyttelton.

The local Maori tribe discovered the beauty of the location long before the legendary British explorer and navigator,

Captain Cook, explored the south sea island and Polynesia looking for the southern continent. Captain Cook sighted Akaroa Harbor in the 1770s, but in 1840, the township was established by French settlers. Authentic interiors are preserved in three heritage buildings: the court house, the customs house and Akaroa's oldest building, the Langlois-Eteveneaux Cottage, which dates from the early 1840s.

Before heading for Christchurch, one hour's drive away, Helena accepted an invitation from the local postal service to enjoy a scenic mail run around the Eastern Bays. Welcoming visitors aboard a rural postal van, the postmaster delivered commentary as he traveled from sea level to crater rim delivering the day's mail.

"We bring our customers the mail," explained the postmaster, "and they show their thanks with delicious homemade treats."

A visit to the farmers market allowed Helena and the other cruise guests to see why Akaroa has become an international destination for its fine dining and wines. A veritable feast of local produce is on offer and visitors are encouraged to try the handcrafted cheeses, hazelnuts, olives and olive oil. Stallholders tempt visitors with samples of their wares of locally grown fruit, smoked salmon, vegetables, herbs, honey, olives, nuts and flowers, plus preserves of pickles, jams, sauces and breads, pastries, lavender products and plants.

"Breakfast *was* a long time ago," Helena agreed with the stallholder who insisted she try one more sample of his exquisite French pastries. "They look delicious but I don't think I'll have room for lunch. We're taking a trip to Christchurch and I hear there are excellent restaurants there."

In contrast to Akaroa's French heritage, Christchurch, the largest town on the South Island, with a population of some 400,000 people, is fiercely proud of its British past and street names that are all comfortably familiar to visitors from the UK. Grey and white buildings in the newly restored city boast wide-open, uncluttered streets with modern restaurants and world-class shopping. A circular streetcar makes getting around the inner streets easy and cheap. There are even unscheduled stops for vendors to board the streetcar and offer complimentary fudge, toffee and chocolate.

The pace is unhurried and city dwellers go about their business in a relaxed manner displaying openness and tolerance to the ever-increasing numbers of tourists who visit their city.

On February 22, 2011, Christchurch was devastated by a magnitude 6.3 earthquake in the Canterbury area, and the epicenter in Lyttelton killed 185 people and injured several thousands. The earthquake destroyed or damaged around 170,000 buildings, a series of aftershocks delayed rebuilding and many disputed insurance claims remain outstanding.

Tales of heroism remain. In one high rise building, the elevators and stairs collapsed—a resident of the city, an experienced mountaineer, gathered materials from the debris and made a rope. He guided the trapped people down the outside of the building but refused to accept that he was a hero.

The city have spent billions of dollars reconstructing civic and public buildings and vow to regenerate and create a spectacularly beautiful city, allowing a great vision to come from destruction now that they have the opportunity to build from the ground up. The driving force has been to create a purposefully designed and integrated new city. Rising like a phoenix from the ashes, art galleries, cultural centers and civic buildings embody the spirit of the modern city.

In the heart of the city, the once magnificent cathedral had only its walls standing; all of the interior was razed to the ground. Finally, after years of arguments and disputes about the cost of rebuilding versus knocking it down and constructing a brand-new edifice, the city agreed to rebuild the cathedral brick by brick at a cost estimated at over 34 million dollars.

Helena had two missions while in Christchurch. First, she wanted to see the famous "pop-up church" built as a temporary space for worshippers, as well as the extent of the damage to the original cathedral.

"Where is the pop-up church?" she asked passersby as she wandered around the streets close to the cathedral. As it turned out, she had been mistaken and was looking for something different than she expected. Time was always of the essence on a day trip and, though she was leisurely sightseeing, she needed to find the pop-up church.

"I have always wanted to see the pop-up church. Look out for it when you go to Christchurch," the Captain instructed her as they shared lunch.

"You're not going?" she asked.

"No, we have crew training onboard," he told her. "But you go and report back to me."

"Oh, you mean the cardboard church," said one middle-aged lady who was sitting and eating her lunch on a bench near the town square. "They say it's the most famous building in Christchurch," she explained. "I go there sometimes, most people who live in the city do. It's a reminder of what happened and what is being done to restore the buildings and infrastructure.

"Of course, it's not really cardboard, so if you are looking for some flimsy structure, you won't find it. Its official name is the Transitional Cathedral. The diocese paid over $2 million to build it, but what we really want is for the classic cathedral to be rebuilt. Instead of its roof being open to the skies and the inside a pile of rubble and home to pigeons. Some architects have suggested building a new structure on the existing ruins.

117

That may work. As long as we get rid of that ugly destructive reminder of the earthquake scarring our beautiful city."

She tucked away the remains of her lunch into her handbag and told Helena, "I'm on my way back to work. I'll walk you to the church; it's not far."

Helena made a donation to the restoration fund as she looked around the multicolored front-peaked entrance of the so called cardboard cathedral, reminiscent of the shape and structure of the cathedral itself. She marveled at all it symbolized. She promised herself that she would visit Christchurch again one day when the city's reconstruction was complete.

The symbolism moved her, and she acknowledged a feeling of sadness inside that pointed to the fact she felt her reconstruction as a human being was not yet totally complete. "I'm still a work in progress," she was fond of saying.

Hopefully she could find enlightenment from her second Christchurch mission: to find the Wizard of Christchurch. He held court in Cathedral Square where, before the earthquake, he used to climb a ladder and preach from alongside the church's walls. She soon found her quarry. It is claimed that, thanks to him, the area has been declared a public-speaking zone.

Approaching an old man with a long beard, black cloak and wizard's hat, she hardly needed to ask the question. But did anyway. "Are you the Wizard of Christchurch?"

"I am indeed," he said, stretching out a gnarled hand and indicating she should sit at his makeshift table and join the other acolytes seeking his wisdom.

Among more esoteric amblings, the Wizard seemed to confirm the perceived wisdom about him. He claimed to be an educator, comedian, magician and politician. "Born in London, I'm now over eighty years of age and I came to New Zealand from Great Britain over forty years ago. The New Zealand Art

Gallery Directors Association designated me as an authentic Work of Art and in 1990 my old friend, the Prime Minister of New Zealand, Mike Moore, appointed me the official 'Wizard of New Zealand.'"

After the earthquake, the Wizard declared his intention to retire and leave Christchurch but returned to oppose the proposed demolition of the cathedral.

A cathedral square stallholder, selling Wizard hats, spoke in support of the Wizard, "He's an eccentric, but somehow he has managed to embody the spirit of Christchurch, and, in speaking out about the need to preserve Christchurch's heritage buildings, he gives a voice to what a lot of people think. On the other hand, a lot of people think he's a public nuisance, but people come from all over the world to see him, and they even made a documentary about him."

Helena ventured to ask the Wizard to cast a spell for her.

"It's traditional to offer him a gift—money will work," explained one of the youths who form the Wizard's inner circle.

Helena passed over a couple of NZ dollars. "Now, what is it you require?" asked the Wizard. "I'm excellent with requests for specific weather."

"It's a personal matter," said Helena as a blush of embarrassment spread over her face.

"Okay, write it on a piece of paper, and I'll put it in my hat," the Wizard instructed.

Helena did as asked. Keeping the message cryptic in case he was going to share it with his followers, she wrote, "A love spell to join our hearts."

The Wizard accepted the piece of paper that she folded into a small neat parcel. "It is done," he said confidently. "If it doesn't work, you can always come back and get a refund; you know where to find me."

Helena thanked him and said, "Goodbye," conscious as always of the need to get back to the ship. Leaving Cathedral Square, she ran into a small group of cruise ship passengers all heading back to the same place. They compared notes for the day and spoke about the remarkable story of the city of Christchurch and its cathedral.

"What a weird character," they joked as they talked about the Wizard of Christchurch. "He's got some funny ideas."

"He told me," said one woman, "that wars are caused by women spending too much money."

Helena smiled and crossed her fingers. She dared to hope that her recent spending would bring love, not war. The last rays of the sun reflected a subtle glow on the clouds and cast the whole city in a mystical light that illuminated the cathedral and celebrated the promise of this beautiful house of worship— restored one brick at a time.

At Sea
Day 44

"I missed you yesterday," he said as he settled at the lunch table. "Even though I knew you were on a shore excursion, I like to have my lunch companion beside me."

Helena narrowed her eyes. "Is that what I am, a lunch companion? There must be many colleagues, your officers or other passengers who would be glad of your company."

"Of course," he said enigmatically, "but they are not like you. Is it a problem for you that I like to sit with you?"

"It is the highlight of my day," Helena admitted. "You must know how I feel about you."

She watched carefully to see the reaction her remark might provoke.

"How can I know what you feel?" he asked.

The color was rising in Helena's cheeks. She desperately wanted to have a conversation and lay bare her feelings, but she was worried she had misinterpreted the situation.

"I enjoy talking with you, laughing with you, looking at you," he told her.

She considered accepting the compliment and moving on to talk about everyday things, but could not resist admitting, "I like all those things about you." There was no denying that his dynamic good looks, his smile, his humor, his intelligence, his status, his authority all added up to an attraction that had become an obsession.

She refused to play games such as staying out of his way and hoping he would come looking for her. The previous night after dinner, she excused herself and passed by some of the places he frequented. From afar she glimpsed him but resisted the urge to approach. She walked on purposefully when a male passenger who was having a drink in one of the lounges observed her as she retraced her steps and told her, "He went that way."

On another circuit of the decks, Meredith insisted on tagging along and asking questions to which she must have already known the answer, "What time does the disco start? Is the second show over yet? Why did you leave dinner early?"

Helena dreaded bumping into him when Meredith was with her. No way was she going to introduce her or risk her asking ridiculous questions.

The private world she and the Captain shared at the lunch table did not extend to other times of the day. Much as she would have loved to spend the evenings with him, that was when he performed his official duties.

The night before, a Gala night, a presentation of crew awards took place in a public lounge and the passengers were invited to go and watch. Helena claimed her seat, always carefully chosen so that she could see him but not be seen. She watched in admiration as he greeted each crew member with a smile and said, "Well done," sometimes with a hand on their shoulder. He stood genuinely engaged as photograph after photograph was taken; photographs that would travel the world with the employees and hold pride of place in family homes around the globe. The Captain took the hands of a young laundry worker who shed a tear as he was handed his certificate and an envelope containing the cash reward that came with the award.

Helena watched the presentations with almost a thousand other passengers. The interest confirmed the public acknowledgment and value placed on the tireless dedication of the behind-the-scenes staff who work long hours in the bowels of the ship, far away from the sunshine and bracing fresh air enjoyed on deck by the passengers. The Captain stopped for a drink in the cocktail bar after the presentation with one of his officers, It was a quiet night and there were only half a dozen guests in the lounge.

Helena was dressed to impress in one of her exquisitely embroidered, gold-beaded Chinese gowns and wore a glittering tiara in her long blond hair. She did not doubt he would notice her, but, because he was with another officer, she was not sure he would show any favoritism towards her.

She need not have worried. To her delight, he introduced her to his companion and made room for her to sit down beside them. "You want something to drink?" he asked,

She shook her head and smiled. "No, thank you."

He looked into her eyes, and her stomach lurched; the longing she felt for him never diminished. His flashing black eyes showed his appreciation as he held her gaze and nodded his approval.

"This is my special friend, Madame Helena," he told his colleague. "We share many interests."

Helena smiled at the compliment. The more she saw of him, of how he conducted himself with integrity, control and competence, the more she fell under his spell.

The next day at lunch, she thanked him for the introduction.

"I like being your special friend," she said. He smiled, and she was sure that every day his smile, which showed white, even teeth, was wider yet always held a hint of amusement.

"You called me your special friend." She watched as he laid down his cutlery and prepared to give her all his attention.

"That is what you are," he said. "Yes, no?"

"Yes," Helena confirmed, "but is that all we are, and all we will be, friends?"

"What are you asking me?" he said.

Feeling out of her depth, not knowing how to proceed, Helena struggled to articulate what she wanted to say.

Helena lowered her eyes and her voice as she admitted, "I want us to be more than friends. I can't stop thinking about you. I don't want to settle for a friendship. I want to believe that it will become a relationship. A romance. This cruise for me has become all about you."

Unsure how he would react, Helena tried not to look at him. She blurted out what was to her the truth, but how would he feel about it? She wished she could take back what she had said.

He pushed his chair back and stood up from the table. She was afraid she had driven him away by speaking so openly. Instead he towered over her as he positioned himself on her side of the table and said, "Thank you," as he reached down and gently touched her shoulder. "I'm not unaware that something is happening between us, but I have no idea what it means. Things are complicated, not straightforward."

Relieved that at least he had not been offended, Helena reassured him. "We have plenty of time to work it out. We're only halfway around the world."

The Captain picked up his radio from the table and clipped it to his belt. "Let's see what happens," he told her, turned on his heel and walked away.

Helena felt like a fool. Having expressed her feelings, she feared she would lose even their friendship because she asked for more. In all their hours of conversation, she avoided asking personal questions, though, she told him everything about her. She hoped to live in the cocooned world of the cruise ship and not have to consider anything or anyone outside.

Helena knew her experience with relationships was so out of date. Like a woman looking to return to the corporate world after years of having no work experience, a long-term happy marriage did not prepare her for the situation in which she now found herself. She should have realized that expecting a relationship with the Captain of the ship was not going to be straightforward. Were there considerations like the professional restrictions imposed on a doctor/patient relationship? Captain/passenger—was it out of bounds? Forbidden? But when all was said and done, he was the one who had moved the situation onto a new level by coming to her table.

She dared to hope he was as attracted to her as she was to him. And whatever boundaries were in place, he had chosen to cross them in his desire to be close to her. But in his defense, nothing had really happened. He maintained a professional integrity, and, apart from some hand-holding, there was no physical aspect to their attraction, certainly not a kiss. Helena worried she had blown the whole situation out of proportion. Had she made all of this up? But surely their dozens of lunch dates added up to more than a polite social interaction. Helena's head felt like it would explode. It was so full of questions and doubts and fears.

There were three sea days now as the ship headed across the South Pacific Ocean away from New Zealand en route to Sydney, Australia. Several hundred passengers, many returning home from European trips or visiting far-flung family, were scheduled to get off in Sydney, and their places would be taken by others heading for Europe. Helena was forced to admit that she had made few friends among the passengers who were due to disembark. She had, as she had told him, spent most of her cruise focusing on the Captain. Two of the dinner table guests who she had come to know were getting off, happy to be visiting their grown-up son, his wife and their grandchildren, including one grandchild they had not yet met.

She hoped at one point that Meredith would also be ready to leave the ship, especially with the amount of complaining she did about everything from the food to the ship to the countries they visited. The patience of the other dinner guests at their table had long since run out concerning Meredith.

It turned out that the sister she had booked to take the cruise with refused to join her after the two had a massive row. Their home in the Devon countryside had been left to them by their parents, who had both passed away, and they were forced to continue living together to share the stables where they kept their horses and to run a riding school.

"She hadn't really wanted to leave the stables in the care of a manager so she grabbed the chance to stay home and take care of everything herself. As if I'd care. I'm happier where I am."

When she told the story at dinner one night of why she was traveling alone, one or two eyebrows were raised at the proposition that on the ship she was happier than at home. She may have been Meredith by name, but she was not Merry by nature. Helena tried to ignore her and the malicious remarks that were constantly directed her way. That afternoon, Helena took a deck walk to clear her head and was dismayed to see Meredith heading toward her. Though they were clearly not friends, Meredith insisted on stopping to make conversation. Usually to pass on gossip.

She fell into step with Helena and quizzed her about the helicopter ride in the Bay of Islands. "I heard you had company," she said, "only the two of you on the trip. Very cozy."

Nothing ever stayed private when a thousand passengers had little more to do with their time than follow one another around on shore excursions and indulge their love of conversation and intrigue in the bars and lounges, at the pool and around the dinner table.

"You two have certainly become very friendly," said Meredith. "Sitting head-to-head at the lunch table, oblivious to everyone else. I'm wondering what you will do when he leaves."

Helena refused to let her face register surprise, but she needed to know.

"Leave?" she asked, trying not to give her archenemy more ammunition than necessary.

"Yes, he's leaving in Sydney," she said with a smirk. "You did know, didn't you?"

Helena felt a terrible chill run through her body. She could not believe what she had heard. Her eyes stung; her mouth was dry. She didn't know what to do. She couldn't lose him now.

For a crazy moment, she thought she, too, would have to leave the ship.

"Tomorrow's his last day," Meredith smirked as she gathered speed and stomped off down the deck.

Sydney, Australia
Day 48

Helena let out a scream of frustration as soon as she entered her cabin. She was distraught. The thought of him leaving the ship, so soon and without telling her, pierced her heart.

For the rest of the day, she stayed in the cabin, cocooned under the duvet, crying and trying to make sense of the information she had received. The pain was excruciating—the thought of never seeing him again brought on a panic attack.

"Please don't let it be true," she said over and over again.

At dinner time, with no appetite and determined not to give Meredith the chance to gloat, she stayed in bed. Curled up in the foetal position.

She made her way down to the reception area only after she had judged that most people she knew would have left the bars and lounges in preparation for an anticipated dawn entry into Sydney Harbour, sailing under the majestic Sydney Harbour Bridge.

"Please, would you see that the Captain gets this letter?" she asked the pleasant young woman who was manning the late-night reception desk. "It's rather urgent."

"I'll make sure he gets it," said the young woman, "but is there anything with which I can help?"

"No, you're very kind," said Helena. "The letter is marked personal." She had written and torn up several letters because it had proved so difficult to get the tone and words right. She didn't want to sound desperate, but she needed to appeal to him to not leave her without a word.

The version she settled on was short and sweet: "Are you leaving the ship in Sydney? Will there be an opportunity for us to say goodbye?"

Her alarm was set for 6 a.m., but she didn't need the reminder. All night she tossed and turned. Yesterday she had dared to question what would be the next stage of the relationship. Now it turned out, there was to be no relationship. Perhaps, not even the chance to see or talk to him again.

The predawn morning was fresh and cool. She dressed to stay warm. To sail under the Sydney Harbour Bridge had been an anticipated highlight of the Grand Around the World Cruise. This was Helena's first visit to Australia, and she was excited to see the country about which she had heard so much.

Now all she cared about was that the Captain would be on the bridge and she would see him for, maybe, the last time. It seemed that everyone on the ship had surfaced early to experience the thrill of sailing under the iconic landmark.

The Sydney Harbour Bridge measures about three-quarters of a mile long and was once considered to be the largest steel arch bridge in the world. Opened in 1932, the heritage-listed steel arch bridge carries rail, vehicular, bicycle and pedestrian traffic between the Sydney central business district and the North Shore. When the bridge was built, it required so much paint that the original color was grey—the only color that was available in such quantities. Its distinctive shape gave the bridge its nickname: the coat hanger.

Helena rushed to the upstairs railing where a crowd had gathered.

Was he there? She could not relax and enjoy the passageway under the bridge until she knew the answer. In a sea of white uniforms, he stood head and shoulders above the rest of the company.

She sighed deeply and her heart settled; he was there. Overseeing all operations. Watching every action of the pilot boats whose job it was to guide the huge vessel into the harbor.

It would not be appropriate to try to make any of this magnificent spectacle about her, but she wished she could at least draw his attention for a second, at least catch his eye. Let him know she was there. Confirm some kind of special relationship.

As the ship docked and passengers jostled and formed queues to be the first to disembark, Helena returned to her cabin. There was no reply to her letter of the previous night.

Reluctantly she gathered her belongings and headed toward the day's designated gangway to leave the ship. Every moment she hoped and prayed that he would be somewhere visible, standing erect at the gangway and bidding farewell to the passengers. Not that she knew how she would conduct herself if she did see him; she could hardly throw herself into his arms and plead with him to take her with him. Embarrassment and fear kept her from asking anyone who might actually have the answer, like the officers she had come to know.

"Will we see the Captain before he leaves?" she asked a couple of the administrative staff manning the gangway. They looked at her blankly. One shrugged.

Helena walked ashore and completed immigration procedures before she emerged into the cruise terminal. She had waited for this visit for so long and had no intention of allowing her personal disappointment to overshadow a great experience.

Sydney, the most densely populated city in the entire Oceanic continent, is internationally famous, and, though Canberra is actually the capital of the country, Sydney, located in the

New South Wales territory, is the jewel in the crown. Australia is a member of the fifty-three country Commonwealth and Her Majesty Queen Elizabeth II is Head of State. Sydney was founded as a colony in 1788, but it officially became a city in 1842 and, currently, is a city inhabited by young people; the median age of its residents being less than thirty-five years.

Modern, vibrant and pulsating with high energy and enviable weather, the city is a mecca for adventurers, sunseekers and world travelers. A monument to feel-good urban living and human achievement, Sydney's cultures, languages and minds mix to create inspired architecture, fabulous food and iconic art—and the impression is that every street is crammed full of life and full of surprises.

Helena headed for the place she dreamed of visiting for so many years, the iconic Sydney Opera House, the white-sailed, world-class performing arts venue that dominated the harbor and proclaimed Sydney as a center of culture and enterprise.

Climbing the multi-storeyed staircase to the higher levels of the Opera House filled Helena with a sense of the spiritual, and she felt an emotional connection to the beauty of the building. Work commenced in 1959 and construction was expected to take four years, but it took fourteen. It was estimated that the cost would be $7 million dollars, but the final cost was $107 million, largely paid for by a state lottery. More than 10,000 construction workers worked on the building.

An international competition was held by the city to choose the design for the building, on the site of what had been proposed as a streetcar yard. Held in 1956, 233 designs were submitted to the competition. Jorn Utzon from Denmark was announced the winner and received $5,000 for his design.

"There are more than one million tiles covering the

structure, all made in Sweden and more than 10 million people visit the Opera House every year," Helena read on a plaque.

"You are more than welcome to stay and listen to the rehearsals for tonight's performance of the opera *Turandot*," the tour guide informed Helena and her party. "Also there will be a special lightshow illuminating the building this evening to celebrate Chinese New Year. Our famous white sails will be lit up red."

"Unfortunately, we will not see the illuminations. Our cruise ship sails before the lighting up ceremony," Helena explained. "Unless we see the display as we head out of the harbor en route to our next port of call. We're only scheduled to be here for one day."

"It's the nature of the cruising world," commiserated the guide, "sometimes you wish you could stay longer in a port."

Helena felt her whole body fill with the anguish of leaving Sydney. The kindly Aussie woman became worried when Helena suddenly burst into tears. "Hopefully you will come back one day," she consoled her.

A guided tour of the Opera House and a visit to the Joan Sutherland Theatre confirmed to Helena that she would plan a return visit. One day. She stood before an elaborately robed portrait of Dame Joan Sutherland, one of Australia's most celebrated opera singers.

"Dame Joan," she whispered to the painting of the diva, which resembled a religious icon and portrayed the great woman whose career made her a legendary figure. "Opera is about passion, drama, love and death. Please show me a way to embrace the powerful events that are driving my life and show me, by your example, the way to conduct myself with grace and dignity."

Helena had long been an avid opera lover and the visit to the Opera House delivered a soul-enriching, as well as a cultural, experience. In the underground gift shop, she selected items that would remind her of her visit: an intricately decorated and colored-enamel pen, a carved model of the Opera House and a leather-bound notebook. She had them gift wrapped inside a polished wooden box bearing the signature sails of the building. "I know who the gifts are for," she admitted to her inner self. "Perfect gifts for a Captain who promised to open a new page in his logbook for me."

* * *

Feeling restored and ready to accept the circumstances of the Captain's departure, Helena returned to the ship and refused to succumb to sadness, even when there was no reply to her letter. Instead she played opera music, Dame Joan singing one of her favorite arias, while she dressed for dinner.

"I am still on a world cruise," she reminded herself, "still undertaking a trip of a lifetime. Now I get to tick Sydney off my wish list."

To deflect any suggestion, especially in Meredith's presence, that she might be in mourning, Helena wore to dinner a tailored yellow trouser suit offset with her beautiful black Tahitian pearls and black patent high-heeled shoes.

"You look like a ray of sunshine," said one of the male guests, who always championed Helena and complimented her, especially if his wife was not within hearing distance.

"Thank you," said Helena. "I loved the visit to Sydney. I'd have to say it was my favorite port of call so far on the world cruise."

"Strange that," said Meredith, almost under her breath.

Helena enjoyed sharing the highlights of her day and

listening to sightseeing stories from the other diners. "One day really was not enough," one of the couples agreed. "There was so much to see and do. We didn't even get to Bondi Beach."

Dinner was almost over when they heard the familiar electronic sound that signaled an announcement over the radio broadcast system.

Glass in hand, Helena stopped as still as a statue when she heard his voice; he was still onboard. He hadn't left the ship in Sydney.

"Ladies and Gentleman, this is your Captain speaking from the bridge. I trust you all had an enjoyable visit to Sydney. If so, I'm sure I will make you very happy when I tell you that we have a change in our planned schedule. I have taken the decision that we should stay overnight here in the harbor and spend an extra day in the city tomorrow."

The passengers burst into applause. "Great decision," they assured one another.

Some questioned the reasons for the decision, but, as no explanation was forthcoming, the consensus was that to stay in Sydney one more day was a win-win situation all around.

Helena cast a glance at Meredith. It was too early to celebrate. Maybe tomorrow was the day when he would leave her life for good, but for today, she was delighted that he was still onboard. One day at a time, anything could happen tomorrow.

Sydney—Day 2
Day 49

Helena had no intention of missing the opportunity presented by an extra day in Sydney. To ensure that she could enjoy the freedom of sightseeing without anxiety about whether or not the Captain would leave the ship while she was elsewhere, she kept her tone light as she casually asked the cruise director, "There was a rumor among the passengers, you know how it is, that the Captain is leaving the ship in Sydney?"

"May have been part of plan A, not part of plan B," he answered as he stood behind a desk in the reception area and handed out details of a new hastily arranged shore excursion.

Helena smiled to herself, disaster averted for another day. She knew from the previous day's visit that Sydney was a well-laid-out city: very accessible and easy to get around. She collected water at the hospitality desk and headed into the city.

Map in hand, she made her way to the designated stop for the Big Bus Tours. In hundreds of destinations all over the world, Helena, along with thousands of tourists, discovered that the quickest way to get an overview of a city was on the hop on, hop off bus. The route generally covered all main points of interest, and the option to hop off to explore an area and hop on again was a method of transport she found convenient.

On the open-top deck of a red bus in glorious sunshine, she sat captivated by the grand buildings of the city center. The bus passed by Sydney Town Hall, a civic landmark combining venue facilities with spectacular heritage architecture; the Mint, Sydney's oldest building; the Art Gallery of New South Wales where works of art by Australian international artists past and present are exhibited; Hyde Park, the oldest public park with monuments, statues and the Anzac Memorial building; and the State Library containing documents and artefacts of the history and heritage of Australia. Sky Tower, the tallest building in Sydney, dominates the city skyline, and Helena knew where she was headed.

Queen Victoria Building, a stunning example of Romanesque Revival architecture, a heritage-listed late-nineteenth-century building named in honor of Queen Victoria in celebration of her Diamond Jubilee in 1897. In Sydney's oldest and grandest Victorian arcade, Helena challenged herself to check out as many of the 180 elegant and unique boutiques as possible. Designer-led fashions typified Sydney's youthful, devil-may-care temperament and Helena succumbed to the temptation offered by unashamedly feminine clothing ranges and bought an extravagant midnight-blue satin dress with a low-cut corset top and a billowing skirt.

The perfect accessory to the low-cut dress caught her eye in an exotic, Arabian store. She approached the store owner. "I've fallen in love with the beautiful piece of jewelry displayed on the marble statue of a woman in your store window."

Removing the piece from the neck of the statue, the store owner cradled it lovingly in both hands. "You have a good eye." He smiled at her, and she saw that he had two prominent gold teeth at the edges of his mouth so that when he smiled, the gold glinted. "The necklace on the statue is a replica of the wedding necklace worn by a very beautiful and famed Arabian princess. I designed this particular piece myself. I selected every jewel to ensure that all the colors of the spectrum were represented: sapphires for the sky, rubies for the blood mingled at the sharing of the sacred vows, jade for fertility and to mark the cycle of life and, at every seventh jewel, I inserted a gold band to represent the joining of two in marriage."

Helena listened enchanted. "It is very beautiful. Thank you for your art and for sharing your story with me. When I saw the necklace, I thought it would perfectly complement my new dress." She held up the shopping bag from an exclusive boutique.

"Please, may I have a look?" said the store owner. "Place it here."

He swept aside small pieces of jewelry and draped Helena's dress over the black marble and gilt-edged counter. At the neckline, he placed the string of jewels. Whatever the price, Helena already knew that she had to take ownership of the necklace.

Numbers were written on small pieces of paper, crossed and discarded as Helena joined in the haggling process. The store owner started high; Helena started low. Both knew a deal was inevitable but the ritual of bartering added to the excitement of the exchange.

Finally, an acceptable median number was reached. "Only for a beautiful lady like you would I let my special design leave the shop at this price. The necklace belongs to you," said the now happy store owner.

Helena was a well-satisfied customer, and she accepted the gift of a pair of matching earrings. "I have enjoyed our encounter," Helena said and watched as the two gold teeth added a glint to his smile.

Hand on the door handle, she turned and gave her own dazzling smile as he told her, "He is a lucky man."

With a spring in her step and her purchases swinging in their bags, Helena headed for the Big Bus stop. She waved to a couple of passengers on the top deck whom she knew from the ship but, with her bags, chose to stay downstairs.

Bondi Beach was her next planned stop, and, following the previous night's conversation, she guessed they were all going to the same place. With its rolling breakers and golden sand, Sydney's world-famous Bondi Beach lives up to expectations. Shoes off, Helena slipped her dress off; she was already prepared and underneath wore a bikini. Asking permission from the cruise ship couple who were sitting on the beach and eating ice cream to leave her clothes in their safekeeping, Helena strolled along the water's edge.

Paddling up to her knees, she soon found that the force of the breakers made for unsteady progress. Luckily she was not intending to swim because a lifeguard shouted into his bullhorn, "Clear the water," every time anyone attempted to move too far into the sea.

Back on the sand, she asked the couple she knew to take photos of her to supplement her selfies. "Bondi Beach, another check on the wish list," she wrote on the caption as she used WhatsApp to send the photos back home.

The contrast between a bleak winter day in London and a summer day at a dream destination with sun, sand and rolling surf did not bear comparison.

"Thanks for the photographs," one of her friends responded. "It was kind of you to think of us. Not."

"Do you want to share a taxi back to the ship?" asked the couple with whom she had struck up a friendship. "If the traffic is bad, we could be cutting it close to boarding time."

In the cab on the return journey, as Helena sat in the front seat and they sat in the back, husband and wife shared highlights of their day in Sydney; happy finally to say they had been to Bondi Beach.

"Didn't expect to see the Captain on the beach," said the wife. "Sitting there with a pool towel from the ship wrapped around his shoulders."

Helena felt her whole body tense. She was furious. How had she missed him? Why didn't they tell her? Why hadn't he sought her out?

She leaned forward in the seat and pretended to check the contents of her shopping bags. She wanted to scream or cry. She grabbed tightly onto her shopping bag and tried to keep the annoyance out of her voice. "Where was he?" she said.

"Near to the café. We saw him when we went to buy our ice cream. We hadn't run into you at that point."

"At first we thought you might be with him," said the husband. Like most people on the ship, they obviously knew that the two of them shared a lunch table in the restaurant and about her trip to the Captain's table.

Helena's Sydney sightseeing, her gorgeous dress and the perfect piece of jewelry, all designed to catch and keep his attention, faded into insignificance.

How cruel is fate that the one person she longed to see eluded her. He was so near to her and yet so far. Damn him, she wanted to yell. What game was he playing? Why didn't he behave like other people when they wanted to pursue a relationship? Send a text, make a date, pick up the phone. Make contact, for goodness sake.

The emotional roller coaster was fraying her nerves to breaking point. After days of anguish that he might leave the ship, in the last hour she had been so close to him and yet so far.

Back onboard that evening there was a carnival atmosphere. The trip to Sydney was a great success and the Captain's decision to give them an extra day made him the most popular man on the ship. Helena gritted her teeth and agreed that Sydney had delivered a visit to remember.

* * *

The Captain was on the bridge to sail his ship out of Sydney Harbour, back under the Harbour Bridge, and plough out into the ocean to continue the itinerary and visit other places of interest in Australia.

On the next sea day, Helena made her way to the restaurant at the usual time and sat in her usual seat. She did not take her eyes from the headwaiter as he ruled over his domain in the buffet restaurant and monitored the situation. The restaurant was almost empty, but serving staff stayed alert and the chef popped his head out of the swing door between restaurant and kitchen.

The headwaiter checked his watch as the time crept near to the official close of the lunch buffet. "Close the line," he called. Staff started to put up the green curtains on the counters signifying that serving was over for the day. Everyone relaxed a little and went about their tasks.

Helena's heart sank. From the moment she woke, she had counted the minutes until she could be here, opposite him, speak to him, see him.

She sat dejected and sipped her tea as a waiter asked if he could clear her plate away.

Out of the corner of her eye, she saw a signal between the kitchen staff and the headwaiter—a last minute phone call told them, "He's on his way. Take the curtains down."

Helena's heart leaped.

He entered the restaurant from a staircase on the outside deck, walked slowly down the line selecting his food, stopped, looked around and, seeing who he was looking for, headed to where Helena sat.

"May I?" he said. She nodded and smiled a welcome. "Anytime," she assured him.

Helena could hardly believe the calm demeanor she was able to present, knowing she had been to hell and back in the days since they last shared a table.

In the privacy of her cabin she cried and raged, suffered pain and powerlessness and prayed and plotted to find a way to end her desolation. In the cold light of day, it seemed extreme that she had invested so much of her mental and emotional energy on a person and a situation over which she had no control.

"How are you, Helena? Did you enjoy our port call in Sydney?" he asked and waited for a reply. His smile dazzled and his voice held the seductive tone she found so hard to resist.

If only she dared tell him, "I'm a hot mess. I'm crazy about you. I fall apart all the time."

Instead she stared into his eyes and tried to transmit wordless messages.

"Did you get my letter?" she asked.

"Yes, I was a little surprised," he said. "A long time ago the plans changed. My vacation was supposed to start in Sydney. The company asked me to stay on when the Captain who was taking over had a personal crisis and could not fly out here. I won't leave till maybe Singapore. More than a month away."

With no attempt to hide her relief, Helena breathed deeply and told him, "That's wonderful news. I was so sad at the thought you were leaving us—well, leaving me, especially as you hadn't mentioned it."

He looked serious. More serious than she had ever seen him. "You must not rely on me, Helena," he said. "You will be let down. My life is complicated. I have responsibilities. To the company, to the ship, to the passengers, to my family. To my wife."

Determined not to let him see her cry, Helena turned her head away. How stupid of her not to have realized. Of course, he was not a blank canvas waiting for her to paint herself into his life. "Thank you for your honesty," she said.

He nodded. "I don't want to have the conversation now, but when the time is right, I may tell you about me."

Pain and Healing
Day 50

Pain seared Helena's body. Intense heat burned her skin and radiated from the point of contact to penetrate to the deepest recesses of her being. A pulse of high energy shocked her nakedness and threatened to break her fragile spirit. At the point when she believed she could tolerate no more, the pressure was released and with it came her tears.

Years of self-development and healing practices had taught her that every painful experience triggered previous events: The trauma was felt and the memories of the past were replayed in the present. Our hearts, like the mind, hold on to memories, good and bad.

"Are you okay?" asked the therapist as she removed the hot stones from Helena's back and legs. "We can stop anytime you say."

Helena's mind was miles away and years apart from the comfortable towel-covered treatment couch where she lay in the cocooned ambiance of the ship's spa while relaxing music played and sweet smells encouraged the mind to drift. Escaping to the beauty room for a series of therapeutic procedures and deep tissue massage ensured she would not have to socialize or take part in onboard activities, but it did not isolate her, unlike when she sought solace hiding out in her cabin.

She knew that the sense of abandonment she suffered owed more to grief over her husband than the loss of a man she met only a matter of weeks before. However, the intensity of the feelings overwhelmed her and tapped into all the previous pain, thus magnifying the emotions.

"I'll leave you to get dressed," said the empathetic young Polish girl who had become the person with whom Helena shared healing time without needing to express reasons for her dilemmas. Whatever she may have heard about Helena and the Captain, she kept to herself but did confide the uncertainties of her own strained relationship with one of the entertainment company.

"I came on board to be close to him," she admitted, "but now I question the depth of his feelings for me. I thought we had a future. Now I don't know."

Helena listened and compared that situation to her own without opening up about the real reasons for her own insecurity.

"The hot stone treatment was a revelation," said Helena. "I hadn't expected it to release so many emotions or leave me feeling so exposed. Like an empty vessel that needs refilling with positive thoughts and emotions. I need to start doing my affirmations more conscientiously."

One of the dilemmas on her mind during treatment was whether to go to lunch in the Terrazza.

Was it childish to throw her rattle out of the stroller or was it an act of self-preservation? He had made his situation clear. It should have cleared the air for them to start again.

Even as she made her way to the cabin, clutching a robe around her reinvigorated body, Helena knew she would go to lunch. "You always attract attention with your clothes," one of the receptionists told Helena. "Every day, we check out what you are wearing. Even in the daytime, you manage to make an impression."

Helena was flattered. "Thank you for noticing," she said. Life onboard a cruise ship allowed plenty of time for indulgence and dressing up was one of Helena's favorite indulgences.

Dressed ultra-casual and smart in a pair of leopard-skin trousers and a bronze-and-black sweater with puffed, bronze organza sleeves, her long, blond hair brushed out around her shoulders, Helena sat at her window table overlooking the ocean and waited.

Her heart was beating far faster than usual, but she tried to remain calm and relaxed.

Maybe he would choose to return to his high table far away from a woman who expected more than he could deliver. The fruit on her plate was not so fascinating that it demanded her full attention, but she was determined not to look too anxious or expectant.

The first indication of the Captain's arrival was when the headwaiter gave a discreet nod to the girl behind the soup counter. Everyone knew how much he liked his soup.

Helena kept her head down but was conscious of his every move as he made his way deliberately and unhurriedly down the buffet line. He gave his full attention to the vast array of dishes and showed respect for the many staff who worked tirelessly to produce appetizing meals day after day. "Very good, I like the look of it." He smiled at the serving staff. His gracious, courteous manners endeared him to the hardworking team.

At the end of the line, he stopped, turned, sought out Helena and gave a wave.

Be prepared, that may be the extent of your connection from now on, Helena warned herself.

She kept her eyes fixed on her plate until she felt rather than saw his presence beside her.

"Is okay if I join you?" he asked.

"Of course," said Helena, "it is my pleasure."

His smile was as wide as always and he sat comfortably eating his food. Companionable silence reigned. Helena was annoyed that she was still as enamored of him as ever. His closeness meant she no choice but to succumb to the immense attraction she experienced from the first time she saw him. If love at first sight existed, and she knew it did from her first encounter with her husband, then that was her surely her experience. Sadly, it now seemed that this was a game for one—he was not part of the equation. Helena did not know what to say. Only he could steer the ship.

She inhaled and exhaled in a measured way, replicating the rhythm of his breathing, and allowed him to speak first. "We are still friends?" he asked.

"Of course, friends, that's what we are. Friends."

He looked at her and his expression was one of puzzlement. "Yes, friends. It's okay to be friends?"

"That's what this has been all about?" she asked, "Friendship? Did I misunderstand? I thought it was more."

He raised his eyebrows. "You know it is more," he challenged her. "There is something that has happened between us, but I don't know how to explain it. I have a fascination for you. Of course I believe you have the same feelings, but what can I do? It is not easy for me. I have tried to explain about my responsibilities. I will do nothing that reflects badly on me or my office. While I am in charge of this ship, I am not free to be involved with you or anybody else."

He rose and made his way to the counter where he selected pumpkin bread.

Helena liked that she had riled him. She had never before seen him lose control. At least she had not been mistaken about the attraction. The only question now seemed to be what happened next. And there was the matter of his wife to consider.

When he returned, Helena tried to pull back from what she now perceived to be her unacceptable behavior. "I'm sorry," she told him, "I have no right to question you. You told me what you needed me to know. I was disappointed. But, of course, I want to be your friend and I would never encourage you to compromise your office. I'm sorry if I appeared to be asking for more than you are able to offer."

She smiled and leaned in close. "But I did want to be sure that I had not misread the signs. If it's okay with you, while we continue our friendship, I will continue to flirt with you and imagine that there may be a time when friendship becomes relationship."

"It's okay." He nodded. "You can flirt with me. I like the way you do that. Why do you think I sit with you every day?"

Helena laughed and then listened as his voice became serious.

Reaching out his hand to touch her arm lightly, the Captain took her into his confidence. "Yes, I have a wife. She lives with my family in Odessa. I have a grown-up family, a son and a daughter. That's all I want to say about them. My wife and I have problems. I am traveling all the time so we do not separate, but we are rarely ever in the same place. The marriage continues, and I will not do anything that would make it even more difficult."

"Now I understand," said Helena. "It really is NOT me; it's you."

They both laughed.

Grigory relaxed and out of the blue asked, "Why don't you use my name?"

"It's a mark of respect," Helena explained. "I do not want to forget who you are."

"This is one of the things I like about you," he said. "You are different. Not like other women. I can be honest with you. You have class. That is something I knew from the time I first saw you arrive on the ship."

Helena blushed. Glad to have all her assumptions confirmed that he had singled her out.

"My life is complicated," he admitted. "Now all my vacation plans have been changed and I need to make arrangements to fulfil my commitments. I hope my grown-up children will come to meet me in maybe Singapore. They like to travel. My wife will refuse. It is understandable."

Allowing him to proceed at his own pace, Helena resisted the temptation to ask questions.

"I have another commitment to fulfil," he said with a sigh. "My youngest son lives with his mother in America. I need to make a visit there to meet them. The boy is at school."

Helena struggled to make sense of what she was hearing. In reality, she wished she could avoid hearing what he was about to reveal.

"He is ten years old. His mother and I had a brief affair when she was commissioned for a project on the small speciality cruise liner where I was second in command. She was an interior designer contracted to make changes to certain aspects of the shopping galleries. I am not proud of the fact we crossed the line professionally and personally and had an affair. She was on board for only a short period of time, but to complete her work, she returned again. Of course, I honor my responsibility to both her and our son, but it has meant the end of my marriage."

Helena felt like she was drowning in memories of the past. The story played out again. The pain she buried so deep and then the obsession that surfaced and threatened her very existence. But this time she was not the wife. She did not have to decide whether to stay or go.

One question demanded an answer before she could begin to process the situation. "The mother, what is your relationship?"

"There is no relationship," he owned up. "I cannot even say I am a good father, but I do support them. My son knows who is his father, and I make it a priority to stay in touch. We Skype and visit when possible. It is not ideal for any of us, but we make the best of it."

The restaurant was empty. The headwaiter had long since let the staff go on to other duties.

"It is late, I did not mean to stay so late," said the Captain. "I have to get back to work. Maybe you now understand why I need your friendship. It is all I can offer."

"Thank you, I accept," said Helena. "It is not what I contemplated, but life unfolds in its own strange way. You know where to find me."

Kuranda, Northern Territory, Australia
Day 55

"This is the closest you will ever get to the rain forest without actually climbing a tree," said the unofficial guide on the Kuranda Skyrail Rainforest Cableway. In the glass cable car, Helena marveled at the rain forest as the hydraulic cable car skimmed the trees of one of the largest rain forest in the Northern Territory of Australia. A sky train journey of 4.7 miles with birds flying by the windows of the cable cars and creatures on the ground that were close enough to observe. She was flying in the sky across the oldest rain forest in the world, in existence for 150 million years.

Gliding a few feet above the rainforest canopy and built in the 1970s, the Kuranda Skyrail transports passengers on an interactive experience in the ancient rain forest. Almost within reach to touch, the sights, sounds and smells of the rain forest are brought to life as the sky ride offers a chance to explore one of the most botanically diverse places on earth. The rain forest is home to tree wallabies, possums, tree dragons, owls, eagles, butterflies and one amazing species of flightless bird, with a black body, royal-blue neck and a plume.

Back on the ground, walkway lookouts present breath-taking views of Barron Falls, Barron Gorge and the Rainforest Interpretation Center.

"We are passionate about protecting the environment," explained the Aussie forest ranger who did indeed look a lot like Crocodile Dundee who he claims is his cousin. "Our explorations are entirely sustainable, and countless ecologists have testified that our impact on the rain forest is negligible. We preserve and maintain every plant, creature and tree."

A passenger in the sky train who had decreed himself something of an expert asked the question, "What about the tourists who visit every year; do they not have a negative impact?"

Crocodile Dundee (he calls himself that) shook his head, and his bush hat moved from side to side. "Rain forest first, tourists next," he explained. "Sure, we welcome and encourage visitors so that we can explain the work we are doing, but the work goes on whether the visitors are here or not. My job is 24/7—if a tree falls in this rain forest, I know about it. My concern is to support the bio atmosphere and ensure that our animal habitats are protected."

Crocodile described encounters with the largest land animal in Australia, the cassowary, and took delight in telling the story of the female who is known to pursue male birds, demand that they impregnate her and then leaves them to look after the chicks for a year. This bird is still known to wander wild in the territory, as does the Australian bush turkey, which looks like a regular turkey but the tail feathers are arranged vertically, not horizontally.

"We don't capture and incarcerate our wild animals," he explained, "but they can be seen, if you're very lucky, around rainforest campgrounds."

"Is it okay to take photographs?" asked one woman shyly.

"You better believe it," he said, "but we haven't got a cassowary or bush turkey for you to photograph today. You'll have to make do with me. I'm happy to pose. That's part of my job, getting my photo taken with beautiful women from all over the world who are interested in nature and saving the planet."

Following on from the rain forest and Kuranda, a trip to the Koala Gardens was on the agenda. In complete contrast to the untamed rain forest, the Koala Gardens offers one of the best exhibitions of cultivated tropical plants and flowers in Australia. The small local market sells fruits and vegetables, sugar products and macadamia nuts baked and packaged in dozens of different products.

Local talk has it that the village at one time thrived on hippies who, when not growing their own vegetables, farmed marijuana. Bird World and Australian Butterfly Sanctuary also attract tourists. A highlight of the trip is a visit to the beachside community of Palm Cove where exotic plants line the shoreline. Helena slipped away from the other visitors and, barefoot, walked on the sand and paddled in the warm clear waters.

Next stop was one she looked forward to but that also made her nervous: a visit to a nature reserve where she would come face-to-face with a live koala bear. There was to be a photo opportunity. She had heard koalas could be temperamental. And she had to admit, so could she. Live animals made her nervous, but the bundle of fun with which she was presented did look adorable. He was heavier than she expected, but she cuddled the bear and put on her best smile. A red-carpet event complete with koala. Some things you never actually imagined doing in your life.

"Where are the kangaroos?" she asked.

"Now, they are very temperamental. Getting them to do photo calls is harder than herding cats," the guide explained. "And, of course, kangaroos are not native to this environment. You will need to go into the bush to see them up close."

The nearby city of Cairns provided a welcome opportunity for some serious retail therapy, and Helena made her way to the vast shopping mall where box stores like Kmart and Target have outlets. She had forgotten how comforting it was to be able to buy everything from a new battery for her iPhone to a special shade of red nail polish to a fresh supply of essential toiletries.

In the shoe department, a pair of silver lace-up boots caught her eye, and, once started on a shopping spree, she returned to the ship laden down. Euphemistically she called it, "supporting the local economy."

Retail therapy always lifted her spirits. One attraction of traveling the world was to study the fashion in other countries and visit the local shops and markets to purchase artworks and crafts. Several examples of original Aboriginal souvenirs found their way into her gift packages, and genuine boomerangs were welcome gifts for the family back home, as well as ethically sourced kangaroo wallets. She took the word of the stallholder whose family had been selling them for generations. "No animal has been hurt in the procuring of these genuine articles."

★ ★ ★

On board ship, Gala nights are a highlight of any cruise, and guests are encouraged to dress up and show their ingenuity when participating in the themes of the event. Popular themes for Gala night include masked balls, Victoriana, Arabian nights and a black-and-white ball. Sail-away from Australia was designated a black-and-white party night and Helena knew exactly what she was going to wear: a long, white Grecian gown was the perfect backdrop for her Tahitian black pearls and, in her hair, she wore a feather headdress. The production team presented a spectacular evening of entertainment with a range of costumes and music showcased in the classic black-and-white montage in the film *My Fair Lady*, as well as songs from the popular musical, *Chess*.

Helena sat in the front row of the theater and signaled to the cocktail waiter. "For me, please, a Virgin White Russian. That's a White Russian cocktail with no alcohol. The bartender made it for me once before with vanilla extract, white coffee and crushed ice. Then he sprinkled white chocolate on top and blowtorched it to melt the chocolate. It was delicious."

Constantly alert to the possibility of seeing him, especially when a lunchtime rendezvous was not an option because of a scheduled shore excursion, Helena made a discreet tour of the public areas of the ship before taking her place in the theater. Her vigilance was rewarded.

The Captain was the host at a cocktail party, she saw him across the crowded room. She did not approach, but to see him gave her a warm glow. Despite everything he had said, she knew that her obsession for him was still very much alive and well. She was also very conscious not to do anything to embarrass or pressure him. Her mind was in a turmoil about the situation, but everything was out of her control.

She didn't notice Meredith slip into a newly vacated seat in the row behind her.

"What are you drinking?" asked Meredith. She signaled the cocktail waiter to order a drink.

Helena was reluctant to tell her, knowing the kind of reaction it would provoke, so she said, "It's a drink the barman made especially for me. Not to everyone's taste."

Not to be deflected, when he arrived, Meredith asked the waiter, "What's in the glass?"

Helena tried to intervene as she swirled the ice in her glass. "I told you, it's not really a cocktail. It's a mocktail the barman concocted for me."

In an effort to be helpful, the waiter blurted out, "It's called a Virgin White Russian."

Meredith could not contain her delight at this revelation. She burst out laughing. "Virgin White Russian," she repeated, "well, that's not what I heard."

Soul Searching at Sea
Day 58

Every way she looked, Helena saw a different and disturbing image. As if in a fairground hall of mirrors, the images were distorted, and face after face assaulted her senses, which were distorted by time and distance.

The Captain's revelation about his young son and an affair that wrecked his marriage rocked her world. The pain and betrayal of the confession over seven years before from her husband, Antonio, as he revealed his extramarital affair and the subsequent pregnancy, felt as real and devastating as if it were yesterday.

Helena stretched out on her sun lounger, high up on the top deck in a small secluded area that she had made her own. She wore a wide-brimmed hat and sunglasses; the only thing missing was a DO NOT DISTURB sign. However, she was generally left alone and allowed her privacy. She rotated the chair to follow the changing direction of the sun, and, for most of the day, she had a clear line of sight to watch the churning waves out at sea. Eyes closed, she performed the breathing exercise taught to her by her therapist to be used when anxiety was at its height.

In her mind's eye, she saw a graphic representation of a tangled family tree of husbands, wives, lovers and children. Like dynastic rulers, Antonio and Grigory headed the dual lineages. In pride of place alongside them, cameos of their official marriage partners, their wives. Both couples sat atop strong, enduring branches of a proud family tree. Sacred vows of husbands and wives charged till death do us part to preserve the sanctity of the legal partnership.

In shadow, undermining the structure, smiling shyly and feigning innocence, malicious forces snaked up under the sturdy boughs. Invasive vines inveigling their way into nooks and crannies, causing cracks to appear in the carefully constructed and preserved branches.

At the bottom of the tree, low hanging fruit—two sons born out of wedlock to absentee fathers. Helena clung to the belief that her husband had fought not to separate from the deep roots so long nurtured and cultivated in his marriage. Over the years, there were many women who had taken a fancy to him, and why would they not? He was handsome, successful, rich, accomplished. He would tell her about the outrageous invitations he received. His answer was always, "Why would I want hamburger when I have steak at home?" She totally trusted his integrity and his commitment to her. The fact that he had succumbed even once tore her apart. She totally blamed the invader. Nothing would convince her that the woman who had seduced and enticed him was not an opportunist, striking at a point of male vanity and weakness. If the objective was for a one-night stand, even a trophy to say she had seduced the world-famous doctor, still the mystery remained. How did the encounter lead to an unplanned pregnancy with a man she hardly knew?

All her good intentions to open her heart had been driven out by the revelation from the Captain. He had had an affair, not a relationship. A coupling of opportunity. He had not spoken of love or commitment when he talked about the affair that ended his marriage. Mutual attraction, yes, but no deep ongoing commitment.

Sex, not procreation, was patently the objective of the seduction.

Helena had taken Antonio's side so completely that he had not been required to explain his behavior beyond saying it was a moment of madness. A lapse of judgment that left him with very serious consequences.

"Do you love her?" she had asked Antonio on that first night when they held each other and closed ranks against the catastrophe that had befallen them.

Explanations and recriminations could come later, but on that first night they locked and bolted the marital door against anyone or anything that threatened to destroy the relationship and lifestyle they had lovingly constructed.

"Do you want to be with her?" Helena asked again, desperate for reassurance that whatever else happened, she was not to lose her husband, the man she adored, depended on and defended against the world.

"No, no, no," Antonio was adamant. "There is no relationship. There is no romance. We don't even know each other."

Helena looked daggers at him. "I think you do," she said. "Biblically at least."

"You have to believe me," he said. "I admit, I was a fool.

Maybe I was naïve. Perhaps she did foresee some kind of ongoing situation, but that was never my intention. How can I convince you of the difference between a sexual encounter and an extramarital affair? There is no other woman; there is a woman I slept with and now I must do the right thing and face the consequences. She is pregnant. I cannot ignore that situation."

Helena had a sudden thought in the midst of Antonio's confession that he had had sex with her: It occurred to her that there may need to be clarification that the sex with her husband had indeed led to pregnancy.

"Have you demanded a DNA test?" she asked.

"Not yet, but I'm sure that will be a prerequisite of any financial settlement I make with her and the child."

"Has she considered an alternative?" asked Helena.

"I didn't ask that question," said Antonio, sounding strangely quiet and embarrassed.

"Don't be so bloody stupid," Helena erupted. "You are entitled to ask. She's a grown woman. Surely she needs to take some responsibility for her own body. Why would she not have been able to prevent the pregnancy or take care of it?"

Antonio looked crestfallen. "I wanted to do the right thing by her. She's a nice girl."

"Don't you dare tell me that," shouted Helena. "She's not a nice girl; she sleeps with other women's husbands and gets pregnant. Nice girls don't behave like that!"

At that, Helena burst into tears. "Antonio," she begged, "make her go away. Make this horrible situation go away. She has no part in our lives. Get rid of her."

Like a bad dream that she didn't chose to remember, Helena avoided thoughts of the woman and the situation. She didn't want to know details. She trusted Antonio and the lawyer to do what was necessary. Fortunately, Antonio was a rich man so there were no financial repercussions and no court orders to obey.

The matter was dead and buried. Until Antonio's death fueled her obsession to know who the woman was and to see pictures of the child. She had been driven to distraction for months; her mental health had been in jeopardy—she did not chose to reopen that wound. Helena had been determined to return that particular pain-inflicting genie to the bottle and get on with her life.

The incredible replication of the problem and its impact on the relationship she so desperately wanted to develop with the Captain made her question whether some God or other divine presence was laughing at her. She had no idea what karmic lesson she was being forced to face and resolve, but it was not a challenge she wanted to embrace. Not that that ever stopped the Great Universal plan.

* * *

"This is your Captain speaking from the bridge." She heard the sound of his voice and knew he was about to deliver his noontime, updated meteorological, navigational and weather report.

On the sun lounger she left her book and suntan lotion to show that she was coming back.

Showered, dressed and made-up in record time, Helena raced upstairs to the restaurant. She had to cover all her bases and be there even if he came early. Or maybe he would not come at all. Or if he came, maybe he would not sit with her.

Friends do not have to lunch together every day, she reminded herself.

On his way into the restaurant, the Captain stopped by his old table, the one he used to sit at before he began choosing

Helena as his daily lunchtime companion. She didn't see what he dropped off, but it appeared to signal that he had moved on, or moved back.

Helena made a big show of staring intently at her phone. He walked past her as he moved from the high table to the buffet counter. He waved but did not smile.

Pressing buttons on her phone and typing texts, she kept her head down.

"Are you busy?" he asked as he stood by her table holding two plates of food.

"Not too busy for you, ever," she emphasized.

"Good." Now he smiled. "I left my papers on the other table," he told her. "I do not like to carry things."

Helena laughed. "I've noticed. It seems to be a man thing. Women are happy to carry handbags; men want to be free."

Everything she said sounded as though it carried a deeper meaning. "I mean they like to have their hands free."

"You're right." He nodded. "As long as I have my radio and phone, I don't want to carry anything else. Please, remind me to collect the papers from the other table when I leave."

Cutlery in hand, he asked her, "How are you?"

"Always better for seeing you," she told him.

"Thank you. I feel the same about you," he said.

Helena knew she was beaming; it meant so much to hear that he really did care about her.

"Actually, I have a gift for you, but you don't have to carry it. After you've opened it, I'll rewrap it and leave it at reception."

Helena cleared a space on the table and passed over the gifts she bought at the Sydney Opera House. He stopped eating and leaned across the table to reach the package. "You don't have to buy me gifts," he said.

Helena smiled and watched as he opened the gift bag.

He lined up the notebook and pen on the table. "Thank you," he said, "I am a big fan of the Sydney Opera House. I have visited many times."

Helena rewrapped the gifts and read the card out to him, "To use when you open a new page in your logbook for me."

"You always surprise me," he said as he resumed eating his meal of fish, salad and rice. "Are you not eating?"

"I had something," she lied. "It pleases me to share your mealtime and keep you company."

"You are a remarkable woman," he told her. "You please me and I can relax in your company. You are a light in my day and I am so glad that we are . . . that we are . . ."

"Friends," Helena finished the sentence for him.

"Yes, friends," he said, "but please believe I wish we could be more."

"Thank you," Helena responded. "That's really all I need to know."

"You gave me a gift, now I have one for you," he told her and his hand brushed hers, as if by accident. He gently drew his fingers through hers. The effect was electrifying. Never before could she recall being so affected by the touch of a hand. The hairs stood up on her arms, and a shiver ran through her. She longed to take his hand, kiss it, hold it. This was such sweet torture, to want him and to know he wanted her. To rein in all outward shows of passion and speak to each other with their eyes and the subtlest of furtive touches. Surely, if they got close to each other, all restrictions off, they would explode.

Helena sighed. "There's no need for you to get a gift for me. Being here with you is gift enough."

"Well, I hope you will be pleased," he said. "It is a personal invitation from me. To be my guest at the next Captain's table. Is it okay with you?"

Helena dared to reach out and touch his hand. "Thank you, Captain." She smiled.

Rabaul, Papua New Guinea
Day 60

"Rabaul is not a pretty sight," Helena had been warned before leaving the ship. Now she regretted not heeding the warning. Walking the forlorn streets of eastern Rabaul was like stepping into an apocalyptic film. In 1994 a volcano on Mount Tavurvur erupted and spewed huge amounts of ash over the town leaving a desert like landscape of black-and-brown ash. Over 80 percent of the buildings were destroyed. The still active volcano looms over the devastated town and ominously steams, belching huge plumes of smoke into the sky. Rabaul dwellers accept the inevitability that one day the town could again be buried, but bravely the townsfolk struggle on, dependent on port facilities and the associated industries to keep the town alive.

Living alongside the docks, there is a thriving community, but farther inland, whole areas are abandoned. Located in the southwestern Pacific Ocean, the town was founded as a German Colonial headquarters administered by the Australian Territory of New Guinea.

Unstable tectonic plates means the area experiences earthquakes, tsunamis and volcanic eruptions. Aside from natural disaster, Rabaul was also invaded by the Japanese Imperial Army in 1942. The invasion turned Papua New Guinea into a major theater of war in the battle for the Pacific, and there were many brutal encounters between the invading Japanese and the defending Allied Forces. Occupied by the Japanese from 1942 to 1945 and destroyed by Allied bombing, Rabaul was rebuilt after 1950.

The Kokopo War Museum contains a large collection of relics and parts of airplanes shot down in the Rabaul region during World War Two. Local art and culture from the German Colonial period and artillery pieces and tanks from the Japanese occupation are displayed in the museum.

The volcanic eruption in 1994 buried the town under ash, but thanks to a well-planned evacuation of between 10,000 and 30,000 residents, casualties were kept to a minimum.

"We were moved by the authorities," Helena was informed when she joined a gathering of women in the local Kokopo marketplace. "Housing had been prepared for us. Most of us still live there now."

With all their misfortunes, natural and man-made, Helena was humbled when she realized the degree of acceptance and fortitude displayed by the villagers.

Surrounded by locally made clothes and goods, including spices for sale, villagers sit on the ground in the remains of the volcanic ash. Whole families, including old people and children, gather around the makeshift stalls. "Everybody comes to market," one vendor explained. Fruits and vegetables are piled high and, at the rear of the market, tobacco growers sell dried leaves and cigars wrapped with sticky tape.

With loud, raucous laughter and good-natured bantering, the villagers encourage interactions and conversation with the cruise ship passengers. Helena observed that, considering the variations in their circumstances, the villagers often seemed happier than many passengers, who looked distinctly unhappy as they picked their way through pot-holed dirt roads and the dust of volcanic ash.

The villagers display an amazing resilience, and women and children are eager to express thanks for their lives and community. "We have a good life," Helena was told by one of the older women who acted as a spokeswoman, and her friends nodded in agreement. "We love our families. We have enough to eat, we have places to live and we share what we have."

Several villagers spoke English and also variations on the 853 other languages that are alive and used in Papua New Guinea. Linguistically, this independent state in Oceania is one of the most diverse countries in the world. Many of the indigenous people have no contact with the outside world, and, like the communities and the languages, it is believed that many species of animals and plants in the interior of Papua New Guinea are still undiscovered.

Teeth stained red from the constant chewing of betel nut, the women laugh and share jokes. "You travel far," said one woman, "but where are your family, your husband, your children?"

"At home," said Helena, "my family are at home."

"You bring them with, we like to see," said the women.

In honor of the visitors and a day trip into town, many of the children wore traditional costumes and head dresses. "You take a photo," urged the mothers.

Helena realized that the costumes are designed to produce an exchange of money for photos. Along with the earlier warning about the very basic facilities of Rabaul, which was designed to deflect her from even taking the trouble to visit, Helena was told that there were no ATMs or banks in the port areas, but to look out for a small shopping center at the Rabaul Yacht Club.

Helena owned up and admitted to her new friends, "I have none of your local kina money."

"No problem," they told her, "we take Australian dollars, US dollars and British pounds, also the Euro."

Helena checked her purse and one of the women called her child over to be photographed.

"It's not a problem, you don't need to give us money," she said kindly. "But the children like to have their picture taken when they are dressed up."

Helena felt deeply grateful and humbled by the genuine humanity of such simple people.

"Come, I will take a photo of you with my son."

"Do you have your camera?" Helena asked.

The mother laughed loudly. "No, I have no camera. I will use yours."

As she made her way back to the ship, still treading warily through volcanic ash and black dust, Helena realized how much her life was enriched by the visit.

"May I walk with you back to the port gates?" asked a young, local man as he fell into step alongside her.

Helena was concerned. What did he want? Should she try to get rid of him? The cruise companies always impressed upon passengers the need for vigilance on port calls. Exotic, far-flung countries with strange sounding names always raised the possibility of unwelcome attention or theft.

He smiled and his teeth were not coated with betel juice. Helena judged him to be in his late teens.

"Why do you want to walk with me?" she asked.

"You are pretty," he answered, "and I have nothing else to do."

Helena appreciated his honesty. "You speak English well," she said, and they proceeded to walk together.

"I learned at school," he told her.

"What do you do when you're not at school?" she asked.

"There is not much to do, but I like talking to the people from the cruise ships. I learn a lot."

Like two friends out for a stroll, in the blazing hot sunshine, they walked along and Helena answered questions about her travels and asked questions about his home and family.

At the port gates he said goodbye and turned to leave. "I'm afraid I don't have any money," she said having given her last few Euros to the mother and her son.

"What do I need money for?" he asked. "My home is close by here. Maybe I will see you again one day. Goodbye."

"I hope so," said Helena, "it's been good getting to know you."

The ship was moored yards away and Helena looked up at the bridge to see if the Captain was there. She looked forward to telling him all about her experience in Rabaul the next time they had lunch together.

"What an experience," she said to the passenger who shared the gangway with her as she returned to the ship. "Amazing town, amazing people."

"Yea, like walking through a coal mine," he said. "I won't be coming back here."

Helena reflected on the Oscar Wilde quote from his play, *Lady Windermere's Fan*, "We are all in the gutter, but some of us are looking at the stars."

★ ★ ★

That night Helena danced on deck beneath a midnight-blue Pacific Ocean sky and thanked her lucky stars. At the midway point of the Grand Around the World Cruise, the ship had traveled 18,251 nautical miles from its departure port. Sail-away was designated a joint celebration for being halfway around the world and to mark Mardi Gras. The entertainment team proposed a party to transport passengers to the carnival in a colorful, vibrant show in the fresh air and a night of hip-swaying songs and dancing.

In a fiesta to rival Rio, the vibrant young singers and dancers pulsated with high energy and spectacular carnival costumes and insisted on audience participation.

"Seize the day," was Helena's motto as she dressed in an extravagant multicolored blue-and-purple beaded kaftan bought for just such an occasion in Cuba a couple of seasons before. To top it off, she wore a feather plumed headdress and a gold mask.

On the swimming pool deck, colored lights twinkled around fake palm trees and the dance floor was decorated with gigantic flowers and grotesque masks. Tropical cocktails overflowed with exotic fruit and blossoms, and plates of delicious hot and cold canapés and bite-size desserts circulated among the guests. The drinks and foods were carried shoulder high on silver trays by male waitstaff wearing red-and-yellow ruffled shirts and the ladies of the team in pink-and-lime sparkly off-the-shoulder blouses.

"Look into my eyes and dance the rumba," said a masked lothario as he spun Helena around the dance floor in a swirling mass of chiffon, feathers and row upon row of colored beads. The warm night air was made for seduction and the anonymity of masks shielded everyone with an air of mystery. The best of Latin beat provided by the musicians, show singers and dancers blasted out over the decks, and the party atmosphere reached epic feel-good levels with hips swaying, bodies spinning and feet cha-cha-ing.

"Conga line, conga line," called the cruise director as he stepped up to take first place and lead the procession. "Do-do-do, do the conga," chanted his enthusiastic followers as they joined and gathered fellow partygoers into the fast-moving line snaking around the decks. Helena stepped up and grabbed the waist of a man in front of her and was in turn grabbed by someone behind who helped her waist sway to the beat.

"Leave no man or woman behind," instructed the cruise director. "Everyone must join in." An unstoppable human column of dancing, singing partygoers made several circuits of the swimming pool and dance floor as they headed up the outside staircase to the observation deck and onto the disco dance floor. "Do-do-do, do the conga," was accompanied by alternate legs kicked out, as in a chorus line, to the side as the procession swayed from side to side all around the top deck, then headed down the stairs again. Helena was somewhere near the head of the procession and could still hear the voice of the cruise director. She felt a man's strong arms on her waist and held onto the person in front of her, who was regularly replaced as people joined the line.

The pace of progress became more and more frantic, and one or two dancers stumbled, unable to keep up with the pace. Somewhere in the back of the procession several drums kept the beat, and rattles and whistles were acquired to add to the general chaos and excitement.

"Once more 'round the ship," shouted a passenger as he broke off from the main party and started an opposing team composed of fresh bodies and balloon-carrying dancers.

Helena moved up in the line and was now behind the cruise director. She was the first to receive the instruction to halt as the conga line crossed the navigation deck and a door leading to the bridge opened. A uniformed officer appeared.

"Now we're in trouble," joked the cruise director. "Good evening, Captain," he said as the uniformed officer came into full view. "Care to join us?"

Helena knew there was no hiding place. She could have hoped her mask would save her, but she'd already pushed it up onto the top of her head.

He looked straight at her and laughed, as he said, "Glad to see you enjoying your cruise."

To the cruise director, he said, "Carry on, but without me."

At Sea
Day 64

Helena counted the hours till lunchtime. Aimlessly she walked around the ship. Wherever she settled, passengers stopped to talk about the Mardi Gras party. "Yes, it was a lot fun," she agreed. "No, the Captain didn't join in, but that's the rumor going around the ship today."

She fussed and fretted, killing time till she could head for the restaurant and wait for him.

The library was normally a haven, but not when the card players were in attendance. Acting like a bunch of unruly children, they spoke too loud and called across tables to one another.

Truth was, all Helena wanted to do was sit somewhere quiet and meditate, but for once she could find no peace. The restlessness, she knew, was inside herself.

The Captain consumed her thoughts. She had done what she had determined she would not do—allow him to become a full blown obsession. And even more worryingly, she had fallen in love with him.

At the carnival party, she had enjoyed herself, until she saw him. Unable to sleep, she tried to get her thoughts in order. She wrote in her journal: *Romance is not on the menu. He has made it very clear about what is and what is not an option. We are to be friends. Why then do my body and mind go into freefall when I see him? To be close to him every day actually makes the situation more troublesome rather than less. Amazingly, every day I become more enamored of him. I have come to know him and, in my eyes, he is a wonderful person. Intelligent, observant, good-natured, competent and confident. A mature man who is not afraid to show his emotions. His smile is beautiful; he smiles with his eyes as well as his mouth. Up close, I even see the stubble on his chin. I feel such a deep connection to him. My heart cries out for him, and the longing never ceases.*

Helena closed her journal, turned off the light and held against her heart the polished rose-quartz crystal she chose as a symbol of physic connection on the day she performed her love-candle ritual. It all seemed so long ago. Yes, she had attracted him to her but what now?

The Captain was already seated at the window table when she arrived.

"Sorry, I'm late," she said. "Choir has restarted and rehearsals ran late."

"More love songs?" he asked and gave her a wink.

"No. More complicated. At our next show we are to perform "Bohemian Rhapsody." Are you familiar with the Queen song?" she asked.

"Yes, I am familiar," he said. "You're right; it does seem ambitious. When is the show?"

"Not till Singapore," said Helena. "You will still be here, won't you?"

"Till Singapore, I think, yes. After that, who knows?"

Helena's voice was sad as she asked, "Will I ever see you again after you leave the ship?"

The Captain shrugged, and the gold epaulets on his shoulders almost brushed his ears.

"I am not sure how that would work," he said. "I travel the world constantly."

"So we are to be ships that pass in the night?"

"I'm not familiar with that expression." He looked puzzled. "What does it mean?"

"It means that, while we are coming toward each other we are aware of the other's presence, but once we pass in the night, we move on and never again do our paths cross."

"Yes, a life at sea is all about moving on," he said. "It is the life I have chosen. I don't look back. I need to keep the ship moving forward."

He saw the sadness on Helena's face. "Of course, we do not leave everyone behind," he said kindly. "There are people who have a special place in our lives and our hearts."

Helena admitted she knew something of that desire to keep moving on. "You are a traveler," she said. "Me too. I call it the gypsy in my soul. I find it hard to stay in one place for too long. Before I married, I traveled and moved countries frequently. When my husband was alive, I made a home for us and allowed him to be the one who went out into the world and then return to find me waiting for him. Since he died, there is no one coming home. I am reluctant to stay alone and wait."

In the midst of their private conversation, an imperious looking woman approached their table.

Without opening niceties, she stated her case, "Captain, I need you to come to my cabin."

Helena looked away; she was afraid if she looked at the Captain they would both laugh.

"For what reason, madam?" he asked and Helena saw that he struggled to keep a straight face.

"The tap in my bathroom is leaking, and no one seems able to fix it."

"And you think I can?" he asked.

"Well, you are the Captain," she said. "I thought you were in charge of everything."

"I will see what I can do. Leave it with me," he told her. "Thank you for letting me know about the problem. We'll get it sorted out for you."

The passenger walked away, and it looked very much as if she was unsteady on her feet.

The Captain raised his eyebrows, and Helena laughed out loud.

"I'll get maintenance to sort out the problem," he told her, "and tell customer relations to send over a complimentary bottle of wine. It's not the strangest request I've ever had. Everyone expects the Captain to make sure things run smoothly. I'll make sure the problem is solved—or get her moved to a new cabin."

Helena teased him, "She's given me an idea. If I ask, will you to come to my cabin?"

"To solve what problem?" he asked.

"Don't even go there," said Helena.

"Unless there is a very good reason, it is not appropriate for me to go to the cabin of a passenger," he told her. "I hope the taps in your bathroom are working. If not, I will send a plumber."

Helena knew the subject was closed. The interruption had changed the mood, and she knew better than to raise the subject she had hoped to get him to discuss.

He pushed back his chair and turned to leave. "You looked beautiful last night." He smiled. "I'm sorry I could not accept the invitation to dance. Maybe one day, we will dance together."

"I'd prefer a waltz to the conga," she told him, "or even a rumba. The dance of love."

"Yes, that would be better," he agreed. "Captain's table tomorrow night. I'll see you then. Enjoy your afternoon."

Helena had plans for the afternoon. She was to attend a lecture in the theater about International Women's Day. Guest lectures on the cruise generally covered upcoming ports of call giving an early insight to the country, history, people and culture. Helena made it a point to attend talks in the enrichment program, as she found it invaluable to be prepared. Everyone had their own favorite activities onboard ship, and the opportunities to hear guest speakers was one of the major attractions of the cruise, long before she ever heard the name of the Captain or dreamed he would distract her and take up so much of her time and attention.

In the theater, the guest speaker stood at the podium, ready to present information about the origins of International Women's Day, and later the entertainment team were due to perform a show dedicated to International Divas. Celebrated in many countries around the world, International Women's Day recognizes women for their achievements without regard to divisions, whether national, cultural, economic or political.

At the turn of the twentieth century in North America and Europe, labor movements began to unite around the idea of a special day to celebrate women's activities. The Socialist Party of America designated a day to honor garment workers in New York who went on strike to protest working conditions.

That day had become a rallying call to address challenges faced by women across the globe. Empowerment of women in their social, economic and political struggles is the central focus of the day. The stated mission was to achieve gender equality and empower all women and girls.

The guest speaker, a lecturer in women's affairs in one of the American universities, delivered her lecture and asked if there were any questions. The almost exclusive female audience were quick to address the questions that mattered to them.

To loud laughter, one woman asked, "Why do we strive for equality with men when all women know our sex are superior?"

Helena had a question, "Do you believe that when women run countries, there are less wars?"

"There is some truth in that," said the lecturer, "because we expect women to negotiate from a place of emotion, not ego. However, gender equality is changing attitudes among the millennial generation, and many women are now thinking more like men on a rational level and men are learning to get in touch with their feminine side."

"I have one more question," said Helena. "Will men and women ever learn to speak the same language so that they can understand each other better?"

"In my opinion, the book *Men Are from Mars and Women Are from Venus* by author John Gray sums it up perfectly," said the lecturer. "Men and women are from different planets, but thank goodness there are spaceships to connect us. Thank you, ladies, for your attention. Enjoy International Women's Day."

Helena was tempted to ask the expert on women's studies about the situation between her and the Captain. Of course, she would not because that would be breaking his confidence, but Helena was now beyond confused.

What does it mean that we are friends, but there is a subtext to all our conversations? We flirt and the silences say more than the words. It is obvious we are attracted to each other, but will we ever be able to reconcile the attraction with something more tangible?

Where do we go from here? It's not an affair, it's not a romance, it's not a relationship. Perhaps this is what it means when celebrities are quoted in the paper as being "just good friends" when everyone knows they are actually having an affair.

In a blinding flash, Helena had the answer to all her questions. Or at least a name for what was troubling her. *We are having an emotional affair. An affair of the emotions.*

The relief was overwhelming. She remembered that she had heard emotional affairs were often more powerful than physical ones. In certain circumstances, they challenged and divided conventional relationships because the people involved were engaging on a deeper emotional level than a physical one. They shared thoughts and feelings and emotions that were not necessarily explored in sexual relationships. Sexual relations often happen very early in a relationship, before the people involved have gotten to know each other. They let their bodies do the talking. Sexual relationships are often short-lived because once the deed is done—there is not much more to say or do. For Helena and the Captain, relationship exploration was through the emotions.

Her mind had led her to the answer. No solution yet, but she felt ready to accept that what she was experiencing went beyond friendship. An emotional affair. She liked the sound of it.

Helena headed for the open deck and then regretted it. She had the distinct feeling she was being stalked.

Whenever she really didn't want to see her, which was all the time, Meredith showed up. Today she was deck walking—in her riding boots. An affectation she had adopted lately. So far, she was not wearing jodhpurs, but Helena wouldn't put it past her.

"You look like the cat who got the cream," she taunted Helena.

"Yes, and you look like a cat who needs to be declawed."

Captain's Table
Day 66

Helena froze. About to enter the cocktail bar at the appointed time to meet the guests at the Captain' table, she could hardly believe her eyes. Center stage, in the exclusive circle of VIPs waiting to be escorted into the restaurant, sat Meredith. Thankfully, not wearing her riding boots.

"Hello, Helena," she said brightly, "fancy meeting you here."

Of course she did not wish to be rude, and the guest list was not part of her gift, but Meredith was the last person Helena expected to turn up here and more likely than not, it was a foregone conclusion that she would take pleasure in such an obvious opportunity to rain on Helena's parade.

Helena braced herself for a bitchy comment. Instead Meredith was sweetness itself.

"I love your dress," she complimented Helena on the midnight-blue, off-the-shoulder satin sheath she had bought in the designer boutique in Sydney.

"You look very nice, too," Helena returned the compliment, with caution, indicating Meredith's black trousers and floral chiffon top. She was not about to let her guard down. An instinct that proved right.

"Strange, I was sure you would wear red," said Meredith and smiled at Helena. "Red for danger and always designed to attract."

A senior officer approached. "Welcome, please sit down. The waiter will pour you a glass of champagne, and I can introduce you to the Captain's other guests."

Without making it too obvious that she had no intention of sitting next to Meredith, Helena enthusiastically greeted one of the guests she knew vaguely and settled herself into an armchair next to him and his wife.

"Everyone got a glass of champagne? Good," the senior officer addressed the guests.

"The Captain sends his apologies, but he has been unavoidably delayed. He will join us in the restaurant as soon as he has finished his other business."

Helena strategically chose a large comfortable armchair with an empty one next to it, in preparation for the Captain's arrival. Walking through the bars and lounges in step with the Captain as he led his guests into dinner was a showpiece moment she had been looking forward to for days. "Bloody Meredith," she said under her breath, though what Meredith actually had to do with this turn of events was not clear, even as she blamed her. With a monumental effort, Helena made herself breathe normally and took the view that whatever will be, will be; she could not control the situation. Expectations always led her astray.

In a good light with makeup on, Meredith looked rather more attractive than usual; her country girl ruddy complexion with her hair pulled into a messy bun did not generally do her any favors. Tonight for once, she had an important addition: a smile.

Helena reminded herself that a pout and a sulky attitude would do nothing to improve her own image. She asked polite questions and joined in small talk as the guests drained their champagne flutes and prepared to be escorted into dinner. Only one guest was totally unknown to her. Ships are small villages, and, at some point, especially halfway through a world cruise, in some situation or other, she had seen or been introduced to all the other guests. Or at least knew them by sight.

"We haven't been introduced," said the gentleman rising

from his chair. He wore a red velvet tuxedo with a black velvet cravat tucked inside a snow-white shirt.

"My name is Emile Beauchamp. Enchanted, Madame," he said as he kissed Helena's hand and offered an explanation as to why they had not met previously. "I'm a stowaway," he joked. "I sneaked onto the ship in Sydney."

Helena liked him immediately. "Are you French?" she asked.

"French Canadian," he told her. "My hometown is Quebec, but I live in Paris."

Emile's dark good looks and curly black hair did not escape Helena's keen eye. Though she preferred clean-shaven men, his designer stubble and a tiny gold stud in his right ear certainly gave him a dashing appearance. She judged him to be only slightly older than her and certainly at least a decade younger than the Captain.

"If you hadn't admitted to being a stowaway, I might have taken you for a pirate," Helena returned his joke.

As when entering into the ark, guests were lined up two by two to make the formal parade toward the restaurant. Helena was still in pride of place at the front of the line, escorted by a senior officer. "As the Captain is not yet with us, the official photographer will delay the group photograph till after dinner," he explained.

"Are we all ready?" Helena nodded her head and discreetly looked behind to see who Emile had been designated to escort.

Please don't let it be Meredith, she thought.

But no, Emile was standing beside the wife of the man Helena had acknowledged earlier. The one she had sat next to on a tender journey when his wife had been feeling queasy and gone upstairs to get fresh air. Meredith was his walking-in partner.

At a sedate pace, the line proceeded through the communal areas and Helena perceived that, without the Captain leading the parade, the theatrical value was rather less than the last time she had been a guest. The Captain's table is, after all, the Captain's table.

Inside the formal dining room behind the voile curtain, the table was set to perfection.

Snow-white tablecloths and napkins, a white rose centerpiece, gleaming silver cutlery, silver-edged crockery and dazzling crystal glassware sparkled in the twinkling electronic tea lights that Helena remembered from last time.

Nameplates designated where each guest should sit.

Helena identified the Captain's place in the center of the table and looked to see if she had again been seated opposite him. No, her name was not engraved on the place card at that place. Nor was her place card at either of the seats alongside him.

"You're here beside me," said Emile, leading her to a seat at the far end of the dining table. Meredith was at the other end of the table, alongside one of the administrative staff.

Next to the Captain, the table plan placed the seasick wife from the tender; on her other side, the wife was seated beside the senior officer who had been hosting the proceedings so far. The officer, who, to put it politely, was sturdily built, was on Helena's right hand and Emile was on her left.

If he had even been there, she had no line of sight to the Captain. She would hardly be able to see him, nor him her. He arrived a few minutes after they were all seated. No courses had been served, but wine was poured and hot olive and walnut bread passed around.

Unhurried but apologetic, the Captain greeted his guests. Assessing the state of play, his eyes searched the table and Helena hoped he was looking for her. "My apologies," he said with a smile that could have charmed a snake out of its skin. "I had company business to attend to. I trust you have been well taken care of by my officers and staff?"

"Yes, thank you, Captain," the guests dutifully replied. "We are all happy you could join us. The Captain's table would not be the same without its guest of honor."

"You are the honored guests," he told them graciously.

Around the table, the invited guests nodded and smiled their appreciation, relieved that he had finally arrived. As he headed to his place at the center of the table, he sought out Helena in her place at the far end and asked a silent question with his eyes and raised eyebrows. She answered with a barely noticeable shrug.

"Our Captain is certainly a charmer," said Emile.

"You can say that again," said Helena. She was tempted to add, it takes one to know one, Monsieur Emile Beauchamp.

"How fortunate that at our first meeting, we are seated together and have a chance to get to know each other," he told her. "I want to know all about you, Madame Helena. Since I arrived on the ship, I have been fascinated by you. You are a seriously interesting woman. And if it's not a breach of protocol at the Captain's table, may I say how much I admire your style and tonight's choice of the blue dress that so perfectly matches your eyes."

"Thank you, kind sir. I appreciate and accept your compliments. And I must say that for a stowaway, you, too, have a very dashing fashion sense."

Emile raised his glass and caught the eye of a passing waiter to top off their wine. "To us," he said, "Travelers on the high seas. Who knows what adventures await?"

Course after course of delicious food was placed before the

guests, and Helena relished the mastery of the chefs in producing such wonderful combinations. From appetizers through main courses and onto dessert, the selections of the gourmet menu satisfied the gastronomic senses.

Helena failed to see around the bulk of the officer seated next to her, but she did once or twice notice the Captain lean forward so that he could see her. He did not look happy.

"Good food, good wine and the best company," said Emile. An award-winning architect, he explained that the purpose of his trip was both pleasure and business. Returning to Paris from a trip to Australia, he had been in discussions with designers at the Sydney Opera House.

"A world-class performing center constantly needs to be updated, upgraded and have certain ongoing design requirements addressed. I have submitted plans for necessary improvements to the main theater stage. We shall see. If and when the commission comes through, I will spend some months in Sydney. Returning home by ship was an indulgence as I have time before the powers that be make their decisions. Sea air will inspire my imagination."

Dinner table conversation continued all around, but Helena became aware that one person was holding court and captivating everyone at the table with her story. Meredith took center stage and began to reiterate the story that had grabbed the attention of her dinner companion.

"I'm so sorry. It's such a sad story," said the woman on the other side of the Captain, who had leaned over when it was obvious the conversation was getting really interesting.

"Do you mind sharing with the other dinner guests what happened to you?"

"The Captain already knows all about it," said Meredith giving him a soft-eyed puppy dog look.

"He has been very kind."

Helena had been extremely curious about Meredith's qualification for an invitation to the Captain's table. She had expected to get a chance to subtly ask the Captain at some stage how he made his selection for invited guests. Meredith had never indicated that she held Diamond or Platinum status. But she had everyone's attention.

"I never intended to be a solo traveler on this cruise," she said. "In fact, the opposite. It was not my sister who let me down and refused to come on the Grand Around the World Cruise, it was my fiancé." She paused for dramatic effect and to allow the full force of the revelation to sink in.

"One week before we sailed, he broke off the engagement." No one spoke a word.

Now her eyes filled with tears. "Of course, I was heartbroken. But the worst of it all is that we were due to be married on the voyage by the Captain. It was a dream I'd had since I was a little girl—to be married by a captain onboard a ship."

The Captain accepted the acknowledgment of how much he had figured in the lifetime plans.

"The date was chosen to coincide with the date of our first meeting and to celebrate our two years of being together. We were due to make our marriage vows in a ceremony onboard and then be invited to dine at the Captain's table. Isn't that right, Captain?"

The Captain nodded his agreement. Other guests offered their commiserations.

"It is very sad," he said, "but I am hopeful that Meredith and her young man will find a way to work through their problems. Of course, I will miss the opportunity to officiate at the ceremony."

"I'd love to be married to you, Captain. I mean, married by

you," said Meredith, as the guests laughed. The mistake lightened the moment.

"Let us drink a toast," said the Captain, "to the course of true love, which doesn't always run smooth. But, remember, we must never give up hope."

"Ladies and gentlemen, raise your glasses, please. To Meredith."

Free Spirit
Day 66

"Smile, please, and look directly into the camera." Guests gathered around the Captain at the end of dinner as the official photographer recorded the moment for posterity. Meredith clung to the Captain's side, and Helena distanced herself by tagging on at the end of the line-up with Emile. He was still by her side when she stopped by the double glass doors at the exit of the restaurant as the guests took their leave and thanked the Captain for his hospitality.

"Thank you for a wonderful evening, Captain," said Helena as she indicated the ribboned gift box in her hand, "and for the chocolates." He took her hand and held it. His grasp was firm, and he seemed reluctant to let go. Wordlessly, he looked into her eyes and nodded a polite smile, but his smile did not extend to his eyes.

"Have you already met Mr. Beauchamp?" she asked.

"Yes, I know Mr. Beauchamp, the famed architect. He attended the welcome cocktail party when we sailed from Sydney."

To Emile, he gave a curt nod and thanked him for coming. Helena and Emile walked together out of the restaurant, and there seemed no polite way of asking her new friend not to put his hand on her back as he guided her out through the glass doors and into the main restaurant.

With a backward glance, Helena confirmed that the Captain was watching their every move.

"What would you like to do now?" Emile asked. "We can join the other guests in the lounge for a nightcap or find our own entertainment."

Helena laughed. "I'm not sure I want to join Meredith's pity party," she said. "Sorry, that sounded very unkind. I don't mean to be a bitch, but I suspect that Meredith will be taking hostages to hear her story for the rest of the voyage. She deserves an audience; the breaking off of the engagement must have hurt very badly, but she doesn't need my attendance. We have not exactly been friends on this cruise, but now I understand better the reasons why she has been so unhappy and perhaps also why she has behaved badly."

Emile nodded. "Poor girl, but as you say, there is still plenty of mileage in the story. At least she gets her fifteen minutes of fame on the ship. Plenty of passengers will befriend her and sympathize with her experience. For me the funniest thing was when she said she wanted to be married to, not by, the Captain. It wouldn't surprise me. She looks at him so adoringly."

"Yes," said Helena. "The Captain is a bit of a babe magnet. Seems all the women on the ship have a crush on him."

Emile laughed. "It's a perk of the job. Women love men in uniforms, and he is the one wearing all the gold braid. I'm sure you are far too sensible to be dazzled by the illusion of power."

Helena could think of nothing to say to defend herself. Obviously, he had not heard any of the rumors that had circulated about her and the Captain. And she had to accept that the novelty of their relationship probably wore off as other new news took its place. Meredith would certainly knock her off the front pages now.

For the first time almost since she joined the ship, Helena felt the burden of being obsessed by the Captain begin to lift. Mostly because of the fact that their encounters were, on many levels, unexplained and unfinished. Certainly, they were not able to walk around the decks of the ship comfortable in each other's company, strolling, talking, laughing, as she and Emile were doing now.

Over dinner, they had shared highlights of their lives and history. "For seven years I have been a widow," Helena told him. "My husband was an internationally recognized doctor, a member of an Italian aristocratic family. He and I lived in London and were blessed with a happy ever after until his sudden death from a heart attack. I won't go into details of what happened. Even now it pains me to talk about it and I prefer not to open up the wound."

"Do you have children?" Emile asked.

"No, we had no children and I had no career. Once we met and married, I stayed home to be there for him. His professional life was busy enough for both of us, and we had a glamorous and extensive social life. He loved Italian opera and I love the ballet, so we had the best seats in the house at the pick of London's cultural, musical and theatrical events. Of course, we also attended fund-raisers for many charitable organizations. We had a wonderful life together."

Emile probed. "Where did you meet?"

"At a friend's art exhibition," Helena told him. "I was helping out at her gallery in London's West End, and Antonio attended an opening. Art was a passion of mine, and, although I was never an expert, my education and research allowed me to appear somewhat knowledgeable."

They talked all through dinner and, while the ship's officer entertained the passenger on his right, Emile and Helena were totally engaged in getting to know each other.

Emile declared that he had always known that he wanted to be an architect. "It sounds fanciful, but even as a boy, I wanted to design houses that were different, unique and innovative. Homes and houses in locations that previously had other uses: warehouses, farm buildings, institutions. Grand designs. I reject the everyday. I glory in extraordinary. My first subject at university was photography. Before I designed buildings, I learned to photograph them."

His family had lived in Canada but moved to France, and as a twentysomething, Emile joined them. "I grew up on the French-Canadian styles of chateau and gothic railway that were supposed to show how different we were than our European past. But I always longed for the grandeur of Europe. Paris is my passion; I love living in the city."

Helena loved his enthusiasm and the joie de vivre that suffused his whole personality.

"And do you have the opportunity to design your grand buildings?" asked Helena.

"I've had my moments," he said with a wink. "My designs have won awards and that gives credibility for me to work on other projects. Companies I work for design outstanding structures and I am part of the team. The project I discussed at the Sydney Opera House is very exciting, and it would be amazing to work on that building. To live and work in Sydney for a few months would be great."

Helena trod carefully but did want to ask one personal question. "Are you married?"

"Free spirit," he said. "I wouldn't want to disappoint someone when I can't stay true to a commitment. I have to be able to go where the wind takes me. Over the years I've had relationships, and they work for a time, but I don't see myself in a forever partnership with anyone—not for a long time. Monogamy in this modern world doesn't strike me as very realistic."

Emile was an engaging companion, and he certainly seemed to know his own mind. Comfortable in his skin, he said what he thought and appeared to be someone who did not follow the rules. Helena loved his candor and identified him as a maverick, the pirate-like figure she had first perceived.

"I am a francophone," he told her, "that's what they call the cultural mix of French and Canadian. The French influence gives a seriousness and Gallic intensity; the Canadian side of my character is liberal, egalitarian, a free spirit."

Helena breathed easy in the freedom of his spirit. She gazed at the vastness of the star-filled sky and the depthless sea on which they traveled and saluted the moon that shone on the waters.

In the warmth of the night, they stood side by side, close but hardly touching, and, lost in their thoughts, they savored the moment. Turning to face each other, it was as if kindred spirits united. They gazed into each other's eyes, and the sparks that were ignited when they first met burned bright. "Two travelers adrift on the high seas. Who knows where the winds will cast us up?" Emile reminded her. "Madame Helena, are you ready for our adventure?"

Emile took her in his arms, and, to the sound of the music floating from the ballroom one deck below, he guided her in a slow, sensuous dance. She rested her head on his shoulder and felt the soft red velvet of his jacket against her cheek. His hand stoked her hair, and he whispered in her ear, "We needed no introduction. We are already in step. There is a grand design at work."

Taking her face in his hand, he leaned forward to kiss her.

Helena broke free from his romantic embrace. She took a step back and breathed deeply.

"Tonight has been wonderful," she told him. "I've loved every minute in your company. I'm so glad you chose to stow away on this ship, and I really hope we can pursue our adventure. I'm game but . . ."

"There's a but?" he asked.

"Yes, there's a but," she answered. "This Cinderella doesn't function well after midnight. Please excuse me."

"Can I walk you home?" he asked. "Yes, thank you," she said. "I'd like that."

Emile took her arm and headed for the staircase leading to the navigator area of the ship.

"It's quicker for me to go the other way," she said steering him away from the bridge.

Passing the cocktail bar where the guests had gathered before dinner, Helena noticed that a couple of them were still drinking. Emile's arm was around her shoulders as they stopped to say a final good night to their fellow guests.

"Where did you two get to?" they wanted to know. "A table was reserved in here for the Captain's guests. We've had brandy and nightcaps and petit fours. You missed it all."

"You also missed the Captain," said one of the male guests who by now was a little inebriated. "He came back twice and asked after you. You missed your chance there."

Helena ignored the remarks and changed the subject, "Was Meredith okay?"

"Yes, she's gone to bed," said a female guest, "but I think she felt better for not having to keep her secret any longer."

"Do you want a drink? The bar is still open," asked the passenger who had passed on the messages about the Captain.

"Not for me," said Helena. "Nor me," said Emile.

"See you all tomorrow. Good night."

Emile and Helena fell into step alongside each other and walked to the elevators at the end of the deck.

"Thank you for a great evening," said Helena. "You can leave me here."

"I don't get to walk you to your door?"

"Not tonight," Helena laughed. "I know my way home." She pecked him on the cheek.

"Remember," he said, "this is the start of the adventure. Who knows where it will end?"

Searching Questions
Day 67

Feet up on the railings of her balcony, Helena sat well into the early hours and replayed every detail of the evening in her mind. The universe had given with one hand and taken away with the other. Anticipation about an enchanted evening at dinner with the Captain was very far from the reality. The scene where they gazed with longing into each other's eyes and she dazzled him with her beauty and the outfit she had bought specifically to please him instead translated into gazing into the white wall of an officer's uniform.

The whole evening could have been a disaster and a major disappointment but for the unexpected appearance of Emile Beauchamp. Helena wanted to deny, even to herself, that she was hugely attracted to him.

But, she argued with herself, "How could she not be?"

Smoldering, dark good looks and a devil-may-care attitude

combined in a package as seductive as a Gauloise cigarette and a rich Canadian whiskey. If she hadn't known better, Helena would have believed he'd come direct from central casting destined to set her heart aflutter and cause all kinds of unholy mayhem.

"Well, so be it," she said out loud. "How come men are like buses, no sight of one and then two come along at the same time?"

She lovingly caressed the rose quartz crystal, the symbol of her longing, and repeated requests that asked the universe to deliver her a romance. The Captain had seemed like the answer to her prayers, but now a dilemma was presented, and she did not intend to dismiss Emile's obvious attraction to her. He was not afraid, even at this early stage, to put his affections on the line. She loved the flattery and the heat she felt when they danced together.

The sun was coming up, and, if Helena had thought she would be able to resolve any questions in her mind by thinking, no solutions were forthcoming.

Fortunately, though, she had been tempted, she had not allowed Emile to kiss her. However, she made it clear that she was not completely averse to the suggestion. "I'm game for the adventure," she had told him, and, unless something happened to change that, Helena felt entitled to contemplate the excitement of a new relationship. She appreciated that he was up front about his intentions. He did not pretend he was looking for Madame Right but there was no reason why Helena might not be Madame Right Now.

Helena remembered the advice her best friend offered: "You can't replace your marriage, you can't even replicate it, so it's time for a complete rethink. You have nothing to lose by taking a totally different brand for a test drive. You may be surprised to find that, when you stop looking so hard, you find your dream make and model."

Helena went to bed with a smile on her face. Emile's offer of an adventure had alighted her desire for excitement. "You're a free woman," she reminded herself, "and an Around the World Cruise is the perfect place to accept the challenge."

Words of wisdom she had read by the Chinese philosopher, Confucius, came to mind, "Wherever you go, go with all your heart."

★ ★ ★

"Are you alone?" the sound of the Captain's voice startled her. How could she not have been aware of him entering the restaurant? Day after day for weeks, her routine was to sit and watch and wait. She focused on his every action, noticed every movement. She had studied the signs all around to see when he was coming, what he was eating, was he coming toward her table? Now, for once, she had been distracted. Whether it was a good or bad sign, she could not be sure.

"Of course, I am alone," she said.

"May I join you?" he asked.

"Please, you know that's what I always want."

He sat down, set down his plates of food and made the sign of the cross before picking up his cutlery.

"Last night was a disaster," he said, and she got the distinct feeling he was about to blame her. "What happened? Why were you way down at the end of the table? Why were you not close to me? That is why I invite you, so I can be close to you."

Helena felt conflicted. It pleased her that he was upset and had admitted his desire for her. However, the seating arrangements at his dinner table were hardly her responsibility.

"If I'd arrived on time, maybe I could have made changes. I

couldn't even see you. Instead I spent the whole evening with a passenger complaining about the ship's tender service."

"Some port transfers deliver a very bumpy ride," said Helena, "especially when the tenders are locally contracted. It's not usually so bad when you use the ship's own life craft."

The Captain pursed his lips and held up his hands in frustration. "I spent all last night talking about tenders. I don't intend to spend my lunchtime talking about them."

"Sorry, I was trying to be helpful," said Helena. "I know the woman who was seated next to you."

"And what I'm asking is why you were not seated next to me?"

"I can hardly be held responsible for the table seating plan," she said. "Of course, I would have rather have been next to you. You must know that."

"Well, you certainly made the best of it. When I did try to catch your eye, you were too interested in that architect to notice I wanted to talk to you. Also, I came to talk to you at the bar. You know that is my routine, to come and say good night to my guests. You were not there."

Helena stared straight at him. "At last, Grigory," she challenged him, "you are forced to admit that I am more than a friend."

His face darkened. "I would have thought that was obvious," he said. "And, at last, Helena, you are forced to use my name."

Neither seemed to know how to break the impasse.

The Captain was the first one to speak. "Do you want to know why I was so late joining my guests last night?" he asked.

"If you want to tell me," she answered.

"Conversations with the office in Southampton delayed me. Plans for me to hand over command and leave the ship in

Hong Kong have changed. The company asked me to stay on another couple of weeks and leave the ship in Singapore. That was the plan three plans ago. All my vacations flights have to be rearranged."

Helena could not stop the delight showing on her face. "I'm sorry about your vacation plans," she said sympathetically. "I know you were looking forward to seeing your family. But what is bad news for you is good news for me. Instead of leaving two weeks from now, you will be onboard an extra ten days, at least. I'm betting that you will take this ship right back to where you picked us up. You are going to make it all the way around the world."

"Yes, I had hoped you would be happy," he admitted, "but it makes many complications for me."

"Do you want to talk about them?" asked Helena.

"Not really. There is nothing to be done," he sighed. "My family must change all their travel plans and dates. They are used to it; this has been my life always, but it never gets easier on them. It's not so bad for the older ones, but the young one is upset. He doesn't understand."

Helena wanted to comfort him. He was making it clear that the decisions he was forced to make were not easy. He had to choose between loyalties. When he agreed to the needs of the company and his job, he was put in a position of letting down his family.

"I want to please everyone," he told her. "It's painful for me to let people down. Always, I try to face my responsibilities, but inevitably there is disappointment. Sometimes we have commitments we would prefer not to have, but that doesn't mean we can walk away. There are consequences to actions, and, if they lead to inconvenience, then that is as it may be. I am not one to walk away."

He stopped eating and looked into the distance. He looked tired and under pressure. Helena had never seen him like this. He was always so in control.

"I do not want to choose work over family, but I have a commitment to the company. They need me and it is my job. It is not as if they can easily find someone to do what I do. Even a first-class captain needs time to settle in and get to know a ship. He doesn't arrive today and sail the vessel tomorrow."

He sighed. "I'm sorry, Helena," he said, and reached out to take her hand. "You don't want to listen to my problems."

"You are wrong," she said. "I am glad to be your confidant."

"You like it better than being a friend?" he mocked her.

"There is something I want to tell you," she said. "It is about my husband."

He looked surprised. "Really? I know you always told me your marriage was happy."

"Yes, we were happy," said Helena, "and what happened did not change that, but it certainly tested our relationship. Fortunately, the marriage survived. But it was not easy."

"I'm sorry," said the Captain. And again, he reached out to take her hand. It was quite some time before he let it go, and Helena was reassured by his arm resting alongside hers on the table.

"My husband had a son," she said. "I found out about it not long before he died. He vowed he did not have an affair. But he did father a child with a woman he met through his work. What he told me was that they slept together, twice. He implied that she was the one who made all the moves, but over the years, I've come to realize that, even if she did the pursuing, he should have taken responsibility for his actions. Presumably, she did not force him against his will."

She gave a sardonic laugh and the Captain laughed also. "That would be difficult," he agreed. "And what did you do about it?" he asked.

"From the moment he told me, I was determined it would not break up my marriage. I asked the difficult questions: Like, did he love her? Did he want to leave me? But he was adamant that he had no intention of leaving as long as I would agree to keep the marriage intact."

"That was very brave of you," said the Captain. "I admire you."

"What would I have gained?" she asked sadly. "I loved him. He loved me. I'm tempted to say, 'These things happen,' but you know that, don't you? I almost wish he hadn't told me, but I guess that would have been worse."

"How did you cope?" he asked. "It must have been very painful. The loss of trust. The betrayal. It is not easy to mend."

"I forced myself not to ask for details. I refused to give the woman power in my marriage. She was not so important that she could destroy what we had built over all the years. The lawyers dealt with all the arrangements," Helena explained.

"And after your husband died?"

"That's when the really problems started," Helena admitted. "I became obsessed with finding her, and I finally did through Facebook. I saw a photo of her with her son. He's six now. For a while I allowed it to torment me. I really made myself very unhappy. Then I had a moment of revelation and realized that I had to forgive her. I had already forgiven my husband."

Helena looked to be on the verge of tears, a passing waiter was about to ask if he should remove the empty plates but thought better of it and retreated.

"I sent her a message, it said, 'There's enough love to go around,'" Helena told him. "That's all I said, but it freed me."

The Captain's radio bleeped. He checked it and confirmed with the person on the other end, "I'm on my way."

"Sorry, I have to go," he said as he rose from the table. "Thank you for telling me. I am very grateful. You are a remarkable woman, Helena."

"And you are a remarkable man," she answered. "Go, your ship needs you."

Tokyo, Yokohama and Kagoshima, Japan
Day 68

The Land of the Rising Sun is the first country to greet the arrival of each new day, and with her alarm set for sunrise, Helena leaped from bed filled with enthusiasm for her visit to one of the highlighted must-see countries on her bucket list.

The islands of Japan were a closed society unknown to the world until the middle of the nineteenth century. Yokohama was the first harbor city to open as an entry point for world trade and introduced Japan to its international neighbors after hundreds of years of self-imposed isolation. A major culture clash whereby Christian philosophy was in conflict with Samurai culture led Japanese authorities to ban all contact with foreign countries for more than 200 years.

Yokohama was a small fishing village up to the end of the Edo period, which was the time of Japan's policy of seclusion from foreigners. A major turning point in Japanese history happened in 1853 when Commodore Matthew Perry arrived with a fleet of American warships and demanded Japan open several ports for commerce. The Japanese military government agreed and signed the Treaty of Peace and Amity. Yokohama became the base of foreign trade in Japan.

The opening of the port invigorated the entire country, and new cultures and access to interaction with foreign territories earned Yokohama the distinction of being the birthplace of Japan's modern culture. Yokohama prides itself on being forward thinking and positive, and this attitude is reflected in its people, who are fashionable and sophisticated.

Yokohama, one of Japan's fifteen major government classified cities, is the point of entry for many cruise lines and is located in the center of Japan along the coastline of the Pacific Ocean. Yokohama is the second largest city after Tokyo, and, with car giants Nissan and Mitsubishi located in their city, Yokohama is often hailed as a city of dreams to the 3.7 million people who live there. It is famous as a tourist mecca and a center of business and culture. Yokohama abounds with art and culture and its international museums, classical music venues and commissioned sculptures are subtly incorporated into the city's landscape.

Yokohama is modern but also proudly preserves traditional Japanese values through the Noh, masked dance-drama theaters, and archaic rituals. A very Japanese city, Yokohama is integrated and has a large Chinatown and hundreds of Chinese restaurants and shops. The integration gives a unique blend of cultures. The Japanese use Chinese characters in their one hundred character alphabet, though, they pronounce them totally differently.

After an early arrival into the famous harbor, Helena joined other passengers keen to make the most of the day's shore excursion. "Every tiny element is exquisite," Helena observed as she photographed a pot of white orchids strategically placed at the entrance to a communal bathroom in the cruise terminal. "The sense of style and attention to detail is breath-taking."

Helena claimed she fell in love with Japan the moment she saw her first magnolia tree in blossom. The season had begun and on every street a profusion of the flowers added a white-wedding quality to the simplest outdoor scene.

The iconic image of Japan, with Mount Fuji as its spiritual and natural monument overseeing all the land, perfectly defines the country as 72 percent of Japan is mountain or forest. No wonder the 127 million people live with chronic overcrowding in the cities. Mount Fuji delivers small earthquakes every day and tremors are a common occurrence in the streets and inside buildings.

On a ferry to visit one of the many small islands overlooked by Mount Fuji, Helena gazed in awe at the beauty of the mountain. Emile stood beside her at the railings and, when she shivered after possibly having been caught in a sudden breeze on the open water, declared, "Being in the presence of the mountain is known to bring on profoundly spiritual experiences. It has been said that people who worship at the foot of Mount Fuji have their lives changed forever.

"Buddhism and Shintoism are the religions adhered to by 80 percent of Japanese people. Religion is closely related to nature: God is the Sun, the moon reflects the goddesses and clouds, air and ocean are elements that correlate to every aspect of life."

"You make a very knowledgeable guide," Helena thanked him. Emile invited himself along on the trip, even though he had not signed up, when he realized Helene was planning to go sightseeing in Yokohama and then take a road trip to see the Imperial Palace.

"I've been lucky enough to spend a lot of time in Japan," he admitted, "but I never tire of it. It's a fascinating country. I'd like to see you become enchanted by your first visit."

"The Tokyo Imperial Palace is the primary residence of the Emperor of Japan," said Emile putting on his best official guide voice. "It towers over the parkland in the Chiyoda Ward of Tokyo and contains many buildings, including the private residences of the Imperial Family, an archive, museums and administrative offices. The new palace was completed in 1888. It is located on the former site of Edo Castle, surrounded by moats and massive stone walls in the center of Tokyo. The palace was destroyed during World War II and rebuilt in the same style."

Emile broke off from his commentary and asked, "You do know Japan had to be totally rebuilt after the Second World War? As an architect, I am fascinated by the possibilities presented to rebuild when a city is totally destroyed. Apart from a showcase like the Imperial Palace, most of Japan and certainly Tokyo was rebuilt in modern and contemporary styles."

From Kokyo Gaien National Garden, the large plaza in front of the Imperial Palace, Helena and Emile, crossed the vast open areas to view Nijubashi, the two bridges that form an entrance to the inner palace grounds. The inner grounds are not open to the public except for two days of the year: Jan 2, New Year's Greeting, and February 23, the Emperor's birthday. Visitors are able to enter the grounds and see the members of the Imperial Family as they make stylized appearances on the balcony. It is possible to tour the grounds of the palace on other days, but no inner buildings are open to the public.

Landscaping is regulated by the government who decree that ornamental pine trees are to be manicured to within an inch of their lives to maintain uniformity. In the extensive grounds, Japanese people of all ages join in communal tai chi exercises and joggers, fitness freaks and multigenerational families find space to pursue their health-based activities.

In the Imperial Palace, one single family has ruled for 170 generations and the Emperor is proclaimed as a God—the first-born son becomes Emperor and can last for decades—a new succession took place in 2019. Tokyo is a high-speed, vibrant, electronic city with great wealth, and this is reflected in European-inspired, elegant, stylish buildings designed by world-renowned architects that house global designer shops: Chanel, Dior, Vuitton, Armani, Lauren. Young fashion is showcased on the streets with millennials and under twenty-fives dressed as cartoon characters,

Helena was as enchanted as Emile had predicted. In the main shopping area of Ginza Road, pedestrian thoroughfares on the famous Ginza crossing show nearly all new cars on the road. One major surprise—the traffic lights flash red for stop and blue for go.

Spirituality and commercialism go hand in hand.

At the towering Buddha statue that dominates the skyline, Emile urged Helena, "You need to pay homage to the Buddah. It is a ritual you must not miss. You buy a handful of shiny gold tokens that have been tied with red ribbons and attach them to the praying trees. People pray for their family and ancestors."

The gigantic bronze Buddha statue celebrates the tale of three fishermen who found a tiny bronze Buddha three days in a row as they fished. The priests decided this was a sign indicating that the statue would bring prosperity and health to the area, and in 1300, they built a temple to honor the bronze Buddha.

Following instruction and surrounded by dozens of other worshippers, Helena washed her hands, breathed into the sacred moment, held her face in the smoke from the burning fire of the shrine, clapped her hands three times and said a prayer. "There is one special man in my heart; I long for us to be together."

Much as she enjoyed Emile's company, and if she were honest, she had even contemplated a possible romance, Helena was in no doubt—her prayer was for the Captain.

"What did you pray for?" Emile asked.

"You know better than that," said Helena. "Prayers, like wishes, must remain secret."

"I guess I have to work harder before you include me in your prayers," he answered.

"There is one wish you could help me fulfil," she told him. "Seeing all these gorgeous young girls dressed up in their kimonos has inspired me. I'd really love to try one on—and have a photo to send back home."

"Your wish is my command," said Emile. "I saw a sign in a fashion shop around the corner, offering kimono dress-up sessions.

"Let's go," he said. "I can't wait to see you dressed up as my own personal geisha girl. That's what I call an adventure. But don't forget, when dressed as a geisha, you must walk three paces behind the man. Feudal laws state that the man is always first. Women are not equal."

"Don't hold your breath," said Helena. "I'm a liberated, independent woman and proud of it."

In Tokyo city center, Emile and Helena held hands as they strolled through the bustling Tsukiji Fish Market and sampled street food, green tea, bonito flakes and delicious snacks that rivaled the best of fine gourmet cuisine.

They watched the intricate sushi-making process as a guide explained in Japanese, Chinese and English about the connections between Japanese culture, history and food.

"Here, my friend would like to try," said Emile, when the guide requested a volunteer to learn the art of sushi rolling. Helena looked distinctly nervous as the guide produced a ceremonial dagger and an ugly looking fish. "You must first cut up the fish," said the guide, much to the amusement of the watching crowd. "Only joking," he said as he produced a platter of freshly cut fish. "Your job is to roll the fish with the rice. And then eat."

"I can do the last bit." Helena laughed.

Emile clapped loudest of all when she completed her task and told her, "How are you enjoying our adventures so far? Check sushi rolling off your list. Who knows what comes next?"

＊　＊　＊

Kagoshima, a city on the southernmost main island, holds the title of Japan's friendliest city. It is proud of its past as the capital of feudal Satsuma province, its original Mandarin name. Entering a world of unbelievable privilege and wealth, the first stop on a tour of Kagoshima was the Shoko Shuseikan Museum at Sengan-en. The museum is housed in Japan's oldest remaining stone factory, which was built in 1865 as the country replicated the industrial revolution taking place in other parts of the world. Sengan-en, one of Japan's greatest stately homes, was inhabited in the nineteenth century by the Shimazu family and its head, Prince Shimazu Tadayoshi.

From royalty to the Samurai warrior aristocracy, 260 years of history proclaims the town of Chiran a miniature Kyoto; the fabled city was once the capital of Japan and is famous for its numerous classical Buddhists temples, gardens, Imperial places, Shinto shrines and traditional wooden houses, transplanted into the heart of Satsuma.

The town is a living reminder of the story seen across the ages. Chiran Samurai Residence Garden's houses and gardens are magnificently preserved in a feudal village setting. The Samurai era ended in 1868 and Japan entered another incarnation—the modernizing of an entire culture, heritage and history. Instilled in the warrior honor tradition, Chiran was the main kamikaze base for the Japanese Army toward the end of the Pacific War. The museum has a mission to reveal to future generations the truths about the war and thus lead the world along the road to perpetual peace.

"Amen to that," said Emile, as he and Helena left the village and walked toward the river. "Before we head back to the ship, let's treat ourselves to a meal at one of the traditional restaurants that claims to have the finest local cuisine and amazing views of the active volcano, Sakurajima. I hear that locals raise their umbrellas against the mountain's eruptions when fine ash coats the landscape like snow and obscures the sun like fog. Mystical and captivating. There is even a special ash forecast as part of the weather report. Graves have roofs on top to protect them from the volcanic ash."

"I agree with the sentiment of peace," said Helena, "but I feel so moved by our whole Japan adventure. Listen to the mission statement of this town: 'a town thriving on the blessings of an active volcano.'"

"It's so poetic," said Emile. "The Japanese certainly have a unique way of looking at life. It's been my pleasure to see it through your eyes. I knew you would be a great fellow adventurer."

"I certainly won't forget my first visit to Japan," said Helena. "A true highlight of my world voyage."

Confidants
Day 72

"*Emperor*, that is the name of the film. It was made in 2012, starring Matthew Fox and Tommy Lee Jones," Helena told the Captain as they sat together at lunch the day after the port calls in Japan. "It's an American Japanese historical drama based on the actual life story of Brigadier General Bonner Fellers who was sent to Japan as a part of the occupation forces. He had the responsibility of arresting Japanese war criminals, including Prime Minister Hideki Tojo. After arresting Tojo, the Supreme Commander for the Allied Powers MacArthur informed Fellers that Emperor Hirohito should also be charged as a war criminal.

"After extensive investigations, Fellers told MacArthur that instead of punishing the Emperor, whom they concluded played an important role in ending the war, the Allies should start to discuss Japan's reconstruction. Fellers' wisdom and humanity were said to have enabled him to come to the momentous decision that changed the course of history and the future of two nations."

The Captain looked at Helena with admiration. "Thank you so much for your kindness. When I told you that I would like to see the film again but did not know the name, I never expected you to go to so much trouble to find out about it for me."

"Google makes research very accessible."

"Yes, but you did not have to use your time to solve my problem."

"We talked before about your interest in war history, the strategies, the generals, the worldview. My husband also was very interested. He had a complete bound set of Churchill's war diaries—it was his favorite bedtime reading. That is, when he wasn't watching the classic British television series, *The World at War*."

"I guess it is something else he and I have in common," he said with a wry smile.

Helena talked about her visit to the Chiran Peace Museum in the Samurai village.

"The village is amazing," he agreed. "I have been there on previous trips. It's not always possible because of other duties when we are in port, but I do make an effort to get off the ship and go to visit places of interest. The homes of the warriors were a reflection of the esteem in which they were held and how much wealth they accumulated. My favorite place was a secret house attached to the main residence where one of the war lords hid out for days listening to what people were saying about him and what his warriors were plotting."

"Would you like such a place?" she asked.

"It's not necessary. I have good relations with my officers and good intelligence. There is not much that happens on the ship that I don't know about; someone always tells me."

Helena reached into her handbag, which was sitting on the chair between them.

"I have another gift for you," she said.

"Why, what have I done to deserve this?" he asked.

Helena smiled and asked, "Can't I buy my favorite Captain a gift?"

She handed him a bright red gift box and inside was a shiny, magnetized gold brooch she bought at the Buddhist shrine. The one where she prayed for them to be together.

"The engraved symbol for *shinobi*—it is the Japanese word for 'warrior'; you are a warrior."

"I don't know what to say. You are so kind to me. I feel that I don't understand what I have done to deserve your attention."

Helena beamed. "I want to please you. I don't suppose you realize, but you are always in my thoughts. The gifts are to thank you and show you how much I care."

"What can I give you in return?" he asked.

Helena laughed out loud. "Don't even go there," she told him.

He gave her a look of such intensity that she blushed and looked away. The unspoken messages confused her, and she wished she knew the dilemma that was playing out in his mind.

They gazed at each other for a long time, and it seemed as if he was on the verge of saying something but resisted. Helena allowed him his caution and reminded herself that he was steering the ship. When the time felt right for him, he was perfectly capable of breaking the impasse.

Helena broke the silence. "May I ask you a personal question? If you don't want to answer, that's fine. If you don't even want to discuss the subject, I understand."

"If I don't like it, I won't answer, but you always ask so nicely. It is okay. But first let me get my drink refilled."

Lifting his glass, he signaled a waiter. The headwaiter appeared. "You want another drink, Captain?"

"Yes, please. The usual." He addressed Helena, "A drink for you?"

"No, nothing," she said, though her mouth felt dry as she framed her question. It felt intrusive, but she needed to know and he could always refuse to answer.

"The woman, the mother of your son, do you have a relationship with her?"

He narrowed his eyes, and his expression turned stern. Helena regretted asking the question. She did not want to set up barriers between her and him. It was difficult enough to maintain the status quo that existed between them, and had for two months now.

"Some marriages don't last as long," she told herself. A few more weeks and he would leave the ship for good.

"No, we do not have a relationship. Not a personal one. We are parents, and, of course, we have a relationship about matters that concern our son. We have both tried to do our best by him."

Helena saw the sadness in his eyes and wished she had not pursued the matter. It really wasn't her business.

"I appreciate your answer," she said. "Truth is, I was trying to reconcile the status of my husband's relationship. Not yours. I will not bring up the matter again."

"Do you know if your husband maintained a relationship with the woman?" he asked.

"The situation was rather different," she admitted. "My husband died before the boy was born. But when I checked information on Facebook, the boy was named after his father."

"Is that difficult for you to accept?" he asked, glad that the spotlight was off his personal situation and on hers. "Perhaps the mother thought he needed a connection with the father he would never know.

"I have to accept that my husband's son is a part of him. Whatever the circumstances of his birth and how that impacted my marriage. My husband certainly was insistent that his son was entitled to be supported by him. Financially, if in no other way."

Helena bit the inside of her cheek and tried to stop the tears that had started to fall. "I'm so sorry. I wish I hadn't started this conversation. Goodness knows what you must think of me. I've confused, in my mind, my husband's situation with yours. As if by talking to you about it I am really talking to him."

"What is it that's bothering you?" he asked. His tone was kind, but she sensed his frustration. "This really isn't the right time or place for this conversation. Tell me what you think I can do to help. It is not necessarily anything like my own situation, but at least the fact that your husband is dead means he is not having any relationship with his son or the mother."

"I want to have a relationship with them," she blurted out. "At least with my husband's son and, maybe in time, with the mother. Is that so strange? I'd like to know my husband's son, and I hope he would benefit from knowing about his father: his roots, his family, his heritage. He is entitled to be a part of that if it is what his mother wants for him. His father was an amazing man, an accomplished man.

"My heart tells me that he would have maintained a relationship with his son. I trust to believe that he would not have pursued a relationship with the mother. The son, yes. That's the kind of man my husband was."

The Captain confirmed. "That is the kind of man I am. I believe my son is entitled to know his father."

Helena sighed with relief. "I had hoped you would be able to see my point of view. The mother doesn't know my husband. She has none of the background information or family photographs that I plan to offer to introduce Antonio to his father. I will make contact after the cruise."

"I hope it turns out well, but, if you want my advice, I suggest you leave well enough alone." He pulled no punches. "It is not your business. The mother will tell her son what she wants him to know about his father. She *did* know him even though you don't want to accept that. You are setting yourself up for heartache and resentment."

"What would you think if your wife . . ."

"Stop now," he said. The stern face he had shown earlier returned. "Please, do not drag me into these deep emotional waters again. Our lives seem to have some quite extraordinary coincidences, but I will not discuss the matter again. Instead, we should be concentrating on our relationship."

"Our relationship," Helena teased him. "So we do have a relationship?"

"We have a special relationship, and it is for us to know what that means," he said. "Now, I have news."

"About your vacation?" Helena asked.

"Yes, the plans are now in place. I have made all my flight arrangements, and I will leave the ship in Singapore."

Helena was determined to take onboard what he had said. She had no intention of asking anymore about his family situation or even his vacation plans.

"We have two more weeks together," he said. "Maybe we can make arrangements to spend time together in one of the ports. Shanghai is an amazing place to visit. Have you been there before?"

"No, I haven't, but I've always wanted to go."

"I make no promises," he told her. "Things change around here at a moment's notice, but the new Captain will be on board by then, learning the ropes and getting ready to take over, and I may be able to get away for a few hours."

"I have an ambition to eat noodles from a street vendor in Shanghai," she said. "They say the noodles are the best in the world."

"Maybe not the best in the world," he disagreed, "but a trip up the Oriental Pearl Tower in the financial district is certainly worthwhile. There is an amazing view of the entire city."

"If I'm with you, I don't care what we do," she said and added with a wink, "Noodles on the street or at the top of the tower will be as fabulous as dinner at the Captain's table."

"Every day I spend longer eating my lunch with you," he said. "I'm not on vacation yet."

He leaned close to say goodbye and his hand brushed hers. Helena's heart skipped a beat. The effect he had on her was powerful and, even with familiarity, did not diminish.

He walked away and came back. "By the way, you can tell your Canadian friend his company won't be required in Shanghai. You have an important date."

Tianjin, China
Day 73

All day long the ship's horn sounded as storms lashed the ship. Adverse weather forced the cancellation of many onboard activities, and the outside decks were closed. The Captain was absent from lunch for days.

Helena grew angry at her continuing obsession. The adult side of her knew he had many priorities and lunch was obviously not one of them. The child in her felt abandoned. She began to believe that for all their laughter, conversation, closeness and even the upcoming date in Shanghai, she was not a priority.

"He can find me anytime he likes," she reminded herself, "and there are plenty of methods of electronic communication he could use to check in. Text, email, phone, even a handwritten letter." Two steps forward, one step back, there was never any real progress. Yet for all the disappointments, Helena still felt a compelling attraction to him.

It is such a strange sensation, she wrote in her journal. *Every time I think of him, my arms open wide and I long to embrace him. My heart opens and I refuse to deny we have a deep connection. Somewhere our souls are united.*

Helena deliberately avoided the places she knew Emile would be; at this stage, he was too great a complication. "Meredith has become friends with some people she met at the Captain's table," he told her during dinner in the restaurant overlooking the volcano in Japan. "She is moving off your table. Is it okay if I take her vacant spot?"

"Leave it a couple of days," said Helena. "Meredith may decide she wants to come back."

Life for the passengers continued with those activities that were not deemed a hazard during turbulent weather. Dance lessons and fitness classes were canceled; choir was not.

Helena was relieved. Learning the complicated harmonies of *Bohemian Rhapsody* was proving challenging, and she hoped there would be time to get the piece performance ready, and that the Captain would still be onboard when performance day arrived. But that, like his departure, was subject to rescheduling.

"*Bohemian Rhapsody* used to be one of my favorite songs," she confided to another choir member. "I'm not sure it will be at the end of our rehearsals. Perhaps I shouldn't have watched the Queen movie at the open-air cinema. It was brilliant, but it's set up unrealistic expectations in my head."

Sea days made some passengers restless, and bad weather added to the feelings of confinement. Now a new country was in sight and this particular one brought a general feeling of tension as the liner entered Chinese shipping lines in the Yellow Sea.

In the major shipping channel, a blackout was imposed and no photographs were allowed. "Please respect the blackout," the headwaiter insisted as one male passenger decided to ignore instructions.

"I only want to take a photograph," the man in question complained. He was a small-town politician back in England, and even on the ship, it seemed he expected to wield influence.

"Yes, and you taking photographs could lead the Chinese authorities to deny us passage through their waters," a fellow passenger remonstrated with him. "This is not a joke. The Chinese expect instructions to be followed. There could be serious consequences otherwise."

"Quite right," said yet another passenger. This man's wife added her observations. "He's an idiot," she said. "Always thinks he knows better. Hates following rules. Says he makes them, doesn't follow them."

"Okay, okay, I hear you. I've closed the curtain," the politician said. "There's nothing to see. Only bright spotlights from other ships aimed at us."

"I despair of him," said the politician's wife, rolling her eyes.

The arrival into the port of Tianjin, where the ship docked, also gave a telling indication of the Chinese insistence on rules being followed. Although immigration officials boarded the ship and scrutinized passports, all passengers were subjected to a face-to-face interview with Chinese officials.

Passengers who ignored the strict requirements for visas that were to be obtained before leaving the home port found there was no opportunity to apply for visas onboard.

Long lines formed to leave the ship because the processing was so slow in the cruise terminal.

Helena said, "Hello," to the wife of the passenger who had been trying to take photographs the previous evening. She sat alone in a lounge area.

"Guess who said we didn't need visas," she said angrily. "We're not allowed off the ship in China. He'll take a while to live this down. I've looked forward to visiting Tiananmen Square."

The three-hour drive to Beijing on an arrow-straight highway showed miles upon miles of industrial developments and concrete white high-rise accommodation blocks. They were regulated and ordered but devoid of landscaping.

Ensconced at the front of the coach in a window seat, Helena sat bolt upright, ready to turn on her full concentration as the Chinese-speaking guide lectured and demanded attention. Her accent and the vast amount of facts and figures given made it difficult to keep up with the constant flow of information.

The guide introduced herself. A teacher, when she was not acting as a guide, she explained that her Chinese name was Sun Min, but she was known as Nancy. She had a plan and slackers would not be tolerated. "I want you to learn these two words and I will test you on them at the end of the day. *Nǐ hǎo* [nee haow] means 'hello' and *Xiè xiè* [zh-yeh zh-yeh] is 'thanks.' I will tell you the Chinese for 'goodbye' when it is time for you to leave."

She was direct, "You may prefer to sleep or look out the window, but you are in China for a short time and I want you to learn something about our great country.

"China has led the world in innovation for thousands of years," she proclaimed. "Chinese people from a thousand years ago invented papermaking, printing and gun powder. The Terracotta Army was made in 221 BC and the building of the Great Wall started in the seventh century BC. Both are achievements that have never been rivaled in world history."

Classical history and the powerful dynasties that ruled China were accomplishments of the past, but the guide reserved her admiration for the current situation and concentrated on the Communist party, which focused on New China and the Mao Tse Tung era from the 1960s.

"May I ask a question?" said Helena, putting up her hand. "Can you explain about the one child rule?"

"Before the rule came into force," explained the guide, "families would often have between six and a dozen children. They needed them to help work the land. Now that China is industrialized, we can have only one child. Chinese people like to have boys so they carry on the family name. We say 'Boy is cultural bank. Girl is financial bank.' Girls cost money.

If a family have girl first, after two years they can have another child. They will hope to have a boy."

Once started on social context in China, the guide really hit her stride, "If they want to marry, boys must make a dowry to the girl's family. All girls want for a dowry three big wedding presents. It used to be a watch, a bicycle and a sewing machine. But at the start of private enterprise, the gifts changed to a freezer, a television and a washing machine. Now that China is the biggest market in the world, wedding gifts are a house, a car and a credit card."

In the commercial center of Beijing, cruise ship passengers were led into a vast wooden restaurant and joined hundreds of diners in a traditional family-style meal with everyone helping themselves from fast spinning dishes on a revolving table laden with chicken soup, dumplings, spicy meat, boneless chicken, stir fried vegetables, noodles and rice.

Chopsticks were provided—as well as cutlery. "I show you how to use them?" asked the unsmiling waitress. Her smile soon appeared as she watched the ungainly efforts of western diners trying to transfer food from plate to mouth on the slim wooden sticks. "I think is best you use fork," the waitress concluded.

In a nearby park, the guide wanted to show the imaginative way that Chinese couples go about finding partners. No internet dating. Their method is much more personal. On Sundays, mothers present themselves at the marriage market.

"They take a photograph of their marriage-age child and make a connection with a mother who has a child who may be a suitable match. Together they discuss the merits of the child and talk about the assets that will be offered in a marriage settlement. Arrangements then can be made for the couple to meet. In our economy couples work so hard, they do not have any other way of meeting and finding a suitable partner."

Helena sat alongside the guide on one of the designated marriage benches.

"Is the method successful?" Helena was anxious to know.

"Of course," said the guide. "But it can take a long time. My mother comes here every Sunday for two years and shows my photograph. I do not have a husband yet."

"I'm sorry," Helena said. "I'm sure you will make a very good wife one day."

* * *

The cruise ship company hired policemen to board the coach and deliver the passengers directly to the entrance of the Imperial Palace. "Not so much for safety," explained the guide, "but because there are thousands of people visiting and we are allowed to come to a special entrance. We also leave by this exit with an armed policeman to make sure we are given safe passage through the crowds."

The Temple of Heaven is a pagoda-style wooden painted palace, blue for the sky and heaven, gold to represent the Emperor and green for the earth. The twelve pillars holding up the building represent the four seasons, twelve months, and twelve multiplied by two for the hours of a day.

North and south, east and west, all the land under heaven belonged to the Emperor.

Praying for the preservation of the harvest was the main ceremony performed in the temple that is now a World Heritage Site visited by thousands of people every day.

In ancient times, only the Emperor and his family were allowed access to the Imperial Palace, which is part of the huge site of the Forbidden City.

"How many bedrooms does the palace have?" asked one passenger.

"It is said that if a child was born and slept in a new bedroom each night, he would be twenty-seven years of age before he had slept in every bedroom," the guide claimed.

One particular apartment, a renovated grand showplace visible through a wall of plate-glass windows, fascinated Helena.

"Whose residence is this?" she asked the guide.

"That bedroom and the several rooms behind, for her entourage, belong to the Dragon Lady."

"Please tell me more," Helena urged.

"The famous and very beautiful Dragon Lady was one of the two thousand concubines the Emperor entertained at the Imperial Palace. By a series of daring subterfuges, she caught the Emperor's eye and became his special mistress, then she became one of his wives. She bore him a son and when the Emperor died, suddenly, she became the ruler until the son was old enough to take the throne. She held the fate of two empires in her hands."

"Sounds like quite a lady," said a male voice coming from the back of the crowd who had gathered to peer in the windows and hear the extraordinary story.

"Emile, what are you doing here?" Helena asked. "You weren't on the coach, were you?"

"No," he told her. "I was a late entry for the trip. The excursion was already fully booked, but when two passengers were refused permission to get off the ship, there became room for me in a private taxi tour organized by their friends. We've got a spare seat; do you want to join us?"

"Thanks for the offer, but the procedure is very strict, and I think our guide would have a fit if she lost me in the middle of the Forbidden City."

"Okay, see you back at the ship," he said. "As long as you are not avoiding me."

"As if," said Helena with what she hoped was a reassuring smile.

"Everyone back on the coach, now," shouted the guide, Nancy. "We will lose our preferential position to leave the Imperial Palace and complete today's tour at the tomb of our great leader, Chairman Mao Tse Tung."

The leader of China's Cultural Revolution, Mao Tse Tung, died in Beijing in 1976 at the age of eighty-four. His body was preserved and buried in a crystal tomb in Tiananmen Square, at the focal point of a vast parade ground. In the spirit of a visit to Mecca, Chinese people are expected to visit the tomb at least once in their lifetime. A flag raising and lowering ceremony takes place every day at sunrise and sunset.

Soldiers guard the tomb. Helena approached as near as she dared to take a photo of the tomb and the ceremony.

"Stop, go," a soldier shouted and made to lower his gun.

Helena held up her hands. In any language, the message was clear.

On the Gate of Heavenly Purity, a gigantic portrait of Chairman Mao dominates the square and the painting is designed so that his eyes ominously track visitors all over the square. Nothing escapes his oversight. Despite all the perceived changes in China in recent years, Chairman Mao, his authority and the Communist Party still control everything.

"China welcomes visitors," Nancy explained as the passengers settled back on the coach for the journey to the port, "but we demand respect for our country and our culture.

"Cranes in our culture are a symbol of good luck. We believe that the birds, with their red crown and five-foot height, represent longevity and good fortune. Now I have a gift for you. Made by my mother, who was very excited that I spend my day with foreign visitors. A few years ago, she would not have allowed it. Now she welcomes interaction with people from other countries." To each person, Nancy presented, from her mother, a handmade origami crane "as a symbol of our friendship."

"Do you remember the words I taught you this morning?" she asked. A couple of passengers did.

They called out "Nǐ hǎo" and "Xiè xiè." Nancy acknowledged them with an uncharacteristic smile.

"Our day together has come to an end so now I will teach you the word for 'goodbye.' Zàijiàn [ZYE jeeyen]. See you again."

Shanghai, China
Day 76

Few cities in the world invoke so much history, excess, glamour, mystique and exotic promise as Shanghai. If Helena's fantasy of an enchanting and magical romance was to come true, she could not imagine any place more perfect for her first date with the Captain. The city is located on the coast of the East China Sea between the mouth of the Yangtze River to the north and the bay of Hangzhou to the south.

Shanghai is a cosmopolitan metropolis on the western bank of the Pacific Ocean and serves as a center of finance, trade and navigation. It is one of the most populous and developed cities in the People's Republic of China, has one of the largest seaports and claims to be the most important business and cultural center in the world.

This incredibly beautiful and dynamic city welcomes millions of guests from all over the world who are attracted by thousands of entertainment venues, large-scale shopping malls and cultural events in the city. Shanghai is an international destination with its rich heritage of ancient Chinese culture and is one of the four direct-controlled municipalities of China. It is a global financial center with one of the world's busiest container ports. Shanghai grew in importance in the nineteenth century due to trade and recognition of its favorable port location and economic potential. The city was one of five treaty ports forced to open to foreign trade following the British victory over China in the First Opium War.

Shanghai has a humid and subtropical climate and experiences four different seasons. The city is susceptible to tycoons in summer and autumn.

Citizens of many countries and all continents came to Shanghai to live and work during different decades. In the 1920s and '30s, almost 20,000 White Russians and Russian Jews fled the newly established Soviet Union and took up residence in Shanghai. Helena made a mental note to ask the Captain whether his family had connections with the area.

By 1932, Shanghai had become the fifth largest city in the world behind London and New York, and the current population is over 24 million.

Vision Star sailed into Shanghai down the Huangpu River in the early hours of the morning and berthed in the International Cruise Terminal where the cruise ship would make an overnight stay until the early hours of the following morning.

Helena joined the other passengers for the sail-in on the deck and watched the Captain as he steered the vessel into port. After an early breakfast, she stared out of her cabin window at the Oriental Pearl Tower, the tallest TV tower in Asia and the third highest in the world. The dazzling pink-jeweled spire, standing at 1,536 feet and located in the financial and trade district, dominates the city skyline and is a symbol of the grandeur and prestige the city showcases to the world.

The pink fairy-tale tower, close to Shanghai Disney Land, was to be the meeting place for the romantic encounter she had so long imagined. Helena was as nervous as any teenage girl when she contemplated her first official date with the man who had dominated her thoughts throughout the world cruise on which she had embarked two and a half months before in London on a bitterly cold January day. Now at the spring equinox, the expected temperature was almost 86°F.

Three times she changed her outfit. A sleek black trouser suit was judged too formal, denims and a sweater too casual. Finally, she settled on wide-legged white trousers with a red leather jacket and red suede Cuban heel boots. High heels were not an option. He liked to walk, and she did not want to look like a silly woman tripping along beside him, inappropriately dressed.

To make the most of her time in the morning, she planned to visit well-known sights. The Bund with its eclectic collection of different architectural styles, including colonial, classic and art deco, was within walking distance of the ship across a zigzag pedestrian bridge. From there a visit to China's number one commercial street, Nanjing Road known as 'Oriental Paris', which covers three and a half miles of retail with over 600 shops.

At the Chinese bazaars, shopkeepers stood in the doorway and dazzled buyers with their beautiful merchandise. "Pretty lady, I have a treat for you," said one young Chinese girl as Helena stopped to look at the kaleidoscope of silk scarves fluttering in the breeze.

"Not a scarf, thank you," said Helena, "but a jacket. An evening jacket. Gold color, that is what I want to buy."

In a flurry of activity, drawers, cupboards and packets in cellophane from under the counter were opened and the contents wound around Helena's shoulders, then modeled by the shop assistant. Silk jackets of every shade of gold from palest lemon to deepest bronze were offered for consideration. Plus, a dazzling array of scarves and stoles and embellished evening wraps.

Helena knew what she was looking for; the jacket was to be used as a glamorous accessory over a strapless sequined rose-gold evening dress.

"Thank you, this one is perfect," she said as she chose a silken jacket in a rich golden shade with the most delicate of Chinese pearl buttons that enabled the jacket to be worn several different ways. The eager young sales assistant wrapped the jacket in a pretty silk carrying bag.

Though tempted, she bought only the one. She hoped that before he left the ship, there might be one more formal dinner at the Captain's table. A golden silk evening jacket would be perfect to wear for the occasion.

Well satisfied with her purchase, Helena resisted the temptation to continue shopping.

The morning wasn't half over and she had walked miles. Next stop on her cultural agenda was the Yuyuan Gardens, the largest of Shanghai's ancient gardens with classical architectural styles of the Ming and Qing Dynasties.

Considered one of China's world-class modern museums and rebuilt in 1994, Helena paid a high-speed visit to the Shanghai Museum, knowing she could not possibly do justice to the treasure house of Chinese art, which contained 120,000 precious relics in bronze, pottery, paintings and calligraphies.

Hailing a taxi, she handed the driver the address written in Chinese of her next destination. The journey took her out of the city and brought her close to Shanghai Railway Station.

The driver assured her that he was on the correct route. "Buddha," he repeated several times. A must-see point on the tourist map, Helena did not want to miss the Jade Buddha Temple, a priceless Buddha statue carved from one piece of white jade. The Jade Buddha Temple is set in a beautiful garden landscaped with decorated bridges, colorful pagodas and brightly decorated dragon walls. The whole atmosphere is one of tranquillity and grace.

Helena seriously considered that on her return home she would explore Buddhism. A daily meditator all her adult life, she loved the serenity invoked by elegant Buddha statues and the philosophy of acceptance in their religion. "Nothing is good or bad, all is as it is meant to be."

The taxi driver agreed to wait while Helena visited the temple, and she handed him the address of the ship's berth for the return journey.

Arrangements for her date with the Captain were dependent on his daily program.

"Formalities that I need to attend with the Chinese authorities are unpredictable," he told her. "If you are close to the ship around lunchtime, come to the restaurant and I will see you there. We will go together to the financial district. Otherwise, go direct to the Oriental Pearl Tower."

Carrying packages containing her silk jacket and other items of shopping, Helena decided to go back to the ship. It was only one o'clock. They usually met for lunch closer to 2:30 p.m.

She dropped her shopping bags in her cabin, freshened up her makeup, brushed her hair and headed upstairs to the Terrazza. For more than an hour she sat at their usual table and waited. The restaurant was almost empty. It appeared that almost all the passengers had headed off the ship. Seemed no wanted to miss a visit to Shanghai. The headwaiter closed the line and discreetly shrugged when he saw Helena waiting in her usual place. "Lunch is over for today," he said.

Plan B. Helena knew what to do.

She walked with purpose through the International Cruise Terminal and hailed another taxi.

"Pearl Oriental Tower," she tried saying it, but then pointed to the place on the map.

"There is a ticket booth inside the doors of the tower," the Captain had informed her. "I'll meet you there and we can go up to the Space Module, the highest observatory level from which you can see the whole city. It is a Shanghai landmark that should not be missed."

Helena looked at all the people coming and going around the ticket desk. At any minute she expected to see him. The reception area was filled with photographs of the city and the tower and information panels, which she studied and then walked around again and studied again.

She took out her phone, checked emails, texts, WhatsApp, phone calls. Nothing.

A seat became available in the busy lobby, and she positioned herself so that she could see the ticket desk. After an hour, despite the fact that she felt stupid, she had to take action. Nervously she checked with the young man behind the ticket counter. "Excuse me, this is the Oriental Pearl Tower?"

"Yes," he confirmed. "Do you want to buy a ticket?"

"I'm waiting for my friend," she said.

Another hour passed during which Helena made several trips outside. Inside, outside, she checked everywhere. Every passing, tall male figure in baseball cap and sunglasses briefly raised her hopes. The coffee she bought tasted bitter. She sat on a crowded seat and watched hundreds of tourists come and go. She checked her phone again.

What kind of cruel game was he playing?

An image flashed into her mind of a time, decades before when she was stood up. Deliberately and maliciously. A teenage boy had left her standing outside the local cinema.

Friends of his going in to see the film sniggered as they saw her waiting, knowing he was not going to show. Eventually a friend, who was in on the game, took pity on her. "You've been stood up," he told her. The humiliation was devastating. She dreaded the thought of facing the other kids at school the next day but was surprised when many expressed outrage that a class-mate should have behaved so badly. "You didn't deserve to be treated that way. No one does," her real friends commiserated.

As she waited in the Imperial Pearl Tower, the humiliation and feelings of rejection reactivated the old wound. But, she reminded herself, if the teenage girl survived, so would the grown-up version. "What doesn't kill you makes you stronger," she repeated.

Two hours had passed since she arrived. Disappointment was replaced with indignation. She faced a dilemma. Her inde-cision was acute. Whether to buy that ticket and go up to the observation level or stay where she was in case he appeared.

Mid-afternoon and her date was a no-show. Funny how history repeated itself.

When she had all but given up hope, out of the blue, scores of familiar faces appeared as a coach party from her ship entered the lobby of the tower.

Embarrassment washed over her, and Helena tried to hide behind some German tourists.

"Madame Helena," the shore excursion chaperone greeted her. "Have you already been up to the observation level?"

"Yes," said Helena. "I was on an earlier tour with friends. I am ready to leave."

She dropped her empty coffee cup in a rubbish can and almost ran from the building. Not looking where she was going, she wanted to get away as quickly as possible.

"We can't keep meeting like this," said a friendly voice she knew only too well.

Emile steadied her and put his arms around her shoulders.

"It really is a small world." He grinned. "Especially when visiting a city with a thousand other passengers on a cruise ship. Don't tell anyone, but I keep trying to avoid them by going on private tours. Now I've run into you again. Are you on your own?"

Helena hesitated. For certain, she did not intend to tell the truth—that she had been stood up. "Yes, I was on another tour and got left behind,"

"Happens all the time," said Emile. "I'm on my own, too. I hear the view from the top is spectacular. Would you kindly accompany me?" he asked.

"My pleasure," she said. "I'm something of an expert after having made an extensive study of the information and photographic exhibition."

"You have my undivided attention," he told her as he bought two tickets, took her arm and led her toward the high-speed elevators. "You don't have to take my word for it, but I think we two are destined to be together." He smiled.

Singing from the Same Hymn Sheet
Day 77

The Chinese authorities delayed the ship's departure from the mainland en route to Hong Kong. Two passengers were not accounted for, and it could not be verified whether they had re-boarded or not. Announcements broadcasting their cabin numbers were made over the radio system. Passports were checked and rechecked.

The ship operated a standard procedure that all passports be handed in on returning to the ship. Either two passengers had bypassed administrative staff and not handed in their passports or two passengers had not returned to the ship.

For several hours announcements were broadcast: "Please, would the named passengers come to reception immediately? The ship cannot depart until we have their passports."

On any port call, the absence of two passengers or two passports would be serious; in the People's Republic of China, it was disastrous. A constant Chinese Whisper ran around the ship, telling what was known of events up-to-date. The word was that the Chinese authorities demanded more and more documentation in an effort to track down the passengers.

Acting like a town crier, one officious passenger walked around the ship, stopped in communal areas where he had a ready-made audience and passed on his version of updates. "Last I heard, looks like all passengers will be forced to claim their passport and go through immigration again. We could be here till tomorrow morning because immigration officers are not on duty. We'll be late arriving in Hong Kong. May not get there on this trip."

Helena was among the curious ones on deck watching the action play out in a lighted committee room visible on an upper floor of the International Cruise Terminal alongside the berthed vessel. Armed police officers patrolled the immigration hall, and Chinese officials sat at tables stamping documents as uniformed officers delivered paperwork from the ship.

The Captain did not leave the ship but appeared on the bridge, talked into his radio and checked out the scene in the terminal. Passengers sat in bars and lounges, speculating on the missing passengers' whereabouts.

"For them to be left ashore in China is not an option although that eventually might be considered in other ports. If they're on land, then their passports are in their possession, and the ship could, in theory, sail without them."

"But if they're on the ship, what possible explanation is there for them not hearing the almost continuous announcements?"

"Cruise ships leave people behind all the time. If you don't return at the stated time, the company is entitled to believe you don't want to continue the journey."

"At least a phone call is expected to say that, for whatever reason, you are staying in port."

"Not very considerate for the thousand passengers onboard waiting to leave if you don't even notify the company."

"I was left behind once by the cruise ship," a middle-aged man announced. "I was much younger then, I got drunk and missed the sailing time. The ship left without me. I had to get a flight to the next port, and my travel insurance didn't cover me."

In exasperation, a passenger raised his voice, "That's as may be and I'm all for leaving them behind, but that's not going to work in China. The authorities won't allow it."

"I bet the Captain's tearing his hair out."

"Heads should roll for this. It costs a fortune in berthing fees to overstay in a port."

"Presuming they are onboard, what possible reason can there be for not hearing the announcements?"

"Perhaps they're drunk."

"But there are two separate cabin numbers and the names are not related."

"Perhaps they're together in one cabin, drunk."

"That can't be the case. Staff have been knocking on the doors for hours."

"More drinks over here, please."

The whole conversation reached an impasse before there finally came a breakthrough.

An official announcement: "Ladies and gentlemen, thank you for your patience. The missing passengers have been located. We are ready to sail. We apologize for the inconvenience."

"Tonight's performance in the theater by the *Vision Star* choir will take place later than scheduled: 10 p.m., not 9 p.m."

That was the announcement Helena had waited for all evening. The show must go on.

She ran to her cabin and changed into the black trouser suit she had rejected earlier in the day. To complete the theme of black and white that the choir masters had requested, she pulled on a white fur shrug, piled her hair on the top of her head and added rhinestone hair decorations.

Fellow choir members hurriedly gathered in the theater lobby. "Do you think we'll have an audience?" they asked each other.

For the event, every seat in the house was filled and the performance exceeded expectations. "Bohemian Rhapsody" closed the show and the enthusiastic audience demanded an encore.

The choir gathered on stage for photographs, and there was one question on everybody's lips: "Is it true the two missing passengers were found making out inside a lifeboat?"

The cruise director refused to confirm or deny. "That's more or less the story. Seems they had too much to drink, climbed in and fell asleep. They eventually heard the announcements but were too embarrassed to appear. They will be disciplined. It's against all safety regulations to interfere with the lifeboats. They may be put off the ship in Hong Kong."

Helena hoped she would get a chance to ask the Captain what really happened. He already owed her one explanation for a no-show in Shanghai, but tonight she guessed he had other more pressing matters on his mind.

"You were amazing," said Emile as he embraced her after the show. "I hadn't expected the choir to sound so professional. 'Bohemian Rhapsody' was great, and you had a starring role. I'm very impressed."

"We have over one hundred members. I don't think I had a starring role," said Helena, "but thanks for the vote of confidence. Singing in a choir is all about being unified. I love the opportunity to take part. For me it's a highlight of the cruise to experience different things."

The choir members all went their separate ways and Helena walked with Emile outside and onto the deck. "Let's go upstairs," he said. "It's such a beautiful evening. The star show is spectacular and I'll show you the lifeboat where the missing couple was found."

Helena laughed. "Okay, I am curious. It can't be easy to get into one of those things."

Emile picked up on what she'd said. "Do you want to try?" he asked with a laugh. "I'm game if you are."

"Stop it," she said, and tapped him playfully on the hand. "I've had my excitement for today. Shanghai, the Oriental Pearl Tower, missing passengers and a showstopper choir performance."

"You didn't mention the best thing that happened today," he said. "At least it was a highlight for me. A red-letter day on our big adventure."

Helena knew to what he was referring.

"Our kiss at the top of the tower," said Emile. "With my head way up in the clouds above the Shanghai skyline, I realized

I'm falling in love with you. You seemed so vulnerable, so lovable."

Helena felt the guilt wash over her. She allowed him to kiss her, but it was not for the reasons he had thought. She used him to get back at someone who didn't even know she was exacting revenge.

"Emile, I need to tell you something," she said in a gentle voice. "You rescued me today. You saved me from myself and I'm grateful but . . ."

Without letting her say another word, he leaned forward to wrap his arms around her and kissed her, long and hard.

"You took my breath away," she said. "You didn't let me finish what I was saying."

"Helena, if something is inevitable, why resist it?" he asked.

"I can't think of a good answer," she admitted. "Kiss me again, and I might be able to work it out."

Hong Kong, China
Day 79

A GIFT FOR THE SUPER-RICH BUSINESSMAN WHO ALREADY HAS EVERYTHING, read the sign.

"It certainly is impressive," said Emile. "A bulletproof gold toilet studded with more than forty thousand diamonds at a cost of only one million pounds. Quite a gift for the super-rich businessman who already has everything. The Hong Kong manufacturer was determined it should win the Guinness World Records as a posh super toilet."

Emile invited Helena to a trade fair in Hong Kong. "While I'm in the city, I've promised to look up a few contacts," he told her. "I am excited to check out what new and wonderful inventions the Chinese have on offer. Now, I bet there is nowhere else you would have been treated to the sight of this super toilet."

"You would have to be flush to buy it." Helena laughed at her own joke.

Sailing into Victoria Harbour on the Pearl River Estuary and South China Sea and seeing, for the first time, the iconic skyline was as spectacular as she always envisioned. Hong Kong is a teeming international city where old traditional values blend with a modern Western culture. It is also a global culinary capital. Hong Kong is known as the city that lives to eat. Whether Cantonese, Vietnamese, Japanese or European, some of the world's finest cuisine is to be found in Hong Kong.

Another claim to fame, Hong Kong is rated third in the world after New York and Moscow as the city with the most billionaires. China as a whole has 476 billionaires and ranks number two in the world after the United States, which is credited with having 585.

In 1842, China ceded Hong King Island to Britain after the First Opium War. Over the decades thousands of Chinese immigrants settled in the colony after fleeing domestic upheavals. From the early days as a British colony, Hong Kong served as a center of international trade. In 1984 Britain and China signed a Joint Declaration on the condition that Hong Kong reverted to Chinese rule in 1997. Hong Kong was handed back to China after more than 150 years of British control.

The flag of Hong Kong features a white, stylized five-petaled orchid tree flower in the center of a red field. The color is significant; red is a festive color for the Chinese people and used to convey a sense of celebration and nationalism. The flag of Hong Kong was first officially hoisted on July 1, 1997 in the handover ceremony marking the transfer of sovereignty.

Vision Star arrived in Hong Kong late, as a result of the previous evening's enforced delays. Helena transferred from the cruise ship to a local sampan for a ride around the harbor and to see the Chinese floating villages. Lunch was Chinese style in one of the most famous restaurants in the city, the Jumbo Kingdom Floating Restaurant.

Entering a spectacular traditional Chinese red-and-gold décor foyer of marbled pillars featuring ceremonial dragons on a huge tiled mosaic of ancient Chinese scenes—Emile suggested a photographic dress-up session. Together they sat side by side on a ceremonial throne, dressed in emperor gowns of silk, satin and fur with royal ceremonial robes and Chinese gold headdresses. Back on the sampan, Helena and Emile headed for Repulse Bay, a small resort area with a large temple right there on the beach.

Fine golden sand surrounded the statues of goddesses. Helena prayed, "Goddess, I desire love. Please allow me to receive it and make the right choice."

Hong Kong is 70 percent mountains and sprawling country parks, and Emile was keen to take a trip out into the countryside, but first Helena was determined to check out the legendary shopping opportunities on the small, overcrowded island.

She had been told that the phenomenal variety of products in Hong Kong stores was unimaginable, from bespoke Chinese gowns to speciality knives. Every budget, need and whim were catered to—even a bulletproof gold toilet—in a can-do spirit in an impressive assortment of venues. From glitzy malls where the moneyed people shop in chic side-by-side boutiques to vintage dens where fashionistas find hidden gems and gadgets to bazaars and a mix of markets where you can haggle to your heart's content. The city has no sales tax so prices are generally attractive to visitors. Underneath the glass and steel of Hong Kong's commercial enterprise zones is a dynamic cultural landscape where its Chinese roots, colonial connections and the contributions of its homegrown talent become intertwined.

Emile was excited by the amazing choices of art galleries. "I'm still an artist at heart," Emile explained to Helena, "having gone to art school before my passion for architecture really claimed me. One day I'll show you my painting and artwork. I have a huge collection at my home in Paris. I've had several exhibitions and my agent believes I could make a good living as an artist. I rather fancy it will always be a hobby."

Helena told him, "You've come to the right place. In Hong Kong, you can explore art in any number of contemporary galleries. It's a city that embraces artists. As the ship arrived, I saw people of all ages sketching, dancing and doing tai chi. I'd also like to go to the outdoor performance space where they say you can hear local poets read their work to the drumbeats of a dragon boat."

Culture in Hong Kong also means independent live music by the harbor and Chinese opera in a bamboo theatre, not to mention the thousands of shows staged each year in the city's museums and concert halls.

Emile and Helena were ready to embrace the tourist trail and to explore some of the favorite sightseeing venues. "We must go up Victoria Peak," said Helena, "it's the highest point on Hong Kong Island with an amazing view of the harbor." They booked their seats and joined the long queues for the streetcar ride that went up the peak in under eight minutes. The Peak Tram is Asia's oldest funicular railway and opened in 1888.

"Whoa," said Helena. "I'm getting vertigo. I've never been on a railway with a sheer drop like this one. The perpendicular angle of the cars is so disorientating. I feel like I'm forced forward and trying not to lose my bearings."

The streetcar ride to the peak at Victoria offers, on a good day, a 360-degree view of Hong Kong.

At nightfall in the city, Helena and Emile planned to join the crowds visiting Temple Street night market, the liveliest night market in Hong Kong. This impressive street bazaar is the place to find trinkets, tea ware, electronics, watches, menswear, jade and antiques. Haggling is expected and there are food outlets selling clay pot rice, seafood, noodles and sweet treats.

The Ten Thousand Buddhas Monastery, built in the 1950s, honored more than ten thousand Buddhas in incense-filled temples and pavilions. Helena bought flowers to leave for the Buddha but decided against praying her usual prayer. "Dear Buddha," she said instead, "I trust that I will be presented with all that I need. And the wisdom to know what to do about it. The Universe knows my desires. I have faith that my dilemma will be resolved."

Hong Kong prides itself on its cultural traditions, and Emile and Helena were delighted to see a poster for a Banksy exhibition that recently opened in Hong Kong after a successful tour of Moscow, St. Petersburg, Madrid and Lisbon.

"Come on, I love Banksy, let's go," said Emile.

The exhibition featured over seventy original works, installations, sculptures and photographs of the talented British artist. The title of the exhibition: Banksy: Genius or Vandal? Urban art lovers are treated to an immersive experience with an audio visual presentation specially created to reveal clues about the mystical artist, showcasing his most important and recognized pieces. One highlight was the *Girl with Balloon* artwork similar to the one programmed to self-destruct that was destroyed by the artist at London's Sotheby's auction house.

Together, hand in hand and looking for a new adventure, they followed a trail of artsy posters and set off to experience a Chocolate Bliss Afternoon Tea and an "arteastic" workshop. The Lounge at New World Millennium Hong Kong Hotel features a hands-on craft workshops followed by an elaborately themed afternoon tea. The Lounge is a natural, light-filled, contemporary yet cozy, "living room" environment. With a satisfied sigh, the newly inspired artists sank into deep armchairs and ordered well-earned pots of tea.

Coffee and Art—Arts Afternoon Tea and Visual Art Tea Workshop are instructed by famous artist Michael Lim, who encourages the idea of recycling material while incorporating art into daily life. Coffee and Art was designed for coffee lovers to create their own unique drawing with coffee leftovers. During the workshop, guests paint with liquid coffee on paper, combining images of elements from the natural world. The different intensities and strengths of the coffee paint create depth and varieties of tone for uniquely subtle masterpieces. In the Tea-ny Tiny Canvas Visual Art Tea Workshop, Helena and Emile created a miniature watercolor painting on a couple of tiny tea bag canvases. Michael, the artist, guides participants through basic painting methods as well as landscape drawing skills.

Chocolate Bliss Afternoon Tea indulged artists with a palate of homemade cocoa delights that are made with silky smooth Valrhona chocolat from France. Flavors included Chocolate Cheesecake, Chocolate Crème Brûlée Cake, Chocolate Tart, Chocolate Éclair and Chocolate Raspberry Cranberry scone with fruit jam and clotted crème.

"Shall I be mum?" said Helena, as she lifted the silver teapot, ready to pour.

"Helena, I have a question for you," said Emile, "and you must be honest with me."

Helena dreaded what might be coming next. Her prayers at the holy shrines reflected the dilemma she was experiencing.

Emile made a delightful and charming companion, and she could not deny that she was hugely attracted to him.

The other man who featured on her horizon had the added attraction of being unavailable. She had not stopped her obsession over the Captain, but since Emile arrived on the scene, she had at least been presented with an alternative choice.

"What's the question?" she asked, and held her breath.

Emile kept a straight face. "Hong Kong has provided lots of cultural experiences," said Emile. "Which do you think was the most profound expression of fine art? The Banksy painting of a *Girl with a Balloon*; our own efforts at coffee drawings; or the gold toilet studded with forty thousand diamonds?"

Helena loved the way he teased her and the way he was always unpredictable.

"The image of the golden toilet will live on in my mind. It's definitely one of the most unique objects I've ever seen, but is it art?" she wondered. "What I am sure of is if I had a million pounds to spend, I'd buy the Banksy painting, not the toilet. And your choice?"

Emile gave a mysterious smile and replied, "The title of the Banksy exhibition intrigued me. Vandal or Genius? Certainly, I believe he is a genius, but my vote goes to the original art we produced with coffee grains. Those drawings will never be replicated. They captured a moment in time when two people created masterpieces. For me, that's real art."

* * *

Helena challenged herself not to go to the Terrazza restaurant during the following sea day. She sat out on the open deck and listened to his noontime broadcast. "Good morning ladies and gentlemen. This is your Captain speaking from the bridge. We are on course for our next destination, Ha Long Bay in

Vietnam." He proceeded to give the ship's position, latitude and longitude and confirmed the time. There followed meteorological information including wind speed and sea conditions.

She observed several other women hanging on the Captain's every word and his distinctive guttural accent. *I'm betting they are not interested in the wind speed on the Beaufort scale*, she thought.

"I'm not going to lunch," she told Emile. "You go on ahead. I'll get something later."

The last thing she wanted was for him to run into her sitting at the table with the Captain.

"I'm through to the final of the darts' league," he came back and reported after eating lunch. She didn't even know he could play darts but was grateful that he was now safely out of the way on a higher deck in the games area.

"What's the prize?" she asked.

"Oh, there's no prize, only prestige," he told her.

Helena raised her eyebrows. "I wish you luck. Or it like the theater—bad luck to say good luck? Break an arrow or something."

Emile smiled, bent down to where she lay on a sun lounger and kissed her on the top of the head. "I'll come and find you when the big game is over."

"Here is probably a good bet," she said, "I have a book I'm hoping to finish reading."

She hadn't meant to deceive, but once Emile was safely out of the way and on his own important business, Helena slipped on an animal-print kaftan and gold sandals and hurried up to the restaurant, using the rear staircase.

The Captain was also in a hurry, already on his way out and about to use that staircase to go back to the upper deck where his office was alongside the bridge. They almost collided.

"I waited for you," he said.

"Like I waited for you in Shanghai," she said, not able to keep the annoyance out of her voice.

"I'm sorry," he said with a small shrug. "I told you I couldn't promise. Circumstances meant I needed to stay on the ship. There were so many problems with the Chinese authorities. You know about some of them that happened in the evening. From the minute we arrived in port, it was a nightmare. I couldn't drop everything and leave others in charge."

"You could at least have let me know," said Helena. "You had my contact information."

They stood at the foot of the staircase and occasionally moved to let someone pass, usually a staff member or officer. Few passengers used this particular staircase.

"I know you must have been disappointed," he said, and now he did sound genuinely sorry. "If I am needed onboard, I stay. The ship always comes first. I thought you knew that."

He looked upward as an officer began to descend the staircase. He narrowed his eyes.

"I have to go. We have VIPs onboard; they came on in Hong Kong. I'm due at a presentation."

Helena was annoyed that she had deliberately come to lunch late in an effort to punish him. *Serves you right for playing childish games,* she told herself.

"I'll see you soon," he said. "Enjoy your day."

"Yes, Captain," she said, "I'll see you around."

Behind her, she heard Meredith's voice calling out to him, "Captain, Captain, I need to speak to you."

"Not now," he said as he climbed the stairs two at a time. "Duty calls."

Helena nodded sympathetically at Meredith. Since the

revelation about her broken engagement, Helena tried to treat her with kindness. "He's in a hurry," she said.

"He always seems to have time for you," said Meredith. Suddenly, as if a thought had occurred to her, she remarked, "Funny, I always thought you were quite tall; I guess it's the high heels. But when you were standing beside him, I noticed you kept looking up."

"Thank you for noticing, Meredith," said Helena. "If it bothers you that much, I'll do what I can to grow a few inches."

Helena turned on her heel and walked away. Meredith called after her, "Tall men like women their own height."

"What was that all about?" said Emile as he crossed the deck and saw Helena. "I looked for you downstairs."

"I came up for a cup of tea," said Helena.

"And Meredith? What was her problem? She does always seem to have a scowl on her face when she's in your company."

"Oh, pay her no heed. She's doing her ugly sister act, as usual. Which reminds me—if she still wants to change tables, I have no objections to you taking her place."

"Must be my lucky day," he said. "I won the darts' match. And there was a prize. A set of darts with the ship's logo on the box."

"Come on, let's celebrate," said Helena, "with a cup of tea, hot scones and fresh cream."

Emile reached out to hold her hand, and she deliberately transferred the book she was carrying to her empty hand and clasped her tote bag to her shoulder with the other hand.

"Poor Meredith," he said as they walked back into the restaurant. "I think her fiancé had a very lucky escape."

Ha Long Bay, Hanoi, Vietnam
Day 82

"Somali Pirates Attack British Liner in Pacific Ocean" read the headline. The couple who brandished the newspaper report had been on a cruise the year before when the ship was boarded by four pirates. "We finished dinner and, right by the chair on the open deck where I had been sitting, the attack happened," said the wife.

"We didn't see anything," said her husband, spoiling her story. "But we heard a lot of noise and people shouting. The news got out in the press back home and our family was worried. They gave us a hero's welcome when we arrived back. Fortunately, nobody was injured and the incident was contained. Now the cruise lines employ security protection teams."

In his lunchtime broadcast, the Captain made an announcement: "The ship will soon be entering an area known for pirates. A security team has boarded the ship, and their job is to keep everyone safe. There is no need for concern. Passengers should become accustomed to seeing men in black, with machine guns, patrolling the decks."

Helena was headed for dinner when she opened her cabin door and shut it again quickly as two guards passed. A moment later, they retraced their steps and knocked on her door.

"Is everything okay, Madam?" they asked.

"Yes, thank you," she assured them.

"We're here for your safety and protection," the younger security man told her. "You have nothing to fear. Call us if you need any help."

The Qiongzhou Strait, also known as the Hainan Strait, is located in the South China Sea and all vessels cruising in the strait are subject to strict regulations.

The Captain issued a warning, "It is strictly forbidden to take pictures and videos in the strait. Failure to comply with this requirement could cause the ship to face prosecution as patrol ships will be near the vessel."

In Vietnamese, the name Ha Long Bay means "descending dragon," and, according to locals, the gods sent down dragons to help the Vietnamese repel Chinese invaders by spitting out jewels. These jewels formed the almost 2,000 islands and inlets that formed the bay.

Myth had it that a dragon with a large tail tore up the earth and created valleys and crevices that became flooded when the dragon jumped into a nearby lake.

"Come on, slow coach," said Emile, as he and Helena boarded a wooden junk for a cruise in the picturesque bay. The surrealistic scenery and the beauty of the area with its emerald waters surrounding an ancient fishermen's port meant it had been discovered as a film location, and the bay features in countless movies.

"This land feels so ancient and timeless. Stone artefacts and structures have been uncovered showing that ten thousand years ago a whole culture, the Hoabinhian civilization flourished on this coastline."

"If it's been here ten thousand years, it can wait a few more minutes for me," said Helena.

"Tempting as it is to have a lazy afternoon in this island paradise," Emile said as he hurried her up, "the real highlight on this trip is Hanoi City."

The capital of Vietnam, Hanoi, is home to 8 million people. The map of Vietnam looked like a little dragon and the 19 million citizens claim the symbol of the dragon to invoke prosperity and fear.

A subtropical region, Vietnam is home to over fifty different ethnic groups, including the Viet people in the north and the Nam in the south. Thanks to investment from the government and car giants, Mazda and Peugeot, the country has been called one of the New Seven Wonders of the World. The country shares a thousand-mile border with China and Cambodia.

"Vietnamese people eat rice every day," explained a delightful young man who was assigned as an official guide on the tour of the city. "Dinnertime is seen as a reunion time with the family, and it is traditional for all members to be present."

"Seafood farming and working in the rice paddies have been the main occupations of the country folk," he said, "but now there are more opportunities with coal mining, natural resources and organic farming."

On a new expressway, along the Red River, convenience stores offer a selection of Thai and Western-style food. "Food from the south is spicy—they use more sugar—and the north is salty," explained the guide. Helena and Emile happily tried samples of each of the different styles of food offered by happy, smiling people as a welcome to their roadside stores. Each dish was unique and delicious.

A drive through the Vietnamese countryside showed a rural system of small farms where families lived and worked together in communities with chalet homes in pastel colors: yellow, terracotta and blue with red roofs. Farmyard animals, cows and dogs roam free.

Small lakes and waterways fringed with palm trees, banana trees and lush vegetation shelter wooden buildings on the edge of irrigated fields under dense clouds. More elaborate pagoda houses are built several stories high, with only one or two rooms on each floor to accommodate multifamily living. Workers toil in the paddy fields wearing traditional straw hats and pulling oxen carts while up to their knees in water. Cemeteries are an integral part of every village, with miniature houses and pagodas and Buddhist temples protected by palm fronds.

Helena and Emile listened fascinated as the young guide, his face aglow, happily answered questions about the hundreds of cemeteries in the countryside and the rituals surrounding death. "Every village has its own cemetery and these are built directly on the rice paddies," said the guide and went on to explain the reason. "After burial and three or four years in the water, the body decomposes and we open the grave, open the coffin and pick up every bone of the ancestor for a second long-term reburial. Every bone is washed in perfumed water. There is no greater honor than to be invited to help with this ceremony. For many of my family members, I have been invited to wash the bones and rebury the ancestor. Second time not in the paddy field. Now in the temple. And we have a Catholic priest perform the ceremony. We are Buddhist Catholics. And Confucians and we follow the Tao. We believe in reincarnation: the spirit of everything that is alive lives on in the next world. We burn incense and light candles in the temple to give the spirits the life for the body to go on living. The spirits are happy, and karma means that what you are doing now will impact on your future lives. Instead of buying flowers, mourners bring envelopes containing money to make sure the spirit is well provided for in the next world."

"You live in a communist/socialist country. Are there any restrictions on the practice of religion?" asked Emile.

"No this is a respectful place for religion, people are free to choose," explained the guide who called himself Freddy and was little more than a student. "We also follow the Chinese zodiac," he added, now enjoying the fact that his audience was baffled and delighted by his insights. "Houses and graves are painted in the colors of the zodiac and guided by the fortune-teller. But things are changing and in towns now, some cremations are taking place."

"Nothing like covering all the bases," said Emile. "These wonderful people live a truly spiritual life. Religion is all embracing and completely interwoven into their everyday existence."

Homes, temples, cultural and community buildings co-exist and the countryside is alive with hundreds of small pagoda houses, decorated with graceful columns and dancing spires and pointed roofs and elaborate filigree scrollwork in red and yellow. Most public buildings are painted yellow, the color of the sun.

In Hanoi, elegant French colonial buildings showcase the city's elegance, and on the outskirts of the city there are thousands of high-rise apartments. East and West are depicted in the old Asian buildings and the modern Western structures.

Emile was keen to show off his knowledge, and he explained to Helena that Hanoi is linked with seven bridges, "The most famous Dragon Bridge was designed by the same man who designed the Eiffel Tower. The French Quarter is a flamboyant mixture of yellow paint and green shutters, a combination of French colonial and Vietnamese traditional."

Hanoi assaults the ears and the senses with a cacophony of sound, and at the top of its collective voice noisily crashes together the old and the new. Thousands of people in traditional clothes wearing straw hats, tunics and wide-legged trousers are eclipsed by enterprising and modern young women riding colorfully decorated push bikes and pink scooters in silver, five-inch power heels with masks on to keep out pollution. Death-defying drivers on scooters speed around the streets, their vehicles piled high with a colorful collection of goods and squawking birds in cages, and narrowly avoid vendors whose wares, including fresh vegetables and fruit in boxes, are balanced on poles. Some even wear live, squawking chickens as necklaces or handbags.

The 36 Street district in the Old Quarter entices confused tourists to get lost in a myriad of streets that were originally named after the tradesmen who worked there—Tin Street, Paper Street, and Silk Street.

"You take your life in your hands when you cross the road," Emile admitted to Helena, "but we have to do as Freddy advised. Put your hands on my shoulders, close your eyes and trust me. Do as the locals do. Walk straight ahead, and do not stop for anyone. Be fearless."

With her eyes closed, Helena did not see the tall, confident figure who crossed the road a few yards ahead of her. No stranger to the rules of engagement, he was totally fearless and looked as if he had taken his life in his own hands many times before. He walked into the busy thoroughfare, baseball cap pulled down over his eyes and sunglasses in place. Striding out, he walked as swiftly as he did onboard the ship he commanded.

Hanoi, previously called Ho Chi Minh city, houses the marble and granite mausoleum where the country's father and great leader, Ho Chi Minh, lay in state. Tranquil lotus ponds surrounded the campus where the leader lived and worked in a network of small wooden houses rather than in the Imperial Citadel of Thang Long.

Close by is the Temple of Literature, located within five walled courtyards where "men of letters" recite their poetry. Every school student is encouraged to visit the temple at least once in their academic years.

Helena made her way into the temple, removed her shoes and stepped over the threshold. "Removing shoes removes stress and conflict," she was informed about the ritual and "stepping over the threshold of a temple ensures that we must give pause, stop and be aware that we are entering a sacred place where we give thanks to the Gods."

Making time to visit the gift shop had now become a habit. So that she could buy a present for the Captain, she told Emile, "Go on ahead, I'll see you on the coach."

Several other passengers were in the gift shop. "Did you see the Captain?" one asked her.

"No. Where?" she asked anxiously.

"He went into the temple," the woman answered. "It's hard to miss him. He's so tall and the doorways into those temples are very low."

Helena dropped her purchases and set off at a run. At the Temple of Literature doorway, the necessity to stop to remove her shoes and step over the threshold slowed her down. Her heart was beating as if it would jump out of her chest.

She looked around frantically at the tourist-filled place of worship, lit only with the candles on the flower-adorned altar. He was nowhere to be seen. Without stopping to put her shoes back on, she jammed them into her large handbag. Through the five walled courtyards she ran, desperate and confused. How did this happen? He had given no indication he was making the trip to Hanoi. Now he'd disappeared.

At the entrance to the temple gardens, she stopped. Defeated. Out of hope.

"Where have you been?" asked one of the exasperated shore excursion chaperones, hardly keeping the irritation out of her voice. "I'm rounding up stragglers. I think you're the last. I hope so. The coaches have left—the traffic is crazy out there; they couldn't wait any longer. The Captain was the last person to board. They could hardly go without him. Your coach was one of the first to leave. I did the count. Your partner thought you were already onboard."

"What am I supposed to do?" Helena demanded. She knew it was wrong, but she wanted to make out that the girl was to blame for the dilemma.

"Follow me, I've got a plan," said the chaperone, brightening up. "We'll catch them up at the next stop. I'll phone the guide on your coach and tell him you're with me. Quick, follow me. We're going by scooter, you and me in a sidecar."

Helena was too angry to be excited. On a crazy, harumscarum drive across Hanoi, the driver followed the route of the coaches and was determined to catch up. Or even get there before them. Weaving in and out of traffic, speeding across intersections, squeezing down alleyways hardly wider than his motorbike with the sidecar contraption, the driver skidded to a halt in front of the restaurant where tea was being served.

Helena thanked the chaperone and stomped into the small, overcrowded teahouse.

"I got the message," said Emile as he moved over to make room for her at the table. "Sorry, you were left behind. Still, you must have had great fun on a high-speed motorcycle ride across Hanoi."

"Please, get me some tea," said Helena. "It wasn't an adventure, more a punishment. I feel sick and queasy."

"Sorry to hear that," said Emile. "You can sleep on the coach; it's several hours drive back to the ship. By the way, guess who was here?"

"I don't want to know," Helena snapped. Standing up, she pushed her chair back and almost knocked it over. "I have no interest. I don't care. Leave me alone," she raised her voice. "Don't say another word. I'm going to the coach and don't sit next to me. I want to be on my own. I've had enough of this day and of this stupid cruise. Around the world is not far enough away for me."

Bangkok and Ko Samui, Thailand
Day 86

Helena called Emile the next day as the sun was rising. He had left a note under her door the evening before when she was already fast asleep. "What did I do wrong?"

"Sorry to wake you so early," said Helena, "but I need to apologize for my bad behavior. I had no right to take it out on you. You did nothing wrong. Absolutely nothing. It was all down to me. I got lost in the courtyard gardens after going back into the temple. I thought I'd left my jacket on a bench. I was angry with myself for missing the coach. And I took it out on you. Now you know the kind of person you are dealing with, one who blames others for their mistakes."

"You're forgiven," said Emile. "I was worried I'd upset you, but as long as everything is alright between us, I don't carry grudges. It's all forgotten now."

"You're a good person, Emile," she said. "As long as we are still on speaking terms, I'd hoped we would go together on an adventure today, to explore Thailand?"

"If it's Tuesday, this must be Thailand," he laughed. "See you at the gangway."

Bangkok is the capital of Thailand, and Ko Samui, the port where the ship docked, is a resort island off the east coast of the Kra Isthmus, 420 miles south of Bangkok. The first settlers were islanders from Hainan Island who took up coconut farming over 1,500 years ago. In addition to tourism, coconut farming still provides a major source of income to Ko Samui.

The central part of Ko Samui is the mostly unspoiled natural tropical jungle, including the country's largest mountain, Khao Pom, peaking at 2,083 feet. Inhabited beginning approximately fifteen centuries ago and until the twentieth century, Ko Samui was an isolated self-sufficient community that had little connection with mainland Thailand. The island was without roads until the early 1970s. The economy of Ko Samui is now based on their successful tourist industry as well as the exportation of coconut and rubber.

On a drive-by heading into the town—Helena loved what she saw: the beach resort with its crystal clear, translucent still waters. Red-tiled roofed, wooden shacks with a tangle of electric cables, each abode having an individual line. Restaurants and houses made of bamboo, houses on stilts and mountain roads through lush vegetation. The area is alive with beach bars/restaurants and single-story houses. Roadside stalls all have their Buddha shrines, and in the small towns, a vibrant urban infrastructure provides services in retail and banking. Posters for training with teacher monks to learn how to turn toward nirvana, leave aside the material world and be free of suffering competed with posters for Super Fights in the island's most popular sport, Thai boxing. Upmarket beachfront villas and luxury apartment blocks in new developments are decorated with good luck elephant statues at the entrances; red sandstone rocks and a profusion of tumbling flowers cover the buildings.

Helena had become accustomed to seeking out and worshipping Buddha—and in Ko Samui—she knelt at the feet of the Big Buddha Temple, high on a hill, overlooking the beautiful islands and the bay. All around were bells and smells and a sense of peace, as well as elegant restaurants and local eating places.

On a coconut plantation, a red-bottomed monkey entertained tourists. He had trained for three to six months to collect coconuts from high trees by skimming up to a cluster of ripe coconuts, indicated by a twisted rope, and throwing down the coconuts from the treetops. Nothing is wasted on a coconut tree. It is a perfect example of recycling. The tree are used for building houses and furniture—the leaves for roofing—the coconut shell for bowls—the milk to drink—the flesh to cook.

When the monkey tires of working he starts throwing coconuts at his owner instead of aiming at the ground. "You can't make him work once he is tired," says the owner. "He is the boss. I have to take him home, treat him nice, give dinner and sleep, then he will work again the next day."

The view of Ko Samui's renowned Big Buddha sculpture overlooking the beautiful coastline is reached by a series of staircases leading higher and higher. The Big Buddha Temple has become a major meditation center for local residents and tourists and the showpiece is the impressive forty-foot-high golden Buddha. Plai Laem Temple is one of the most colorful temples on Ko Samui island and features an eighteen-armed Goddess of Mercy statue set in the middle of a shimmering lake full of hundreds of fish. Her eighteen hands each contain a different tool or implement for use depending on the problem she is being asked to solve. Her avowed intention is to be the goddess who helps the most people. She is known to be the protector of women and children, the sick and the poor. The temple's design, though modern, incorporates elements of Chinese and Thai traditions.

Khunaram Temple sanctified the mummified body of Ko Samui's best-known monk, Luang Pho Daeng. At the time of his death, he was in a meditating pose, which is the same sitting position as in the sacred display.

After a cultural tour of the temples, most tourists head for the beach. Chaweng Beach has upmarket hotels where beach vendors offer Thai massages, and sophisticated cocktail bars with a bustling nightlife. One of the best-known festivals on Ko Samui is the Buffalo Fighting Festival, which is held on special occasions such as New Year's Day and selected religious festivals. Unlike Spanish bullfighting, the buffalo fight is not a blood sport. The buffalo are decorated with ribbons and gold-painted leaves. The winning owner typically takes home millions of baht in prize money though the rewards might not be so impressive because the conversion rate probably made millions of baht worth little more than US $125.

The Samui Regatta is an annual sailing tournament. The event is internationally recognized and competitors come from all over the world, including Australia, Singapore and Japan.

The area has become known for partying and also for new age therapies and meditation retreats. Cleansing fasts, yoga tai-chi, herbal steam treatments and chakra balancing sessions are all designed to restore equilibrium, and spas and massage offer feel-good factors of serenity. The laid-back lifestyle and relative affordability of the island attracts many younger people and also a thriving community of retirees.

After a morning of relaxing on the beach, where Emile had a Thai massage while Helena chose a manicure and pedicure, the couple took a taxi to the capital, Bangkok.

Bangkok is a mixture of new buildings interspersed with pagodas and luxury developments of residential and corporate buildings. Golden domes are visible everywhere. Old buildings have been renovated and modern developments of shiny sky-scrapers line impressive wide avenues.

Emile took photographs that expressed the contrast between building styles. "I love how beautifully the styles blend," he told Helena. "No one style dominates and you really could not say one is better than the other. Traditional and modern both have their merits."

New modern, architecturally advanced buildings, offices, apartment blocks, financial institutions fill the city to overflow-ing. As in Hanoi, the primary mode of transport for working people is the scooter, which costs approximately US $2,000, new.

Taxis for hire whizz around the streets; green/yellow, blue and pink; while raspberry-pink buses and *tuk tuks*, three-wheeled open vehicles with covered seating are used for extra quick transport around the city, which has a population of 12 million people.

The elephant is revered and a popular subject for topiary on the streets where bushes are manicured into the shapes of the ceremonial creatures. Thailand is the home of the white elephant, and, if a hunter catches one, he must offer it as gift to the King of Thailand because the king is an angel and so are the elephants.

Buddha was a prince in India, but gave up his royal status following his enlightenment. On a hilltop outside the city, there is a gold-domed temple, a copy of the pagoda in India where the Lord Buddha was cremated.

The current King Ramada the Tenth is almost 70 years old, but all over the city he is honored and photographed dressed in his ceremonial uniform at the age of about twenty-five. His official coronation ceremony lasted several days, and during that time, streets were closed to tourists.

The Grand Palace complex in the center of Bangkok, where the king resides with his extended family, was established in 1782 and consists of not only the royal residence and throne halls but also a number of government offices, as well as the renowned Temple of the Emerald Buddha. The palace covers an area of 2.35 million square feet and is surrounded by four walls, 2,078 yards in length.

On the gallery that surrounds every building in the temple, there are mural paintings depicting the story of the Ramakien; the Thai version of the Indian Ramayana epic glories in the momentous battle between the king of the demons and the human King Rama. The story is told of the kidnap of the queen of King Rama who refused to fall in love with the king of the demons. King Rama had a monkey army and the great monkey warriors under his command. King Rama triumphed and took the queen back to his capital city. The paintings consist of 178 sections and have been repainted many times in the intervening 300 years.

The Temple of the Emerald Buddha is located in an area of the Outer Court. According to ancient tradition, a temple for Buddha has been in the royal palace for more than 800 years. The unique aspect of this temple is that it has no living quarters for monks.

The Grand Palace and the Temple of the Emerald Buddha are symbols for the whole country.

Helena told Emile about the philosophy behind the statue of the Emerald Buddha. Carved from a single block of jasper, a quartz stone, which is reputed to strengthen one's connection to the earth and the spiritual wisdom and sacredness of life that exists in nature. Quartz stone encourages the celebration of beauty in the ordinary and the extraordinary and the harmony found within oneself. Used in healing rituals, it supports through times of stress and brings tranquillity and wholeness. It provides protection and absorbs negative energy. The Emerald Buddha wears three different ceremonial costumes, one for each season; summer, rainy season and winter. The ceremony of the changing costumes of the Emerald Buddha takes place three times a year.

Emile, as usual, had done his homework and told Helena, "There are three thousand temples in Thailand, and I feel that I've seen every one of them." On the horizon in the misty mountains in the distance, temples can be seen rising above the small villages.

Helena and Emile reached the exit of the Grand Palace complex, and as they waited to cross, police blocked the road, stopped the traffic to allow an official car into the grounds. Excited crowds outside the palace gave a small reserved cheer.

"It is the Royal Princess, sister of the King," explained a Thai man who was selling tourist trinkets from a bag almost taller than himself that he carried on his shoulder. "We are blessed," he said, smiling. "We see the Royal Princess."

Helena was close by the gleaming black car with a flag on its front, as it swept into the gates. "She looks like a tiny porcelain doll," she described the princess to Emile, "she is dressed in exquisite satin and lace robes and she shines like an angel wearing gold jewelry on her body and in her hair. She looks like a heavenly being and I'm sure it must be a blessing for us to have seen her today."

Emile pulled Helena close, risking the displeasure of several soldiers who stood close by monitoring the crowd of visitors. "This is a sacred area," Helena reminded him, "not a place for overt displays of affection. Don't forget security at the entrance made me cover up and wear a special shawl because they said my ankles were visible under my long skirt."

"Okay," he said, "but I wanted to tell you that princess or no princess, I already feel blessed being in this beautiful city with you, the most beautiful woman in the world."

"Emile, you won't give up, will you?" She laughed. "I'm not immune to flattery, but I thought we had the talk where I asked you to give me the space and time to work out my emotions. I'm so confused right now. I don't want to say or do anything that gives you false hope. We're friends, I love spending time with you, you've made the cruise extra special, but I don't know where we would go from here."

"You mean after Singapore and India and Egypt and Europe and . . ."

"Exactly," she said, "there's a lot of world left to see before I return to London and you go home to Paris. This voyage was not only about checking off boxes on a wish list. It was a quest to explore my life and make decisions about the next stage. One major issue is resolved; others will become clear when the time is right. Each time I pray at a temple, I ask for guidance as to how to continue the next stage of my life as a human being having a spiritual experience. A Grand Around the World Cruise is a great adventure but also a great mystery."

Emile nodded his agreement. "I'm here when you resolve your matters of the heart."

Helena fell asleep with her head on Emile's shoulder on the journey back to the ship.

Onboard they went their separate ways. "See you later," said Emile as the customer service manager approached Helena. "Can I have a word?" he asked. "I'll walk with you back to your cabin, if that's alright; I'm going that way."

"Okay," said Helena, "what can I do for you?"

"Have you received your invitation to the Captain's farewell party?" he asked.

"No, not yet," said Helena and her stomach lurched. The Captain's farewell. She dreaded it.

"It's not a Captain's table, more a cocktail party with food, but it is exclusive. He asked me to invite you personally," said the manager. "The night after we dock in Singapore. I'll make sure you receive your invitation."

Helena thanked him and, once inside her cabin, made her way to her favorite thinking place, the balcony. The sun had begun setting over the coast of Thailand. Gold domes and pagodas reflected the fading rays and signaled the ending of the day. The gentleness of the country touched her heart and confirmed a growing faith that made her spirit, though seeking, peaceful.

"What do I make of all this?" she asked out loud. "Maybe there is no answer, go with the flow and don't question so much."

Helena turned to the mission statement in the front of her journal where she had written: *In the words of the author, Anais Nin, "We travel, some of us forever, to seek other places, other lives, other souls."*

She smiled. *The Captain and I are kindred spirits*; she consoled herself with that thought. *Though we travel forever, people like us know that the search is never complete.*

Singapore, Malaysia
Day 90

Singapore is not only one island but a main island with sixty-three surrounding inlets. Singapore has grown into a thriving center of commerce and industry. Its former role as a trading post diminished as the republic, with its 6 million people of Chinese, Malay and Indian descent, increased its manufacturing base.

Singapore has the busiest port in the world with more than 600 shipping lines sending super tankers, container ships and passenger liners to share the busy waters with coastal fishing vessels and wooden lighters. One of the world's major oil refining and distribution centers, Singapore is also a major supplier of electronic components and a leader in shipbuilding and repairing, it has become one of the most important financial centers of Asia with more than 130 banks. Singapore's strategic location, excellent facilities, fascinating cultural contrasts and tourist attractions contribute to its success as a leading destination for business and pleasure.

While the earliest known records of Singapore are shrouded in the mists of time, a third-century Chinese account described it as "Island at the end of a Peninsular." Later the island was known as Sea Town when the first settlements were established from AD 1298–1299. During the fourteenth century, this small but strategically located island earned a new name, the Lion City. According to legend, a visiting prince was hunting when he caught sight of an animal he had never seen before. The lion signifies strength and power.

The peace and prosperity of the country suffered a major blow during World War Two when it was attacked by the Japanese on December 8, 1941. When the Japanese surrendered in 1945, the island was handed over to the British Military Administration, which remained in power until the dissolution of the Straits Settlements comprising Penang, Melaka and Singapore. The Kranji War Memorial commemorates the lives of the men and women who sacrificed their lives during World War Two, including 25,000 allied soldiers.

Sprawling Singapore Botanical Gardens provides a welcome respite from the hustle and bustle of the city. Located here is the National Orchid Garden, lauded as the world's largest orchid display featuring over sixty thousand plants and orchids. Dignitaries from all over the world visit the gardens and some, like Princess Diana and Barack Obama, have rare orchids named after them.

Since 1973 Singapore Zoo has been known as one of the most beautiful wildlife park settings in the world. Animals roam free in open and natural habitats. More than 2,800 animals representing over 300 species of mammals, birds and reptiles call Singapore Zoo home.

Marina Bay is a place for people from all walks of life to explore, engage and entertain. The local community and visitors enjoy the parks, waterfront promenade and celebrations held at the bay. Chinese New Year is one of the most eagerly anticipated occasions each year. This marks the biggest and most significant event of the Chinese community and it is observed by Singaporeans from all walks of life. The festival traditionally begins on the first day of the first month in the Chinese calendar and finishes on the fifteenth day. Symbolically new clothes are worn to signify the new year. It is also the tradition for every family to thoroughly clean their homes to "sweep away" any ill fortune and to make way for the arrival of good luck. Chinese New Year brings people together and is marked by visits to relatives and friends.

Chinatown, with its stunning street illuminations, night markets and decorations, is the focal point for Chinese New Year celebrations in Singapore. The streets of the city come alive with the sounds of traditional music, the sight of hanging red lanterns and tantalizing smells.

Dragons and lions are prominent characters in Chinese mythology; these characters' roots originated in ancient China when Nien, a mythical beast that tormented villagers, was discovered to be afraid of the color red. Singapore is a vibrant and colorful city guarded by a white marble statue of the Merlion for which Singapore was named Lion City.

Technologically advanced, there are hotels in Singapore which use robots to deliver water and check coats. In the Blue Mosque the sultan is buried. City Hall is in the shape of a flying saucer, displaying the fact that old buildings were refashioned as new spaces. Old British buildings can still be seen with their colorful wall murals. Iconic hotel structures dominate the sky-line and the city is proud of its triple high-rise buildings with bridges connecting the top floors to iconic hotel structures. A toll operates in the city. Private housing has produced 7 to 8 million luxury apartments.

Little India features a dazzling array of gold shops and flowers destined for shrines and temples; these shops close after 2 p.m. because it is too hot for the gods to listen to prayers. Even gods need to rest. Different ethnicities claim their own areas with streets presided over by Hindu temples or Muslim mosques.

The Prime Minister rules the country. Constant improvement and redevelopment are an on-going feature of urban planning—expanding from the center out—with different areas designated for different ethnicities. A Master Plan is in place to reclaim more land and build bigger and better communities. Singapore faces the South China Sea and has a population of 6 million: 76 percent Chinese, 15 percent Malay and 7 percent Indian. The government has enforced strict laws since independence in 1965 to accommodate people from all over the world.

Helena arrived aboard *Vision Star* in the cruise terminal at 7 a.m. and joined a shore excursion for Scenes of Singapore, which included a harbor-front cable car ride to other islands and the Singapore City.

"The government forms us to be Singapore people," the guide explains. "We are happy because they look after us." She admitted that when her husband was spending his wages in the casino and depriving her family, she reported him to the authorities who prohibited him from entering the casino on more than a certain number of days a month and the amount of his gambling capital was also monitored.

Sir Stamford Raffles, a British governor employed by the

East India Trading company, was sent by the British government to found Singapore as a British colony. Currently there is a movement to disseminate information about this founding and to give credit to other peoples and cultures who came before and established the settlement.

In 1965 the island gained independence. In 1970 the British army left, and Lee Kuan Yew became the first Prime Minister, he ruled Singapore for more than three decades. One of his decrees was that trees were to be planted to give shade and this established the fabled Garden City and Gardens by the Bay. High rises, some with bridges between tower blocks, dominate the skyline; the areas west and north of the city are industrial, to the South is the harbor.

After a morning spent on official tours, including civic centers and urban galleries where town hall officials proudly showed off the ambitious and extensive long-term plans for redevelopment, Helena and Emile agreed to go their separate ways.

Emile had promised to have lunch with an architectural colleague who was currently helping with the redevelopment of the city. Helena was game for a cable car ride that gave a view over the whole city. She experienced a sense of freedom and joy, gliding over the modern high-tech city in a cable car that was surprisingly underused on a day when there were no school children around. An extensive network of cable car gondolas stretches across the harbor and out to Sentosa Island, a resort built for recreation. With its many attractions, Sentosa Island offers Resorts World, Universal Studios Singapore, Tiger Sky Tower, Singapore Butterfly & Insect Kingdom and one of the largest collections of aquatic animals to be found in any city.

Helena donned a bikini for a solitary visit to the small beach area and the Butterfly Kingdom. The Captain had told her about Resorts World and admitted that he often spent time there when the ship was docked. "Will you be visiting on this trip?" she asked.

"I have a presentation in the morning; are you going on a shore excursion?" he enquired.

"Yes, I am," she told him, "it's always a good way to see a place if it's your first visit. Before I was a cruise passenger, I always climbed aboard the Big Bus Tour to check out new cities. They show you everything there is to see and you can always go back to explore particular areas that interest you."

"I'm not making any promises," he was quick to point out, "but when we get to Singapore, go on your shore excursion and then, if it's convenient, come back to the ship for lunch."

Pushing aside memories of the disastrous Shanghai trip, Helena made sure she was back on board at his normal lunch-time. She took the time to change her sightseeing clothes and comfortable shoes for a casual, smart navy tunic and short skirt and white-and-navy pumps.

He was waiting when she arrived, sitting at his high table. There were no plates in front of him.

"The restaurant is empty," he told her. "Choose a table and I'll come and join you."

In the spirit of doing something different, instead of their usual place, Helena chose a counter table under an outdoor canopy overlooking the hundreds of ships in the harbor.

"Do you want to have lunch here?" he asked.

Helena wasn't sure she had heard the question right or whether there was an alternative.

"There's an option?" she asked.

"Yes, if we go off the ship," he answered.

"You have time to go off the ship?" she asked.

"I have arranged it, for you," he said, with a smile. "The new Captain is already onboard and I requested a couple of hours off. He's taking over the whole command in a couple of days so I'm sure he will be fine for the afternoon while the ship is in the harbor."

"Great news," said Helena and, in her excitement, had to remind herself not to embrace him.

"Where are we going?" she asked.

"Where everyone goes when they are in Singapore. To drink a Singapore Sling at the Long Bar in the Raffles Hotel."

Helena smiled. "Thank you, that will be a first for me. I know a major renovation has been completed. We passed the beautiful colonial white building with green shutters and palm trees on the tour."

"Do you need to collect anything from your cabin?" he asked. "A hat maybe? It's extremely hot out there."

"I'm a tourist." She smiled. "I carry a hat with me at all times," and she pointed to where her wide-brimmed hat sat on the chair alongside her.

"What about you?" she asked. "Are you going like that?"

"My uniform is okay for you?" he asked.

"Of course," she was quick to answer. "What could be better for my reputation than to be seen drinking Singapore Slings in the Raffles Hotel with a handsome sea captain?"

"Okay, let's go," he said and walked ahead of her out of the restaurant and down the three flights of stairs. At the gangway, he gave his radio to the officer in charge.

"The bridge knows how to contact me," he told him. "You have my number."

"Yes, Captain," said the officer and smiled as he saw Helena standing alongside him.

"Enjoy your afternoon, sir. Madame."

The Captain pulled from his pocket his baseball cap and put on sunglasses.

Side by side, as a couple, as if it was the most natural thing in the world, Helena and the Captain walked down the gangway and off the ship. They strode through the cruise terminal and several passengers' heads turned as they spotted their Captain and identified the fellow passenger, Helena. A couple smiled and nodded greetings. The men looked impressed, the women envious. "It's too far to walk," he said. "We'll take a taxi. I must be conscious of the time."

"You're in charge." She smiled, knowing that whatever he wanted to do was completely fine with her. This was the dream date she had longed for and nothing could spoil her delight.

On arrival at Raffles, Helena looked around and breathed in the opulence of the luxury hotel. "There is no finer hotel in the world," she had heard it said. Now, here she was with her dream lover as they walked through the exquisitely landscaped courtyard and into the fabled colonnade in the Raffles Arcade.

A world traveler, he had probably been there many times before as he circumnavigated the globe, in his own words, "too many times to count." He needed no directions as he walked straight toward the Long Bar where the Singapore Sling was first invented and is still served today in its original format. Never in her life had Helena identified so strongly with the Broadway musical showstopper from Sweet Charity, "If My Friends Could See Me Now."

Raffles Hotel, Singapore, and the Captain, a life-changing combination.

She had read so many times about Raffles Singapore and dreamed of going there. This one definitely was on her bucket list, a must-see place to visit before she died. As it happened, today she already felt like she had died and gone to heaven. Walking beside him, a striking figure in uniform, heads turned.

A mecca of style and luxury on Beach Road, Raffles Hotel is a spectacular three-story mansion with a gracefully columned portico, arched windows and a circular driveway. Housed in a beautifully restored colonial building, the colonnade walkway leads to the grand lobby with its triple-story beams and wooden black-tiered galleries.

The recent renovation of the iconic Raffles Hotel now presents guests with fourteen dining options and a designer shopping arcade, a destination in its own right—indescribable beauty and majesty. This spectacular landmark hotel exudes opulence and serenity. Recognized as a national monument by the Singapore government the hotel lies amidst extensive gardens and courtyards. Epitomizing the captivating beauty of the Far East the hotel has been immortalized by prominent writers such as Ernest Hemingway, this exclusive hotel stands alone as a world-class hotel. With its white marble colonnades and enchanting tropical gardens, it leaves guests truly breathless. Boasting uncompromising hospitality, flawless attention to detail and unparalleled service the hotel is an oasis amidst the bustle of Singapore.

The Long Bar is the home of the Singapore Sling. The famous counter shines like brand-new amidst the décor that marries architecture and contemporary plantation inspired motifs. Long Bar was located at Cad's Alley in the early 1900s. The earthy décor of the two-story long bar was inspired by Malayan life in the 1920s. Rich, deep colors and greenery transported patrons to the edge of a tropical plantation.

The Singapore Sling, widely regarded as the national drink, was first created in 1915 by Raffles bartender Ngaim Tong Boon. Primarily a gin-based cocktail, a Singapore Sling also contains pineapple juice, curaçao and Benedictine. Giving it the pretty pink hue are grenadine and cherry liqueur. It was originally designed as a lady's drink to disguise the fact that women were drinking alcohol.

Passing through the Grand Lobby with its sophisticated black-and-white décor and imposing staircase, the Captain guided Helena to the Long Bar. They perched on brown leather stools under wooden fans on the tiled floor and, following tradition, brushed their empty peanut shells onto the floor to keep down the dust. The Singapore Sling cocktails arrived with little ceremony, as is the style of the Long Bar, which aims to maintain its unpretentiousness and authenticity.

The Captain raised his glass and clinked Helena's. His eyes were never more direct and loving as he toasted, "To the future. I hope today makes you happy, Helena?"

"There is nothing I love more than an invitation to the Captain's table," she laughed. "I will treasure today. Thank you."

Captain's Farewell
Day 96

On arrival at the cruise terminal, Helena took the initiative. Reluctant to leave Raffles Hotel and the freedom of time away from his responsibilities, the Captain returned later than intended to the ship. Dismissing Helena's teasing suggestion that they take a *tuk tuk* or rickshaw, he frowned. "When I am in uniform, it will not happen." Instead they took a cab and in the back seat, so discreet that even the driver could not have noticed anything untoward, they held hands. Still they did not kiss. Helena knew better than to expect anything different. While he was in uniform, that was not going to happen.

"Go on ahead," she told him as the taxi pulled up alongside the ship. "I have gift shopping to do."

She watched in admiration as he walked swiftly toward his ship and in a couple of long strides moved up the gangway and out of sight. She wondered if he realized how much attention he attracted; wherever he went, heads turned.

At a leisurely pace, Helena browsed the tourist shops and retail outlets before making her way back to the ship. Going up the gangway, she ran into Emile as he was coming down.

"Where have you been?" he asked.

"I'll tell you later," she said.

"You missed a trip to Raffles," said Emile. "A few of us plotted to indulge in Singapore Slings and we wanted to invite you."

"Thanks, anyway," said Helena, desperate to get away before she had to reveal the details of her own visit. "I'll catch up with you later."

She knew it was a forlorn hope to be able to keep the afternoon's outing a secret, but she wanted to hug the memory of it to herself before the rumor factory got up to speed. *The Captain in uniform in Raffles Hotel drinking Singapore Slings*; now that was newsworthy.

Sure enough, by the time she arrived for dinner, that was the sole topic of conversation.

"How was your date with the Captain?" she was asked. "We want to know all about it."

An aura of celebrity now attached itself to her and this new revelation ensured that Helena was the center of attention. They were disappointed by her determination not to reveal anything.

"We had hoped for an exclusive kiss-and-tell," said one guest.

Helena smiled politely and left dinner early to avoid further questioning. All eyes were on her as she walked the corridors alone and went to join friends in the lounge who were listening to the nightly classical music. She chose her friends carefully, people whom she knew would be discreet, an older Canadian couple to whom she had been introduced by Emile.

They nodded, smiled and asked, "Had a good day?"

"The best," she said happily. "Thanks for asking."

Emile sought her out, and, after a brief conversation with his friends, he invited her to accompany him on what had become their nightly ritual: an after-dinner stroll on the open deck.

Helena detected a sadness in him but was reluctant to open up the conversation to discuss what they both knew was the elephant in the room.

Singapore's seemingly endless shipping lanes were visible all around. It would be hours before their ship cleared the congested harbor; tankers, liners and junks jockeyed for position, all lit up like Christmas trees to identify their presence.

Enhancing the balmy, warm evening, tropical breezes blew clouds across the sky and allowed the light show from above to mirror the one on the water. Helena and Emile leaned on the railings and watched the ship churn up foam as the waves lapped the bow and fireflies danced on the surface. "Our evening meditation," Helena called it.

Eventually Emile could resist no more. "How was the Singapore Sling?" he asked.

"Probably about the same as yours," she answered, still keen to avoid talking about what she knew he was really asking. "I'm not a gin girl," she commented, "and it was a little sweet for my taste, but it was on my wish list. Now I've checked off 'Drink a Singapore Sling in Raffles Hotel.'"

"With the Captain? Was that part of the grand plan?" he asked.

"The invitation was spontaneous and came as a surprise," she explained, "but certainly it was not totally unexpected."

"I feel like a fool," he said and, with a sigh, added, "am I the last one to know?"

"Honestly, there's not much to know," said Helena, "but he and I are friends. We lunch together, he invited me to the Captain's table and today we went to Raffles Hotel."

"Friends or lovers?" Emile snapped.

"As if it is any of your business, but, I told you, we are friends."

"Did it escape your attention that I thought you and I were more than friends and I certainly hoped we would one day become lovers? You never said that was not a possibility."

"I did not intentionally lead you on, Emile," she said putting her hand on his arm. "You're a wonderful person. I love your company and, truthfully, it has always been a possibility in my mind that our friendship could develop into something deeper. If you are willing, when we arrive back home, I'd love to keep in touch with you and see what happens. I'm making no promises.

"An adventure, yes, a romance, maybe. I'm not averse to that, in fact I'd welcome it. But you must have realized I'm not the kind of woman who is going to jump into bed on the first date or even during the course of this voyage. Have you seen how many shipboard romances burn brightly for a short time, burn out and leave awkwardness all around? Especially when one or the other party takes up with someone else. You mean more than that to me."

Emile covered her hand with his. "Now I think I know where I stand. And the Captain?"

"I told you, we are friends. In a few days, he is handing over command of the ship. Tomorrow night there is a farewell party, presentation and concert in his honor. Along with other friends and colleagues, I have been invited to the cocktail party. All passengers are invited to the presentation and concert."

* * *

Helena excelled at dressing to impress, and she went all out to make an entrance at the farewell party. She chose a knock 'em dead black velvet off-the-shoulder cocktail dress by designer Gina Bacconi with a glamorous ostrich-feather stole. Her blond hair was pulled off her face with a mass of curls at the back, and she wore a flashing pair of real diamond chandelier earrings and a matching bracelet. Her feet shone in silver strappy Gina five-inch heels and she carried a small rhinestone evening bag, large enough to hold a phone and a lipstick.

She was not too shy about using every trick in the attention seeker's book. Pausing at the bronze double entrance doorway to the VIP hospitality suite, she stood a moment and waited for a senior officer to acknowledge her and head over to lead her into the roomful of guests.

Waiters circled the room with flutes of champagne, and she accepted a glass. The Captain was in a prominent position at the front of the room and surrounded by well-wishers. With a slight nod of his head, he indicated that she should come to him.

Helena believed one of the reasons he had become so enamored of her was that she never forced her position or tried to take advantage. As she had decided at the beginning of their friendship, she respected that he was the one steering the ship.

"Allow me to introduce Madame Helena," he said as he beamed with pride. "She is a passenger on the world voyage. Sadly, as I leave tomorrow, I will not be here to sail her safely back to London, but I leave her and all of you in the capable hands of the new captain."

He turned to her and in a quiet voice said, "Thank you for coming. You took my breath away when you walked in. It is as I have come to expect. You are always the most beautiful woman in the room."

It was Helena's turn to beam as she radiated in the warmth of his praise and attention.

The Captain, his guests, company staff and officers drank champagne and ate canapés until an announcement was made that it was time for the formal presentation to start downstairs.

"It's going to get very busy now," he warned her, "but I will look for you."

Hundreds of passengers claimed prime seating in the downstairs atrium, and every gallery was filled with people crowding the staircases to watch the farewell ceremony.

The new captain made a short speech, thanked his predecessor and handed over a gift-wrapped package. "I promise to take good care of your passengers, on the rest of the world voyage," he said. "You are a very popular captain and will be much missed. Enjoy your well-deserved vacation."

Music started up, and a giant net containing balloons was let loose. The female singers of the show team launched into a set of popular songs dedicated to the departing Captain.

The two captains waved to the passengers and prepared to leave. However, one particularly extrovert passenger had other ideas. Dressed in one of her trademark billowing gowns that nearly covered the small dance floor, she barred the Captain's way and insisted he dance with her.

After a moment's hesitation, he accepted the invitation. The new captain fled before they could drag him onto the dance floor. "Me, next," clamored a line of desperate women as they jostled to maintain their place in the queue. Each was about to fulfil her dream of being in the arms of the Captain.

His eyes sought out Helena, and he gave a slight shrug that said, "What am I to do?"

At one point, as the line of women showed no signs of diminishing, he maneuvered his way across the floor to where Helena, stationed by the grand piano, danced with friends. He two-stepped slowly, and, out of sight of his dance partner, held out his hand and touched Helena's in a gesture of such grace that Helena knew why she had fallen hopelessly in love with this man.

The fan worship eventually drove him from the room but Helena did not approach. She knew that she was to have a private farewell with him.

"I will come to your suite to say goodbye before I leave the ship," he promised.

Mumbai, India
Day 100

Bright and early, Helena woke up. Up on the deck, she noted that the new captain was standing by to observe the outgoing captain sail the ship into the first Indian port on the tour: Mumbai. After all the false premises, this time he really was leaving.

A crowd gathered on the decks to watch the activity on the bridge. As the ship glided smoothly into the dock, the Captain raised his hand and acknowledged the goodbyes of the passengers. "Good job, Captain," they called to him. "We'll miss you."

Helena waited in her cabin. She wore a short red dress that he had once commented on and her favorite pair of red high-heeled shoes. Fully made-up from early morning, not knowing exactly when he was due to visit, she reapplied red lipstick, her signature perfume and brushed her hair several more times.

She rechecked that the mini bar had his favorite daytime drink of ginger ale and that the ice bucket was full. The music of the ship's radio system played quietly in the background.

The knock on the door when it came was firm. Three distinct knocks. She checked the mirror one final time and opened the door wide.

He crossed the threshold and, finally, there he was in her room. She noted that he was wearing civilian clothes. Denims, a navy polo shirt, black leather belt and boots. He took off his sunglasses, put them on the dresser and showed her his empty hands.

"No radio. I have handed it over. I am no longer the captain of this ship," he told her.

They stood in the middle of the room, smiling at each other. He held out his arms.

"Finally, I can do what I wanted to do the first time I saw you. I can kiss you."

They gazed into each other's eyes and stepped together into an embrace as he reached down and lifted up her chin.

"Do you realize this is the first time we have ever been alone?" said Helena. "I've waited so long."

"It has been that way, too, for me," he said, "but that was how it has to be. I have no choice."

Helena sighed with the pleasure of being firmly wrapped in his arms, and he kissed her passionately. Their lips locked, and she felt as if she had known his embrace forever. The connection she felt so strongly now translated itself to their bodies, and they held each other tight in a kiss that seemed endless.

Unsure what would be the next right thing to do, Helena waited for him to make a move. It was not what she expected.

He broke off the kiss and laughed when he looked in the dressing table mirror and saw that he had lipstick smudges on his face.

Taking both her hands in his, he walked them to the settee and sat down.

"I have to go soon," he said. "My flight is earlier than expected."

Helena could not hide her disappointment and looked questioningly at him.

"You are very special to me," he said. "I value you and don't believe you are a woman who would welcome me to your room and your bed and then be happy to say goodbye, never knowing if we will ever see each other again. We are friends and maybe one day we can be more, but this is not the time or place. Thank you for all we have shared on this journey."

Helena gazed at him and the deep emotions that had built up over so many months, so many casual lunches, the formal dinners and all those longing looks erupted.

"You are an amazing man," she said. "You have stolen a piece of my heart. This cruise was all about me meeting you and finding myself. I am all I need to be. You made me realize that. I will never find anyone else like you, however many times I sail around the world."

"Come, kiss me goodbye," he commanded, "and I will tell you what I have written in my logbook about you: 'A most remarkable woman walked into my life. I will never forget her.'"

★ ★ ★

Helena watched him walk down the gangway, off the ship and out of her life.

She knew in her heart of hearts that they would never meet again. Their journey was at an end.

Ships that pass in the night and speak each other in passing,
Only a signal shown and a distant voice in the darkness;
So on the ocean of life, we pass and speak one another,
Only a look and a voice, then darkness again and a silence.

—HENRY WADSWORTH LONGFELLOW,
"Tales of a Wayside Inn"

Adrift on the Shore

Expelled from paradise, Helena wandered like a lost soul. Adrift, aimless, in anguish. Fearful of the future, peace eluded her as she stood at the railings and the ship sailed into port on a breezy spring day that blew the hopeful white blossoms from the trees. In step with hundreds of fellow passengers, she trudged the gangway with no choice but to return to reality. Her dream of romance floated away on the waves as the gleaming liner moored alongside the dock and, without a backward glance, turned its attention to the fresh intake of passengers who, in a few hours, would join the ship for the expectation of fantasy-filled days in exotic foreign locations.

She stared up at the small band of officers gathered on the ship's bridge as it jutted out above the dock and imagined that he stood in his place of command. She conjured up his smiling face and lamented the fact that her great adventure was over.

For months after the voyage ended, Helena was unable to shake off her despair. Like a patient with an untreated broken limb, her body resisted healing. The pain and sense of loss magnified and replicated as unresolved scenarios circulated through her mind. Spinning on a constant spiral of hopelessness, sadness reverberated at the triggered memory of every experience of grief and pain her body had ever endured. Some disgraces small and humiliating, some huge and life-changing.

Constantly she replayed the narrative of her encounters with the Captain; day by day, smile by smile, step-by-step, convinced that their relationship was divine and proved a deep soul connection. If she tried to explain, even to herself, why he continued to exert such an influence on her bodily, mentally and spiritually, all rationalizations left only unanswered questions.

"He is my grand obsession," she admitted to her therapist whom she saw regularly as a protection for her mental health and a sounding board for her strange enduring attachment. "I don't want to lose this feeling. Even though I am dazed, confused and mystified by our relationship, the fact I met him gives me joy and I live in anticipation. I'm adrift and need to search for a way to anchor myself. There is a lesson to be learned."

Emile Beauchamp, her French-Canadian architect friend from the cruise, reached out and suggested meeting up on several occasions. She did not reply; instead she deleted him from her contacts file, from her social media platforms and from her life.

Spring gave way to summer and the long hot days transitioned into autumn. The thought of a British winter held no appeal for sun-loving Helena. Action was the answer.

Without warning, on waking one chilly morning, a suggestion she had rejected many times over the months surfaced in her mind. "I must go around again," she said out loud. "I need to make my hero's journey and return to the place where I faced defeat." The decision brought renewed enthusiasm. "There is nothing to lose and everything to gain." She attempted to convince herself that the decision was not motivated by her desire to see him. A traveler such as he could be sailing anywhere in the world on any number of ships. His restless soul ensured he never stayed long in one place.

Reason fled. By the end of that fateful day, Helena was on her way. A Grand Around the World Cruise beckoned on the horizon.

"Go Around Again"

Deep inside every human being is the concept of God. To know and trust that belief guides and sustains us in moments of supreme hubris when to steal apples from the gods is the avowed mission of a heart in turmoil.

Helena knew she was poised on tiptoes and about to throw herself into the fathomless waters of a desire and a wretched longing that promised to destroy her. She begged the forces that be to let her pay the price. Cast under a spell, she rejoiced that to sacrifice her body, mind and soul would bring a feeling of being alive that eluded her, buried as she was in deep grief at the death of a beloved. She prayed to breathe into each moment with the joy of expectation and absence of dread at unfulfilled anticipation.

Caution was for the fainthearted; to treat herself like a patient was no longer an option. "Let me feel love and pain and suffer a broken heart rather than this nothingness," she begged.

"Four seasons ago, the affair was over, melted into nothingness, went nowhere. Analyzed, processed, moved on, tears dried. Then, without warning, the siren call came and he veered back into the realm of possibility. Sign me up. Here I am hook, line and sinker. The Captain is again in command of the ship—my soul and destiny."

Temptation beckoned and held out the promise of a golden future in Helena's consciousness.

First his name was on the Welcome Aboard Newsletter.

Her heart leaped into her mouth as she confronted the reality she hardly dared consider.

Next, a photograph in full color that should have come with a red warning for radio activity. Danger ahead. Transfixed, Helena stood in front of the portrait that was displayed at reception on the silver-framed "Welcome to the Officers" noticeboard. Captain Grigory Petrovich was leading his team. In the photograph, he smiled, seductive, assured.

Helena had been so sure he would NOT be the master of the ship. Not this year. The colleague who took over command on the last world cruise enticed passengers with a blatant attempt to upstage the so popular departing captain. At the official handover ceremony, the new captain had declared, "Come on the cruise next year and I promise to take you all the way around." As if Captain Grigory had let them down by leaving the ship halfway. Whether she was in denial or not, Helena convinced herself, he wouldn't be onboard.

She warned herself, "Don't take the cruise again with the hopes of seeing him. That ship has sailed."

She froze mid-step, like a statue in a children's game, when she heard his voice again, for the first time since she came aboard, over the ship's radio system.

"This is your Captain speaking." She held her breath and tuned into every word.

By the time he finished speaking and signed off with his usual, "See you around," she was quivering with pleasure from head to toe.

No child was ever happier to receive exactly what they had asked for from Santa than was she in those tingling moments. It was as if he had never waved goodbye as he walked down the gangway and out of her life, leaving her distraught, confused and praying that this was not the end—that the relationship would continue sometime, someplace.

His voice soothed her soul and vindicated the emotions invested in hours of believing he and she possessed an otherworldly connection. Her heart strings reverberated with a joyful song of belief restored, with souls reaching out to complete the circle of timeless devotion. Traveling together through the eons, together forever.

On a deck above, below or alongside, he lived and breathed, and Helena dared to hope that he was already planning a reunion with her. He must know she was onboard. If not through their divine entanglements, then through the guest list that he would have studied to identify the passengers he needed to acknowledge onboard.

Be still, wait for him to come to you, she challenged herself. *Don't go looking for him; don't retrace the steps that you know make up his daily routines.* Discreetly checking out the officers on the bridge as they arrived for their first port of call, she kept the white fur hood of her winter coat pulled low so as not to draw attention. No need, he was nowhere to be seen.

At the mandatory lifeboat drilled practiced on every embarkation day, she averted her eyes in case he walked into her line of vision. She savored the thought of a full-on meeting and knew that, in those busy first few days of a major voyage, he would avoid distraction. Work always came first. At the first port of call, Rotterdam, she disciplined herself not to look for him in the Dutch port. A trip to the Maritime Museum Rotterdam brought him as close as she could bear.

Breathe, wait, delay the gratification. Feed off the anticipation. With a supreme effort of will, Helena controlled her emotions and, with grace, managed to walk, talk and act as if she was not a woman poised on the edge of craziness. Waiting for her lover. Waiting for the exquisite pain to start.

Sinking onto a soft cloud of snow-white bedding, she stared out of the floor-to-ceiling windows, knowing she was finally back in his world, waiting for the random time, morning, noon or night when she would turn a corner and see him face-to-face. Only then would the big screen of her life spring once again into Technicolor. Romance alert on the horizon.

At Sea
Day 3

The Captain's voice awoke Helena. In an unscheduled early morning broadcast he had an important announcement to make.

"Ladies and gentlemen, serious and dangerous weather conditions, which have worsened overnight, force us to alter course and cancel the next stop on our itinerary. Instead of Ponta Delgada we are heading for the beautiful island of Madeira. However, despite rerouting, we are still forced to prepare for a severe gale that is forecast to impact the course of our vessel today. Our officers and crew will take all necessary precautions to keep you safe, but we must ask you to restrict movement around the ship in the upcoming unstable conditions. There is no need to be afraid or worry, but you do need to be aware. Please take care and follow instructions. Your safety is our top priority."

The weather warning proved timely. As passengers settled down to enjoy their midday meals, a severe gale attacked the ship as vicious winds increased and relentless rain battered down on the decks. Gigantic waves harassed the ship and a malicious swell created an aquatic fairground that bounced the vessel on its humped back and pitched her from side to side. The ship developed a life of its own and the air was punctuated with bangs, bumps, crashes and the sound of crashing crockery that reverberated across the decks. In the silences between, guests held their breath. Those seated at tables, held on and wrapped their arms protectively around plates of food, glasses of drinks and clattering cutlery. To no avail, as whole meals slid across the tables and ended up on guests' laps. Tables that looked to be heavily anchored became detached and chairs raced crazily across the restaurant floor, even taking their occupants with them.

When the ride was over, guests found themselves squashed up close against other bemused diners in distant parts of the restaurant. As untamed energy and unpredictable movement built up and the crazy rollercoaster ride began again, the sickening crashes of breaking crockery came from the serving areas and kitchens.

Waves lashed at panoramic windows and climbed ever higher on the decks until the surf pounded, curved and rolled over again, ready to restart its game. Churned-up sea released rocks and boulders that flung themselves menacingly against the ship. Anything that wasn't tied down, and even things that had been covered and roped in preparation, broke adrift and one sun lounger hurled itself down two decks.

"What was that?" asked one guest, clutching hold of her friend as they gingerly made their way down the main staircase and past the gallery of designer shops. Frightening the life out of several passersby, a line-up of fashionably dressed mannequins toppled over and crashed into racks of merchandise. Brave or foolhardy passengers, determined to make their way around the ship, weaved from side to side and needed no reminder to hold on to handrails as every step became hazardous. Paper bags hung on the rails, a stark reminder that the heaving of the ship often led to another brand of heaving. In cabins, doors and drawers opened and closed eerily as if the victim of poltergeist activity. Personal items were thrown off surfaces and vulnerable wine, perfume and aqua bottles landed in heaps on the floor. Top deck restaurants were closed and new dining arrangements hastily implemented. Guests huddled together to share stories and eat from paper plates and drink from plastic cups. Staff did their best to provide service and apologized when soups spilled. Passengers, some of whom had a reputation for being difficult, behaved appropriately and accepted the efforts to ensure that, despite the difficult circumstances, no guests would go hungry, even if the meals were not served in the usual elegant fine-dining style.

Helena ate a salad and drank ice-free water followed by a delicious dish of swordfish.

She bathed in a baseless, deflected limelight as her companions praised the Captain and his mastery at navigating the storm. "It's rough but would be much worse if he were not at the helm." "Captain Grigory is the best master in the fleet. We are in safe hands. He knows what he is doing. There is nothing to fear."

Helena was proud of her friend the Captain and could admit only to herself that all day long she visualized him in his commanding position on the bridge—steering the vessel, totally in charge. Nevertheless she still sent silent prayers for his endeavors and for a safe passage for the *Vision Star*'s guests. Alert to sights and sounds of mayhem and admittedly a little edgy, she jumped in surprise at a familiar voice calling her name. "Madame Helena, so good to see you again. Do you have everything you need?"

One of the senior administrative staff from her previous cruise bounded across the restaurant, shook her hand and offered an enthusiastic welcome: "Wonderful to have you back onboard. Many of your friends are still here. I am sure they will be glad to see you again. Things will return to our best normal when this terrible weather system disperses. In the meantime, on behalf of the Captain and the company, may I welcome you, one of our most valued guests. We look forward to ensuring that you have an amazing journey. It's always a different and unique experience for travelers who chose to 'go around again.'"

Helena felt a warm glow and a genuine feeling of being back at home on familiar territory. The previous journey had been life-changing, and she did not dare to predict what might be in store this time. Yet she was determined to find out. Unfinished business left a sad longing in the soul, a need to try to recapture the past, now that she was in the right time and place. The Universe had placed him again in her sights. To come back was the right choice. Now she needed only to see one special person to make her decision complete. She had no doubt the ship was in safe hands, but was she?

At Sea
Day 4

Stationed at a window seat in the opposite part of the restaurant from where the Captain normally sat, Helena was alert to the familiar signs that would confirm his lunchtime routine. A couple of his senior officers chatted and laughed as they finished their meals. The buffet line was closed. Green curtains were in place. She hardly raised her head when a cold wind from the terrace doors blasted into the restaurant and a figure cloaked in navy waterproof clothing entered. He stopped to remove his outer coat, and, when he saw Helena, his face lit up with surprise and delight.

At the same moment, Helena realized the person she so longed to see was right in front of her. Their eyes locked, their smiles mirrored each other, and he held his hands out toward her, grasped her shoulders and hugged her tightly while kissing her on both cheeks. "I had no idea you were onboard," he said. "It's so good to see you. You look wonderful, as always."

Helena gazed at him as if she could not believe he was really there. Her every thought for the best part of a year was filled with him. In every dream she conjured him up, and with every wish and prayer, she longed for the day when she would see him again.

They talked together excitedly and caught up with all that had happened since their last meeting in India. The day of the treasured kiss that had, ever since, kept Helena under his spell. He had asked her a question that day, "Why do you treat me like I am so special?" She wished she could reiterate all the reasons that captured her heart and imagination but it was mysterious and unfathomable. Especially to her. All she knew was that he was unlike any other man she had met; she was totally besotted by him.

He held her hands and gazed into her eyes as they talked, repeating over and over again, "It's so great to see you."

He reiterated some of the information she had given him in the only message that she had sent in that year. A simple one paragraph note of her travel plans over the holiday season, the most likely time she figured he might be in Southampton as some of the ships in the cruise liner fleet made overnight stops en route to various Christmas destinations.

"Did you get my reply?" he asked. "I never heard from you after I told you the dates when I would be on the South coast. I thought we could meet up."

Helena knew there had been no reply. She checked and searched for it compulsively for days after she saw the indication online that he had received and opened her message. She appreciated the lie. "I'm sorry, I did not receive it. Of course, I would have loved to see you."

"You are here now," he said, "that is good. I look forward to inviting you to the Captain's table on the next Gala night. I know how much you enjoy the formal dinner."

Helena smiled her thanks and took the initiative after he asked for and wrote down her stateroom number on a napkin.

"Now you know where I live, you can come to visit," she told him.

"I will," he assured her. "I promise you, I will."

Helena could hardly contain her excitement. She had secured a promise. Now their relationship could resume at the point they had concluded last time.

"You know the buffet line is closed," she stated. "What about your lunch?"

"I had already eaten upstairs before I came down," he explained. "I came to see one of the officers. I didn't know he had already left."

Holding her close for one last hug, they kissed briefly.

Two days later, Helena put the finishing touches on her outfit for the Captain's cocktail party. She chose again the off-the-shoulder black velvet number with ostrich feathers, as he had admired it so much when she wore it to his farewell party on the previous cruise.

Familiar with the cruise ship tradition whereby the Captain offers a formal welcome aboard to his guests by hosting a cocktail party and posing for photographs, Helena joined the line of guests all decked out in their party best. As she worked her way to the head of the line, the master of ceremonies singled her out. "Wow, you look like a movie star. Captain, let me introduce Miss Fabulous."

The Captain grinned. "I know her already, and she is always fabulous," he said.

Helena beamed as he kissed her and put his arm around her waist as they posed for a photograph. "Please forgive me," he whispered in her ear. "I planned to visit you, but I could not get away from my work. Also, I must apologize, but it was too late for me to add you to tonight's guest list for the formal dinner.

Invitations had already been sent. I am so sorry. But you are definitely first on the list for next time."

Helena never lost her smile, and the photographer continued to take shots as she and the Captain held their private conversation.

"I will call you," said the Captain and squeezed her hand.

Disappointment threatened to overwhelm her. She had felt so wonderful before. Now, the evening was overshadowed with a loss she did not even know existed less than ten minutes previously. Helena was not aware that the Captain's cocktail party and an onstage presentation to passengers of the senior officers and heads of department was followed by a formal dinner, though it made sense. Tears of frustration welled up, and she wanted to turn tail and leave the party disappointed by the fact that she was not to be feted by the Captain and join his guests on this the first official table.

"You certainly made an impression on the Captain," said a male guest whom she had sat next to at dinner one evening. "I hope he saw the full picture. The feathers on your off-the-shoulder dress look great but I was even more fascinated by the black seams up the back of your stockings."

Helena felt a rush of anger at the relative stranger who took such notice of the finer points of her outfit. The compliment made her feel demeaned. The seams had been intended for the Captain's eyes. Maybe she should have waited until there was an opportunity for a private viewing.

"It's none of your business," she said, unintentionally aloud. Her admirer looked shocked as she spun around on her high stiletto heels and walked away.

Helena did not look right or left as she made her way purposefully down the silver-gilded grand staircase from the lounge where the cocktail party was being held, stomped down the corridor to her room and was thwarted in slamming the door as it glided smoothly on its automatic overhead closer.

Black ostrich feathers flew wildly around the room as Helena yanked the dress from her shoulders. She cursed the sexy tightness of the velvet material that held her captive as she wriggled and shimmied out of it, not even caring if she burst the seams. Her anger exploded as she snatched up and ripped the straps off a black negligee she had strategically placed on the bed earlier. Her dreams of the glamorous reunion evening had been thwarted. Another excuse, another indication that he would not commit to a relationship he said he wanted but then refused to follow through. What kind of game was he playing?

She cared less about the missed formal dinner, which she hadn't known about anyway, than his excuse of "too busy" to come and pay a late-night visit. What man refused that kind of invitation, no matter how busy?

Helena endured a white hot night of frustration and restlessness until the light of dawn finally brought short bursts of sleep. Her mind was in turmoil. True, she hadn't known what to expect when she saw him again, but a polite brush-off and "nice to see you" might have been preferable to all the mixed messages. To add to her misery, a last-minute change of itinerary was announced. Instead of Ponta Delgada, the ship was to dock in Funchal, Madeira.

Helena dreaded it. She vowed never to return to Funchal, the place of her worst nightmare. The town from which she had flown home with her dead husband's body after he had died of a fatal heart attack onboard a luxury liner docked in the Madeiran capital on New Year's Eve seven years before.

Helena struggled to wake up and was shocked by the first sight she saw. She closed her eyes immediately because floating by her cabin window was a black-masted ship. "A funeral ship." She shuddered. "Why does this town speak to me of death?"

In reality the ominous vessel was a pirate ship. A tourist attraction, not the real thing.

Still emotionally fragile, though she hated to admit it, for seven years Helena had fought to reconstruct a new identity and regain a purpose in life after her beloved life partner had passed away. Falling in love again had not even figured in her plan until she met the Captain. Was she now paying the price for her obsession with the Captain by being faced with the reality of the day she had become a widow?

On a gloriously sunny Sunday morning, the ornate golden church in Funchal was filled to capacity; catholic mass was being said as Helena walked in through the open doors of the cathedral. The priest on the high altar delivered the sermon in Portuguese and, with no pews available, Helena joined other members of the congregation who stood at the back of the church. With her hands crossed in front of her, Helena closed her eyes and attempted to feel a direct connection to the divine presence who had saved her on so many occasions before when she was in distress and despair.

"Dear God, please hear my prayer," she begged. "Relieve me of this pain. For the emotional torture I inflict on myself, have mercy on me. For the repose of the soul of my husband, Antonio, may he rest in peace. May he never be aware or see how miserable I choose to make myself as I demand love from a man who is not able or willing to return it. This man is not my husband, he does not adore me as you did, this is not the love we shared. I pray for release from my compulsion. Show me what I need to do."

Helena took communion and walked slowly back to the ship through streets that were familiar from previous visits yet cloaked in blackness from when she rode from the town to the airport beside Antonio's body lifeless.

"There is a lesson to be learned," she told herself. "Listen to your heart; God will put the answer there."

* * *

The sun set as the ship left Funchal and sailed on the next leg of its global journey. Helena saw for the first time that day the majestic mountains, towering landscapes and cottages, villas and shimmering hotels that swept down to the cliff-like fortress walls sheltering a botanical garden bursting with colorful flowers and plants overlooking the peaceful ocean. She lamented that, as on the previous cruise, she was so wrapped up in her own thoughts and feelings that she was blind to the wonders of this exotic location where her life had changed forever. If not necessarily for the better.

A bracing wind blew cold off the sea, but she braved the discomfort to go outside and watch the sail-away. From where she watched and waited, she had a perfect view of the Captain on the bridge directing operations. He was stationed there when the cruise ship entered and exited ports. High up on the bridge in uniform, dark glasses on, he looked like a movie star.

All best intentions to distance herself from her constant compulsion to observe him sailed off into the sunset. Helena knew she was entrapped in a glorious obsession; when she would escape, she knew not. She prayed that she would find a way to free herself before the obsession completely destroyed her, mentally and physically.

* * *

Drawn like a moth to a flame, Helena made a circuit of the ship and came upon him standing alone in a corridor outside the entertainment lounge. He waved to indicate that she should come to him. When she was next to him, he smiled sheepishly and covered his mouth with a large white handkerchief before admitting, "I'm sick. I'm on antibiotics."

Obviously fighting a severe case of man flu but still gamely carrying out his duties, he waited to go onstage to take part in a question and answer session. With no time to talk, she felt suspicious, already thinking that here was yet another reason why he would not be paying a visit to her suite.

"I wish you better," said Helena and gave what she hoped looked like a sympathetic smile. Sympathy was the furthest thing from her mind. It seemed too convenient.

Another avoidance, though, surely he wouldn't lie about something as serious as being sick.

Again, if she ever doubted it, she had to accept the fact that she was not a priority to him.

She positioned herself out of his line of vision as he prepared to be interrogated by a passenger who in a previous life was a broadcaster. He lavished praise for the masterly way the Captain took the ship and passengers safely through the recent storm. Huge rounds of applause. Next technical questions were about aspects of shipping.

"Captain," said the interviewer, "can you tell us all the difference between a regular mile and a nautical mile? You quote nautical miles traveled in the previous twenty-four hours in your daily navigational broadcast. Also, we would all like to know, how do you differentiate between a boat and a ship?"

Easy questions for an experienced sailor. The Captain reeled off the difference in distances between nautical and regular miles (one regular mile equals 0.86 nautical miles) and used a simple analogy to explain the difference between boats and ships, "A ship can carry a boat; a boat cannot carry a ship."

Career questions followed, "How many years have you sailed with this cruise line? How long have you been captain of *Vision Star*? When did you first go to sea?"

All perfectly predictable, the Captain maintained his usual good humor and delighted the audience of passengers who were enjoying a late-night drink in the presence of his smiling, cheerful attitude. The relaxed, informative conversation was coming to a natural conclusion when the interviewer turned to more personal questions about home life and family.

"Yes, I still live in Odessa. It is a beautiful city, once part of Russia and now part of independent Ukraine. We have a magnificent opera house in my city." The Captain replied to more questions and further explained, "My son is in the national navy. I often took him traveling with me when he was a boy, and he learned to share my love for the sea."

Still smiling, still good humored until the next question stopped him in his tracks. "Are you married? Is there a Mrs. Captain?"

The Captain did not answer. He looked distinctly uncomfortable, then laughed. "Yes always," he said, making a joke of it, but the interviewer was not to be put off.

"How long have you been married?"

He answered with another joke, obscuring the facts, "Many, some long, years."

But his interrogator hadn't finished. "Where did you meet? On a ship?"

A quiet answer, "Yes."

"What was she doing?"

The Captain gazed toward the outside deck as he searched for a way to avoid answering. His first answer was inaudible. "Sorry, I didn't hear," said the interviewer.

Helena wanted to kill him. The Captain repeated his

answer, "She was part of an interior design team, making the ship look more fancy."

The audience laughed. Now their hero, the Captain, was laid bare. He had no secrets. No personal privacy.

Helena was furious. With the busybody interviewer. With the Captain and with all that had been revealed. She did not want to know the details of his private life. Now everyone on the ship knew. If he had ever seriously considered having an affair with her, she felt that possibility disappear before her very eyes. It was impossible to unravel whether she cared that he was married or was more upset that now everyone knew. Truth be told, she already knew. But not the details. Were they still together? Who was this mystery woman? Why the hell was his life so complicated?

She wished she had never returned to the ship. Whatever she had hoped to achieve now felt hopeless. One thing she did know, the Captain was a man of integrity and pride, and he would not allow his reputation to be tarnished. Helena felt a complete and utter fool for ever believing that she and he would develop a relationship. Even a one-night stand seemed out of the question. Too many prying eyes and ears.

Helena returned to her cabin, threw herself on the double bed and wept bitter tears of frustration and loss. There was no one to wipe her tears. She was utterly and completely alone.

Captain's Table
Day 10

Out of the blue, two days later, she answered an early morning phone call from the reception desk. "Good morning Madame Ringold," said the caller, "the Captain requested that you be invited to his table for dinner tomorrow evening. May I tell him you accept?"

"Yes, thank you, I will be delighted to accept," replied Helena. What a difference a day makes. Now she did a happy dance around the stateroom.

First consideration, as always, was what to wear. Second, a spa appointment for a manicure, a pedicure and beauty treatments to ensure she looked her best. All thoughts of other cruise activities became irrelevant. She was determined to mount a charm offensive that he would not be able to ignore. Game on, she had come too far to fail now. And, what if he still did not move the relationship to the next stage? Helena refused to contemplate the possibility.

The Captain was worth the wait.

Helena entered the cocktail bar on the stroke of eight for predinner drinks. Her appearance was designed to stop the show; it did not disappoint. A shimmering figure-hugging scarlet-sequined ball gown cascaded from a sweetheart neckline and flowed down to cut out mermaid panels that revealed, then concealed, her legs. A diamond collar partnered with chandelier earrings shone as bright as her starry eyes. Golden-blond hair and makeup were styled to perfection. Silver-sequined sandals with five-inch heels ensured that her height complimented that of the Captain. The hospitality director's movie-star comment offered an incentive to upgrade the gloss and glamour.

"Thank you for joining me at this special dinner and choosing our cruise line," said the Captain. "You are all most welcome. Please raise your glasses in a toast to an enjoyable Grand Around the World Cruise."

For all his polished manners and well-practiced hospitality, while going through the formalities, his gaze returned to

Helena. He appraised her appearance constantly and smiled with delight.

"Now, please follow the senior hotels officer who will lead you to our table."

As the guests filed out of the cocktail bar en route to the restaurant, the Captain indicated for Helena to hold back. Taking her in his arms, he held her close, kissed a greeting and told her, "YOU ARE GORGEOUS."

This then was what she had longed for on so many sad days and lonely nights. Previously he held back. Not committing. Not showing his hand.

With that statement, a line was crossed. Helena beamed.

"I instructed the staff that you are to sit beside me this evening," he explained. "Not like the last time when I couldn't even see you. Tonight, I intend to keep you close."

The specially selected guests made their choices from the menu, and the Captain ensured that he made personal contact with each individual, some of whom he knew from previous cruises.

Helena made small talk with the lady on her left and held an animated conversation with the senior hotels officer whom she discovered was new to the ship but a long-time employee of the cruise line.

Dinner progressed and the guests engaged in animated conversations.

"Your guests are very well behaved tonight, Captain." Helena reminded him of other formal dinners on the last world voyage. Especially the drunken sailor, a passenger who had embarrassed everyone by stating, "Every woman on this ship, my wife included, wants to kiss the Captain."

"I remember very well." He laughed and touched her hand. "Don't think I forget anything. You looked beautiful also on those other occasions, but tonight you take my breath away. I am so happy you are here. We will have a wonderful cruise together. I plan to do things differently this time. I have thought about you often since I left the ship and we said goodbye."

Helena could hardly believe what she was hearing. All her dreams were coming true.

"I didn't know if I would ever see you again," she admitted. "But my heart told me that there was a special connection between us. I wanted to believe, but I didn't even know till the day I joined the cruise that you would be the captain. There were so many other options. You could have been anywhere in the world."

Conversations around the dinner table continued, and live classical music playing softly in the background created a refined and sophisticated ambiance. Helena's meal was delicious, though, she hardly knew what she was eating. The Captain artfully conversed with his other guests while he avoided making it too obvious that his primary focus of attention was Helena.

"From the first day I saw you on the world voyage last year, I have been aware that you are special to me," he assured her. "I clearly remember the surprise on your face when I asked you in the Van Gogh Museum in Amsterdam, 'Would you cut off your ear for love?'"

Helena laughed as she recalled the memory. "I told you, 'No, I would not, but that I would not stop you from cutting off your ear to prove your love for me.'"

Their eyes locked and passion electrified the distance of one table space between the couple. The Captain broke the visual embrace. "May I come to visit you?" he asked.

"I believe you know the answer." She smiled. "But yes, of course, you may."

Dinner was over. In a well-practiced ritual, guests were invited to take coffee and liqueurs in the lounge. An officer led the way and the guests departed. The Captain and Helena were the last to leave the dining room. He embraced her warmly and as he noticed the hotel director return to the dining room, the Captain explained, "I know Madame Helena from last year's world cruise. We became friends."

Helena was amused by one of the references that had caused tension between them on the previous journey. She did not want to be a friend. She looked knowingly at her host and watched as he reached into his pocket to withdraw a packet of antibiotics.

"You will forgive me," he said, pressing a pill out of the strip and popping it in his mouth, "if I complete my course of antibiotics and do not come close to endanger your health. Much as I wish to visit you, I will delay for another day or two."

Helena could not hide her disappointment, though, she was grateful for his thoughtfulness. "Of course," she agreed. What else could she say: "No, please, don't worry about that, come and share your sickness with me"?

Such a strange romance, she pondered. Here we go again in a medieval dance of desire deferred. This knight certainly knew how to keep a damsel in distress.

She wished she was bold enough to entreat him, "Please climb up my tower and rescue me."

Instead she accepted one more close-contact hug, a good-night kiss on the cheek and his assurance, "I will come to see you soon. Thank you for your understanding."

Helena reluctantly prepared for another period of waiting.

* * *

She had come to rely on spending time with him in the lunchtime buffet, but even that was thwarted when her schedule ran late because of choir practice and he was about to leave the restaurant as she arrived. They exchanged a few brief words, and he asked "Did you enjoy the dinner last night?" Helena nodded. "Yes, thank you." In her handbag was the thank-you card she planned to leave for him at reception.

In the evening she returned to her suite straight after dinner instead of staying on for any of the dancing or entertainment activities. Frustration was building and in the middle of the night, unable to sleep, Helena put on the bedside light and laid out a tarot spread. She consulted her directory for the meanings of the cards.

"Favorable indications of romance," cheered Helena. "Cups are the suit of cards that deal with emotions; they are related to the suit of hearts in regular playing cards," she read. "A romantic reunion is due to happen." And the warning, "Don't give up on a new relationship. It may look to have stalled, but it will come back stronger than ever."

One major figure who appeared in the cards was the King of Cups, a strong, powerful, mature man. Helena read the description of his character, "The King of Cups is an image of the wounded healer, the figure whose compassion and empathy can heal others, yet cannot heal his own hurt in the realm of the heart. Enthroned on the banks of the waters of emotion, still he cannot submerge himself in it, for he fears the drowning that letting go to another might entail. This individual can only form relationships where they are in control and cannot be hurt deeply again as they have been in the past. He cheats himself by refusing to let go and allow another to become close. Although he may initiate a relationship and talk of it as something desirable, the truth is he will not surrender to the world of the unconscious and a mystery phenomenon called love."

Insight from the tarot cards, over many decades of studying the ancient art, informed much of Helena's understanding of human nature and now she felt as if a profound secret of the Captain's personality was revealed.

Snuggling back down in bed as dawn was breaking, she sighed with relief. "It would certainly explain a lot of what has been going on," she decided. "I can't rush him or even find a way to convince him of my trustworthiness; he will come to me when he's ready. The Captain is in control. If the cards are right about that, hopefully they will also be right about the romantic reunion."

* * *

One more day and he did not appear in the dining room at lunchtime.

Helena joined friends to watch a show in the theater in the evening and before dinner returned to her cabin to change her shoes. It took only a few minutes, but as she walked out into the corridor headed toward the elevator, she saw the Captain in front of her. "Captain," she called out, and, although he was only yards ahead of her, he did not respond or stop. Helena was totally confused. It was such a rare occurrence for him to be seen in the residential areas of the ship. Had he been looking for her? Had he knocked on her door? But, no, surely, she would have heard from where she sat on the bed changing her shoes. *I can't take much more of this*, she thought.

In case he was intent on seeing her, Helena quickly ate dinner in the downstairs restaurant and returned to her room. He did not call or appear.

* * *

Exiting an upper deck, on her way to the restaurant at lunchtime the following day, Helena spied his familiar, tall, white-clad figure through the porthole door. At least a head taller than any of the other officers, it was hard to mistake him. Helena moved quickly and, as she walked through the doors, readjusted her navy-blue minidress to ensure that the dress rose above her knees and showed off her long, tanned legs to the best effect in a pair of gold-and-navy high-heeled espadrilles. He saw her coming, smiled appreciatively and stepped forward to greet her with a double-cheeked kiss. This special greeting seemed to be reserved for her as she had never seen him embrace anyone else in this manner.

"I've already eaten," he said and, after a few more pleasantries, he brought the conversation to a close as he resumed his walkabout of the ship and waved goodbye. "See you later."

Disappointed but determined not to show it, Helena took the opportunity to make sure he could see what he was missing as she sashayed up the stairs. She sneaked a look over her right shoulder to make sure he was watching. Sure enough, he was watching.

Helena's reasons for going to the restaurant centered on the Captain, not food. What small appetite she might have had disappeared, and she nibbled unenthusiastically on a tasteless slice of cheese and a dry cracker. Less than five minutes later, he followed her into the restaurant and sat down at her table. "Is that all you're eating?" he asked.

Helena kept her gaze on her food. "Cheese, biscuits and fruit, my lunchtime menu. I eat more in the evening in the restaurant."

Ignoring their previous brief conversation, he again asked, "How are you? What have you been doing today? Are you enjoying the sunshine?"

"I sunbathed this morning," she informed him, "and attended choir rehearsals."

Reading upside down, he repeated the title of the song on her sheet music. "Can't Help Falling in Love." He grinned and asked, "Is that true for you?"

"Of course," she agreed looking directly into his eyes.

"I'm still sick," he explained, "but I've finished the antibiotics. I hope to be well soon."

With no notice, as suddenly as he had reappeared, he pushed back his chair and stated, "I have to get back to work." A fond pat on her hand and he was gone.

Helena was fast losing patience. Leaving her chair to go to collect a cup of tea at the drink station, she watched as he walked out of the restaurant, stopped at the top of the stairs and re-entered the restaurant. At the dessert counter, he collected a small plate and helped himself to a portion of rice pudding and walked back to where Helena sat finishing her meager lunch.

Too familiar by now to have to ask permission to join her, he pulled up a chair and sat down. Third time lucky, he relaxed and gave her time for a proper conversation.

He talked about the storm and admitted, "It was a nightmare. Not the worst, but one of the worst storms I have ever come through. I hope never to deal with anything as bad as that again. Of course, I would not tell the other passengers this; it is between us."

"You know you can trust me," Helena assured him and laid her hand on top of his. "I like being your confidant."

Here we go again, she thought as they sat together locked in each other's company for close to an hour. It was not what she hoped for, but if confidant was the best offer, she'd accept. Back in the cabin, she stared hard into the mirror and told her reflection, "I don't know whether your behavior is noble or foolish, but I think the hero of the storm needs someone to share his experiences. He deserves a confidant and he's chosen you."

At Sea
Day 12

Vision Star had been at sea for a week since the last port of call. Passengers stripped off and headed to the upper decks as the ship sailed into the sapphire blue seas of the Caribbean. Helena preferred sea days to port days. At sea, her day revolved around the lunchtime ritual. She hardly believed they had established it again so quickly.

Her and the Captain at a table in the restaurant in full sight of servers, crew and passengers. Locked deep in conversation, oblivious to their surroundings, anyone could be forgiven for thinking that they were in a relationship. Helena continued to wish that was the case.

She developed another ritual. A night-time one. Not knowing when he might choose to make good on his promise to visit her, she readied the room in case he stopped by.

Cushions and silk quilt were piled high on the double bed, lights were set low and soft music played.

He did not call or visit.

* * *

"How are you feeling?" Helena asked the following day, not wishing to make the question sound too loaded. Without hesitation, the Captain seized the moment. "I am almost well enough to come to visit you," he said. "What times of the day are best for you?"

At last, they appeared to be making a breakthrough.

She pointed out highlights of a typical day but also made it clear, "I am on vacation. My plans are flexible."

"So it is I who needs to make arrangements," he conceded. "I will come soon. I will come to your cabin and we can have some private time together."

"I'd like that," Helena did not attempt to hide her delight. She had waited too long to start being coy. "I am available. You know where to find me."

"Soon I will come," he said. "But first I want to make sure I am one hundred percent."

" One hundred percent better?" Helena asked.

"One hundred percent sure." He touched his forehead. "I am dealing with some issues," he disclosed. "I am trying to work them out. In my head, I want to be sure. I will come to you, soon, maybe," he stopped and repeated, "maybe, yes, soon."

Helena remembered the tarot card of the King of Cups. Totally in control except when it came to feelings. Adrift at sea. Struggling with his emotions. Reluctant to commit. Scared of being hurt. Wrestling with the dilemma. The reason for his reticence. Why he kept coming and going. Changing his mind.

In a flash of insight, Helena saw right through his reluctance. He was torn by guilt and not yet ready to let go of whatever it was that caused him to hesitate when it was obvious beyond doubt that he wanted to pursue a relationship with her.

"I understand. I'll be here when you are ready," she encouraged him. "I'll wait."

At Sea
Day 13

Helena watched him watching her. High up on the gallery, he gazed down at her in the front row as she rehearsed the Beatles' song, "All You Need Is Love" with the choir. He caught her eye and gave one of his discreet, low-level waves. She smiled.

At the first possible moment, she ran from choir practice and continued running until she reached the dining room. At what she had come to think of as their table, a big, burly man was eating a huge meal of sliced beef in gravy with roast potatoes and a huge Yorkshire pudding. Stalking the buffet line and pretending to make her choices, she kept her eye on him and willed him to leave the table before the Captain arrived.

Luckily the passenger was not one to prolong the dining experience. He cleared his plate, pushed back his chair and rushed off. Relieved, Helena stood aside as the waiter cleared and reset the table. Her small plate contained three portions of fresh fruit.

Without even picking up her cutlery, she sat motionless at the table and waited. All around, the smell of freshly cooked food permeated the atmosphere. She had no appetite.

Ten minutes passed, fifteen, twenty, twenty-five, thirty. Along with the headwaiter she checked and rechecked the door, waiting for the arrival of one individual. Discreetly, he watched Helena as she watched him, and they both kept their eyes on the entrance door. Ten minutes after lunchtime ended, he instructed the staff to close the line. Green curtains in front of the buffet counter signified that service was over for the day. The Captain did not arrive to look over the lunchtime offerings or to sit at Helena's table.

The fruit on her plate remained untouched, she collected her belongings and left the restaurant. Food held no appeal, as full as she was on suppressed emotions. Anger stuck in her throat, sadness constricted her chest and frustration made her grind her teeth.

His nonappearance was not totally unexpected. The following day was a port day, the first after a week at sea. It raised questions of whether or not they would meet offshore. Helena was filled with expectations of an opportunity to spend quality time together—walking, talking, visiting museums, swimming in the sea, eating at a table in a restaurant that wasn't overseen by officers, crew and passenger.

Sometimes he went along with her suggestions. "That would be nice," he admitted, but rarely did he follow through and meet her off the ship. There were a multitude of excuses: "We have a crew training session; I have to attend a presentation from the shore excursions team; I am required to meet with the ship's agent in this port; a sailing magazine is coming to conduct an interview." She was familiar with the pattern. "I don't want to hurt you," he told her during their last almost-relationship. "So I say yes, but I know I cannot come to meet you. It is not appropriate."

Tears of resentment choked Helena. She sat in a deck chair overlooking the indigo-blue Caribbean Sea, and hot, tainted tears ran down her cheeks.

"This Herculean hero has an Achilles heel. He is terrified of emotion. A lone sailor traveling the world, he recoils from getting his feet wet in the murky emotional depths. Why do you refuse time and again to accept that he is emotionally unavailable?" Helena berated herself. "He does hurt you, and you allow it."

Kicking off her shoes, Helena aimed them across the room,

and they landed with a satisfying thud against the edge of the sofa. The shoes came to no harm, but a crazy thought crossed her mind—to hurl herself off the side of the ship into the deep, inviting waters.

"God, in heaven, take away my pain," she repeated over and over again. "I put myself in the firing line every day and every day I expect a different result. I settle for crumbs and pretend he has a deeper agenda that involves me. For God's sake, release me from unrealistic expectations. I am not a priority. He could make this relationship happen in a second should he so choose. I am a puppet on the end of a string, an amusement, a dalliance. Please take away my obsession and relieve me of the hurt and pain. I can't take much more rejection and humiliation. These are dangerous waters. Don't let me drown."

Impatiently she pulled the dress over her head, unhooked her bra and stepped out of her pants as she crossed to the bathroom. Naked, she stepped into the shower.

She waited until the water was as hot as she could stand and unwrapped a brand-new razor blade. Satisfied that relief was imminent, if not from God, she had another way of achieving the desired result. The razor blade sliced into her wrist and a stream of blood trickled through her fingers. Scars from her self-harm would join others she had inflicted over the years.

"Better the pain on the outside than inside," was a mantra she had adopted over many decades, her remedy in times of emotional distress. "No-one hurts me as good as I hurt myself," she conceded. Helena was proud of her secret weapon.

At Sea
Day 15

The woman who stared back at Helena from the mirror was one she hardly knew. It was an image of a person she thought she had left behind years before. It horrified her that deep inside her psyche, the self-destructive streak lived and breathed and was able to inflict harm due to unresolved emotional issues. Repeated promises to herself, her late husband and her counselor over the years provided relief, and she credited herself with having worked through past problems and learned to control her emotions so that she could behave in a mature manner.

She was horrified with her recent behavior and fearful of the angst that drove her to act so destructively. Fortunately, on this occasion, the damage was not serious. The first sight of blood brought her to her senses.

"I have to forgive," she consoled herself. "Out of my depths emotionally, I reverted to old behavior. It won't happen again. I know now that I must never go back down into that dark tunnel of despair."

Helena responded to her own pep talk by making a concerted effort to put the incident behind her. She dressed the wound, a small bandage was all that was required, and put on a long-sleeve blouse. "Don't fret," she said, "no one will ever know."

* * *

A shore excursion to the Caribbean island of Curacao offered a change of pace. Balmy breezes and steamy sunshine restored her spirits. "Today is a Captain-free day," she vowed.

"I refuse to look for him onshore." One indication that she

had failed in her commitment was that she went into several stores looking to find the dark chocolate he liked. She bought him two bars. Also, having seen a giant sculpture at the harbor where lovers linked metal locks of all shapes and sizes to declare their undying love, she bought a small shiny silver lock and added it to the work of art. "With this lock, I bind him to me," she declared.

At Sea
Day 18

"Thank you, singers," said the choir master. "You did a great job today. Tomorrow, a new song. We hope to have six songs for our theater presentation before Sydney, Australia."

Helena debated whether to go to the restaurant or not. She intended to punish him for not coming the previous day and for the fact that the rejection drove her back to old, destructive actions. She readjusted the bandage under her sleeve to make sure it was not too noticeable. "Shall I? Shall I not go upstairs?" She struggled with the answer even while she knew that she would not miss the opportunity to see him.

Minutes after she collected her food and sat at the table, he appeared. No pretense at checking the food or talking to waiters, nodding and smiling to passengers, he headed straight for her table.

He looked so handsome in his tropical white suit with the four gold stripes on the epaulet that she smiled. "How are you?" he asked as he folded his tall frame into a dainty white wrought-iron chair. "I looked for you at the lifeboat drill this morning, but you were nowhere to be seen. Which muster station are you called to?"

The fact that he looked for her, as she did for him, constantly, took away the niggling annoyance she felt toward him. "Alpha, in the theater, Lifeboat Three. I can assure you I was there."

"Okay," he said. "Is everything alright?"

Helena was tempted to tell the truth: "I was so upset you didn't come to lunch the other day that I went home and slashed my wrists. It makes me feel better when I release the pain."

Instead she told him, "My life is very busy. I have a new passion."

His eyes narrowed and he asked, "What does that mean?"

"I've taken up painting," she explained. "The onboard art classes are excellent. I really like the art teacher and his way of describing the techniques and processes of various kinds of art. Yesterday in Curacao, I did my first official sketch. Sitting on the harbor wall, I sketched the colored houses that the island is famous for and even managed to paint the Bulgari jewelry building."

"Well done," he congratulated her. "I like to know you are happily engaged, and learning something new is a great use of your time on the voyage. Perhaps you have a hidden talent as an artist."

All the time he talked, he leaned into Helena and frequently touched her on the hand. The restaurant no longer existed, they were both so totally focused on each other.

They gazed into each other's eyes and smiled together. At those moments, the relationship Helena sometimes doubted they had was so vibrant, so tactile that the world reduced down to embrace only the two of them. Completely absorbed. Food uneaten, tea grown cold. This was the romance Helena envisioned with him. He flirted, complimented her and looked at her with such longing that she knew he craved her as much as she did him.

"You have beautiful eyes," he told her. "I remembered that about you. I want to keep looking at you. I want to be able to explain how special you are to me. You are a distinguished person," he told her, "a very classy lady and I love being with you."

Desire drove her boldness, and Helena asked, "Why don't you come to see me?"

"It's complicated." He sighed. "There are problems I need to resolve. When I am fit physically and my head is sorted out, I promise I will come. Do you think there is any reason why I would not want to be close to you? I am so happy to have you here on my ship."

Deep down Helena believed she knew the reasons, but they never properly discussed his personal life, and she cautioned herself not to pry. By forcing the issue, she was concerned she would uncover things she would prefer not to know. "I trust your judgment," she said. "When you are ready, you will take the right action."

She reached into her handbag. "I bought you a present onshore yesterday. The black chocolate you said you liked."

"You are very kind." He patted her hand. "With my coffee in the morning, I like one or two squares of this dark chocolate. It is good for the heart, and now I will remember every day that Helena gave me this gift."

"Do you want me to leave the package at reception? I know you don't like to carry anything," she recalled from previous times when she had presented him with gifts.

"It is fine. I can carry," he said. "You always spoil me. I remember all the gifts you gave me on the last voyage: the Samurai warrior badge, a brass compass, a jeweled elephant. I never forget anything about you. You are an extra special person," he told her.

Helena chose that moment to answer the question the Captain had asked on the one and only occasion he had come to her suite on the previous voyage. Then they had shared their first kiss. She still sighed at the memory.

"You asked me why I am so enamored of you," she reminded him. "I want to give you the answer." His powerful masculine smell and presence were too close to be ignored, and he gazed at her so expectantly that her thoughts went into a tailspin and she felt light-headed.

"In the seven years since my husband died, there has been no other man," she told him. "When men ask to date me, I make it clear straightaway that I am not interested. But with you, the first day I saw you, I fell under your smell. I was fascinated by you. That has not changed, over a year later. You are the most impressive man I have ever met. You are a hero and so much more."

She blushed. He laughed. "Thank you for telling me," he said. "You may like to know that is how I felt about you. I noticed you the first day you arrived on my ship. We cannot deny the attraction we have for each other. Let us see how it develops. *Vision Star* is not only on a cruise around the world, you and I are on a journey."

Cartagena, Colombia
Day 20

The city of Cartagena, a major port, was founded in 1533. It is located on the northern coast of Colombia in the Caribbean coast region, strategically placed between the Magdalena and Sinu Rivers. Cartagena became the main port for trade between

Spain and its overseas empire and its importance was established by the early 1540s.

During the colonial era, it was a major port for the export of Peruvian silver to Spain. It is the fifth largest city in Colombia. Economic activities include the maritime and petrochemicals industries as well as tourism. In recent decades, Cartagena has expanded dramatically and is now surrounded by vast suburbs and high-rise buildings. Despite increasing urban sprawl, the walled Old Town has remained virtually unchanged.

It was to the Old Town that Helena headed as soon as she left the ship, and hailed a taxi outside the port gates. In her mind's eye she remembered the fine displays of Colombian lingerie seen on a previous visit. From there she would buy the Captain's latest gift, though, it would not be appropriate to hand it over in the dining room or leave it at reception to be delivered to him.

Anticipating the day, or evening, when he finally made the decision to visit, Helena spent a long time finding exactly the right underwear. The specialist shop was a treasure trove of gorgeous, sophisticated, sexy underwear. A tall, beautiful, dark-haired Colombian sales assistant invited Helena into the sensual luxury of an exclusive dressing area. Red velvet curtains screened from view a mirrored boudoir reflecting delicate gold-en-gilt furniture and a glittering chandelier. "Your husband, he can help you decide," the girl, who spoke little English but smiled a lot, said as she indicated the dainty silver chaise lounge.

"Thank you, but he's still on the ship," Helena explained. A sign in the window offered discounts to cruise passengers. Helena stripped off and began the pleasurable task of working her way through a specially chosen selection of jewel-colored silk, satin and lace underwear. The double-mirrored cubicle ensured a 360-degree view.

I wish he were here to help me decide, thought Helena. *He could make his informed choice between the black satin balcony bra with vibrant red edges or the red lace with neon-pink frills. Maybe he would say, "Take both and also the sheer violet set with golden ties."*

"I'll take these three," said Helena, already smiling at the thought of his appreciative eyes on her slim, tanned body in the exotic South American lingerie. She handed over her gold American Express card without considering the price. No expense was too high to enhance the act of seduction for which she had waited so long. "Gift wrapped, please."

Mission completed, she returned to the ship clutching her small package of purchases in a black-and-gold carrier.

* * *

"Did you enjoy your day in Cartagena? What did you do?" he asked as he passed her dining table that evening and stopped briefly as he was exiting and she was entering.

Helena smiled. "Shopping and sightseeing. Usual cruise ship passenger occupations." They had both chosen to go to the buffet for casual dining, a choice many passengers made on shore excursion days.

"I'm tired," he said. "I've been up since five a.m. and have another dawn start tomorrow. One of the officers and I came for an early dinner."

She could not deny that he looked weary, and she knew his schedule was punishing. One indicator that he was on duty for too many long hours was that his beard growth was showing.

Helena was tempted to tease him, "The gift I bought for you today would soon wake you up," but the staff officer was within earshot. "You need to get a good night's rest," she sympathized. "The passage of the Panama Canal day after tomorrow is such a long day and tiring even for the passengers. You need to be one hundred percent fit."

"Thank you for your concern." He smiled. "You are very kind. I need to go now."

* * *

Unlike the previous world cruise the year before when Helena often went for days without seeing him around the ship, now their paths crossed with surprising regularity. The following morning after the ship docked in their next port of call, Colon, Panama, Helena left her cabin on the way to breakfast and, as she stepped into the corridor, he was a few feet away and coming toward her.

Moving fast, following a man in white overalls, he explained, "Can't stop. I'm running," and disappeared into one of the crew only doors.

The day was hot, steamy and intermittent rain showers gave Helena an excuse not to go ashore. She had been to Colon before and was not impressed. The main reason for their port of call was to refuel the ship before traversing the two oceans through the Panama Canal. The refueling vessel was alongside *Vision Star* for most of the daylight hours.

The ship was eerily empty as most passengers went ashore to explore. Helena appeared almost alone in her assessment that there was little of interest to see, and she enjoyed a commitment-free day with no activities or classes to attend.

The theater was almost empty as she attended a lecture on the monumental building and operating phenomena of the Panama Canal, one of the two most strategic artificial waterways in the world; the other was the Suez Canal. The lecturer, a former airline pilot and university professor, explained, "Work on the man-made Panama Canal, now often considered the Eighth Wonder of the World, began in 1881, but the hugely ambitious engineering project, started by France, ran into problems and was eventually taken over by the United States. The USA, in 1904, started one of the largest and most challenging excavation projects ever undertaken and completed the forty-eight miles of locks in 1914. The gigantic undertaking allowed ships to more easily sail between the east and west coasts of the United States, which otherwise would have to round Cape Horn in South America. Vessels shorten their journey by about eight thousand nautical miles. It takes between six and eight hours to traverse the canal, and every day thousands of ships make the journey as the locks raise and lower them high enough above sea level to travel between the Atlantic Ocean and the Pacific Ocean."

The lecturer encouraged the audience to remember the palindrome, a grammatical device where words read the same backward as forward, A MAN A PLAN A CANAL PANAMA.

Helena needed no reminder. She used those very words to encourage the Captain to remember her the year before when the Grand Around the World Cruise made the passage of the canal.

"Are you familiar with this word game, Captain?" she asked as she approached his lunch table the day after he took the ship, guided by a Panama Canal pilot, through the canal. Written on one of her signature gold-rimmed Cartier cards, Helena handed over the words, A MAN A PLAN A CANAL PANAMA. He read through them a couple of times. Then he burst out laughing and told her, "Very clever. I shall keep this. You never fail to impress me, thank you."

Helena credited the Panama palindrome with raising his interest in her to the point where, a few days later, he moved from his usual lunchtime position at a high table in the center of the dining room to approach her table, and ask, "May I join you?"

A year later to the day, as the ship crossed the Panama Canal, she awaited the next stage of their relationship to develop. Without a doubt, this was the longest courtship she had ever known. One kiss, a bouquet full of compliments and repeated promises. She wished this man would have a plan.

At Sea
Day 22

"Everyone is in love with our Captain," said the beauty therapist as she applied scarlet nail polish to Helena's newly manicured hands. "Really," said Helena noncommittally. She wondered if one of the spa therapists reported seeing her sharing a table with him at the lunchtime buffet. The waitstaff were all aware of the situation, and a couple of passengers made remarks that might be considered criticism.

One even barged in on their private conversation. The solidly built busybody passenger who wore a dress that billowed out like a sail and made her resemble a galleon in full flight smiled while dripping resentment. "My husband was the chief engineer on cruise liners for over thirty years," she proclaimed in an attempt to imbue herself with her husband's status. "He would never willingly sit down with a passenger. It was bad enough that he was forced to sit at the officer's table and entertain all the old, rich guests. Much as he loved his job on the ships, he hated the socializing he was required to undertake because of his seniority."

The Captain turned on the full force of his charm and defused the situation by giving her the attention she demanded.

He engaged her in conversation about her husband's service, and she left smiling. Another woman, who hovered out of his line of vision for a few minutes while she worked out how to approach, finally pushed herself up close to the table and stated, "I didn't expect to see you here, Captain. There were a few things I wanted to discuss with you. Is this a good time?"

"Maybe later," he smiled. "I am on my rounds and need to leave now."

She looked from him to Helena and pursed her lips as she walked away.

A young waitress took advantage of the line of people vying for the Captain's attention. "Is okay, Captain, if I have a word?" she asked. "Of course," he said and stood up to listen to her complaint about the fact that she and her boyfriend had not been granted time off together at the last port. From his elevated height of six feet six inches, he bent his head down to her dainty five-foot height. He listened while she stated her initial case and, having got his attention, went on to make mention of other complaints about her working conditions.

"Leave it to me," he said.

The young woman's head of department watched but, without directly interfering, cast a look in her direction that said plainly, "Okay, you've had you say." It took a while for her to respond to the silent order that it was time to get back to work.

"Sorry, I do have to go," he apologized to Helena. "I didn't even get a chance to ask what you've been doing today."

"Art classes," responded Helena. "The teacher is great. I'm really enjoying it."

"Good, good," he said, and patted her on the shoulder. Lowering his voice, now that their table had taken on the appearance of a drop-by center, he smiled conspiratorially. "I will come to see you in the next couple of days. Let me check my schedule."

Helena refused to respond with too much enthusiasm. She'd been down this path too many times before. She almost shrugged a "Whatever," but instead told him, "You know where I live. I'm not going anywhere."

* * *

Head bent deep in concentration on the piece of art she was coloring, Helena did not see him enter the arts and crafts room. But she could not ignore the chorus of excited voices, "Hello, Captain. Have you come to join the art class? Here, sit beside me."

In two voyages, she had never seen him enter the craft studio. She smiled. He was keeping tabs on her. Wherever she said she would be, he managed to find a reason to stop by.

"If only he would take our relationship to the next level." She sighed. "Sometimes I fear he will keep finding excuses not to come to visit until the day he leaves the ship, whenever that may be." She refused to ask, knowing from experience that however firm the arrangements for his departure, they were liable to change right up to the last minute.

At Sea, Sunday
Day 25

Sunday, a day of rest, maybe he would choose that day to follow through on his promise.

Taking advantage of the warm sunshine, a gift for having sailed into the sparkly blue Pacific Ocean, Helena stretched out on a sunbed close to the pool and used the holy day to pray, "Please, please, please, please, please God. What can I do to convince you that I need to get close to him? I need to have him make love to me. I've waited so long. I crave him. Please, please, please, please. I don't know what else to say. I know it's not the right thing to do, to keep petitioning you to plead and beg and entreat when you already know my heart's desire and reward according to need, not want. But, please let me know if there is anything I can do to make you grant my wishes."

She pulled out all the stops in getting ready for their regular lunchtime assignation. The first time he had seen the outfit she chose, he complimented her. "You sure know how to dress to get my attention."

She wore a tight-fitting, vibrant-red V-neck sweater that showed off her curves, a figure-hugging black miniskirt and Valentino studded high heels.

The red color was a testimony to the Chinese Dragon Lady whose extravagant boudoir she had visited in the Grand Palace. The infamous Dragon Queen, who had won the heart of an emperor.

"One captain shouldn't be too hard to capture," Helena assured herself.

In the packed dining room, the female passenger who was insistent on trying to make the Captain notice her had taken ownership of the table where Helena and the Captain sat every day. Perched on a high stool at the lunch counter, Helena awaited his arrival and hoped a table would become available. It didn't. The woman sat alone at the table; she had no food or drink.

"Captain." The woman smiled as he came through the doors. "You were too busy yesterday. Can I talk to you today?"

"I will come over before I leave," he said.

Helena seethed but tried not to show it. She knew how courteous he always was to the passengers. To show her annoyance would not be appropriate. "Smile if it kills you," she reminded herself.

"I looked in at the art class this morning," he told her. "I didn't see you."

"I was there," she said, trying to keep the petulance she felt out of her voice.

"I thought I'd missed it," he said. "I slept till 10 a.m. That never happens, but I was exhausted after the Panama Canal and three dawn starts in the last three days."

"Did you have your dark chocolate with your morning coffee?" she asked, determined to remind him of their special relationship. He leaned against her chair but did not sit down.

"Tomorrow is a formal night," he informed her. "I am hosting a table. If you agree, and have no plans after your own dinner, may I come to see you? It would be good to spend some private time together."

Annoyance melted away and a smile brightened Helena's face. "I have no plans. You are welcome to come visit. I look forward to it."

"I have to talk to these people." He raised his eyebrows. "Tomorrow."

* * *

Helena lay on her bed to meditate. She blocked out all noise with headphones that played relaxing pan pipe sounds to allow her to concentrate and a frilly eye mask to block out the sunshine.

"Be careful what you wish and pray and beg for," she warned as her body angst set in. *He's never seen me with my clothes off. What if he's disappointed? We've only kissed. What if we don't fit together. He's so tall. What if my body is not up to the job? Is it like riding a bike? Is it true that you never forget? It's been seven years and then some since I last had sex. What if I don't remember how to do it? What the hell am I going to wear? Can I switch the lights off? Dive under the covers? Oh no, what have I let myself in for? I'm practically a virgin. Surely after seven years, I'm born again? Renewed. Restored. HELP.*

Captain's Table
Day 30

Canceled. The ship went into lockdown due to a virus, a common bacterial virus that strikes without warning. Within a day, dozens of passengers became infected.

The Captain phoned her cabin at the time his formal dinner would normally end. He had a predictable routine: finish dinner and then do a walkabout of the communal and entertainment areas. Helena rushed from her own dinner and dressed in a sexy little black dress with black-and-red underwear.

He called, "Helena, this is Grigory, the Captain. I'm sorry, but I cannot come to see you. We all have to take extra precautions to protect ourselves from this virus. Many passengers are sick, and I need to do whatever is necessary to keep well."

Helena ticked off yet another excuse but had to admit there was a legitimacy to what he was saying. "I understand," she said, disappointment in her faux relationship with him had become a most unattractive feeling. She tried to shake it off. A sulky voice was not appropriate.

"How are you?" he asked. "How was your evening?"

"Better if I could see you," she admitted.

"I know," he said, "but this is serious. We need to avoid infection."

Helena finally felt ready to let go. She had tried so hard to control the situation. *Maybe it really was not meant to be. I surrender. This is the end of the road. I see no way back from all these false starts.*

* * *

She wished he had been honest from the start and admitted their relationship would go nowhere. Whatever the facts of the matter, virus or not, he always made an excuse to not follow through with his commitment. It was over. Time to get real and accept that the cruise must take on a life of its own, without him. Bye, bye, Captain.

Helena felt sick. And so did at least another hundred guests. Norovirus, a bacterial illness, known to affect cruise ship passengers, was present on the *Vision Star* and about to get worse.

Overnight the ship was subjected to stringent sickness preventative measures, and an army of staff wearing white plastic hazmat suits overran the ship cleaning, wiping down and spraying antibacterial fluids on every inch of the ship's surface. Passengers were instructed to implement increased standards of hygiene regarding hand washing and to resist personal contact. Sanitized sprays were administered by staff at every entranceway to restaurants, cafes and bars. On every staircase, in elevators, in restrooms and in dining areas, crew members worked twenty-four/seven to wash, scrub, spray.

As the problem increased and the number of passengers affected rose each day, large areas of the ship became subject to closure or quarantine. Pools, Jacuzzis, the gym, the launderette. Entertainment events and activities changed venues to areas considered easier to maintain and manage, or they were canceled altogether.

The upstairs buffet closed to allow staff to fumigate and perform a major cleaning process. Crew members on the cleaning details worked double shifts and all personnel undertook extra duties. Passengers with any indication of symptoms potentially linked to the norovirus sickness faced enforced cabin isolation for forty-eight hours. To aid recovery, all meals were to be taken in the cabins and only restricted diets with bland food were on the menu.

Helena opened her cabin door to yet another white-suited man who looked like he had landed from Mars. "Your dinner, Madame," he said through his mask. "Did you enjoy?"

"Thank you, yes, as much as you can enjoy hot water broth, sugar-free fruit jelly and tea with no milk."

The visitors from outer space arrived regularly to deliver food, clear away, clean the cabin and check if there were any special requirements. A member of the medical team visited a couple of times a day. On her first visit, the young henna-haired nurse carried out well-versed instructions.

Helena attempted to illicit information by commenting, "You seem to be very busy. It is a couple of hours since I was told you were on your way. Are a large number of passengers reporting symptoms?"

"We are busy with many medical matters," the nurse's tone was firm as she brought that line of questioning to a close. "You are confined to your cabin. You are not allowed outside for any reason, not even into the corridor, and you will have no personal visitors. Take the medication as prescribed, drink lots of water and rest. You are to be isolated for forty-eight hours. Then we will review. Hopefully, you will soon recover. If you need anything, call reception and they will contact us."

She moved with speed, carried out her duties efficiently and was soon on her way. "Also." She stopped at the cabin door. "Please fill out the feedback form in as much detail as you can remember. We need to know how the virus is being spread."

Helena followed instructions, took the medication, ate her tasteless meal and rested.

She was grateful for her private balcony, which added an extra dimension to the cabin and allowed her to breathe fresh air and stretch out on a sun lounger as if she were simply enjoying a relaxing day at sea without care or worry.

It was a relief to be isolated from the daily round of ship's activities where passengers congregated to gossip while trying to outdo each other with horror stories of their norovirus experiences. "I was on a voyage when 500 passengers went down with norovirus." "My ship returned to port from a cruise in the Caribbean because there were so many sick passengers." "People died every day on my last cruise."

Helena's illness came on suddenly after dinner one evening in the first week the norovirus had been detected on the ship. Her symptoms were thankfully mild. To report the occurrence was obviously the responsible thing to do, but she wished her cabin number did not have to appear on the roll call of sick passengers. Following the initial uncomfortable onset of symptoms, she was left with a headache and dehydration. Both easily fixed. Within twelve hours, she was symptom free.

The day before she was taken ill, the Captain sought her out in the dining room. He appeared in the buffet, which was then still open for business, and joined her table. She smiled, happy to see him, despite good intentions to sever all ties. True, she was, as usual, still sitting at their preferred table, but she had convinced herself that he would stay in the confines of his working area—the bridge and his private quarters—until the virus crisis passed. She had not expected him to be downstairs mixing with passengers and increasing his chances of picking up the illness.

"I'm sorry I had to make that late-night phone call," he apologized. "The virus was detected and I was forced to implement an emergency course of action."

"Thank you for telling me," said Helena and gave him a long, hard look as she added, "I was worried it was personal. That you found a reason for not wanting to come to visit me."

He shook his head. "You really don't understand how I feel about you, do you?"

"How can I?" Helena tried not to sound angry. "We never have a normal conversation. We sit at this silly little table, surrounded by passengers and staff all highly interested in why the Captain singles out one person to sit with every day. For a year now, on this world cruise and the last, you have gazed into my eyes and asked me in a deep, meaningful voice, 'How are you?' and I tell you, 'Always better for seeing you.'"

"It will not get easier with the contagion on the ship," he admitted. "I do not even shake hands anymore. Not with anybody. No touching, that's my rule."

Helena felt like that was the rule she had lived all through their relationship in the making.

"Keep well and take care," he said as he stood to leave and, in a final gesture, touched her clothed arm with his elbow.

Helena sighed, as she continued to sit at the table, and cradled her cold cup of tea. The refrain of an old song ran through her head, *A fine romance, my friend this is; a fine romance, with no kisses.*

At Sea
Day 35

A wild wind whipped in from the open decks through the restaurant sliding doors every time they opened. Helena felt the chill in her bones as she looked up in hope and trepidation that the next person to enter would be the Captain. Fears that their fledging relationship would be broken beyond repair plagued her. The fact that she was part of his current problem rather than part of the solution left her in despair. The suspected bacterial outbreak was under control, but constantly the situation needed to be monitored and, according to insider information, the authorities had yet to confirm whether *Vision Star* would be allowed to berth on the next island of her itinerary.

Helena watched as the Captain made his way down the outside stairs and walked quickly across the open dining area. At the automatic doors, he paused. Helena held her breath. Before the doors had time to activate, he turned and walked away. Rejection. In that moment, she froze with a fear that he would never speak to her again. Surely, he now saw her as one more sick passenger—best to keep his distance.

"Captain," she heard the voice of the waiter as he acknowledged the arrival of his chief. The doors opened and closed, but lost in her misery, Helena was no longer aware of her surroundings.

Always focused on the task at hand, the Captain pulled out a chair. He sat down and stretched across the table to pat her arm. "Always a passenger wants me to listen to their complaint," he said with a nod toward the outside area where his attention had been claimed as Helena waited in purgatory for him to enter the restaurant. His eyes shone as he looked at her and said, "How are you? I've missed you."

If it were remotely possible, Helena would have thrown her arms around him and thanked him for not casting her out of his life.

"My life has been a nightmare," he confided. "I am exhausted. But." He laughed as he stole her words. "I am always better for seeing you."

This man never failed to surpass all expectations of how a mature, compassionate individual should behave. Helena had worried he would blame her for getting sick, but of course any reasonable person could see those circumstances were beyond her control.

Happy to be in his presence, she listened and smiled as he shared experiences of the current storm at sea. "There is always a new challenge to face," he admitted. "It is one of the reasons I love life on the ocean, but it would be welcome to have some smooth sailing. Things are getting better, though. This morning I received the news that we have clearance for our next port of call, Nuku Hiva."

"I've never been to the island," Helena reminded him. "Last year there was another crisis. We changed our course and went to rescue a US yacht in distress on the sea. Yes, there is always a challenge."

The rescue at sea was a turning point in their relationship on the first voyage. Helena had written a feature story that she posted on social media in which she had interviewed and quoted the Captain, and the two thereby established a professional relationship. "You write very well," he told her. "I see all the time that you are a woman with many talents."

She thrilled to the compliments he gave, but always there were too many words left unsaid. In their private world of a small white wrought-iron dining table, the clatter of the busy lunchtime restaurant faded into insignificance. Helena softened her eyes and her voice, "It matters little to me. Wherever we are in the world, all I see is you."

"I know." He nodded, and reached out to touch her hand. Their hands reluctantly stopped a few inches from contact, but their hearts reached out to form a connection.

Nuku Hiva
Day 38

Vision Star anchored in the sparkling azure-blue bay as small sailboats and craft bobbed all around. A tender service operated to ferry guests ashore. Tender ticket and allocated number safely in her pocket, Helena sat on the open deck, contemplated the waves and breathed in the goodness of pure French Polynesian island air.

Most passengers congregated in the busy communal areas, always afraid they might miss their tender slot. Up on deck, Helena and one elderly German lady shared the vast open space. Finger to her lips, the German lady nodded to Helena and indicated that silence was indeed bliss.

Notebook in hand, Helena played around with the words of a poem that ran through her head. She completed it as her tender number was called. Through the healing medium of words, she expressed the angst and confusion that clouded her heart.

My heart wants to know why you broke it,
How could anyone be so cruel?
Shredding a gift of devotion into confetti,
Scaring the tearstained face of the fool.
In the joy where my heart once lived and breathed,
Now only a Grand Canyon of space,
Waterfalls rush from the tears of my loss,

Cutting off sunlight in this dismal place.
Did you mean to wound with your words?
Tell me the reason you inflicted such pain,
If I knew what you were trying to say,
My heart may heal and one day be free to love again.

* * *

Helena strolled the uneven pathway alongside the bay of Nuku Hiva in the Marquesas Islands. One of over 118 tiny island formations in French Polynesia in the South Pacific Ocean, an overseas collectivist of the French Republic, Nuku Hiva is one of the handful of inhabited islands. Second in size to Tahiti with a population under 3,000, the island has one notable landmark, Notre Dame Cathedral, a wooden structure towered over by the imposing statue of a patriarchal God-like figure.

Myth has it that the ancient God Ono promised his wife he would build a house for her in one day. He chose various islands to represent the building and Nuku Hiva was the roof. The story goes that at the end of the day, not quite finished, he heaped all the leftovers onto one island, sometimes known as Pearl Lodge or less picturesquely by the natives as "Rubbish."

Overlooking the harbor, a gigantic sculpture stood guard—a twenty-foot, wooden spear–carrying statue of a Polynesian warrior—to welcome visitors to the island. At the tender arrival pier, the warriors are real. Screaming their tribal chants and blowing on horns, the warriors attempted to intimidate tourists, but intermittent smiles assured that the arrival of dollar-rich cruise ship passengers was welcome and indeed essential to the local economy.

Helena visited the waterfront palm-fringed craft shop and bought a colorful sarong and a handful of postcards from a jolly Polynesian woman who resembled the familiar national symbol of a generously voluptuous female. "It is one size," she assured and, for proof, wrapped the long, floral-printed material around her substantial body.

The calm bay and gentle waves provided a smooth tender ride back to the ship. But not all passengers were happy. There were complaints that the wait time between tenders was too long and passengers were forced to wait in the hot sun—albeit under a shade erected by the cruise line and with iced water on offer.

In his evening announcement, Helena heard the resignation in the Captain's tone as he explained, "This small, unspoiled Polynesian island has very little infrastructure. The pier can accommodate only one tender at a time. We thank you for your cooperation and understanding."

On one of the postcards bought in Nuku Hiva, Helena wrote a message that she left at reception in an envelope addressed, "Personal, Captain Grigory, *Vision Star*": *"No wonder Captain Bligh threw the complainers off his ship! Be assured, most passengers respect and appreciate the wonderful job you and your company are doing under difficult circumstances. This storm will soon pass. Take Care, Helena."*

The mention of Captain Bligh was a reminder to him of one aspect of their shared history: when they had discussed the *Mutiny on the Bounty* at length and she had amassed a small collection of books, information and artefacts for him.

At Sea
Day 39

Lifeboat drill for all passengers. Helena dressed carefully in a tailored pair of navy-blue suede trousers, matching silk blouse and gold boating shoes. The effect was decisively nautical. Even wearing a life jacket, she managed to look stylish.

Personifying the role he completely owned, the Captain stood on the deck in his tropical white uniform. Tall, erect, proud. Dark glasses in place, gold braid reflecting the sunlight. Rock Star Captain. He looked like a Hollywood movie star.

Captain Grigory watched a thousand passengers file past him in an inspection to ensure that all procedures were being administered correctly—and singled out Helena. She responded to his discreet smile, accompanied by a low-level wave. If there was ever going to be a time when she stopped fantasizing about him, it was not going to be today.

* * *

There was always a Meredith. A supremely annoying person, a fly in the ointment, a pain in the butt. Originally Meredith showed up on Helena's first Grand Around the World Cruise and made a complete nuisance of herself. She was a self-appointed ugly stepsister, always ready with a bitchy remark and an attempt to undermine Helena's self-confidence. Her classic comment, "Your hair looks ridiculous," as Helena, dressed to the nines, made her way to dinner at the Captain's table, had become a watchword for all jealous and bitchy behavior.

Helena first encountered Meredith Version Two at a cocktail party when, swiping yet another glass of bubbly from the waiter's silver tray, the blond and blowsy woman was overheard as she declared to friends, "My first job on this cruise is to grab a man to keep me company and top of my list is the Captain."

She dogged the Captain's footsteps. On one occasion, Helena was horrified to find the middle-aged woman, cleavage spilling out of the top of her skimpy summer dress, at their favorite table and boldly waving to the Captain as he entered the restaurant. Allowing his attention to be distracted by a member of staff, the Captain moved at once to another part of the restaurant and signaled for Helena to follow him. Indignant that the woman had the nerve to think she could step in and replace her, Helena repeated to the Captain the overheard conversation at the cocktail party.

He wrinkled his nose in disgust. "These women," he spat out the words, "I cannot understand how they would throw themselves at someone they do not know. As if I would be interested."

Helena smiled as she felt the gentlest of pressures on her foot under the dining table, and he confirmed, "You, I chose the first day I saw you. You are the woman who attracts my attention. You are a classy lady. I am happy to share my time and attention with you."

Totally sure of the integrity of his character, Helena knew he spoke the truth. He did not need to lie. That many women were attracted to him was obvious—how could they not be?—but he did an admirable job of keeping himself at arm's length. Even when, on some social occasions, he was forced to take to the dance floor as the women passengers lined up to be partnered with him. Helena once took him to task. "Everyone knows sailors have a girl in every port."

"Not true," he answered, "it is a myth."

"Pity," Helena flirted with him. "I was going to ask if you had a vacancy."

If he were a different kind of man, Helena judged that their relationship would have progressed much more quickly, albeit maybe nothing more than a one-night stand or a brief fling. In a modern world, the strange drawn-out courtship they endured was decidedly unusual, and he could easily have used her obvious attraction to him to his own advantage. Instead, he played a quiet and thoughtful game of expectation. His behavior was never predatory. Helena always felt respected.

* * *

"You asked me once why I was so enamored of you?" Helena brought up the subject again as he laid down his cutlery after having eaten, with obvious pleasure, a thick pink salmon steak that the chef cooked to order and served him at the lunch table.

"You are not like most other men," she continued. "You are a gentleman. You conduct yourself with grace. Despite all the challenges and constant pressures and decision-making of your job, you always ask about, and listen to, what I have been doing every day. You genuinely take an interest in my long, leisure days filled with passing activities and meaningless social small talk and interactions. You give me your full attention, and I love that we laugh so much together. With you, I can be my authentic self and not have to act a part. You make me feel like the best version of me."

He nodded. "It is important to me that you are happy and fulfilled," he said. "I would not be a part of your life if I didn't feel I could contribute to making you feel special and valued. What would be the point?"

His eyes never left hers as he explained his position. Helena blushed. "I am flattered."

"Good," he said. "You should be. I am very discriminating about where I place my time and attention. I like to be in your company. You make me feel good. You are special."

Helena cupped her chin in her hand to give protection to the intimate thoughts she shared, as she opened her heart. "When my husband died seven years ago, I expected to have boyfriends or marry again. It never occurred to me that there would be no one who appealed, even if I made compromises. I gave up all hope of romance. After the love affair I enjoyed with my husband, it was not a big sacrifice. Romance can be overrated. But from the day I first saw you, I was captivated. I fell under your spell and began to yearn to know you better. I longed to be close to you, to be a part of your life. I am so grateful my wish came true."

As always, when she laid bare her inner most feelings, Helena watched and waited for his reaction, fearful that she may have overstepped a boundary.

"Thank you for your honesty," he said. "I am glad to meet with your approval."

There was a long silence while they looked directly at each other and spoke only with their eyes.

The Captain broke the silence. "It will not be long now before we resume our unfinished business," he informed her.

Helena laughed. "With everything else you have to take care of, you managed to remember?" she teased.

"Oh, yes, I have not forgotten," he said. "You are about to find yourself at the top of my priority list. No matter how many other responsibilities vie for my attention, I refuse to put off that pleasurable task much longer."

As he walked out of the restaurant, she blew her beloved Captain a kiss.

Bora Bora, French Polynesia
Day 40

Slowly opening her eyes as the sunrise painted her room with a pink cloud of rosy anticipation for the day ahead, Helena marveled at the sight of the majestic mountain proudly framed in the panoramic windows. Immortalized in the classic 1950s film, *South Pacific*, set on the French Polynesian island of Bora Bora, the volcanic crater of Bali Ha'i towers to the highest clouds and cloaks itself in the mystery of a mist-shrouded pinnacle and emits a strange, hypnotic siren song. Illuminated by a Technicolor rainbow in a pink-and-purple-and-violet skyscape, the island wise woman, Bloody Mary, sang her song of the beauty of the island and its power to call and whisper to the soul, "Here I am your special island / Come to me, come to me."

Helena stood transfixed, her hands gripping the balcony railings. She was still unclothed as she rose from her bed and allowed herself to be seduced by the untamed power of the brooding mountain. "I will come to you," she said aloud. "Bloody Mary knows I cannot refuse."

"You have come to see Bloody Mary?" asked the baby-faced Polynesian woman who drove the mud-splattered silver jeep taking Helena and her companion to a date with destiny. "You have been here before." It was not a question.

Helena nodded. She demurely pulled at the hem of her silken, multicolored, floral minidress. In the confinement of the well-used front seat of the ancient jeep, the slinky dress rode up around her upper thighs and she felt exposed.

"My name is Brunetta," said the driver. "The spirit of Bloody Mary speaks through the hearts and minds of all the island women. We honor her and the power of the volcano. She is our mother."

Bora Bora is a major international tourist destination famous for its exclusive aquatic resorts. In the middle of the South Pacific, on tiny private islands at the edges of palm tree–fringed beaches, luxurious tiki huts on stilts offer picture-perfect sanctuaries that many visitors claim to be the closest thing on earth to heaven. Modern conveniences, personal butlers and chefs ensure state of the art five-star service.

Bloody Mary's Restaurant is famous throughout the islands of French Polynesia. Its own version of a tropical paradise, the restaurant has a bamboo structure with soft, white sand floors and overflows with palm fronds, extravagant greenery, exotic flowers and soothing stone water statues. In a tiki hut at the entrance, a band of local musicians play traditional instruments and smile a warm island welcome as they place garlands of floral leis around the necks of guests. There is no pressure to drop a dollar in their collecting hat, but many patrons do.

Helena slipped off her gold sandals and walked barefoot as she and her companion were led to the alfresco garden at the rear of the restaurant. A dark-haired, muscled, tattooed and handsome Polynesian youth took their order.

"You came to Bloody Mary's for a Bloody Mary?" His smile was wide and amused as he addressed Helena rather than her male companion. "You have been here before," he said. "I never forget a beautiful woman."

It was extremely unlikely to be true as the restaurant is the go-to place for thousands of cruise ship passengers who arrive several times a week. Still, graciously she accepted the compliment.

"You seem to have made quite an impression; how many times have you been here?" her date asked. Helena smiled. "Just the once, a year ago. But I made a wish that I would be able to return."

"Come, Captain" she said. "I'll show you," as they waited for the spicy tomato juice and local liquor cocktail to be delivered. On a huge noticeboard, she pointed out thousands of dollars' worth of notes in every currency imaginable pinned, stapled, stuck, glued and hanging on simply by the pressure of deep layers of other notes. "Tradition has it that if you leave an offering, write your name on the note and make a wish, you will come back again to Bloody Mary's."

Helena deliberately avoided adding the last part of the spell. She was not about to tell him that she had previously written the name of the person she wanted to be with when she returned. And this date's name was not on the note. The universe may have been playing a game because the man who shared her lunch date was actually a captain but not *the* Captain. A fellow passenger, he flew commercial jets and had invited Helena out on several occasions. Today she accepted the invitation.

Her reasoning was sound. The Captain was always too pre-occupied with his ship's duties to find time for her on port days. Crew exercises, customs inspections and goodwill presentations to local dignitaries took up his time.

"I never know if I will get off the ship until the last min-ute," he explained more than once. "If the opportunity arises, I go. If not, I stay onboard. You cannot be waiting for me. You must go and enjoy your visits at the port. You can tell me about it when I next see you."

Helena refused to demean herself by stating, "I'll wait for you. I don't mind, honestly. I'd rather go with you than on my own."

She was proud of the fact that she had trained herself not to question him. Independently, she made her own way, with friends or, as today, at the invitation of a fellow passenger. Ryan Starling, a flying ace, had acquired his nickname from the car-toon character of a kids' comic book flying hero.

The Bloody Marys tasted great. Sharp, tangy and decidedly more-ish.

"One more toast, one more photo and one drink for the

road," said the pilot, as the couple clinked glasses and smiled into the camera. To help down the drinks, they consumed large portions of island food served in wooden bowls decorated with palm fronds: Bloody Mary's house salads of kebab shrimps, smoked fish, fresh fruit and rocket leaves in a juicy raspberry vinaigrette dressing.

Helena was startled to look around the restaurant and realize they were the last two lunch guests. The other cruise ship passengers had already left.

"We need to head back to the ship," she said. "I had no idea of the time. I was having so much fun."

It was true. The conversation and laughter flowed effortlessly and her new friend regaled her with a wealth of fascinating stories. The pilot, an Anglo-American, shared details of his flying career with Helena. Originally from New York, he joined the US Air Force and for many years was stationed at bases in Britain. His family was originally from Ireland and his home base since leaving the military had been Sarasota on the west coast of Florida. He had flown with large commercial airlines but currently piloted smaller independent airlines. "I'm a joyrider pilot," he freely admitted, "mostly retired but still licensed to instruct. Flying was my life until I was forced to retire. Now I refuse to give up the thing I love."

Helena was curious, "Isn't cruising a bit tame after all that high flying?"

"Took me a while to get used to it," he admitted, "but now I've learned to relax and let go of the adrenaline rush. It suits me just fine."

Pilot Ryan Starling achieved what few men had managed, especially during the world voyage—to take Helena's mind off the Captain. She had not looked up once when the restaurant door opened on the off chance that he would appear.

Comfortable in Ryan's company, she relaxed and enjoyed the ease with which he conducted himself and the pleasure of a socially skilled and good-looking man's attention.

His presence never made her feel pressured, but in subtle ways he made it obvious he, too, was enjoying their interactions and those early stages of getting to know each other. Helena rather regretted that she had turned him down so many times in some misguided sense of loyalty to her infatuation.

"Head always in the clouds," she admonished herself. Then, she laughed, "Well, at least this one also has his head in the clouds; he's not all at sea."

"Do you have your note ready?" she asked Ryan as he paid the bill. "That's if you want to come back again."

"You betcha," he said, "especially if it's with you."

Helena beamed. "I've already written out my wish and you can't look."

She tucked a dollar bill high up on the noticeboard behind a French Pacific franc.

"Please grant my wish to return to Bloody Mary's with ?????" The name, she left to fate.

Brunetta stood next to the battered old jeep, which she had pulled off the main road and into the restaurant courtyard while waiting to take them back to the ship. Her services had not been requested. "I was driving past," she explained.

Squashed between Brunetta and Ryan in the front seat, Helena stretched forward to see out of the window and look up at Bali Ha'i. "Bali Ha'i called to you," said Brunetta. Again, it was not a question. "Bloody Mary will call you back."

Gala Night
Day 41

Helena could feel his eyes on her as she deliberately crossed and re-crossed her shapely, tanned legs. The hem of her sequined navy-blue minidress rode up her thighs and she dared him to look away. Her provocation was intentional. She needed to know once and for all where she stood in the relationship. Although she was normally very discreet and did not try to attract his attention in public situations, on this occasion she threw caution to the wind. As he performed his task of handing out certificates to employees of the month, she challenged him to not look at her.

Ceremony over, he crossed the main lounge of the ship in a few strides. Passengers who tried to impede his progress had to be satisfied with a smile and a nod.

Helena watched him approach. Each time she saw the man, she fell further under his spell. In his formal white evening tunic, he looked more than ever like a movie star. "You are more handsome than any man has a right to be," she murmured under her breath. All around fellow female passengers watched him and she knew what they were thinking. She knew because she shared their thoughts.

"Where have you been?" he demanded as he stood a mere few inches away from Helena. She breathed in his manliness and concentrated on hypnotizing him with her powers of persuasion.

The sound of violin strings and piano chords from the resident classical duo started up and Helena pointedly turned her back as she moved herself from blocking the audience's view of the entertainers. He followed her, determined to receive an explanation. "I've been looking for you," he said. "Everywhere. It's been days since you were in the dining room."

"Shore excursion. I went off the ship to explore the islands," she said feigning innocence.

"You weren't with your usual friends," he persisted. "I saw them several times and you were not with them."

"Ah, yes, I have a new friend," she said staring off into the distance as if conjuring up an image. "He's a captain, like you, but he doesn't sail ships. He flies airplanes."

He digested the information as he scanned the music-filled lounge and tried to identify by sight a professional pilot. Helena enjoyed his discomfort.

"I've had a great time," she said pointedly. "And you?"

Cutting short the game of cat and mouse, he asked, "What time are you going to your cabin?"

Helena checked her watch. "Half an hour," she told him.

"Good. I have to socialize here, then I will come to visit if you agree."

"I'll be there," she assured him.

As soon as he descended the spiral staircase and disappeared from sight, Helena made her way to her balcony cabin on one of the highest decks of the ship. She knew exactly how she planned to stage the seduction scene: curtains closed; light from only one small glass table lamp in the farthest corner of the room; cushions from the settee piled high on the bed; perfume sprayed everywhere and mood music on the video channel.

Without stopping to hang up her sequined party dress, she pulled it over her head and threw it on top of the shelf where her best underwear was already awaiting an excuse to be worn. Bra and panties in shiny black satin with a decoration of scarlet ribbons. She brushed her hair, brushed her teeth and swilled a cup full of mouthwash. Quick makeup touch-up, more bright red lipstick and Chanel N°5 perfume dabbed on her wrists, breasts and behind the knees. Over the underwear, she tied a figure-hugging black wrap from which her cleavage escaped and then changed her shiny silver evening shoes for red high heels. Preparations were complete seconds before the phone rang. Helena could not believe it. History repeated itself. This was where he had left her hanging last time.

"This is Helena," she said as she spoke into the receiver and dared the voice on the other end to let her down again.

"Sorry, I was delayed," he said, "now I am on my way."

At last. Helena approved her gift-wrapped appearance in the mirror. She felt like a kid who, beside herself with excitement, had religiously counted down the days and was fit to burst as Christmas Day finally dawned, full of promise.

She answered his knock on the cabin door and stepped aside to let him in. No words were spoken, but joyful smiles signaled realization that the longed-for culmination of their mutual attraction was about to be realized. In one movement, they held out their arms and embraced each other. For long minutes they stayed that way, sighing with relief that all hurdles were overcome. They were alone, together. Their expectant breathing filled the air.

Helena remembered this powerful emotion from their last goodbye almost a year previously when words were not enough to express all the emotions that bound and separated them. The Captain held her tight and squeezed her to his chest. He stroked her hair and sighed into her ear. He still wore his uniform and Helena worried that her makeup and lipstick would stain the pristine white tunic.

She cupped his face between her hands and prayed that this was not yet another dream where he would suddenly disappear. She had longed for his embrace for so long, she hardly dared believe it was true.

They kissed and lips locked, fevered, urgent, wild and breath stopping. His kisses made her swoon and the full force of the open-mouthed contact took her breath away.

"You are so beautiful," he whispered over and over again between kisses. Locked in his arms seemed the most natural place in the world to be. His eyes fixed on hers, and they smiled together in delight. While clasped in his powerful arms, she reached up, put her arms around him and, as they moved together, she felt his hardness.

Head bowed, he pulled aside her silk wrap and kissed her ample breasts. He took her hands in his and walked her to the bed. When he stopped to take off his jacket, she slipped out of her cover-up. He held her hand as she stepped out of the wrap, then undressed himself. Helena gazed in admiration at his imposing, well-toned, masculine frame. His skin was a light golden tan, smooth and muscled and blemish free. He wore a gold cross. Flashes of silver streaked the jet black hair on his chest, which was rugged enough to be manly but not overly so. He had strong, powerful limbs, and, totally assured, he stood before her naked. Helena gave thanks for the beautiful body she had coveted.

"I knew you would be everything I dreamed of," she told him. "You are perfect."

"Thank you, I am happy you approve," he said. "I want to please you."

He undid the clasp on Helena's bra, discarded it on the floor and his hands stroked her tummy and hips. With his fingers inside the silky fabric, he slipped down her panties. In every movement, he was assured, unhurried and proficient. As in every action she had seen him undertake, the Captain gave total concentration to performing the task at hand to the best of his ability. He knew what he was doing but attended to the undressing ritual as diligently as if it were a navigational procedure.

They kissed and hugged and held each other close. He caressed Helena's legs and ankles as he undid the straps on her shoes. Naked and ready for the final act, he positioned her, slid her lower body toward him and inserted himself deep inside. The pain was exquisite. Helena could not remember a time when she had felt more loved or more sure of any man's prowess. He held her in his strong arms, and together they rode the waves of pure sexual energy.

She felt protected, safe and truly connected to another human being in the deepest reaches of her body and soul. Helena cried out in agony and felt it reflected in every moment of the ecstasy. Taking care to ensure she was satisfied, the Captain took his pleasure holding on to Helena's hips and moving them in rhythm with his own to coax every last ounce of pleasure to overrule the pain.

A spot of blood on the sheets told a story.

"Oh, God, what happened?" he exclaimed.

Helena lowered her eyes to hide her vulnerability. "Seven years of celibacy. I was a born-again virgin."

Not knowing what to make of this development, he looked unsure but nodded.

Helena sank into the bliss as she succumbed to her first sexual encounter for over seven years. "It's mythic." She smiled, as they lay together wrapped in each other's arms. "You reached deep down into my soul and awakened me, and the incredible thing is it happened from the first minute I saw you. No man interested me after the death of my husband. I accepted that he was a hard act to follow. The day I met you, I was bewitched. I knew you were an extraordinary human being. I don't know if you believe, but for me it is destiny. You mesmerize and intrigue me. Now you have opened the gates to let me love again. Everything you do charms me. Thank you for choosing me."

His hands were powerful yet gentle. He stroked her hair and her face and the soft skin on her shoulders. "You are a very special woman, Helena," he told her. "The day I met you, I knew we would have a relationship. You delight me every day. Especially today." He kissed her hair and let out one of his well-used, deep, good-humored laughs.

Their bodies entwined as they lay together. For a few moments, the Captain closed his eyes and seemed about to go to sleep. "I am so comfortable I may drift off. I must not do that. But you must. I leave you alone now to go to sleep. Are you happy?"

Helena sank deeper into the plumped-up, snowy-white coverings of her double bed and sighed with delight. By choice it had been over seven years since she had considered any man worthy to share her bed. She congratulated herself for rejecting them all. To now be able to bring the gift of her years of celibacy to a worthy individual gave her a sense that there was truly something divine about their relationship. For over a year, which felt like an eternity in the modern world of romance, they had courted, gotten to know each other, valued each other.

Helena was elated. This man who commanded respect, admiration and longing, choose her. Wherever the relationship led, they had a bond, an unbroken union.

Dressed again in his gold-braided uniform, the Captain kissed Helena and attached his radio to the back of his trousers. "I want you to be aware," he told her, "that you will make a very favorable appearance in my log tonight."

"Please tell me what you will write," Helena asked.

He obliged. "Here in the South Pacific, I am on a voyage of discovery in unchartered territory."

Helena wrote in her journal, *My heart is free to love again. The Captain kissed me—and made passionate love to me. I am floating in a happiness bubble.*

Suva, Fiji
Day 42

Fijian warriors surrounded Helena. Bare-chested, powerfully built, dark-skinned young men who wore grass skirts and brandished three-foot wooden cudgels. One held her tightly around the waist, two others entwined her arms and another wrapped his diamond-hard muscled arms around her shoulders. "Sway your hips," they encouraged her as around and around they circled in a ritualistic tribal dance.

The young men contorted their features into fierce faces calculated to scare off enemies, the image enhanced with black smoke–marked symbols on their faces and chests.

Ancestors of these young men were the most fierce and feared group of all Fiji warriors. Now, their proud history is re-enacted in colorful ceremonies that keep the cultural traditions alive—and entertain the tourists.

On a visit to a traditional Fijian village high up in the hills above the island's capital, Suva, Helena participated enthusiastically in the welcome dance performed to the accompaniment of a twenty-piece band made up of villagers and visiting locals who beat out the pounding rhythm of the dance on wooden instruments and guitars.

Helena thanked the male dancers for the welcome serenade and responded to their request to lead her fellow cruise ship passengers in what could only be described as a Fijian congo followed by the Hokey-Cokey—universal dance moves performed all over the world. The men of the village provided the entertainment; the women provided lunch.

"We cook all of our food in firepits," explained one of the young local women. In Fijian schools, English is compulsory, ensuring that communication between the tribe and their visitors is effective. "Today, for your visit, we cooked chicken and sweet potatoes and roast pumpkin. The pit is dug deep in the ground and kept going with coconut palms, and the fire burns for several days. Everyone in the village brings their own food and places it wrapped in tinfoil on the cooking bars. On ceremonial days, the firepit is burning all day and at night-time, we share the food we have cooked all day."

"It tastes delicious," Helena thanked her hosts and listened as they told stories of the history of their home, Molituva village. "Our families have lived in this village for over two hundred fifty years. There are fifty houses here," said one of the spokeswomen, an attractive, dark-haired mother of three, named Connie. "Our families now are seventh and eighth generation, there are two hundred ninety-eight villagers, and every member of the family is entitled to live here and work the land. Even when our children grow up and move away, they are still part of the family and retain their homes in the village."

Lunch was served in the community hall, a wooden hut large enough to accommodate the whole village for their ceremonies and family gatherings. Oil skin floor and wall coverings depicted traditional symbols and fund-raising had allowed the small communal kitchen to be decorated with ceramic tiles.

Connie explained, "It is the responsibility of every villager to help with the upkeep of the community center. It is here we preserve our culture and remember the hardships our ancestors endured. They did not have the luxuries we have of running water and power. Donations we receive from visitors are all used to renovate and update the hall and the church we have built."

Traditional crafts are practiced by women in the village, and Connie proudly took Helena to see the basket and mat weaving, artwork for souvenirs, and husking and scraping of coconuts for eating, cooking and building everything from houses to children's toys. Fiji has one of the most developed economies in the Pacific thanks to its abundant forest minerals, fish resources and international tourism. The Ministry for Local Government, Urban Developments and Public Utilities supervises Fiji's local government, which takes the form of city and town councils.

"Before you leave the village, our women would like to walk with you up the hill to the church," said Connie. "Will you come?"

"Of course," said Helena. "I'd be honored to visit your church."

In a small procession of women, small children and two skinny dogs, Helena climbed the hill to the beautiful wooden church, which had its windows and walls open to the cooling breeze.

"Why you on your own?" asked one of the women as they walked side by side up the stony incline. "You have no husband?"

"My husband died," Helena explained.

"You need to find another one," said the lady, who gave her name as Sarah. "My husband died," said Sarah. "I have three daughters to look after, but they all growing up now. And they look after me. You have children?"

"No," said Helena.

"You are still beautiful woman," said Sarah, "you need another husband. You must not be on your own."

Knowing that any confidence she shared was safe in this remote village, Helena admitted, "There is someone. Someone I love."

Sarah smiled. "What's the problem, why is he not here with you?"

There was no answer to that question.

At the door of the church, Helena stopped to catch her breath from the steep climb and looked around appreciatively at the peaceful simplicity of the sacred space. "We are Christian Methodists," Sarah told her. "Would you like us to pray for you?"

Helena nodded. "I'd like that very much."

Sarah took her hand and led Helena down the aisle and past the carved wooden pews to the wooden altar piece at the front of the church. The women gathered around her and joined hands as the children and dogs ran up and down the aisle.

"We will pray in our own language, Fijian," Sarah informed her.

Loudly in unison, they intoned prayers that reverberated through the wide-open spaces that reached to the sky, and they held hands out to the surrounding forest. The women embraced one another, and Sarah reminded Helena that they needed to hurry because her coach was due to leave the village for its return trip to the *Vision Star*.

"We prayed for your safe journey back to England," said Sarah, "and we prayed that the next time you visit us, you will not be alone. We have joined you with your love in prayer in God's mind. Your prayers made here in Fiji and witnessed by the women of my village will be answered."

The whole village turned out to wave goodbye to their guests and the women made a special point of blowing kisses to Helena and smiling in anticipation of her forthcoming romance.

All the way back to the ship through the beautiful countryside and forests of Fiji, Helena hugged the secret to herself.

★ ★ ★

Helena's feet hardly touched the ground as she skipped along the dock, up the gangway, into the elevator, then entered her corridor. From the opposite direction, the Captain approached. Stealthily stalking the empty corridor, handsome in his white tropical uniform, he had his radio in hand. In her mind's eye the scene slowed until it played out frame by frame, like in a movie. They walked toward each other, there was not another soul in sight and, suspended in time, their eyes locked, focused solely on each other.

Within touching distance, he stopped. "You're looking very pleased with yourself," he remarked. "Want to share the secret?"

Helena resisted the urge to kiss him there and then. "I'm having a wonderful adventure, Captain," she said. "A Grand Around the World Cruise offers so many opportunities for life-changing experiences."

"My day has not been so much of an adventure," he said, "but it is certainly challenging. Due to an outbreak of a global virus that is affecting travel all over the world, we have to alter our course and cancel ports of call on our itinerary. I have today been working out a new route."

Helena listened attentively. "You know, I always tell you that I want to be part of the solution," she assured him. "Whatever happens you can count on me being at your side. I'm not sure what I can do to help, but I'm here if you need me."

"Of course, I know that," he said. "I am so glad you are onboard. I never know when I will run into you unexpectedly."

He reached out his hand and squeezed her shoulder. "I will see you soon," he said.

"You know where I live." She smiled and nodded toward the general area of her cabin door. Maybe one day, she would tell him that, even in remote villages in the forests of Fiji, prayers were said that they should have a future together.

"Captain, you know that I and the other hundreds of passengers totally trust and respect your judgment. But, remember, whatever happens, I have enough faith for both of us," she told him.

He raised his eyebrows. "Good, that is good," he said, looking completely mystified as the radio crackled into life, and he continued on his way to fulfil his myriad duties.

That night, on her knees, she sent a silent prayer of thanks to Sarah and the other village women for keeping her dream alive.

At Sea
Day 45

Helena made an executive decision. "Today I refuse to get up out of bed and attend an art class to learn about drawing—puddles." Puddles were due to be the subject of the daily landscaping class she attended to prove to herself that the entire focus of her costly and exclusive Around the World Cruise was not the Captain. She told herself that she had already reached the depth of her artistic education by learning to draw sheep, and now Helena obstinately drew the line at sketching puddles.

Truth was she was reluctant to take part in any activities that did not include the opportunity to see the object of her desire.

An exhausting ride on the emotional roller coaster ensured that her moods and perspective changed by the hour.

Since the last port of call she had waited patiently at "their" table in the dining room at lunchtime. On sea day one, he didn't show. On day two, she waited until she heard the headwaiter tell serving staff, "Close the line. The Captain is not coming." Day three she stared forlornly at the entrance doors, every glimpse of a tall figure or crew members in their white uniforms caused her to take her eyes off her scant meal of cheese and fruit and glance up expectantly. The headwaiter watched and waited and offered a discreet smile of sympathy as she again collected her belongings and hurried from the restaurant.

His instruction to the serving staff to hang green curtains and close the buffet line signaled that once again the Captain had failed to turn up. The headwaiter crossed to where Helena sat alone at her table. "Can I get you anything before I close the line?" he asked.

"No, no, I'm fine, thank you," she answered.

The choir concert she had rehearsed for since joining the cruise six weeks before came and went. "How are your rehearsals going? I will come to see you perform," the Captain had told her. Then added, "If I am not too busy."

On a gently swaying stage, as the *Vision Star* ploughed its way through the South Pacific en route to New Zealand, Helena joined the other hundred choir members. Words of the song, "Can't Help Falling in Love," left a bad taste in her mouth as she remembered how, on seeing the sheet music she had placed on the dining table, he had joked, "Is that true? You can't help falling in love? I will come to hear you sing the song."

Helena's nerves reached breaking point as she replayed, over and over again, the one night of passion they shared and the disappointment of the subsequent days.

"He's got more important things to worry about than you." She tormented herself with arguments. "He's responsible for the lives and safety of thousands of passengers and crew and still there is the warning of a cyclone on the way. Weather conditions are dreadful. He's on the bridge. He's in his office. He's answering hundreds of emails on his computer. He's dealing with immigration officials. He's in conferences with the cruise ship's head office about possible further changes to the itinerary."

Then the frustration would erupt, "All of that doesn't prevent him from making a two-minute phone call or taking a short break at lunch to pass by and see how I am."

As they lay wrapped in each other's arms after their first night of lovemaking, Helena had told the Captain, "I want to be part of the solution. You have enough people giving you problems. You can rely on me to be at your side and to support you whatever is happening."

He had squeezed her more tightly. "Thank you, I appreciate that. You are always my special friend. I know I can tell you anything. I'm glad you are here."

Unfortunately, the opportunity to show how reasonable, understanding and compassionate she could be had not happened; apart from a random encounter in the corridor, he had not made contact.

She fought hard to rise above the chilling sense of loss and shame that overcame her. The glittering prize of having him in her arms had been snatched away and, in its place, a bitter taste of humiliation and defeat pervaded her whole being.

Helena fell to her knees beside the bed in her cabin. Another day loomed and she felt bereft. "Please God, do not let my emotions drive me to overreact. I must not act out. Why am I so fragile? I want to scream and shout and let him know how he has let me down, but I can't even see him. I told him it had been seven years since I had allowed any man to touch me. Now I feel so rejected. I am in despair. Please God, let me find some peace."

Tauranga, New Zealand
Day 46

Tauranga is the most populated city in the Bay of Plenty on the North Island of New Zealand. It was settled by the Maori tribe late in the thirteenth century and by the Europeans in the early nineteenth century. The city is one of New Zealand's main centers for business, international trade, culture, fashion and horticultural science. Tauranga is subtropical with a temperate climate. One of the most popular holiday destinations in New Zealand, the population triples in the summer months.

There are 15,000 earthquakes a year in the area known as the Land of Shaky Islands. A fruit growing area, the main produce is kiwifruits, with 200 million being exported annually, and the second major fruit export is avocado.

New Zealanders are outdoor people. Bays and harbors teem with water sports, and 80 percent of the islands have designated bike tracks and hiking trails. The rolling hills and wide-open spaces provided the perfect location when New Zealand born writer, director and producer Sir Peter Jackson and his production team conducted an aerial search to scout for suitable film sites for his classic Hollywood blockbusters, *Lord of the Ring* and *The Hobbit* trilogies, adaptations of the classic works by J. R. R. Tolkien. It is said that every person in New Zealand played a part in the films—either on-screen or behind the scenes, with outdoor filming and studio-based production set up in 158 locations.

"I am off on an adventure," Helena repeated the iconic words that open the Hobbit film as she boarded the special bright green bus taking visitors to Hobbiton village.

With the towering Kaimai Mountain Range in the distance, the family-run Alexander 1250-acre sheep and beef farm just outside Matamata in the heart of the Waikato was transformed into Middle-Earth. The lush pastures and homes of the Hobbits in the village of Shire, including Bag End, were right there and awaited the magical director's touch.

"In September 1998, Sir Peter Jackson 'discovered' the perfect location and site construction started in March 1999," explained the Hobbiton guide, Paul, a local schoolteacher and Hobbit fan long before he became part of one of the most famous movies ever made. Paul quoted the characters while standing in the exact place where filming took place.

"Initially this involved heavy earthmoving machinery provided by the New Zealand army who built a road over a mile long and undertook initial set development. The New Zealand government totally supported the project and passed a law in parliament banning aircraft, primarily the media, from flying over the site.

"Even the neighbors of the Alexander family were kept in the dark about what was really happening. The story outsiders were told was that the Army was conducting maneuvers on their land." The construction process took two years and at its peak over 400 people were onsite, including, at various times, Sir Peter Jackson, Sir Ian McKellan (Gandalf), Elijah Wood (Frodo), Sean Astin (Sam), Ian Holm (Bilbo Baggins) and Martin Freeman (young Bilbo Baggins).

Helena gazed, enchanted, at the fully replicated original

thirty-nine Hobbit holes. Quaint wooden constructions with brightly painted round doors were almost hidden in the profusion of wildflowers where butterflies played and added authenticity to the lifestyle of the Hobbits. Tiny items of washing hung on lines, axes stood upright as if laid down mid-cut through the chopping and sawing of logs to fill the outdoor storehouse. At the gateways of Hobbit houses, produce stalls stood complete with jars of honey, fresh baked bread and a selection of cheeses for sale. Real smoke curled from chimneys of the houses and it was fully expected that at any moment a Hobbit resident would open their door and ask, "Who comes knocking?"

"The set is maintained to keep the magic of the Shire alive," the guide Paul enthused. "This is a working, living movie set. Hundreds of people work here over the year: to landscape the grounds, water the plants and flowers and maintain the Hobbit holes."

"Here, take a seat on Bilbo Baggins bench, mind his pipe and ignore the sign that says NO ADMITTANCE EXCEPT ON PARTY BUSINESS," Paul encouraged Helena.

Looking out over the Shire with familiar scenes from the film of Hobbiton, the Watermill and North March East Farthing, Helena experienced a sense of peace and serenity. "At last, a place and time that transcends my thoughts of the Captain. This visit has truly been a highlight of the cruise."

The voice of Paul, a well-practiced, loud and instructional teacher voice, cut across her thoughts. "Come along," he called in his best Gandalf gruff roar. "A wizard is never late."

Hurried along the perfectly kept pathways to the reconstructed village inn, the Green Dragon, visitors can choose from a selection of favorite Hobbit beverages. Black Stout, Amber Ale, Apple Cider or Ginger Beer to wash down homemade muffins and hot cheese scones. Helena sat on a bench outside the Green Dragon tapping her foot to the madrigal Hobbit music being played in the garden. A butterfly landed on her arm. "Butterflies only live for a day," she reminded herself. "I must live one day at a time and remember I am blessed, come what may. I shall remember this wonderful adventure in Hobbiton."

At Sea
Day 47

Lifejacket under one arm, warm clothing and head gear under the other, Helena walked quickly down the open lifeboat deck. She knew by heart her evacuation procedure in an emergency: Muster Station A, Lifeboat Three. Regular training in the SOLAS (Safety of Life at Sea) requirements ensured that passengers knew the drill and were assisted by crew members, fire crew and all members of the ship's company who provided direction and guidance at stairwells and passageways.

Helena was on an important mission. She needed to see the Captain face-to-face and gauge his reaction to her. Apart from brief, random encounters, she had not an opportunity to talk to him since the night of their intimacy. She dreaded that the whole connection would end up being a one-night stand.

He stood in his usual place to oversee the emergency procedures and, at its completion, thanked passengers for their cooperation.

When he spotted Helena, he walked quickly toward her. He kissed her on both cheeks and told her, "Sorry it is so long since I have seen you. I meant to call you a couple of nights ago, but there has been no let-up in my workload. I'm up to my eyeballs."

Helena smiled. "No problem. I understand."

"How are you?" he asked.

She replied with the comment that always brought a smile to his face, "Always better for seeing you."

"That's good. The same is for me."

She did not know whether to move on and leave because a line of passengers had formed at the side of the railings, all waiting for their moment with the Captain.

He was in no hurry to terminate the conversation with her.

"Did you receive your invitation?" he asked.

Helena shook her head.

"I invited you again as my guest to the Captain's table the day after tomorrow."

Unable to hide her delight, Helena almost reached up and kissed him.

The treasured invite told her all she needed to know. This was not an invitation from the customer service desk to acknowledge her status as a Diamond guest. This was a personal invitation from the Captain.

"As before, I told them to make sure you are seated next to me," he continued. "I want you close to me. This is the best way to be able to see you."

The day had started overcast. Now the clouds cleared. Helena's heart was light. She suffered such anxiety not knowing what was to be the next stage in their relationship. Had she offended him? No, she was again a privileged guest at his table. She knew of no one else who attended the VIP occasion as often as she did over the course of two voyages.

Her first call, once she was back in her cabin, was to the spa to book beauty treatments, a manicure/pedicure and a hair stylist on the evening of the formal dinner. She marveled at how quickly the day had turned out differently than expected. The sorrow she had experienced was immediately lifted.

At lunchtime he arrived to join her at their favorite table. Helena basked in his closeness and accepted the admiring stares of the other passengers and the solicitations of serving staff. All was right with the world. Together, she and the Captain laughed and chatted. He told her about the visit he had paid in the town of Wellington to a wartime exhibition mounted by the Te Papa Museum of New Zealand. Claimed to be the most successful exhibition currently on display in the world, the subject was the Anzac troops in the Battle of Gallipoli, Turkey, during the First World War. A graphic, deeply moving reconstruction manufactured in the New Zealand workshops of the master filmmaker, Sir Peter Jackson, featured triple life-size models of the soldiers whose personal stories were tragically told in words, letters and commentary.

The Captain was an aficionado of world war history and regaled Helena with his hours spent in the museum. "When I get off the ship," he told her, "I need to be able to move fast. See what I want to see and clear my head of the job and the responsibilities."

"I know," she nodded, though, really she would love to accompany him on his outings. Even if it meant that he was visiting a war museum and she the home of the Hobbits.

"I need the time to be alone," he explained as he patted her hand. "But maybe one day soon, we will go together."

"I'd like that," she admitted. "You know I would, but I would not want to deprive you of your personal time. You get little enough of it. For me, a trip to the Captain's table is a glittering prize. And I get to wear an evening dress and high heels, not walking shoes. Thank you for my invitation."

He pushed back his chair. "I'm needed on the bridge," he said. "We have a weather warning that there is a cyclone in the area where we are headed. Take care of yourself."

"I will leave that to you, Captain." She winked. "I know I will be in safe hands."

Captain's Table
Day 49

Helena chose a full-length rose-pink sequined gown for dinner at the Captain's table. As the dinner guests assembled at the cocktail bar and drank champagne, she took her place at the Captain's side.

"Always you look gorgeous," he told her. "Thank you for being my guest."

"There is nowhere I would rather be," she told him, "than at your side with a cyclone on the way."

He laughed, and his whole face lit up. "It could be even worse than a cyclone," he admitted.

"You must have been adored all your life," she once remarked to him. "You have so much confidence and a total belief in the fact that life is to be enjoyed, not endured."

Walking in procession through the communal areas of the cruise ship on their way to the private dining room, Helena reflected on her good fortune. She felt well blessed. All my prayers have paid off, she acknowledged, and gave thanks.

The other female dinner guests seated beside and opposite him, though with their respective spouses, clamored for the Captain's attention. Helena turned to speak to the shy couple seated at the end of the table. Charming, quiet people, they came from a part of middle England that she knew well, and quickly connections were established as conversation flowed. They lived close to the area where J. R. R. Tolkien originally wrote his Hobbit trilogy.

"Our visit to the film set was such a wonderful experience," they enthused. "It is certainly a highlight of our world cruise so far."

Helena agreed with them as they talked about the master moviemaker Sir Peter Jackson and his impact on the New Zealand film industry.

"Are you enjoying yourself?" the Captain asked as the two shared small secret smiles.

Helena nodded and in the silence that followed she waited for him to say he would visit her after the dinner ended. He didn't. In fact, dinner was brought to an abrupt end as the one of the ship's officers arrived and, after a brief private conversation with the Captain, made an announcement. "Ladies and gentleman, the Captain thanks you for being his guest at dinner tonight, but he must make his apologies that duty calls and a last-minute meeting means we will leave you to finish dessert while he returns to his boardroom. You will be well taken care of by the restaurant staff."

Helena resisted the temptation to ask the nature of the emergency but understood that it must be important. Cyclone business, perhaps. Shortly after his departure, leaving a reasonable length of time so that it did not look too obvious, she made her apologies to the other guests and returned to her cabin. Disappointed and annoyed that again expectations had led her to imagine more than was on offer, she gazed out beyond her balcony at the dark night sky and the white waves as they bounced alongside the ship. She sat in the armchair, still wearing her beautiful evening dress, and drank a cup of tea.

"The invitation was for dinner, nothing else," she reminded herself. "He did not say he would come to visit. More's the pity. When, if ever, will this relationship start for real?"

She sighed and concluded that the best solution for her

melancholy mood was to get into bed and pull the duvet over her head. In the bathroom, she brushed her teeth and removed her makeup. The phone rang and she ran across the cabin to answer it.

"I hope I did not wake you," he said, "but my meeting has finished and I would like to come to see you. Is that okay?"

"Of course," she told him, "I'd like that very much."

"Give me fifteen minutes," he said, "and then leave your cabin door open."

Helena agreed, then made fast decisions to prioritize things she needed to do in that fifteen minutes. Close the curtains, turn down the lights, turn on the music channel. Sexy underwear on, shoes on. Because he was so tall, she never wanted to greet him barefoot. With high heels, she reached to a comfortable position and could look into his eyes. Brush her teeth again, renew her makeup, brush out her hair, which was already pinned up ready for bed, spray on favorite perfume.

The stage was set. She opened the cabin door and waited. Within minutes he walked through the door, took her in his arms and kissed her long and hard. They stood for a long time, holding each other close. With sighs of delight, they began to undress each other. "You are beautiful," he told her over and over again. "It takes all my discipline to sit beside you and not reach out to touch you."

On this occasion, their lovemaking was slow and sensuous. Touching, feeling, stroking, exploring each other's bodies. Two lovers confident in their togetherness. Helena was grateful that, with him, the act of sex truly did feel like making love.

The crashing waves of the angry sea outside the window echoed their powerful rising and falling climax. Words became less and less important as they talked with their bodies, hands, mouths, heartfelt sighs of pleasure and deep growls of satisfaction.

Afterward, he took her in his arms and whispered into her ear, "Thank you for your gift to me. Thank you for waiting seven years."

Assured and happy that he was as mature and experienced as she had hoped, Helena stroked his beautiful face. "I told you before, it's mythic," she reminded him.

"I agree," he said. "You are mythic, Helena. You make me happy. Thank you."

Dreams did come true. Helena smiled to herself. "Our relationship reached the next level tonight."

At Sea near Sydney, Australia
Day 52

Halfway around the world, as *Vision Star* approached Sydney in Australia, the atmosphere was electric. Many passengers were scheduled to embark the following day. Some for the holiday of a lifetime, many looking forward to family reunions and a handful of brave souls who left behind lives in Great Britain for a once-in-a-lifetime opportunity to emigrate to Australia. Farewells to the newfound friendships developed onboard were said and a party fever prevailed. The last night onboard made people nostalgic and excited. Bars and lounges filled to overflowing with passengers determined to make the most of their final evening at sea.

Helena, aware that in her obsession with the Captain she had mounted barriers around herself to maintain a secluded existence, rarely socialized except with her well-trusted dinner companions. They were a friendly, interesting set of people. Helena counted herself fortunate that her friend the maître d' placed her with a colorful group of characters with whom she shared many happy evening meals, an international collection with two English couples, one Scottish and one French.

The older Englishman, a Liverpudlian born and bred, was a great mimic and kept the company laughing with his impressions of everybody from President Trump to Prince Charles. His wife rolled her eyes as he turned on yet another accent. The Midlands-based karaoke singer talked of his glory days in a pop group and his wife loyally agreed he could have given Rod Stewart a run for his money. From a small village outside Glasgow, a professional, fun-loving Scottish couple were excellent company and Helena observed that they would be welcome guests at any dinner table. Enjoying their third Grand Around the World Cruise, they generously shared invaluable knowledge and information on all matters cruising. The true extrovert of the group, an immaculately dressed Frenchman and his petite, timid wife excelled on the dance floor as they tangoed and chachaed like professionals. They struggled to understand the British sense of humor but persevered and deliberately added to the confusion as they introduced Gallic jokes into the conversation.

Conversations around the dinner table were intelligent, far-reaching and if on occasion they became heated, good-natured laughter soon restored international relations. From the outset they welcomed Helena and became friends and entertaining companions. Helena valued their company and the opportunity to connect with fun-loving people without expectations or social pressure.

The subject of her friendship with the Captain was never mentioned, though, she knew they were aware of her lunchtime assignations. They respected her privacy, and she was thankful for their good manners and making her feel at ease. If she could not attend the Captain's table every night, Helena felt well blessed by her new and loyal set of cruising companions.

On this special night, she made an exception to her early to bed habits and accepted an invitation to hear one of her dining companions sing in the karaoke competition being held in the traditional English pub. She sipped a tropical cocktail and joined in with several well-known songs. Even seriously bad singers got an enthusiastic response. Her friend sang a Rod Stewart song to which the audience clapped and sang along, and his cheerleading group's high level of support ensured a high placing in the final result.

"I should do this more often; I enjoyed it," Helena called to her companions over the raucous music and brain-numbing level of chatter and laughter. "Now, if you'll excuse me, it's my bedtime."

After exiting the pub, the noise level subsided, and she made her way along the deck toward the elevator. "Glad I caught you," said Ryan Starling, the US pilot, who reached out to steady himself as the ship rolled suddenly. He stumbled and almost collided with her. Tonight, he looked rather less handsome than she remembered; his complexion was flushed and his voice slightly slurred. Perhaps he had overindulged in the complimentary farewell cocktails.

Helena hoped she would not be forced to admit that she had made a point of avoiding him. Several times he had left messages for her at the reception desk, asking her to telephone him. She did not. On deck, seeing him on the opposite side of the ship, she would duck down a stairway or into a gallery shop.

"Don't worry, I won't trouble you anymore," he said. "I leave the ship tomorrow in Sydney."

"I wish you all the best for your onward journey." Helena smiled and held out her hand. "It was good meeting you and thank you for your company."

Ryan did not return her smile. "I soon realized why

my attentions to you were not welcome. I was warned off," he snarled. "Everyone knows you are the property of the Captain."

Anxious to get away, Helena had no intentions of confirming or denying the statement. "Good luck," she said, and attempted to make her getaway. Ryan was too fast for her. He grabbed her wrist and asked, "Don't I get a goodbye kiss?"

Taken by surprise, Helena stepped back and pulled her hand from his.

"No, you do not," said the uniformed figure behind him.

Ryan did not see the figure approach. Now he attempted to disengage from his actions.

"No harm meant," he said. "Helena is a friend of mine. I wanted to say goodbye before I disembark."

The Captain nodded. "You've said goodbye. Now I suggest you go back to your cabin and finish packing. You have an early start in the morning."

"Good night Helena, good night Captain," said Ryan as he weaved unsteadily down the corridor.

Before she could thank him for intervening on her behalf, the Captain had a message. "I've been calling your cabin," he said. "You're usually home at this time." Helena smiled at the familiarity of his statement. He looked around to ensure they would not be overheard. "When I visited you last night, I may have inadvertently left behind my gold cross."

On his first visit, he had left behind the onyx stone pendant he wore around his neck. She noticed him carefully remove it before they made love. The following day he called and asked if he could come by the cabin to retrieve it.

"I have it in an envelope, ready for you," she confirmed. As he left the previous evening, she asked, "Do you have your pendant?"

"Yes, thank you," he said tucking it inside his white, short-sleeve T-shirt.

No mention was made of the cross that she had also observed he wore. She was well aware that he was a man of faith.

"Sorry, I have no knowledge of the cross," she said, "but I'll make a thorough search when I get back to my cabin. Give me half an hour and I'll check if it was left there."

The search was fruitless and Helena relayed the news when he called.

"I'm sorry," she said. "I'll look again in daylight."

"Thank you, it is precious to me," he informed her. "I feel sad that I have lost it."

"Hopefully, it will turn up," said Helena.

"Okay, that's as may be," he sighed. "I wish you a good night's sleep. Enjoy your day in Sydney. As you know, it is a very beautiful city."

"Good night," said Helena as she blew a silent kiss and hung up the phone.

Sydney, Australia
Day 54

Sailing under the Harbour Bridge to moor alongside the magnificent Sydney Opera House felt truly iconic. Though the word is overused, this landmark never fails to impress and unquestionably lives up to its description as *awesome*. Helena felt a strange emotional connection as she revisited the city that topped her list of favorite destinations on her previous Grand Around the World Cruise.

"How fabulous it would be to live here," she had decided then and agreed still.

Standing in front of the Opera House in the warm autumn sunshine, she was overcome with a feeling of gratitude and a wonderful sense that all was indeed well in God's world. She hopped on an Explorer Bus and revisited all the places in the city she had seen and enjoyed on her previous trip. Plans to visit the world-famous surf beach at Bondi were put on hold till the afternoon as she jumped off the bus and headed for the Queen Victoria Building, a restored colonial building that housed a graciously elegant shopping emporium Helena considered one of her favorites in all the cities of the world.

It is here that the wealthy ladies of Sydney indulged in traditional high tea served in delicate watercolor china crockery with rainbow-colored macaroons while seated under the grandeur of the huge Queen Victoria four-sided gilt clock suspended from the ceiling above the glass and dark wooden-framed galleries and staircases. On the half hour, the clock strikes and on the hour, it opens to reveal painted landscape scenes of colonial life. It is easy to be transported back and imagine the whole experience of a visit to Queen Victoria Building that took place in a time warp two centuries ago.

Helena was on a mission. In a moment of inspiration during the night, as she lay in bed reliving, as she did constantly, the wonderful, loving feeling of his arms embracing her and his lips pressing down on hers, she decided that she needed to replace his lost cross.

"You are too kind; you spoil me," he told her as she presented the gifts chosen at the Te Papa Museum in Wellington: a set of enamel cuff links with Maori symbols and a gold pen filled with glittering fragments of precious metals found in the local rivers and presented only to chiefs of the tribe and personages of status and authority.

"What did I do to deserve my gifts?" he asked.

She widened her eyes and smiled. "Want me to tell you?" she whispered.

Fact was that, apart from the intimacies they now shared, Helena would forever be grateful to her handsome, heroic lover for restoring her faith in herself. Personal doubts and fears melted as she looked into his eyes and realized he saw the best version of herself.

Over a period of two years and over a hundred lunchtime assignations, he sat next to her in the revealing rays of the noon-day sun and saw her without soft focus filters, photoshop or the benefit of moody night-time lighting. He knew her. He really looked at her. They had enjoyed an extended courtship period in which they talked, laughed and got to know each other. Despite the public nature of their lunchtime encounters, they managed to conduct personal conversations and develop a deep understanding of and insight into each other.

Helena responded to his question about her desire to buy him gifts in every port, mostly only local souvenirs or the dark chocolate he loved.

"I want to reach out to you. I want to touch your heart," she admitted, "and ensure you will think of me from time to time when you see the gift or eat the chocolate."

"You can be sure that I do think of you," he replied and laughed deeply. "Especially when I am eating the chocolate. It reminds me of how good you taste and how good you make me feel."

Conscious that their time together was limited because he was due to leave the ship sometime during the voyage rather than go all the way around, Helena asked, "Do I embarrass you when I buy you gifts or admit how much I care for you? Or remind you how long I waited for the man of my dreams to come along?"

"You never embarrass me," he assured her. "You always act like a perfect lady. I am happy you are able to tell me how you feel."

One remark Helena did regret, and she tried hard to cover up, happened as they lay side by side on the bed, happy and satisfied after making love. "I love you," she said. As soon as the words were out of her mouth, she wished she was able to claw them back.

"I'm sorry, I didn't mean to say that," she told him. "What I meant was that I love the way you are, I love the essence of you, I love your integrity, I love the way you look, I love the way you make me feel."

He nodded. "I understand. You love all of these things, but you do not love me."

Helena blushed. "I'm sorry. I don't know how to talk myself out of this," she admitted.

"I hear what you say," he told her and stroked her cheek. "Thank you. There is nothing for which you need to apologize."

* * *

Queen Victoria Building was the perfect place to find the farewell gift Helena had in mind. Fashionable galleries, each one more eycatchingly window-dressed than the last, showed off their pyramids of dazzling jewels that reached up to the magnifcent ceiling. Stunning collections of priceless antiques, contemporary designs, authentic native pieces and original creations in gold, silver and platinum; rings, necklaces, bracelets, collars and earrings studded with diamonds, rubies, emeralds, sapphires; a kaleidoscope of precious and semiprecious stones polished to shine to perfection and displayed to attract and delight the eye are artfully laid out as an exclusive, expensive feast that dances with fire and flashes of pure beauty on red, ebony and white velvet that reflected the open caskets of lighted glass cases.

Helena pressed her nose to the jewelers' shop windows. She knew what she was looking for: a cross, a golden cross, a cross to embrace the Eastern Orthodox religion found in Russia where Captain Grigory grew up. She indulged in learned discussions with enthusiastic store staff and occasionally a disinterested sales person as she looked in the various shops.

One young girl, obviously not happy about having been left to mind the shop, shook her head without taking her eyes from her laptop when asked to show her range of traditional Christian and Eastern Orthodox religious crosses. "We only have in stock one cross," she said. "It's got a little figure of a guy on it."

Helena laughed, though the girl did not see the joke. Store after store produced no results. Helena was not to be deflected from her mission, but it took all of her willpower not to become distracted by looking at jewelry items she might like to buy for herself.

"This is his farewell gift," she reminded herself. "He will not be allowed to forget you."

On a store-lined gallery at the top of the four-story building, Helena walked through the doors of the Museum of Contemporary Art, New York's world-famous Met. She smiled at the synchronicity that today she was wearing a pair of Colombian gold medallion earrings bought for her as a gift by her friend, a wealthy South American soap opera star by whom she had been accompanied on a visit to the museum in New York. Laid out in free-standing glass cases by country and classical art and culture, the collections were breath-taking. A wave of excitement ran through Helena. "Surely here I will find what I seek," she whispered.

Leisurely she reveled in the mastery and quality of the works of art. The Met's gift shop was a treasure trove of beautiful artefacts and she indulged her fascination for the history of jewelry design and adornment from the earliest times.

In one glorious moment, as if touched by a divine spark, the golden cross was lit by an inner fire. There it was—the perfect gift to show her love and pay homage to the faith he held so dear. What more could she have asked for than a man of honor with values and integrity. In her eyes, the Captain shone as a bright light, a hero, a lover. Helena smiled in her delight. Loving him had brought a new and wonderful dimension to her life. She felt valued, happy and yes, she could admit it to herself, "I love him."

Delicate and finely balanced on a spun-gold chain, the golden cross represented a contemporary design linking the scrolls of an ancient text of the alpha and omega symbols, expressing God's words as "I am the Alpha and the Omega, the Beginning and the Ending."

The cost of the pure gold pendant far exceeded any previous gift she had purchased for the Captain, but without hesitation, Helena handed over her credit card. Her gold credit card. It all made perfect sense. "The Gods are shining on us," she said.

Helena's time in Sydney was almost over so a trip to Bondi Beach was out of the question, but she ran out of time doing something she loved and following her heart.

"He's a very lucky man," said the sales assistant as she wrapped the pendant after questioning Helena. "So, who is the lucky person who will receive this gift?" she asked.

Helena often took the opportunity to talk of her "special person" to people who were far removed from shipboard life. "It's a farewell gift for his next voyage. He's a ship's captain and sails around the world constantly," she told the girl. "I want him to remember me—and return."

"Wearing this pendant close to his heart, certainly he will remember you," said the young woman who gave a sentimental sigh as she handed over the gift-wrapped package. "Good luck with your romance. I wish that for myself one day."

Back onboard Helena joined the crowds of passengers who gathered to watch the sail-away from Sydney. Passing the Sydney Opera House and out through the Harbour Bridge, she was in no doubt that this was indeed one of her favorite cities. *Who knows if I will ever come back*, she thought, *but I will never forget the beauty of this city. Goodbye, Sydney.*

Under the twinkling Southern Cross in a cloudless sky, Helena enjoyed the feeling of freedom as sea breezes whipped through her long hair and seagulls swooped and flew around the ship. "Life is so perfect," she said as she gave thanks.

Sydney's brightly illuminated high-rise skyline disappeared into the distance as Helena leaned over the railings and waved goodbye. As she did so, the Captain looked up from his position on the bridge, and, for a second, their eyes met. Dread crept over her as she remembered the gift she had bought in Sydney was to mark his farewell.

"Dear God in heaven," she prayed, "you control the beginning and the ending of all. Please do not let my romance end, not yet, not ever."

* * *

Stars in the southern hemisphere really do shine brighter than those in the northern, and the sound of the lapping waves and the warm breeze that drifted into Helena's darkened cabin brought the day to a joy-filled conclusion. She lay naked on her bed and celebrated her womanhood. Since that first magical time when he stripped her clothes off and made passionate love to her, she had regained a confidence that was lost—she felt whole again.

How could she not love someone who made her feel alive? No longer did she need to cover up and hide those parts that did not come up to her exacting standards. He had no complaints, and he kept coming back for more. She was rejuvenated.

Propped up on freshly laundered, fluffy white pillows, through headphones so as not to disturb her neighbors, Helena listened to music for crying to, from the self-penned albums of broken love songs of the British singer Adele.

"If this is my last night with you . . ." she sang along to "All I Ask."

Soon he would leave. Again, she would be alone. Helena kissed the rose quartz pendant she kept under her pillow. The same one she wished on all those months ago when she joined her first world cruise, saw him and immediately fell under his spell.

"I, too, saw you that first day," he assured her on many occasions. "You speak of destiny. Maybe. I agree we have a special connection. But it is not easy. My job is to sail the world. Every day I move on to somewhere new. Do not ask for anything. It will be as it is meant to be. Today we are both here in the same place on the same ship. We are together."

Helena fell asleep with a smile on her lips. The music played on and she said, consoling herself, "Love songs hold meaning at last."

At Sea
Day 55

The cruel voice inside Helena's head cackled, "Yea, sure, any man will agree you have a special relationship when you're lying naked on the bed. Let's see how it plays out in real life when he doesn't bother to contact you. Anyway, where is he tonight while you lie waiting, amusing yourself by humming along to love songs and hoping that he will show?"

All doubts and fears that there would be no future relationship disappeared when they spent time together. Lunchtimes could not come soon enough for her on sea days. She spent the morning being pampered in the spa before dressing to go sit at a table in a half-empty bistro.

Either reading her magazine, studying pages of sheet music for upcoming choir practices or checking emails, Helena sat alone and watched the door for his arrival.

She felt relief as he came in and made his way to her table. He pulled up a chair and sat down while leaning forward to speak in a quiet, private voice. "I have important information. This afternoon I will announce final details of our upcoming port destinations. My departure plans are finalized and I will leave the ship at the last scheduled call in Australia—one week from today."

Helena feigned enthusiasm. "That's wonderful news," she told him. "You certainly deserve your vacation; this cruise has been phenomenally challenging. As they say, one damn thing after another. I know you have been under a lot of pressure. Now it's time for some rest and relaxation."

He acknowledged that she was pleased for him but knew that did not diminish her disappointment that he would be leaving his command. "It will be exactly halfway through the voyage when I leave," he told her. "We are lucky to have had our journey together."

"When I joined the Grand Around the World Cruise, I was so thrilled that you were the captain. I have tried hard not to think about when you might leave. Now that it is confirmed, I am happy for you."

She took a deep breath and held back a tell-tale tear that threatened to escape and show him her true feelings. A pretense that she had developed a sudden tickle in her throat did not fool him.

"We have experienced a lot on this cruise," he pointed out. "I have been glad of your support and presence onboard. You are the first passenger to know about the new plans for our itinerary and when I will be leaving the ship. I know you will keep our confidences."

At a small, white, wooden dining table marooned in a large, airy eating area, he brushed her hand and looked into her eyes. "Helena, I will not forget you," he said. "You have been so kind and given me many thoughtful gifts. I will especially remember the gold Maori pen and the Japanese warrior fridge magnet."

Helena burst out laughing. "My first romantic encounter for seven years and I am to be remembered for a fridge magnet."

Together they laughed and laughed even more as they contemplated the absurdity of the situation. "A fridge magnet," Helena repeated.

"A fridge magnet," he echoed her words, but added with a twinkle in his eyes, "and much more." As so many times since their special connection had started over a year before and now spanned almost a hundred private lunchtimes conducted in the full glare of passengers, officers and waitstaff, Helena and her beloved Captain existed in a magical zone where only the other was visible—real life disappeared. Only their version of love existed.

Determined not to appear needy or high maintenance, Helena effected a light hearted tone. "Now I can concentrate on my world cruise without you to distract me. There must be many sights in the world as beautiful and enchanting as you. But when you're around, I see only you. I am so blessed to have experienced getting to know and love you."

She did not correct herself having said the *love* word. What else had this amazing experience shown her but that she was in love and could love again? Central casting could not have sent along a more appealing star player. Every single thing about this man charmed her. If this was being under a spell, she did not want to be freed.

"Okay, it is time for me to go," he said.

Helena's face fell. "Only from lunch," he said. "I told you, I have one more week. Of course, I will see you before I leave the ship."

He stood up and walked away, but when he saw Helena leave the table and move toward the door, he stopped and came to her. He did not hesitate. "Let me kiss you," he said as he held her shoulders and kissed her on both cheeks.

Often, when he saw her around the ship, he would greet her with a two-cheeked kiss. Helena had never seen him greet any other person with this familiarity. She smiled. Today was a good day despite the news of his departure. Whatever happened next, she thanked the love goddess for the romance she wished for on every new moon.

"A woman comes alive and looks beautiful when she is seen through admiring eyes." She read that in a self-help book and she believed totally. Helena's courtship with the Captain restored her faith in her physical desirability and renewed her feelings of being a woman. She dismissed criticism that a woman should not need a man to validate her.

Before the day she saw him and knew that he was the man for her, Helena was accomplished, independent and well-traveled. She knew her value, but the look of appreciation in his eyes made her shine. "I am the best version of myself that I can be at this moment in time," she conceded. "I truly believe that the love connection adds a wonderful spiritual connection to the experience of being a woman. Maybe the creation myths were right," she joked. "God created man and man created woman. I celebrate my creation. Thank you, Captain, for choosing me. I know that what we have is special, and I will endeavor to not ask for more. One day at a time. What will be, will be. We have a destiny."

At Sea
Day 56

"This is your Captain speaking from the bridge. All passengers must stay clear of open decks until the instruction to return is given."

The helicopter was heard before it was seen. Out of a cloudless blue sky and flying over the Great Barrier Reef, the air/sea rescue aircraft made a direct approach to the *Vision Star*.

The upper restaurant deck was cleared in preparation for the helicopter to make a close encounter but not land, several floors above the medical center. The white helicopter hovered in the air and nosed as close as was practical to the open deck without endangering its swirling rotors.

A crowd gathered on the upper decks and disregarded instructions that photographs and videos were not permitted.

Loud-voiced passengers, anxious to show off their experience and knowledge, or lack of it, offered a running commentary, "Steady, hold her steady. Winch down. Paramedic ready to descend. Stay above the railings. Hover."

The pilot of the helicopter assessed his position and, with a sudden movement, lifted away from the deck, rose into the sky above the ship and flew off and away from the vessel. Making a wide arc over the small islands, coral reefs and atolls of the Great Barrier Reef, he circled and came back for a second attempt.

"Medical emergency, 3 p.m. helicopter evacuation," the Captain told Helena in a quiet voice as he rushed past her door an hour earlier. Ready to leave the cabin to keep her lunchtime rendezvous with him in the restaurant, she stepped back inside the open door as he made his way quickly down the corridor. Without breaking stride, he hurried on his way.

The leisurely three days at sea in which she envisioned them spending time together, discussing plans for future meetings and making his preparations to leave were dashed. His responsibilities carried on twenty-four/seven. There was no easing back, taking it easy, adopting a holiday mood. He was, as always, fully engaged and committed, right up to the moment of handing over the master's role at their next Australian port of call.

His priorities were always crystal clear. Ship, passengers and crew demanded all his focus and attention. Helena mused that a lesser man might have taken his eye off the ball to indulge in a romantic flirtation, not him. That was why she admired him. He never delegated without being available to oversee and take command of any eventuality.

The medical evacuation in progress reminded Helena of the fragility and uncertainty of everyone's life. At the second attempt, the helicopter reached its optimum position for the scheduled evacuation. A winch appeared, a paramedic descended and, within minutes, he returned maneuvering a swaying cradle containing the patient. Into the cockpit the patient and paramedic disappeared and the door closed from the inside. The helicopter rotor blades whirred and, with a swift elegant movement, the aircraft lifted off high above the ship and flew off into the wide blue yonder toward the nearest onshore hospital. The crowd of watchers on the upper decks heaved a communal sigh of relief, and a couple of women sent the patient off with thoughts and prayers for their safe delivery. All were conscious that the next causality could be any one of them or their spouses.

A male voice echoed a more practical sentiment, "Hope they've got medical insurance. Those helicopters don't come cheap."

Excitement over, the Captain's "all clear on decks" announcement gave passengers permission to return to onboard activities. Many of them said a silent prayer for their own deliverance.

* * *

Another day closer to his departure and Helena tried to learn the lesson of acceptance. "God grant me the serenity to accept the things I cannot change, courage to change the things I can and the wisdom to know the difference."

* * *

Helena took advantage of the warm equatorial sunshine and stretched out on a lounger on the open deck at the rear of the ship. She enjoyed the peace and a quietness in her thoughts as she lazed and gazed at the white dancing foam, wondering at the beauty of the Great Barrier Reef. The largest living organism in the world, and a natural phenomenon that can be seen from outer space. The Reef contains coral colonies, mangrove estuaries, sandy cays and continental islands; sea-grass beds, algal and sponge beds, sandy and muddy bottom communities, continental slopes and deep ocean troughs. The *Vision Star* sailed around the coastline of Queensland en route to the North Western farthest point of the tip of the continent of Australia.

"There are definitely more wonders in God's world than are visible to the human eye." She sighed with pleasure. Maybe she had devoted too much of her time and attention on a Grand Around the World Cruise to her love fantasy, but she refused to deny that the feelings and emotions she experienced were worth all the times of doubt and uncertainty.

"The Captain is also a wonder of the modern world," she mused. "And don't forget, it is he who steers this ship."

"Every day is a challenge," he told her. "There is nothing predictable about life at sea. That's why I love it."

Helena picked up her pen to write a brief message of fare-well on the postcard she happened upon in the last Australian town the vessel visited. On the front, a stunning Persian blue butterfly, the breed, Ulysses. Perfect for him, as was the shiny gold cross.

"I wish you fair weather on your homeward journey," she wrote, "and until we meet again, may God hold you in the palm of his hand."

Two sea days left before his departure. Helena was determined to enjoy whatever may be.

At Sea
Day 57

Helena re-created, in her suite, the seductive late-night boudoir scene she had perfected. Soft lighting, soft music, double bed piled high with plumped-up cushions and wrapped in colorful coverings.

Dressed in her finest red satin lingerie and black, shiny hold-up stockings, she stepped into black patent high-heeled shoes and loosened a silky robe to show off her ample breasts. Helena stood in front of a full-length mirror and checked her image. She was determined to ensure her visitor was left with a powerful impression of her beauty and sexuality. She fluffed up her long, blond hair, worn loose, and checked her freshly applied makeup, complete with signature scarlet lipstick.

Chanel N°5 perfume sprayed liberally on her body and into the room tantalized the senses. The stage was set. She craved the privacy of his after-hours visits. Earlier that day, they shared a long, extended lunchtime ensconced at their chosen table. They talked about the plans for his departure, and, though, he gave some details of the countries he would visit, she refused to ask for details. What good would it do for her to know where he was, even less who he was with, though, she had established on the previous year's cruise that it was traditional for him to spend the Easter season at home with his family in Odessa.

With time to talk and enjoy each other's company, the lunchtime conversation covered the subjects that interested both of them: current affairs, politics, the stock markets, issues of global health and a virus that already controlled their destination and formed the basis for a revised itinerary.

The Captain also enjoyed hearing stories of the many rumors that circulated among passengers on the ship. He particularly relished the dramatic suggestion that he handed over the captaincy and was whisked off the ship aboard the helicopter the day before.

Helena was way beyond any attempt to hide her feelings for him. "I am conflicted," she told him. "I know you need and deserve your vacation, you are exhausted, but understanding that won't stop me from missing you. Our lunchtimes, and other times together," she smiled, "are a highlight of my day and my world cruise."

He reached for her hand. "I know," he said, "but we had the opportunity to go halfway around the world. When you arrived on the ship, you didn't even know I was onboard."

"I know, I know," she said, "I am not complaining. But I will be sad."

"I will come to see you," he assured her. "We can say goodbye properly."

Helena smiled happily and stared after him as he walked down the central aisle of the restaurant and went on one of his walkabouts to meet and greet passengers. The demanding voice of Meredith Two, the passenger who had vowed to have the Captain at the top of her man list, broke into her thoughts. Meredith Two and Helena had never exchanged a word, though, Helena saw her frequently sneaking around and following the Captain's movements.

"They might as well put a RESERVED sign on this table for you and the Captain," she said with a sneer. "Oh, no sorry, it won't be needed after today, will it? He's leaving the ship and returning home to his family. I hear he has a wife and several women in ports all over the world."

Helena ignored Meredith Two and her deliberately provocative remarks. With a curt nod, Helena picked up her handbag and walked out of the restaurant. Helena refused to allow one insignificant person's nastiness to add to the sadness she was already experiencing. She called Meredith Two's bad behavior the Ugly Sister syndrome.

"Never mind," she said under her breath, "Cinderella will go to the ball. Or certainly, Prince Charming will come to her."

She reminded herself of this conversation as she sat in her empty suite late into the night waiting for the phone to ring or for him to appear. At midnight she stripped off her beautiful new lingerie and climbed into bed. Alone.

At Sea
Day 58

"Good afternoon, ladies and gentleman, this is your captain speaking." In his regular noontime announcement, the Captain delivered navigational and weather information about the ship's location and upcoming sea conditions. Until noon the following day. Helena dreaded today's announcement. After delivering all the nautical information and facts and figures, he paused.

"Ladies and Gentlemen, I want to tell you that this is my last announcement to you. Tomorrow I will hand over control and leave the ship. I thank you all for your understanding through the challenges we have faced on the Grand Around the World Cruise and I wish you an enjoyable time on the rest of the world cruise. At our arrival in our next port of call in Australia, you will have a new captain. It has been good sailing with you and getting to know you. Now I am signing off. Enjoy the rest of your world voyage, wherever it takes you."

Helena sighed. She knew it was coming. She had counted the days ever since he confirmed his departure plans, but now there was no going back.

Even at this late stage, there was massive uncertainty. *Vision Star* was one of a number of vessels sailing in ever-decreasing circles in a stately procession of Queens and Princesses, Vikings and Norwegians, Anthems and Rhapsodies, who were seeking safe harbor as country after country, including Singapore, Vietnam, Malaysia, Japan, Sri Lanka, India, Jordan, Greece, Malta, Mozambique, South Africa, Cyprus, Norway, Spain, France, Belgium, Malta, Namibia, Portugal and an increasing number of Australian ports, refused them entry. Cruise ships had become as welcome as a black-masted galleon of marauding pirates. World cruises all over the globe were being referred to as Magical Mystery Tours. In reality, they were sailing in the eye of the storm of a global pandemic.

Much as she wished it were otherwise, Helena was forced to accept that when the ship next docked, he would disembark. After two world cruises together, she would be left to finish the last leg and upcoming sixty days without her love interest, her daily fix. Slowly, reluctantly, she dressed for lunch. She always made an effort, knowing or hoping that he would join her in the restaurant. Scarlet was her color of choice. Strong and powerful to attract and keep his attention. Dressed fashionably and always wearing high heels, Helena had adopted the ancient wisdom she learned in China from a visit to the Summer Palace of the Dragon Lady during the last world cruise.

The Dragon Lady, a courtesan who stole the heart of an emperor, used her beauty and her elaborate dress style to get herself noticed and enchant the Emperor as he passed by on official duties in procession between royal palaces attended by his courtiers and entourage.

The Captain was not an emperor, but he was certainly the glittering prize on *Vision Star*. The most handsome and charismatic man onboard—and he chose Helena.

On this, the last day, Helena selected an above-the-knee, red silk dress and red buckled shoes. Her long, blond hair fell loose around her shoulders. To accessorize, she wore gold jewelry.

Dressed and ready to go, she held her rose quartz necklace close, clasped it to her heart and prayed, "Don't let him go without saying goodbye. My heart will surely break."

Out of sight, under the neckline of her dress, she wore the rose quartz love necklace upon which she cast a spell way back at the beginning of the last cruise. With her talisman in place, she reminded herself, "He may be about to hand over command, but he is still the captain of this ship—and of your destiny."

At Sea
Day 59

Helena was determined to be upbeat and cheerful. She sighed with relief as he entered the restaurant and made his way to join her. As he had done on almost a hundred previous occasions, he pulled out a chair, sat down, tucked his long legs under the small bistro table and placed his radio on the table.

He smiled briefly but could not sustain the pretense for long.

"All packed and ready to go?" she asked.

"Almost," he said. "I had other more important matters to deal with."

Agitated and unsmiling, he said nothing more. His usual good humor and ready smile deserted him. His whole being quivered with agitation. Never before had she seen him like this.

"Is everything okay?" she asked, though, she already could see it was not.

"No, no, it is not alright," he said. "I have some major problems."

"Are you still leaving the ship tomorrow?" she asked, knowing that, as usual, her first thought was how this new development might affect her.

"You know I have to go," he said, his tone kind but firm. "It is time. I am exhausted. I need my vacation."

"I know, I know," Helena answered, annoyed she had not acted in the mature and caring way she intended. "I was thinking only of myself. Of course, I would rather you stayed, but I also want you to have a holiday and recuperate from this extraordinarily challenging voyage. You deserve some quality 'me' time."

"There is no question. I am going," he said. "My onward flight arrangements are confirmed." Helena was conscious of the need to tread carefully. She did not ask him to disclose his vacation plans. She had no reason to know, and he had a right to his privacy.

"So, what is wrong?" she asked. "Can I help?"

"No, no, you are very sweet," he answered. "The problem is not with the ship or my departure; the problem is a personal one. It is unexpected and complicated, and I need to sort it out. People rely on me. It is a bad time for it to happen, but there is no good time."

Helena wished she could reach out and take him in her arms. He looked so tired.

Through all the storms and difficult experiences, he never wavered in his strength and commitment. "This is what I am trained to do. It is my job," he told her whenever she expressed concern at the level of constant and ever-changing problems. However, it was no secret to everyone onboard that the last few months were challenging far beyond what would normally be experienced on a well-established annual voyage. Weather conditions, sickness and global circumstances all conspired to produce daily dilemmas. The pressure on him, the Captain, the ultimate authority on the ship was immense, and she was privileged to have helped in her small part as a support and confidant.

Their regular lunchtime encounters gave him a place of sanctuary where he could relax and enjoy stress-free conversation, laughter and appreciative company. Now, right at the last hurdle, twenty-four hours before he was due to leave, an outside problem of which she knew nothing threatened to overwhelm him.

"I will take care of it," he assured her. "This problem is unexpected, and I need to deal with it as soon as possible."

Remembering the elaborate farewell celebrations on the last voyage when he departed the ship in India, Helena asked, "Are there to be no farewell celebrations this evening?"

"No," he said. "I requested that there should be none. I have said goodbye to the passengers in my last broadcast."

"Last year," she reminded him, "we were treated to a huge party with music and food and dancing." He started to grin as he sensed what she was about to say. "Almost every woman on the ship lined up to dance with you after one overenthusiastic passenger dragged you onto the dance floor."

"Yes, I remember." He laughed. "I kept trying to get away."

"That's not how it looked," said Helena, happy she had been able to get him to put aside his problems for a moment.

He blushed. "It's true, I enjoyed it," he admitted.

"I was the only woman who did not get an opportunity to be held in your arms," she reminded him. "Am I to be denied again? Will you come to say goodbye to me tonight? Or is this our farewell?"

He shook his head. "Helena," he said. "Please understand. I have serious problems. I am not good company right now. There is so much on my mind and so much to sort out."

Try as she might, Helena failed to hide her overwhelming sadness. Her eyes pleaded with him.

"Of course, I will come to say goodbye. I will come," he promised her.

Night-time
Day 60

Filled with anticipation and dread, all evening Helena waited. She ordered a light meal from room service. Watched a movie. Played different types of music: classic, pop, romantic.

With no way of controlling the situation, she felt fearful, tearful. What if he didn't come?

The phone rang. "I am on my way. Leave the door open."

Helena walked slowly to the door, unlocked it and assumed the position she had come to know so well as she waited.

"How are you?" he said, as he stepped into the room. He stayed with his back to the closed door and did not attempt to move toward her. "Are you alright? I'm sorry I kept you waiting. You should be with your friends, enjoying your evening.

Not waiting for me." Though he tried hard, it was apparent he was simply going through the motions of politeness. He looked even more uncomfortable than at lunchtime.

Helena's heart went out to him. Distress clouded his features. If only she knew the magic formula to take the pain from his eyes. He was always so rigidly stoic. Discipline and status were the elements that held together the conflicted person she witnessed before her. He held out his hand and, for a dreadful moment, she thought he was going to say goodbye, shake her hand and walk out the door.

Instead, he pulled her into his arms and held her tight. They stood holding each other, breathing deeply to a secret rhythm. His kiss, when it came, was tender, not fierce and demanding as she had come to expect. Without shoes, Helena felt small and vulnerable against his tallness. Not the strong, powerful woman she wanted him to see.

"I'm sorry," he said. "This is not how I wanted to take my leave of you."

"It's okay," she said, "I am happy as long as I can hold you."

For all her dreams of romance bound into a sexual fantasy, the reality was this man, whenever he was close to her, took her breath away, stole her heart, brought her to the brink of tears with the realization of how much she cared for him. She wanted to whisper, "I love you." She resisted. This was not the time or place. But her heart knew the truth. It felt like it would break there and then into a million pieces. He was about to walk out of her life, into another dimension in which she did not even exist. And whatever was troubling him tonight had thrown up yet another barrier. One she had no chance of transcending.

"Come," he said, and took both her hands. He led her gently to the waiting bed and sat alongside her. Cradling her hands in his, he kissed her. "You are a very special lady," he said. "I am so glad we had our time together. I will remember you and your many kindnesses to me."

His strong arms encircled her and he sealed his mouth to hers. Locked in a perfect embrace, their lips and bodies refused to be parted. Suddenly he let her go. He raised his hand to his forehead and let out a long sigh. "I am dealing with a very serious problem," he told her. "My head is full of it. I cannot think of anything else."

Helena stroked his cheek. "I'm so sorry. I wish I could help. Do you need me to lend you money? I know you are going on vacation; maybe you need extra cash?"

He laughed. "You are a strange person, Helena," he said. "You think in a very strange way. But no thank you, I do not need money. That would be easy to arrange. My problem is a health matter. Not so easy to fix."

Helena felt panic. "You? You are ill?"

"No. Not me," he said. "A family member. It is very serious and I need to be there to take care of things."

"I am sorry," said Helena. "You must feel so helpless being here and so far away. It's fortunate you are on your way home tomorrow."

"Yes," he agreed, "though, it does not totally solve the problem. The situation will persist, but if I am there, I can work out what to do. I don't know. What am I to do?" He shook his head. "So many people are dependent on me. I wish it were not that way, but, because I care, I accept my responsibilities. Thank you for listening to me."

Helena realized that the subject was closed. He was not about to reveal any more details, and, as usual, she did not ask. The time when he talked and told her of some of his family issues had long since passed.

Always very guarded, he had nonetheless on their first voyage told her some of his personal situation. She knew he was or had been married and also that he had a young son by a woman he had met when she came onboard ship to complete an interior design project. Helena's deceased husband, a prominent doctor, had also fathered a child by a younger woman with whom he had had an extramarital affair.

"Oh, what a tangled web we weave when first we practice to deceive," she commiserated with him. Helena forgave her husband, and they went on to rebuild their previously happy married life. The Captain never confided to her what really happened in his circumstance.

Everyone is entitled to their privacy, Helena convinced herself and adhered to this belief all through the months of their growing relationship. "His personal business is strictly that, as far as I am concerned. We all have our histories." Whatever the current situation, the Captain was more capable than any man she had ever met; he would take whatever action was necessary. Her feelings for him were not swayed by the events of his past life. His past, previous or even current relationships did not affect her opinion. Her judgment was based on what she saw and heard and observed in his relationship with her. She saw before her a man of supreme integrity. She watched his interactions day by day and made a vow. Her love for him, she decided, needed to be unconditional. He deserved that and she was proud to give it to him. Never should she have doubted him. The time and attention he gave her was precious. In those final moments together, she realized the enormity of his commitment to her.

Even the times when he failed to appear, when other responsibilities took priority. She vowed that in their next incarnation, whenever, wherever that may be, she would understand

and always give him the benefit of the doubt. His honesty and humility shone through and she loved him for it.

"You don't know the half of it," he admitted. "I have tried to make time for us to be together. Sorry it didn't always work out."

He kissed her again and held her face between his two hands. That touch reached somewhere deep inside her and released a tell-tale stream of tears. He wiped them away. "I know you are sad," he said, "but you must be brave and promise me you will enjoy the rest of your cruise. We are only halfway around the world."

Helena choked on her words as she tried to stop the flow of tears. "Don't worry, I am a big girl. I'll get over it. But I may not get over you."

"There is nothing to get over," he said. "We have enjoyed a special time together. It is natural to be sad that it has come to the end."

Helena leaned her head on his shoulder. "You have transformed me," she said. "I am not the person I was before I met you. You opened my heart when I thought I would never love again. However, now I know I will never find another man who speaks to my soul as you do. Why would I even want to try to find that magical connection? You are my hero. My Ulysses. I will wait for you. However long it takes. One day you will come back to me."

Instead of presenting him with the beautiful golden gift of faith she had bought in Sydney, Helena made a decision and gambled on the future. "This is not the end – not goodbye. I will give him his gift next time we are together."

Helena had revealed her true feelings earlier in the day, now it was her turn to blush as she admitted, "If it were in my power, I would have written tonight's script differently. Your departure would have been more peaceful and joyous. Now, all I can do is pray for you, send loving thoughts and every time I visit a church, I will light a candle in your honor so it may keep alive the flame in your heart."

"Helena, you are an extraordinary woman," he told her as he cradled her close to him and stroked her bare shoulders while avoiding placing his hands any farther down on her willing body. "You soothe me and amuse me and delight me and you are incredibly beautiful. You hold a special place in my heart; you do not need to question or doubt that. This situation between us should not have happened, but I could not resist and I will not regret it."

His face brightened with a genuine light for the first time that day. "You are right. It is mythic. I will write that in my logbook. I will not forget you."

Their closeness, even in the many times of trouble they endured over the course of the voyage and now in this present situation, assured Helena that what they shared was above and beyond the realms of the ordinary.

"As you always say, "Every day another challenge," she told him. "Life at sea is unpredictable."

Their farewell kisses went on for a long time. Both were reluctant to let go.

Helena repeated to him the words she had written on the blue Ulysses butterfly postcard, "Until we meet again, may God hold you in the palm of his hand."

* * *

Some people we meet for a reason, some for a season. But somewhere in the world, our hearts will reach out and touch each other.

★ ★ ★

One final kiss and he walked out of the door and out of her life. He gave a backward glance and winked as she blew him a kiss.

Helena felt strangely at peace. Into the early hours, she curled up in a chair on her balcony. The equatorial night was seductively warm, and she felt caressed by the gentle breezes. The moon was full in a cloudless sky, and the glittering diamond necklace of stars shimmered toward the horizon and dipped gracefully into the inky ocean.

The universe combined all its most spectacular natural elements to create a picture-perfect night-time. Helena felt a deep joy and a sense of being loved. On the brightest star, she wished and gave thanks for her beloved Captain and her beautiful romantic adventure.

Love transformed her. She knew she would never be the same again. She was deeply happy and fulfilled. This was the purpose of her two world voyages: to find herself and to know love. Helena would never forget her magical shipboard romance.

★ ★ ★

Halfway around the world, the Captain handed over control of *Vision Star* and flew off on his well-earned vacation. Helena knew that, as much as her heart hurt, it would not break. She convinced herself that their love story was not ended—only paused.

She was excited for the experiences still to come. She looked forward to at least half a world voyage spinning around again. They would surely meet as they sailed the great oceans.

Have Faith. Look up and believe. The sun and the moon are the same ones we see, wherever we are in the world. They were still ships that passed in the night, but this time she knew—he would not disappear or leave only silence. On the final day as *Vision Star* sailed back into its home port, having completed over 30,000 nautical miles, her faith was rewarded.

His message arrived: "Captain's Log: Our journey is not over."

Chapter Three

"What Goes Around, Comes Around"

Classical music played on the sound system and a coal fire burned in the cast iron hearth of the tastefully furnished chintzy sitting room of a pretty Victorian terraced cottage in Central London. Colourful floral Tiffany table lamps cast a diffused glow and royal blue embossed satin curtains kept out the chill of an English evening. Helena curled up on the well-used deep buttoned wine-colored velvet Chesterfield sofa and for added comfort, snuggled under a cashmere throw. She popped a square of smooth milk chocolate into her mouth and settled down to write.

On her lap she opened a black leather-bound journal with gold lettering, *"Grand Round the World Voyage"* and endeavored to make sense of the strange parallel universe in which she found herself living.

"Before the world went into free fall, I was circumnavigating the globe on a 'Grand Round the World Voyage' aboard the luxury liner," M/V Vision Star" from London to the Caribbean through the Panama Canal and on to the Pacific, New Zealand and Australia and returning through Indonesia, Asia and Europe back to our home port, a 120-day adventure. At the beginning of the year 2020, we were in Australia when news began to reach us of a global pandemic. A much-anticipated upcoming visit to China and other Asian countries was cancelled and gradually ports disappeared from the itinerary having refused entry to our ship and the battalions of cruise liners sailing the world and looking for safe harbors. We continued our journey though many other cruise lines curtailed their trips, and some flew passengers' home from Australia. Our company took the bold decision to sail back to the UK with British and American travelers still on board and instigated a unique and daring maritime adventure of exchanging passengers at anchor mid-ocean by tenders to allow all who chose, to be repatriated close to their homelands.

The company did everything in their power to ensure that our trip continued with little disruption to normal onboard cruising life, and we were able to enjoy our fine dining, entertainment, deck parties and Gala evenings. For six weeks we sailed across the ocean stopping only occasionally to refuel at sea, we were not allowed to disembark. With limited and unreliable internet access we were hardly aware of the catastrophe unfolding all across the globe. News reports of quarantines and deaths on other cruise ships, were all happening to someone else somewhere across the world. Like gloriously cocooned passengers on the *Titanic,* we lived in a surreal bubble unaware of what was about to hit us. Real life was a long way off at the end of another six weeks as we sailed on valiantly. The company are to be applauded for the fact that almost a thousand passengers and hundreds of crew members were delivered back safely to the United Kingdom without a single case of Corona virus.

Arriving back in our home port, the great reality finally hit. Having been issued with personal protection equipment including face masks and instructions from the government for restrictions that were to be followed in the lockdown that had been imposed. We were met dockside by men in white protective hazardous material suits with masks and headgear. They man-handled our luggage while maintaining social distancing, staying six feet away from each other and from us, the aliens who had landed in their strange land.

An observation by the brilliant travel writer, Paul Theroux about the end of a cruise never felt more apposite.

Theroux described the scene as passengers trudge down the gangway and lamented "this is the closest most of us will ever get to knowing how Adam and Eve felt when they were expelled from Paradise."

In a state of shell shock and uncertainty, we left to continue our onward journeys having been cleared by health and immigration authorities. Transport police were informed of passengers' destinations, and we were provided letters of authority for our necessary onward journeys. We were not quarantined but advised to self-isolate. Unable to go home to where older family members, classified as 'vulnerable adults' were already in the isolation of a new state known as 'shielding' I head to the home of a relative who was and is still in America, one of the epicenters of the virus. I had arrived bearing gifts of souvenirs and fridge magnets from early ports of call on the cruise and was eager to share the stories of my adventures on the ocean waves. Instead for many weeks I have seen no family or friends and live in this disembodied world of virtual reality where we chat on zoom and Skype. We talk a lot and laugh a lot all designed to hide the fear and anxieties we experience as a mass killer stalks our streets. On infrequent trips outside the home for essential shopping or exercise. I wear a black satin mask, made for me by the ship's tailor; latex gloves and a head covering. I call it corona chic. The atmosphere is one of suspicion where we cross the street to avoid people and eye up strangers, wondering if they are the individual who will pass on the deadly virus to us. We fear for ourselves, our loved ones, our community and humanity.

With all my cognitive skills, fertile imagination and ability to build a complex narrative based on the premise of 'What if?" I could not have envisaged the strangely quiet and weird world we now inhabit. Who knew that life as we lived it would disintegrate so completely and fatally in such a short period of time? We would be alone, thrown back on our own resources.

The personal mission of my Round the World adventure was to explore, experience, embrace other cultures, other worlds and 'Find Myself' as I set out on the next stage of wherever the life path would lead. Little did I know all I was required to do was Stay Home and endeavor to be part of the solution, not a part of the problem. The Hero's Journey always brings challenges, unforeseen circumstances, threatening foes and unexpectedly inspiring friends and allies. Our strengths and weaknesses are revealed. We will all be changed by this world disaster - this time it's not happening to someone else. We are all in the firing line. Stay strong, face the battles ahead, follow instructions and have faith that one day there will be a new normal. We will all live out in the sunshine again. This war will be won. "

The global pandemic that swept the world in 2020, killed hundreds of thousands of people, mostly the old and infirm and often those with pre-existing medical conditions. Hospitals in London and elsewhere were always on the brink of being over-whelmed, medical and health staff reached the point of exhaus-tion and vital equipment constantly threatened to run out while hundreds of patients lay in hospital beds, struggling to breathe and dying. 24hour news broadcasts reported apocalyptic sce-narios and drastic new laws eroded personal freedom. Families were not allowed to visit, workers were ordered to stay at home and businesses, retail and restaurants shut up shop and boarded up their premises. International travel was banned—trains and boats were stagnant and planes were grounded. The streets were deserted and emergency vehicles, police cars and ambulances screeched through the streets, escalating fear, alarm and dread. Terrorized by a global pandemic sweeping the world, causes and cures remained a long way off and each day produced new stories of further horrors. The world was broken and behind closed and locked doors, individuals dreaded the emergence of each new catastrophe.

Alone in a borrowed house in an unfamiliar area of London, Helena curled up on the sofa and wept for the life she had lost.

The unthinkable prospect that she would never again be able to travel and more importantly, she would never again see the man who filled her life with hope and romance, consumed her with a sadness that she could not even share. Everyone was living through the nightmare, Helena's doubts and fears were dwarfed by real life situations others, even within her own family, faced. She hid her grief and nursed her broken heart. Alone.

Every day brought more news of businesses that had gone under because they were unable to operate during the pandemic. A friend called to tell her the news that the cruise line on which they were frequent passengers, with future cruises already booked, had gone bust.

Helena joined in sending messages of commiseration to those who would lose their jobs. Polite thanks you for the concern shown by colleagues, friends and passengers, came back from locations all over the world as company employees already back in their home countries, or in some cases still awaiting repatriation, faced the stark fact that the cruise line they worked for was bankrupt.

In July, three months after the end of the cancelled voyage and the Captain's cryptic message, "Our journey is not over," Helena sent a personal message.

Greetings Captain Grigory,

Such a sad day for the company and staff and passengers who love the cruise line. However, I am confident that the most popular Captain in the fleet will be able to step aboard and command a ship anywhere in the world, whenever he is ready to set sail.

You are in my thoughts. Stay well. Take care.

Kindest Regards, Helena de CR

The speed of the reply to her email took Helena by surprise.

Hi, dear Helena,

It's nice to hear from you and know that you're okay and safe. Indeed, it is sad what happened to the company, this virus is destroying so many lives. I'm on the ship in the docks at Southampton and there is much uncertainty among the crew. Every day we are awaiting further instructions.

I am well and hope that you are managing to enjoy your life without cruising!

You are in my thoughts, too. It is not easy to forget a real lady and a beautiful woman like you. At least we managed to come closer. Take care wherever you are and stay safe. We'll keep in touch.

Many kisses, Capt. Grigory

In the midst of all his turmoil, the Captain found time to write a love letter. Helena danced around the kitchen, here was a gift from heaven. She read and reread "It is not easy to forget a real lady and a beautiful woman like you."

The words filled her heart and Helena hugged the sentiment to her. They were connected, again. Who knew where the journey would take them?

The following day he sent a watt's app number for her to contact him.

Helena observed some of the texting etiquette she read was appropriate. Do not respond immediately. Do not open the message or the sender will know you've seen it. Best to leave 24hours before you reply!

She certainly did not want to appear over-eager, nor did she want to appear as if she did not consider his messages important. *Strike a balance, be approachable, but maintain a distance. This is not your first rodeo.*

Two days later, Helena responded to his message.

"Hopefully there will be a solution for the excellent teams of your vessel. I am sure plans will be put in place to take care of the people whose lives have changed so suddenly and dramatically—and of course your presence on board will be a reassurance.

My life was not as expected after I returned from the World Voyage. Covid 19 regulations mean I have been unable to visit family or friends. My wings are clipped but without travelling, I enjoy a peaceful retreat in a safe place living on my own. There are many restrictions in place, but if I can find a way to make it happen, would you like to meet up? Helena x

She finished the message with three kisses but deleted two and before she pressed send, deleted the final kiss.

His reply came though within the hour.

I'll be glad to meet you after all these months. I am willing to come to London. I can take the train and of course will observe all necessary precautions. Captain Grigory.

Helena was ecstatic. She could hardly believe it. A date with her beloved Captain, in London.

Travel in the capital needed to be navigated carefully.

Helena spent the next two days planning her outfit and as fashion shops remained closed, she settled for a smart beige trouser suit with an amber V-neck silk blouse designed to look semi-formal in partial London lockdown, and minimal gold jewelry.

"This is not the time for frivolous cruise wear," she reminded herself.

Taking a commuter train into Central London, Helena became acutely aware there were only a handful of people on the train. Mask wearing was mandatory, and the passengers spread out through the train, taking up almost a carriage each. At stations along the suburban route, staff, police, and security outnumbered passengers. Facilities and retail on station platforms were closed.

At the mainline station, the scene was the same. Helena waited anxiously for the arrival of his train from Southampton, a 2-hour journey from Central London. She prayed she would not attract the attention of one of the many police or security patrols. She rehearsed the reason for her travel, she needed to visit a family member who needed medical assistance. Fortunately, she was not forced to offer any explanations. She wore her mask and maintained social distancing with the few people in the terminal. She counted every minute till his train arrived.

Even in the midst of a rush hour crowd, she would have seen the Captain immediately. Amongst the handful of passengers, he surely stood out.

The sight of him took her breath away. Dressed in denims with a black leather jacket, baseball cap and ray-bans, he maintained his charisma and movie star looks. Despite the mandatory mask. She could have bet that the ship's tailor had also made that one.

He smiled with his eyes as he saw her. They walked quickly towards each other and stopped. Hugging people in public is no-no under covid rules. He touched her shoulder, then her back and briefly brushed her hand.

"Thank you for meeting me," he said.

"My pleasure," said Helena. "How was your journey?"

"My first time off the ship," he explained, "I am very happy to be here in London—and see you,"

Helena longed to rip off both their masks and hug him to her in the tightest embrace possible. Instead, they maintained social distancing. Six feet apart, they walked together out of the station.

"Is there anything you need or want to do?" asked Helena.

"You mean apart from wanting to kiss you?" he asked.

She hoped her mask, hid her blush.

"I thought we could go for a walk along the River Thames on the embankment," she smiled. "There are bound to be some pop-up outdoor coffee stalls."

'Sounds good," he told her. "As long as I can be close to you today, that is all I need. I've thought of you often."

Somehow, though she knew of her own longing for him, and the daily thoughts that filled her mind, she was surprised and delighted to hear him say that he too thought of her.

The easy familiarity and pleasure they so naturally found in each other's presence, had not diminished. Like old friends, new lovers, they smiled and enjoyed each other's company. The normally bustling thoroughfare of London's South Bank was deserted but an enterprising vendor sold coffee and baked goods —and brightly colored masks.

Helena and Grigory held hands discreetly as they sat on a bench outside the National Theatre overlooking the River Thames and the panoramic glass revolving sightseeing wheel, the London Eye.

The talk was all of global pandemic and the terrible catastrophe that swept the world. Grigory recounted that he had been under curfew and locked down in half a dozen countries as he traversed the globe moving ships from port to port trying to find safe havens. Cruising was at a standstill but hundreds of ships still languished out on the high seas thousands of miles from home ports. On some vessels, crew members were unable to leave because of enforced restrictions in their home countries. Ghost ships going nowhere sailed aimlessly on the world's oceans.

Contrasting stories of lockdowns meant that while Helena was forced to stay in one place, allowed only to venture out locally, Grigory became a world travelling trouble-shooter navigating constantly changing worldwide restrictions. Now he and an international crew awaited news of their fate in a British sea port with little prospect of a resumption of the passenger sailing business or the comfort of a return to home.

"I have chosen not to attempt to return to Russia," he explained as they walked and talked. "The country denies that they have any cases of covid but that is not true. As long as I can be employed in my profession, even the sad task of taking ships to what is likely to be the end of their useful life, I keep moving."

Helena, pained by the sadness in his eyes, wordlessly conveyed her empathy. The world was in chaos and yet here they walked in the summer sunshine by Old Father Thames hand in hand, united in a relationship that over two world voyages and a global pandemic, endured and survived on a bond of caring and trust. From time to time, they stopped, stared out across the river and kissed. Not passionate, not desperate, but an embrace full of love and mutual understanding.

Helena pointed out landmarks along their route as they walked from Waterloo station, past the iconic OXO Tower, under Blackfriars Bridge, past the Tate Modern museum, a former power station; around Shakespeare's circular Globe Theater, past the old Clink Prison, Southwark Cathedral, London Bridge, Borough market, Cross Bones graveyard, St George the Martyr Church and ending at London Bridge station.

"You never cease to amaze me," said Grigory.

Helena looked puzzled.

"Walking for miles. I never had you down as a walker."

"There is an easy explanation," said Helena. "I am not wearing high heels. In the pandemic we have all become accustomed to dressing less formally. Wearing flat shoes or trainers, we are better equipped to run from the virus. Trotting along in high heels is not practical."

He cupped his hands around her face and kissed her forehead. "I like the new look. It makes me feel protective *of* you. Usually you stride out so tall and confident. Please, don't ever underestimate how important you are to me."

Life was so uncertain, so unpredictable, so threatening, that Helena was filled with love and gratitude for the blessing of this beautiful, gracious man in her life.

Grigory checked the large world watch on his right wrist.

'I need to be getting back to the ship," he said.

"It will take too long to walk back to Waterloo," said Helena. "We can flag a black cab, there are still are some plying their trade on these deserted streets, though they are not doing much business. "

The short cab ride back to the station from where they would go their separate ways, provided the perfect opportunity to finally enjoy private space in which to embrace and indulge in the physical contact they had been denied through the wearing of masks and social distancing in public.

The black cab driver had been around the block many times in all his years of driving a taxi, he was not about to object to a couple kissing and cuddling in the back of his cab. As long as they kept the partition fully closed.

Masks firmly in place, in the mainline station, Helena and Grigory touched elbows and waved goodbye as they went towards their respective platforms.

Then Helena had a thought. She turned and ran back towards where Grigory was about to go through the automatic barrier.

Breathless from running, she leaned towards him.

"Next time we meet, I'd like to invite you to my home, it's on this rail route. Not far from here."

"I'd like that, very much," he nodded, "but I can't make plans. We'll talk nearer the weekend —if I am still in Southampton —not bobbing about on the ocean, three miles off the British coast. Keep well. Keep in touch."

That evening, he sent a loving message, "*I am back on the ship. Thank you very much for the wonderful day. It was really great to see you. Have a good week. Kisses, Grigory,*"

Helena walked on air all through the following week and counted the days till the weekend. On Friday she texted him.

His reply sent her into a spiral of despair. Her expectations were unrealistic.

Major complications. I won't be leaving the ship this weekend. Enjoy the sunny weather. Grigory x

Helena replied, "I know you are always equal to any challenge. I send out my best thoughts to you. Take care —and you know where I am if you need me."

She retreated to the couch and binge watched Netflix.

Always two steps forward, one step back with this man," she was forced to accept as she ate more chocolate than she knew was good for her. Might as well load up on the sugar and feel disgusted, sick and unworthy.

Helena's feelings veered between disappointment, anger and hurt. What could she ever do differently? What did she mean to him? Why did he keep allowing her to think she was special, then let her down?

There was no one to talk to, no one to confide in. She had been alone throughout the pandemic, now she felt the agonizing pain of loneliness.

After an early evening bath, ready for bed, Helena picked up her phone to set an alarm. Not that she had anything to get up for but it was habit. She was not a woman to lie around in bed all day, not even when nursing a broken heart.

Now she saw a message, one she had missed earlier.

My dear Helena, I realize it is short notice but if the invitation is still open, I am available to meet with you tomorrow, Sunday. Perhaps I can come to your house as you suggested. Kisses, Captain Grigory

And the icing on the cake— a row of bright red emoji kisses.

Frantic that she had missed her opportunity and her reply would fall on deaf ears, Helena sent a message.

"Sorry missed your text. Sure, tomorrow still works for me. Instructions attached. Details of train service and I'll send a taxi to collect you at station. Shall we say you will arrive around noon?"

Sleep was out of the question. A clean sweep of the house was indicated. She surveyed each room, put things away, straightened, tidied and generally ensured that everything was in order and showed itself to best advantage. She chose an at home outfit for the following day, a low cut short tribal pattern red dress and silver mules.

The contents of the fridge revealed that she could knock up a passable lunch but an early morning trip to the local deli would supply salad ingredients, fresh fruit and newly baked bread. Local food stores were open as some lockdown restrictions were eased but the precautions of only two customers indoors at a time were rigorously observed.

In the early morning hours, Helena set out candles, incense and sweet-smelling oil. There was much to do to make everything perfect.

First in line when the store opened the next morning, she rushed home to put final touches to her preparations and set out two beautiful table settings. On the large double bed, she put silk sheets and cushions and sprayed the room with perfume.

As perfectly as on the cruise liner all those months ago, when she would stage dress her cabin to welcome her special guest, the Captain, her home was set to provide the same ambiance. The music station was set to love songs and while she awaited the time of his arrival, she played her favorite singer, Adele.

Everything went to plan. He caught the train from Southampton where his ship was still birthed, reconnected onto a local train line and arrived in the local taxi service Helena had ordered.

She opened the door and there he stood. Handsome, as ever. He held out a white gift box. "As you know," he said, "the onboard pastry chef makes delicious desserts. I brought you Russian honey cake. We call it seductive, beautiful and absolutely unforgettable. Like you."

Helena laughed with delight. Still holding the box between them, they kissed.

Grigory took the box from her hands, placed it on a small table and turned his attention back to his mission, their kiss. The two locked lips and bodies in a passionate embrace and the kiss was seductive, beautiful and unforgettable.

"Now I can show you how much I missed you and how much I wished to hold you close to me. It was very difficult to keep up the rules of social distancing last week. Now we have our time alone."

Grigory walked Helena backwards from the front door to the lounge couch and all the time, their lips stayed locked.

Side by side on the couch they kissed and he encircled her in his strong arms. Always respectful, his advances went no further than the powerful kisses and an amorous embrace.

Helena made the next move.

"Do you want to go upstairs?" she asked.

He nodded, smiled and after removing his jacket, took her hand. He led her up the staircase of the small cottage and she guided him to her bedroom.

Gently he began to undress her. Helena remembered from their encounters on the cruise ship the fact that he always took his time. A mature and patient man. He knew what he wanted and was willing to savor the moments leading up the main event. He slipped her front wrapped dress down over her shoulders. At his touch, she tensed.

"Please, do not be shy," he told her softly. "You are beautiful. Let me see you, naked."

He proceeded to peel off her silky scarlet bra and panties.

"I value the fact that you are a woman who always retains her grace and dignity. You are feminine and lovely. Thank you for sharing your virtue with me."

Helena sank into his arms, melted by his mesmerizing Russian accent and the poetic murmurings of his seduction.

The two of them naked, stretched side by side, head to toe on the bed, he ran his hands over her whole body. He kissed her and whispered to her in a stream of evocative Russian.

During their developing relationship on the ship, Grigory and Helena had made love many times. Now they clung to each other and fell into a rhythm which reached a crescendo as their bodies moved in ecstasy and they soared together in passion. Higher and higher he took her and as they reached their peak, Helena dared to cry out, "I love you, I love you."

Grigory kissed her tenderly and closed his eyes. Mission accomplished. Helena draped a sheet over his resting body and headed into the shower. Powdered and perfumed and dressed in a silk robe, Helena made her way downstairs.

All preparations were already made and by the time the salmon steaks, a favorite of the Captain, were cooked, she heard Grigory moving about upstairs.

"Towels and shower gel in the bathroom" she called to him. "I'm sure you can figure out how to use the shower. Lunch is almost ready."

Helena instructed voice activated Alexa to play a special piece of music.

"Play *Perfect Day* by Lou Reed," Helena directed.

Grigory came into the kitchen while the song was playing.

"Yes, I agree," he acknowledged the Lou Reed classic. "Sorry about falling asleep. It takes a lot to make me feel so relaxed these days. But you envelop me in a warm glow."

Helena smiled and turned to take plates off the kitchen counter. He came up behind her, lifted her long blonde hair and kissed the back of her neck. "Thank you for everything," he told her. "Especially for my invitation to the Captain's Lady's Table."

Over lunch in the dining room, the conversation flowed as easily as it always did on the hundreds of mealtimes they shared on the cruise ship during two world voyages.

They talked about the past, the present and the future.

"Hopefully we will move the ship soon, possibly as early as this week," he confided.

Helena had to exercise all her control not to start crying. This was the news she had been dreading.

"You call our relationship, mythic," he reminded her. "That connection is too powerful to be lost and forgotten but we must accept that things are not to be the same again for a very long time. What is meant to happen will happen. It is always for the best even when it does not feel that way at the time."

Helena choked back her tears. True, neither of them knew what would happen but they certainly could not doubt that they had a deep, spiritual connection. "I will not forget you," he told her over and over again. "You are very special to me."

As they said goodbye that magical day, Helena made a vow: *I will be grateful for the amazing experience we shared. I will not cloud the memories with regret or wishful thinking.*

Despite her best intentions, Helena's sadness sprang to the surface constantly. Heightened emotions brought on by music, films or items on the news left her in floods of tears.

The Captain's ship left Southampton soon after for parts unknown.

The style of his text messages by now familiar.

My dearest dear, lovely Helena, please come. Come and wave goodbye to the ship as she leaves port. You once asked if you could be my girl in the port, you are, but also so much more than that. You are a shining beacon in my life. I cannot promise much time with you, but I do want to say farewell. Please grant me one last kiss.

He finished off with his new signature, the one Helena treasured every time the whoosh of a text sounded, informing her there was a message from her beloved Captain. He signed off, *Capt. Grigory, kisses and hugs, followed by a row of bright red emoji hearts and kisses.*

* * *

All over the world the pandemic continues to cause devastation. The world has closed, and countries ban travelers, tourists, and visitors. Quarantines are enforced and the best laid plans cancelled and reversed at a moment's notice. Captain Grigory continues to sail the world always fulfilling maritime maneuvers, collecting, delivering, and relocating ships. Hearts and kisses and loving messages from the world's oceans and the seven seas tell Helena that she is in his thoughts and will always remain so.

Every day, on a flower-filled altar with framed photographs of the two of them dressed for the Captain's Gala Dinner, Helena lights a candle to guide his way.

"We are not apart," he assures her, "our hearts are entwined. Our souls speak to each other. I look at the moon and the stars and know you see the same ones I see. Love is eternal. There is no distance between lovers. Sleep tight, my dearest Helena. Your Captain holds you in his thoughts. Do not dream only of tomorrow, I am here now."

If it comes, let it come,
If it stays, let it stay,
If it goes, let it go.
—Nicholas Sparks

The End

With Gratitude

Wherever I am in the world, my heart is always at home—be it London, Miami, or Spain. My books are brought to life—and the bookshelf—by an excellent creative and production team.

Thanks go to graphic designer Gary Rosenberg of The Book Couple in Boca Raton, Florida, line editor Lori Lewis in Vermont, USA, and Jo Ware of Type It Quick in Brighton, West Sussex. Always by my side, to cheerlead and guide, Doctor Michelle Ruger.

My thanks, as ever, to those loyal readers who challenge and inspire me to write and share my stories. I am grateful for a blessed life. Love really *does* make the world go round.

ELLEN FRAZER-JAMESON is a professional communicator working in media, print, and theater. A former BBC broadcaster and Fleet Street journalist, Ellen is a published author, producer, theater director, and performer. She co-presented the largest late-night audience show in Europe on BBC Radio 2. Ellen lives in London and Miami Beach, and to relax dances Argentine tango.

Ellen has written several non-fiction books and six novels. Ellen's round-the-world travels provide her with research, inspiration, and adventure—*An Invitation to the Captain's Table* is an amalgamation of several ocean-going cruises.

All her current titles are available on www.Amazon.com and www.Amazon.co.uk:

Love Trilogy: The story begins with *Love Mother Love Daughter,* the love affair continues with *Love Refuses to Die,* and reaches its thrilling conclusion in *Love Kills with a Kiss.*

Set in New York and Miami, *Dark Hole in My Soul* is the first edition of the retitled *Flame Island.* Ellen's novel *Once Upon a Lie* takes place in Spain and England.

Seven Steps to Fabulous and *Seven Steps to Cruising Fabulous* are Ellen's two must-read nonfiction life-style guides.

Travels with Otto and *Slim with the Stars* are now available for the first time on Amazon.com.

**Contact Ellen at ellenfrazerjameson@gmail.com
or visit www.ellenfrazerjameson.com**